Power (

Book Three

# Thicker Than Water

## SF Mazhar

Also in the Power of Four series

Run To Earth

Playing With Fire

The Elementals (Novella)

ISBN-10: 1537489712

ISBN-13: 978-1537489711

Dedicated to my family and friends.

(Blood Is) Thicker Than Water - to emphasize that family connections are always more important than all other relationships

- English Cambridge Dictionary

# ACKNOWLEDGEMENTS

Writing may be my passion, but it wouldn't be a possibility if it wasn't for the love and care of all those around me. My first thanks has to go to my husband. He is my rock. He gives me all the support I need, in every aspect of my life. Without him, I would never have come this far as to be publishing my third book in the series. So thank you, Mazhar, for pushing me to pursue my dream and for supporting me through it.

Thank you to my Mum and Dad for being so proud of me. A big thank you to my sisters; to Yasmeen and Samena for being the best sisters I could ask for. To my M&Ms, thank you for putting up with mummy's countless 'laptop' hours, so I could get this book finished.

A big, big thank you to Gerard Donnelly from Contribute, for designing the gorgeous cover, and for putting up with my constant requests to 'tweak' some aspect of it. You truly arc the best.

Thank you to my wonderful editor, Melissa Hyder, for editing the book with great enthusiasm. Your kind words make the rewriting process a lot easier.

And a massive thank you to all the readers that send me messages and reviews, expressing their love for this series. I wouldn't be here, doing this, if it wasn't for your love and support.

# 1

# A STOLEN BIRTHRIGHT

The alcove was perfectly hidden behind the mighty waterfall. Gallons of water pounding into the lagoon below drowned out any noise from the dank enclosure. The torches hanging from the moss-covered walls gave nothing more than a dull glow, but the demons didn't need much light to see their captive bound and kneeling before them. The shifters could take on any form they desired, but all chose to look like men – each one six foot tall, with beefy hands and thick necks. They had square faces with menacing features. It did nothing to intimidate the boy, though, who despite being tied down in chains, still held his head high, his vivid green eyes narrowed with impatience.

"Well? Do you have an answer or what?" he asked.

One of the shifters swung a fist, striking him across the face.

Kyran shook his head, clearing it after the blow. He looked up at the demon and smirked. "I'm pretty sure that's not the answer to my question."

The shifter stationed behind Kyran took a fistful of his hair and wrenched his head back. "Who do you think you are?" he growled in Kyran's ear. "Coming to us with such brazen demands?" His grip tightened. "How did you find us?"

"I'll answer yours if you answer mine," Kyran replied.

The shifter let go and shoved Kyran forward. It was only the chain bolted into the ground, holding Kyran's hands behind him, that stopped him from falling face-first onto the stone floor.

"You think this is a game, boy?" he asked, joining the other two shifters in front of Kyran.

Kyran chuckled. "If it is, then you lot are sore losers."

Another punch, and this time it toppled Kyran to his side.

"I'll enjoy ripping that tongue out," the demon hissed, "once you tell us how you found us."

"Answer my question first," Kyran said, straightening up as much as he could in the chains. "Then I'll tell you all you want to know."

"What good is the answer?" another shifter asked. "You're not getting out of here alive."

"Humour me, then," Kyran said. "All I'm looking for is a simple *yes* or *no*." His eyes glinted in the limited light. "Is that it, or not?" he asked, tilting his head to the side, gesturing to something in the corner of the alcove.

All three shifters turned their heads to glance at the small rectangular box they had taken from Kyran the minute he entered their cave. They shared a look with one another before grinning.

"Yes," one answered. "It is."

A look of immense relief flooded Kyran's features.

"But," the demon added, crouching down to meet Kyran's eyes, "it's useless without this."

He held up a hand, and a silver dagger materialised in his hold. Its sharp edge looked like any other steel blade but from what Kyran could see of the handle, it was made of glass with a strange mix of liquid and gas swimming inside it.

"You can't use the box," the shifter said, "without its key." He turned the blade in his hand as if admiring it.

"That's what I was missing," Kyran murmured in understanding, staring at the blade.

The shifter chuckled. "A pulse will be the next thing."

Kyran looked at the demon and smiled. "Funny," he commented. "You know, it's almost a shame I'm going to have to kill you."

The shifter grinned. "And how are you going to manage that," he asked, "bound as you are?"

"Like this."

Kyran lunged at the shifter. The chains that had been holding him turned red, melted and fell to the ground in pieces. The shifter didn't see the hidden blade in Kyran's hand until it slashed across his arm. The silver dagger fell from his grip and the demon dropped back with a hiss, a blue gungey fluid seeping from his injured arm.

With a snarl, the demon looked up to see Kyran leap to his feet with the blade he had used to attack him in one hand, and the silver dagger now in his other. Kyran pocketed the dagger-key before sweeping a hand through the air. All three shifters were knocked back by a blast of unseen power.

The first shifter to sit up changed his form, turning from flesh and bones to a puddle of water in a heartbeat. It stretched across the rocky ground, twisting and turning. Even in the dim light of the cave, Kyran saw the silvery blue water take on another form – a lion like beast this time, with keen fangs and claws.

The beast shook its mighty head, fur rippling. It bounded forward but Kyran was quick to move out of the way. The other two shifters changed form too, each choosing the same lion creature. They surrounded Kyran, circling him, inching closer.

"You should never have come here, boy," one of the demons snarled, speaking in a deep and gruff human voice. "You're not leaving here, especially with that key."

The ground reverberated with the force of Kyran's attack as he slammed the first demonic lion to charge him down using the element of Air. Another jolt caught the second demon, knocking it bodily into the wall, taking out one of the torches.

The third shifter reverted to his human form. He came at Kyran with his fist raised, but Kyran delivered a solid kick, right in the solar plexus, making the shifter double over. Kyran grabbed him and threw him to the wall, holding him there.

The demon was about swing his other hand when something caught his eye. The cave was darker now, so the glow coming from Kyran's chest was instantly noticeable. A small, circular light, just to the left of Kyran's chest, was shining through his shirt. He looked down to see four silvery lines on the back of one of Kyran's hands had started to glow too. The shifter looked up at Kyran in surprised horror.

"No," he choked. "It can't be. You...You're the *Scorcher?*"

Kyran smirked and held up his hand, the four lines a blinding white now. "The one and only," he said, and slammed his hand to the shifter's chest.

The demon froze, his body arched, back curved. His mouth was open, but no sound left him. Thin black lines began to form under the skin of his chest – surfacing around Kyran's fingers. They seeped into Kyran's hand, travelling up his arm and across his chest to the white circle, which drank in the darkness but still continued to glow. Kyran lifted his hand and the demon fell to the ground, dead.

Kyran turned his head to find the other two shifters transfixed, still in their beast form, their yellow eyes on Kyran, watching him with fear. The four lines on the back of Kyran's hand were still glowing white as he flexed his hand and moved towards them.

*** 

It was a strange sensation that Aaron awoke to. His eyes were still closed, sleep ebbing from him like thinning fog, yet he was already aware of it. He didn't even have to rely on his ears to pick up the telltale sound of soft pattering. He knew it was raining before he even woke up. Aaron could sense the droplets of water clinging to the glass of the window of the room. He could *feel* them.

Aaron struggled against stubborn sleep, lifting a hand to rub at his eyes. Even an action as simple as that cost him more effort than it should. Bleary-eyed, Aaron peered around the room. Gradually, the familiarity made sense: he was in one of the Empath huts in the City of Salvador. The room still bore scars of the vamage attack the city had suffered only days before. The walls were stained, cabinets smashed, and chairs and tables had been reduced to rubble and now lay in one corner of the room. Nothing had been cleaned yet.

Slowly, Aaron propped himself up onto his elbows. He felt fatigued, his body heavy and stiff. Lifting his head was a feat in itself. Looking down, Aaron saw his clothes were filthy; mud and sand covered his front and legs. On his chest was the dried blood print of a hand. Aaron reached up to touch it. The blood wasn't his and neither was the print. It was Neriah's. It was the last thing Neriah had done before dying.

But that wasn't the only thing that Neriah had left with Aaron. The pitter-patter of the rain made Aaron turn his head to look at the window. The drops of water streaked down the glass and Aaron felt his breath quicken. He could feel that; he could *feel* the trickle of the rain, as if it were on his very skin. Aaron looked down at his chest again, at Neriah's hand-print.

Neriah had transferred the legacy for the element of Water to him. That's why Aaron could sense the rain. More than that, Aaron realised the heavy feeling in his bones was actually the sensation of the lake, only quarter of a mile away. Sitting in a room in the Empath hut, Aaron knew *exactly* where the lake was, how deep it was and what life was currently residing in it. He could tell which part of Salvador was forming puddles and where each and every drop of water was landing. This strange awareness pressed down on him, overwhelming him until Aaron felt like he couldn't breathe; he was drowning in it.

Aaron scrambled to get out of bed. His legs shook under his weight but Aaron forced himself to stand, holding on to the bed for support. He was panting, gasping for air, his panic making it impossible to calm down. What had Neriah done? He wasn't meant to get the legacy for Water. He was an Adams. It was the power of Earth that was his element. The legacy for Water was Ella's birthright, not his. But as Aaron recalled the memory of Neriah on the ground, wounded and dying, he knew Neriah didn't have a choice. Ella was on the other side of the fire Kyran had conjured to defend Hadrian. Aaron was the only one beside Neriah and so he had given Aaron the legacy to save it from Hadrian, the vamage who was prepared to drink Neriah dry to get to it.

The panic passed as Aaron forced himself to take deep breaths. The feeling slowly returned to his legs and Aaron straightened up. Shakily, he made his way to the window. He had to hold on to the windowsill to stay upright, but he stubbornly stood there, watching the rain. Aaron felt each drop as it hit the glass, as if it were his heartbeat. He lifted a hand and his fingertips started buzzing. Before his eyes, the rain pooled together. Defying gravity, a stream of water twisted and curled up, like a snake raising its head. It moved forward, trying to get closer to Aaron. It tapped against the glass, as if knocking and asking for permission to enter. Aaron watched it and then gave an unspoken command: *Come inside.*

The stream of water dipped down and trickled past the bottom edge of the window. Aaron watched, mesmerised by his own power, as the water lifted up into a stream, floating in the air before him. Tentatively, Aaron reached out and touched it. It was cold on his skin, but it filled Aaron's being with a warmness he'd never felt before. The water twisted over and under his fingers, playing across his hand. The coolness of the water against his skin felt like the most natural thing in the world, and it soothed Aaron in a way he didn't understand. A small smile came to him.

The door behind him opened, startling Aaron. The water fell from his hand, splashing into a puddle on the floor. Aaron turned to find one of Salvador's Empaths at the door. The girl's unseeing eyes moved from the bed to the window, searching past Aaron.

"You're awake," she said, sounding surprised and relieved.

Aaron heard the hurried footsteps behind the Empath almost at once. It was his mum and dad with his uncle Mike, followed by Sam and Rose. They ran into the room, past the Empath. They all looked like they hadn't slept in days. Aaron took a single step and found himself in his parents' embrace. They were cupping his face or holding his shoulders, asking him repeatedly if he was okay.

"I'm fine," Aaron assured them. His gaze darted to his dad's legs before meeting his worried eyes. "Are you okay?"

The memory of how badly his dad had been burnt would never leave Aaron. The flames had leapt up both his legs, searing his skin horribly. But Aaron knew his dad; the pain of the injury was nothing compared to the heartbreak that it was his own son who had sent the flames his way. It was Kyran, Aaron's big brother, who had attacked Chris to protect Hadrian.

Chris nodded tightly to Aaron's question. "I'm fine," he said.

His uncle Mike engulfed him in a bear hug. "You had us worried, kiddo," he said in a muffled voice.

Aaron pulled back and saw his best friends waiting for him. Things had been a little tense between them, with both Sam and Rose angry at him for making contact with Kyran in secret. They blamed Kyran for the vamage attack on Salvador, as did the rest of the mages, and were upset with Aaron meeting him. But as soon as Aaron stepped past his uncle, all seemed to be forgotten as Rose rushed forward to throw her arms around him.

"You're okay," she breathed. "Thank God, you're okay."

Sam just grinned at him. "Bloody hell, Aaron," he said. "You scared us."

"We didn't know what had happened to you," Rose said, pulling to stand back. "You've been unconscious for days."

Aaron's eyes widened. "What?" he asked in astonishment.

"Everyone we asked kept saying you were adjusting, but no one explained to what," Rose added.

"Adjusting?" Aaron frowned. He turned to his parents to see the relief had faded from them, replaced by fury.

"Adjusting to the legacy," his mum explained quietly. "The one that Neriah *forced* on you."

"He did it to protect it from Hadrian." Aaron found himself defending Neriah, without even thinking.

"And in doing so, he's made you a target," Chris said, his voice trembling with anger. "You've got the legacy that Hadrian wants – the *last* legacy he needs to take control of this realm."

He didn't say any more but his unspoken words didn't go unheard – Aaron felt his stomach clench tightly. He was now the only thing standing between Hadrian and his rule as the one and only leader of the mage world.

\*\*\*

It had stopped raining by the time Aaron got discharged from the Empaths' care. The sun had set hours before and floating lanterns now lit the way as Aaron, his parents, uncle and friends walked down the cobbled path into town. The Empath in charge – Amber – had tried to keep Aaron in for one more night, promising release first thing in the morning, but Aaron had insisted he wanted to go home.

The air was cool and fresh following the downpour. Aaron walked in silence, his gaze picking out the reflection of the lanterns in the puddles on the ground. The water moved towards him, stretching out to try to touch him as he walked past. Aaron wasn't sure if it was doing that of its own accord, or if he was unintentionally pulling the element to himself.

His attention shifted to the crowd of mages sitting on the ground where once the communal table had stood. The vamage attack on the city had destroyed it, along with several cottages and buildings. That was nothing, though, compared to the lives lost that night.

Aaron's gaze searched through the tightly formed crowd, spotting several Hunters – Zhi-Jiya, Ryan and Bella. They were talking in low whispers, leaning in towards one mage in particular. It took Aaron a moment to realise who it was, which brought him to a standstill. Ella sat in complete silence, her eyes red-rimmed as she stared at her knees. It didn't look like she was taking in anything the others were saying.

A surge of pain, mixed with empathy, rose inside Aaron at the sight of Ella. Her uncle Neriah had been her only family, but now he too was gone. The legacy for the element of Water was now with Aaron. She had lost everything.

As hard as he tried, Aaron couldn't stop guilt from overwhelming him. He shouldn't have the legacy. It was never meant for him. It was always Ella's. She was the Elemental for Water.

Aaron felt Sam touch his shoulder. He looked around at him, but Sam's eyes were on Ella.

"She's been like this ever since she buried Neriah," he said.

Aaron's heart twisted. Neriah had already been buried. He had missed the funeral, being unconscious for the past few days.

A flash lit up the street. Everyone turned to look at the Gate, to see it slide open. A subdued Skyler entered the city.

A sudden and tense silence fell across the street, with every eye on Skyler. No one had seen the blond-haired Elemental since he'd buried his girlfriend, Armana, and left the City of Salvador days before. He hadn't been there when Neriah planned the counter-attack on Hadrian. He hadn't been with them when the Hunters left to face Hadrian and his vamages in a bid to get back the Hub that had been stolen from their city. Skyler hadn't been there when their leader, Neriah Afton, had fallen.

Skyler made his way down the street with slow steps. One look at him and Aaron knew that somehow Skyler had learnt of Neriah's death. The anguish rolled off from him in thick waves. Skyler may have had issues with Neriah and the secrets he kept from him, but it was clear to see the death of leader of the mages had left Skyler broken.

Ella stood up. Aaron could sense the fresh tears forming in her bloodshot eyes. Ella moved past the group of Hunters, heading towards Skyler, walking at first, before breaking into a run. Aaron watched, waiting for her to reach him and throw her arms around him. He knew how close they were – like a brother and sister who only had each other.

But Ella didn't hug Skyler. The minute she got near enough, she swung her arm, punching him. Skyler reeled from the hit, staggering to one side, but he straightened up and stood before Ella without a word.

"You son of a demon!" Ella screamed. "You left! You left Salvador. You ignored me and walked away."

Her clenched fists hit Skyler again and again, on his chest, his shoulders and his face. Skyler didn't do a thing to stop her.

"You walked out on me!" she shouted. "How *could* you, Skyler?"

Skyler's eyes were filled with tears. He reached out to her, trying to pull her into his arms. "Ella, I'm sorry—"

"No!" Ella yelled, pushing his hands away. "You left and didn't come back!" Her voice cracked and she grabbed Skyler by his collars. "Why didn't you come back?" She shook him, but her strength was fast leaving her. "He's *dead,* Skyler," Ella sobbed. "He's gone. You weren't there. You—" She collapsed against his chest, crying. "You weren't there. If you had been, maybe...maybe—"

Skyler hugged her fiercely. "I know," he said, cradling the back of her head. "I know, Ella. I'm sorry. I'm *so* sorry."

Ella sunk to the ground, and Skyler went down with her, with his arms still tightly around her, supporting her as she cried against his chest. Aaron watched, not having it in him to go to Ella's side. What could he say to comfort her? Aaron didn't think he could even face her, not when he had the legacy that was rightfully hers.

# 2

## NOBLE LEADERS

It took another two days for the fatigue to completely leave Aaron. He'd spent most of his time recuperating in one of the cottages he was living in with his parents, Sam and Rose and two other Hunters. Most of the houses were left devastated after the vamage attack, meaning everyone had to share the residences still left standing. Work had already begun to repair the cottages, along with the Stove and other buildings, but Aaron doubted Salvador would be the same again. Buildings they could restore, but the people who had died – like Armana, Jason and, of course, Neriah – they had taken a part of Salvador with them, and nothing could bring that back.

Neriah, Aaron had learnt, had been buried in the same graveyard as Armana, right there in Salvador. At first there had been talk of burying him in Marwa, as that was the City of the Elementals, and where other Elementals had been buried. But Ella decided Salvador was Neriah's city. It was the place he'd built with a lot of hard work and dedication. It felt like the best resting place for him.

Aaron had an insatiable desire to visit Neriah's grave. He didn't know why, but he felt like he needed to go and pay his respects. Or maybe he wanted to stand where Neriah was buried and scream at him – to ask why he had done what he did. Deep down, Aaron knew why Neriah had left him with the legacy, but he was too angry to accept that right now.

Aaron splashed his face with cold water, again and again, until he couldn't breathe. Panting, he looked at his reflection in the mirror, watching as water dripped down his face. The element clinging to his skin drove a strange comfort into him, taking the bite out of his rage. Aaron closed his eyes, breathing out a difficult sigh. He hated that he held the legacy that was never meant for him, but he couldn't help but feel connected to it too. He ran a hand through his hair, tired from battling his own demons.

He left the bathroom and went downstairs, surprised to find only his mum in the living room. "Where is everyone?" he asked.

"They're outside, helping with breakfast," Kate said. "Are you feeling up to having a meal with them? Or shall I bring a plate inside again?"

"It's okay," Aaron said. "We can go outside."

Kate smiled. She walked over to him, raking a hand through Aaron's messy hair. "You really need a haircut," she chuckled.

"You've been saying that for months," Aaron said.

Kate headed to the cupboard in the corner and opened a drawer. She rummaged through it until she found a small, thin pair of scissors.

She sat Aaron down, wrapped a towel around his shoulders and began snipping at his hair. It didn't take long for Kate to trim Aaron's hair to the way it had been before he'd come to this realm; before he ever found out he was a mage, an Elemental.

Kate put the scissors down and pulled the towel away, brushing the stray strands from his neck. She walked around to face him and smiled. "There's my Aaron," she said. But she wasn't fooling anyone. Aaron could read her pain in her eyes.

Aaron wished he knew what to say to her to quell her fear. Cutting his hair didn't mean Neriah's legacy had also been cut from him. He could go back to looking the way he did when he first came to this realm, but it didn't make him that same boy again.

"I know you're scared, Mum," Aaron started quietly. "You didn't want me to get involved in this war, but now..." He faltered, trying to find the right words. "Now that I have Neriah's legacy—"

"It puts you at the centre of this fight," Kate finished for him. "I know." She looked down at the towel in her hands. "There's no use in trying to keep you away from the battle now," she said. "You're the one Hadrian will be looking for so he can take the last legacy and win this war."

Aaron got up and walked over to her. "It's okay, Mum," he said. "We'll come up with a plan. I'll be fine, I promise."

Kate reached out to lovingly cup his face. Tears that had been lurking in her eyes finally brimmed. "I'm sorry, Aaron," she said. "I'm so sorry."

Aaron shook his head, taking her hand from his face to grip tightly. "Why are you sorry? None of this is your fault."

Kate closed her eyes, lowering her head, trying to hold back her tears. "I know you blame me for keeping you from this realm," she said. "You hold it against me, against us, that your father and I didn't tell you the truth about who you are, what you are capable of."

"I did," Aaron said, "but I don't any more. I get it. You were just trying to protect me." He paused, considering how to say this without upsetting his already emotional mother. "But I can't help think if you had told me from the very start, I could have been prepared for this war."

Kate didn't speak right away. She took in a breath. "When your uncle Alex turned thirteen, he was supposed to choose what career path he wanted to take," she told him.

Aaron was thrown by the sudden mention of his dad's brother; the uncle he lost to the Lycan attack that had separated them from Kyran. But he stayed silent, eager to learn more about the family he never knew he had until recently.

"Almost all Elementals choose to be Hunters. It's the natural fit – they are the ones who rule the realm; they need to know how to protect it," she continued. "Your dad had always been overprotective of Alex. It was understandable; he had raised him, even when he was a kid himself." Her eyes glazed over, as if reliving memories in her head. "Chris didn't want Alex hunting. So he chose a less dangerous role for Alex and enrolled him for Lurker training. But Alex wanted to be a Hunter. They argued about it for a while. I was dating your dad then, and I remember the fights between the brothers." She smiled sadly. "Alex was always the one to give in, always trying to keep the peace." She shook her head. "He gave in on this too, and started Lurker training. It wasn't until a few years later that we learnt he was secretly training to be a Hunter instead."

Aaron's eyes widened. "How did he manage that?" he asked.

"Hadrian," Kate said quietly.

Aaron felt a chill wash through him at just the name.

"Hadrian was our Controller. He was the one responsible for training new Hunters and Lurkers," Kate explained. "Hadrian had always had a soft spot for Alex. He let him get away with things others couldn't even dream of. Chris may have been Alex's actual brother, and even though Alex loved him more than anything, the rest of the Elementals were like an extended family. It was no secret that from all of his 'Elemental brothers', Alex liked Hadrian the most. They were close. So when Alex asked Hadrian to help train him to be a Hunter and keep it a secret, Hadrian did it without a second thought." She met Aaron's eyes. "When your dad found out, he was angry, but Alex eventually talked him into accepting it. Your dad took over Alex's training. He taught him everything he knew, put him through gruelling regimes, worked him from morning till night, until he was confident that Alex was ready, that he was *prepared* for taking down demons."

Aaron felt his hair stand on end, understanding at last why his mum was telling him this story. Her hand tightened in his.

"That day, when the Lycans attacked the City of Marwa, Alex leapt into the battle with all the confidence your dad had instilled in him. Alex went into that fight thinking he was ready, that this was just going to be like the hunts he had fought and won in the past, that he would be able to protect his city, protect his family...protect Ben." She choked on his name, but she pushed past it. "Alex was an incredible fighter. He had all the skills a Hunter could wish for, but that still didn't save him." Tears leaked out of her eyes again. "You can never be fully prepared, Aaron. Training, hunting, learning to fight; it doesn't mean you'll always win." Her eyes held so much pain it was hurting Aaron to hold her gaze. "Your dad blames himself for what happened to Alex. He filled Alex with too much confidence and not enough fear. He regrets giving in to Alex's pleas. If he had forced Alex to give up his Hunter training and go back to being a Lurker, Alex would never have jumped into that battle with the Lycans. He would have known he couldn't defeat them." She stared at Aaron. "That's why we didn't tell you who you were, and what powers you possessed. That's why your dad won't train you, why I won't ever tell you it's okay to go out there and fight, because we know now – we know after losing Alex – you can *never* be fully prepared to survive a battle."

Aaron didn't know what to say to that. All his arguments were falling short. So he settled on nodding, agreeing with her. He gave his mum's hand a squeeze, before pulling her into a hug.

"I know you can't avoid it now," Kate said, dipping her head low to speak into his ear. "Neriah's made sure you're a part of this fight, but remember, Aaron: you're not invincible. You *can* get hurt. Please, *please,* be careful." Her voice cracked at the last word and she tightened her arms around him.

Aaron nodded against her. "I will," he said. "I promise."

*** 

When Aaron and Kate finally stepped out of the cottage to get breakfast, Aaron found the residents of Salvador seated on the ground in two lines, a long stretch of cloth between them. Mary, Alan and Ava were bringing platters of food from the Stove and putting them on top of the cloth. Aaron's dad and uncle were helping to distribute the food. The sight hit Aaron hard. The table that used to stand in the middle of the street was where everyone in Salvador united to sit and eat as one. The table was gone, but the residents of Salvador refused to let that get in the way. They still gathered together to share their meals.

While Kate hurried to the Stove to help serve the food, Aaron sat down to head nods and smiles from almost everyone. Sam and Rose looked surprised that Aaron had joined them. They grinned at him with relief, glad he was walking around. Sam gestured to his hair and raised an eyebrow. Aaron shrugged in response.

A quick look around and Aaron noticed both Ella and Skyler were missing.

"Where's Ella?" Aaron asked Zhi-Jiya, who was seated across from him.

Zhi-Jiya's expression showed her pain. She shook her head. "She's not very hungry these days."

"Know the feeling," Ryan said, playing with the few pieces of fruit on his plate.

"Come on now," Mary said, her tone mildly scolding. "Eat up. Breakfast's the most important meal of the day."

No one said anything, and neither did anyone make any attempts to eat. Mary, Chris, Michael and Kate headed back to the broken building that was the Stove, to bring out more dishes, hoping to stir the mages' appetite.

After a few quiet minutes, Zhi-Jiya looked up from her plate. "What are we going to do?" she asked in a voice that betrayed her fear. "Without Neriah...What...What happens now?"

Everyone looked amongst themselves, but no one had an answer.

"I still can't believe he's gone," Bella said. "I saw it happen with my own eyes, and yet...I don't believe it."

"I know what you mean," Omar said. "I feel the same way."

"We should do something," Zhi-Jiya said. "To honour his memory."

Murmurs of agreement started amongst the mages.

"I'm sorry," Ryan started, dropping his fork, "but are we all just going to ignore what was said?"

The mages turned to Ryan with furrowed brows.

"What do you mean?" Bella asked.

Ryan looked around the seated Hunters. "You know what I mean," he said. "Don't try to tell me that any of you have *not* been thinking about it." He paused for a moment, his eyes dark and full of pained anger. "What Hadrian said to Neriah."

Like a bolt of lightning, the memory hit Aaron: Neriah on the ground, wounded and bleeding. Hadrian standing over him, accusing him...*You turned on me when I did this, all of this, for you. I became what I am to fulfil your dream. You played me. You used me to take out James, then locked my powers. Chris left of his own accord, otherwise you would have got him out of the way somehow too. And all for what? So you could take over. Rule the realm as the one and only Elemental; the one and only leader.*

"Ryan," Zhi-Jiya said, her tone one of warning. "Don't start again."

"You heard him too, Zhi-Jiya," Ryan said. "We all did."

"What we heard was probably nothing more than lies," said Bella.

Ryan turned to look at her. "If they were lies, Neriah didn't put up much of a defence against them." He looked back around at his furious girlfriend. "I know you don't want to hear it, Zhi-Jiya," he said, "but we need to question what secrets our leader was keeping from us."

"He's right," Omar chimed in. "If what Hadrian said has even a grain of truth, then we need to know exactly what Neriah's intentions were. If Neriah really did plan for Hadrian to turn into a vamage so he could take out James Avira–"

"Are you listening to yourself?" Bella interrupted.

"You can't deny that's what happened," Ryan said. "Hadrian was punished for killing James Avira, and Christopher Adams left for his own reasons, which made Neriah the one and only ruler of this realm. But what if that happened not the way Neriah told us, but the way Hadrian said it happened?"

"Why are you so sure Hadrian was telling the truth?" Zhi-Jiya asked.

"Because I saw Neriah's face," Ryan said. "I saw the guilt in him when Hadrian said he did everything to fulfil Neriah's dream."

"Neriah denied it," Bella reminded them.

"Doesn't mean it's not true," Ryan said.

"Neriah would never have wanted to get rid of the other Elementals, just so he could rule," Zhi-Jiya said with conviction. "I don't care what Hadrian said, I believe in my leader."

Ryan paused to look at her. "Zhi-Jiya, Neriah lied to his own niece about how her mother died."

Everyone fell quiet. Sam turned to Aaron, wordlessly asking him if that was true. Aaron gave him a small nod. Hadrian had revealed it wasn't Lycans who killed Lily Afton. He had killed her, and he blamed Neriah for it.

"If Neriah could do that to his own blood," Ryan went on, "then what makes you think he was ever truthful with us, about anything?"

No one had a response.

"We have to face it," Ryan said. "Neriah wasn't the mage we all thought he was."

"Ryan," Zhi-Jiya protested weakly. She caught sight of something behind him and her face dropped.

Ryan turned around, as did Aaron and the others, to see Ella standing behind them, motionless. Her eyes were still red, but they were fixed on Ryan.

"Go on," she said. "Tell us what kind of a mage Neriah really was."

Ryan stood up to face her. "Ella," he started. "I'm sorry–"

"For what?" Ella asked and her voice was sharper than Aaron had ever heard it. "What exactly are you sorry about, Ryan?" she asked. "For believing Hadrian? Or for doubting Neriah?"

"Ella," Ryan pleaded, "you were there, you heard–"

"I don't care," Ella cut him off. "I don't care what Hadrian said. It's not true." Her grey eyes narrowed at the mages. "Neriah was our leader. *No one* will tarnish his memory by doubting his intentions. None of us can imagine what it was like for him to lose his Elemental brothers. Neriah didn't *want* to be the only ruler, it was a crown forced on his head." Ella took in a breath in an attempt to calm herself. "Neriah fought to protect this realm from demons. He gave his life to this cause. I don't know if he played a part in making Hadrian a vamage, but Neriah dedicated his life to defeating him. That's what matters. That's what you all should remember of Neriah Afton." She looked to Ryan. "And if you can't respect him, then leave his city and don't bother coming back."

***

The manor was still and quiet. It was the early hours of the morning, but Kyran knew his father was already up. He had to be careful; this was the third time this week Kyran had missed breakfast with Hadrian. Another one, and the inquisition would start. The last thing Kyran needed right now was his father asking questions.

Kyran turned the corner and cursed under his breath. Leaning against his bedroom door was the red-haired vampire Layla – his father's beloved pet, and the bane of Kyran's existence. She had a necklace in her hand and was idly playing with the long chain, one leg bent at the knee with her foot pressed against the door. She turned her head, spotting Kyran. Her pale blue eyes lit up and she smiled brightly.

"Good morning," she called. "How was your night? Restful seems doubtful, judging by your dishevelled state."

Kyran didn't say anything as he walked towards her, only gestured for her to move out of the way. Layla obliged.

"Where have you been?" she asked.

Kyran opened his door and paused. "Why?" he asked with his back still to her. "What does it have to do with you?"

"I'm just curious," Layla said. "Especially as you've stayed out all night and have come home smelling of blood." Layla grinned. "And it's not yours."

Kyran turned to glare at her. Layla stepped closer and put a hand on his jacket. She leant in and took a long sniff. "Mmmn, warlocks, yummy. Two nights ago it was shifters." She stared into his eyes. "Remind me, when was massacring warlocks and shifters on Hadrian's agenda?"

Kyran pulled her hands away. "What I do in my own time is of no concern to anyone, least of all *you*."

"Everything you do, Kyran, is of great concern – to everyone around you."

"Then stay away from me," Kyran said.

Layla shrugged. "Don't want to."

"What *do* you want?" Kyran asked.

"Countless things, Kyran," she replied. "But at the moment, what I want is to figure you out." She tilted her head, her eyes narrowing before she smirked. "You're up to something." She pushed herself closer to him. "And it's going to be so much fun finding out what it is." She winked at him and sauntered away.

Kyran turned and went into his room, slamming the door shut behind him.

***

Aaron was seeking solitude. He needed to sort his head out. He understood Ryan's mistrust of Neriah, after Hadrian's accusations. A part of Aaron too wondered why Neriah lied about Ella's mother's murder. Why blame the Lycans when it was Hadrian who had killed her? Why did Hadrian say he changed from a mage to a vamage for Neriah? Aaron felt a cold shiver run down his back. Why did Hadrian imply that Neriah was the one to get rid of the rest of the Elementals, just so that he could be the only leader?

Aaron may not have known Neriah very long, but what little time he had spent with their leader, Aaron knew Neriah could do no such thing. He had sensed it in Neriah's interactions with his dad; he could see just how much he despised Chris for leaving the realm and trying to live a life in the human world. He had felt Neriah's pain when he shared memories of Hadrian from the time all the Elementals were together. Aaron could tell how much Neriah missed them, all of them, even Hadrian. It couldn't all be an act. Aaron was sure Neriah hadn't wanted to be the only ruler. Hadrian, on the other hand, wanted nothing more.

Aaron set out to go and find Neriah's grave, but found himself walking towards the lake instead. It was the one spot in Salvador that Aaron always went to when his mind was burdened, so he knew it wasn't the legacy calling out for its element. But Aaron found he wasn't the only one seeking the solace of the water. Ella was sitting at the bank, the cold air whipping her long hair behind her. Aaron almost turned back. He didn't know how to face her, what to say to her. But he couldn't leave her sitting all alone, looking so dejected and lost. She must have heard him approaching, but she didn't acknowledge him. Aaron silently sat down next to her. For a long moment, neither one spoke. Both just sat staring at the calm water of the lake.

"You okay?" Aaron asked at last.

Ella didn't say anything. She stayed as she was, sitting on the ground, her arms around her knees.

"For what it's worth, I don't think Ryan said what he said to be hurtful. He was just—"

"He was just being Ryan," Ella said. "Yeah, I know."

They lapsed into silence. Aaron had noted that Ella had been avoiding meeting his eyes ever since he woke up with her legacy inside of him.

"Ella," Aaron started. "Ella, please look at me."

Ella took in a deep breath and turned her head. But she still couldn't look directly at him. Her grey eyes darted behind Aaron and her expression changed from pained to surprised.

"Scott?" she breathed. "Scott's awake!"

Aaron turned around and sure enough, the Controller of the realm was slowly walking down the street.

Ella and Aaron leapt to their feet to race to Scott's side. No one but Empaths had seen Scott since he had been gravely injured in the vamage attack.

"Scott!" Ella yelled.

When Scott lifted his head, Aaron saw how weak the battle had left him. Even after recuperating for so many days, Scott was still horribly pale. His cheeks were sunken, and he had dark circles under his eyes. He looked thinner, his face gaunt and devoid of its usual charm. But when he saw them, Scott stopped and smiled. He opened his arms to Ella and she ran to him, hugging him tight. For long moments, they simply stood there, their whispers muffled. Then Aaron caught Scott's words and realised he was paying his condolences for Neriah. Ella didn't say anything but just held on to him, her face buried in his shoulder.

They pulled away and Ella wiped her sleeve across her puffy eyes. "I was so worried," she said. "The Empaths said you would wake up days ago."

"I've been awake," Scott confessed. "I just – I didn't have it in me to get up, not after I heard about Neriah." He stopped and seemed to gather himself. He looked over at Aaron and smiled. "How are you, Aaron?" he asked. "You coping okay?"

Aaron nodded. "And you?" he asked.

Scott paused. "I'm..." He was struggling to find the right words. "I've healed from the attack. Physically, I'm fine, but without my Hub, I feel...lost." He looked at Aaron. "It's like they took the strength from my bones along with the Hub."

Ella held on to Scott's arms with both hands. "We'll get it back," she said with such conviction even Aaron believed her. "The Hub belongs to the Controller. I'll get you your Hub back, Scott, I promise."

Scott's eyes glistened and he cupped her cheek with his hand. "No, you won't," he said. "I'm not risking another life. We can't afford to lose anyone else."

"Scott–" Ella started.

"Neriah should never have attempted to get the Hub back," Scott cut across her. "I won't repeat his mistake."

***

Aaron walked back to the cottages with Ella and Scott. The moment the Hunters saw their Controller on his feet, they let out cries of joy and raced to his side, hugging him with great affection. Mary hurried to embrace him, kissing him on the mouth with great passion, surprising Aaron. He hadn't known Mary and Scott were involved with each other.

Aaron spotted his dad's friend, Drake Logan, and his orchard workers making their way through the crowd to meet Scott too. Drake clapped a hand on Scott's back, grinning widely, before hugging him as warmly as a brother would. Chris and Kate shook Scott's hand, expressing their relief that he had survived the vamage attack. Michael wasn't far behind them.

It was the first time since Neriah's death that a hint of happiness was in the air. Aaron couldn't help but smile at the sight of Scott, surrounded by rejoicing mages. It was a moment Aaron wished would never end.

And in that same moment, a sudden darkness fell over them. Everyone stopped – the street came to a standstill. All heads tilted upwards to see thick, darkened clouds rolling in. A bolt of lightning hit the sky.

Fear, sharp and as excruciating as a knife stabbing into his flesh, seared through Aaron. He recognised the phenomenon. Somewhere in this realm, a Q-Zone had just opened – a Q-Zone that Hadrian was controlling with the Hub.

# 3

## NEW LEADERS

Aaron couldn't move.

Thunder boomed overhead and forks of lightning lit the sky. Everyone stood where they were, rooted to the ground by sheer horror, staring at the sky. No one spoke a word. The essence of fear hung heavily in the air. Aaron managed to tear his eyes away and looked around him, searching for the glittery walls of the Q-Zone. He couldn't see anything to suggest they were the ones inside a makeshift zone, designed to obliterate them. But Aaron knew, from previous hunting experiences, that the walls of a Q-Zone could be kept invisible until the very end of its forty minutes existence. If Scott could open a Q-Zone and hide the walls until the last countdown, why couldn't Hadrian?

Is that what Hadrian was doing? Were they sitting inside a zone designed to collapse any minute? Why were they just standing around, staring at the stormy sky? Shouldn't they run? But Aaron knew running wouldn't do them any good. The Q-Zone could be as big as the whole zone. They would never get out in time.

The clouds continued to darken with lightning flickering against them. The clap of thunder had mages jumping. Everyone in Salvador had gathered out onto the street. Aaron saw Skyler and Ella standing shoulder to shoulder, eyes trained on the sky, their hands on their weapons – their familiars. Everyone waited, watching the clouds move in.

The storm disappeared in a flash, leaving bright sunlight momentarily blinding everyone. It was over; the Q-Zone had ended – wherever it had been. Aaron let out the breath he had been holding. Relief flowed like a wave through the street. Some mages started laughing nervously, others hugged one another. Aaron realised how weak his legs had become when he tried to take a step forward. His mum was quick to hold on to him, pulling him in for a hug, but he could feel her shaking.

The euphoria died almost at once, as the realisation dawned on all of them: their city wasn't destroyed by the Q-Zone, but somewhere in this realm, another had been.

Scott started forward, breaking into a run, heading towards the pathway that led to the circular glass building that had been named after the Hub it used to hold.

*** 

Aaron learnt hours later where the Q-Zone had opened. It was the City of Dharkesh, a small population in one of Neriah's safe zones. Why it had been targeted was anyone's guess. Hadrian's Q-Zone had wiped out ninety mages in a single strike. The thought of how vulnerable mages were now to Hadrian's attack was sickening. The feeling of helplessness sat heavily in the pit of Aaron's stomach, not leaving any room for food. Aaron noticed he wasn't the only one ignoring his dinner. Practically no one lifted a hand to eat anything.

The lake was calling to Aaron, urging him to come and sit by its bank. It was tempting to go to it, to surrender to its tranquillity. He closed his eyes and breathed out, trying to quell the craving deep in his core.

"Aaron?"

Rose's voice made him open his eyes, to see her looking at him with wide, shocked eyes. He glanced down and saw why. Water from several pitchers had spilt out and was spreading towards him, pooling into a puddle before his plate. Everyone was staring at Aaron with uneasy expressions. Amongst them was Ella, trying in vain to hide her pain at Aaron's control of her element. Aaron quickly got up.

"Aaron, where are you–?" Mary started.

"I'm not hungry," Aaron said, heading towards his cottage. Two sets of footsteps hurried after him. He didn't have to turn around to know who was following him. "Really, guys, I'm fine. Finish your dinner," he said.

Sam and Rose jogged to reach his side and fall into step with him.

"We've eaten more than you," Rose said.

"Which isn't exactly a feat," Sam added.

Aaron didn't say anything and kept walking.

"What was that?" Rose asked after a moment's pause. "That thing with the water? Did you do that?"

"It wasn't intentional," Aaron said. "It just...happened."

"That was crazy," Sam said. "And sort of cool," he added with a grin.

Aaron dug his hands into his pockets, hunching his shoulders. "It's anything but cool, Sammy."

Rose touched his arm. "It's not your fault," she said softly. "You didn't ask Neriah to give you the legacy. Ella can't be mad at you–"

"Yes, she can," Aaron said. "She has every right in the world to be mad, at me and at Neriah."

They reached the cottage and Aaron heard the raised voices the moment he stepped past the door. They were coming from the living room. Aaron walked in, and his mum and dad abruptly stopped their arguing. Both Chris and Kate seemed out of breath, their faces a little pink as they turned to look at him. Aaron noted at once that his mum's eyes were red, like they got when she was beyond furious. Aaron stood at the door, unsure of what he should do. He had never witnessed a fight between his parents before.

"What's going on?" he asked.

Kate and Chris didn't speak right away, but their eyes went to Sam and Rose.

"Nothing," Kate said, pushing back her hair, tucking it behind her ears. She folded her hands against her chest but Aaron saw the tremble in them before she could hide it. "Have you finished dinner already?" she asked.

Sam and Rose backed out of the room. "We'll see you upstairs," Sam whispered and left with Rose.

Aaron closed the door and stepped towards his parents. "What's wrong?" he asked. "Why are you fighting?"

Kate's lips pressed together. She gave Chris a hard look. "Ask your dad," she said.

Chris didn't speak right away. He took a minute before turning to face Aaron fully.

"I'm leaving," he said. "To find Ben."

It took Aaron a moment to fully understand what his dad had just said. "Ben?" he asked. "You mean, you're leaving to try to find Kyran?"

"His name is Ben," Chris corrected.

"No, it's not," Aaron argued. "He's Kyran now. The same Kyran who tried to *kill* you a week ago."

"It wasn't like that," Chris started.

"I was there!" Aaron snapped. "I saw what happened, Dad."

"He was trying to protect Hadrian," Chris said. "That fire was to keep everyone away. He wouldn't have attacked me otherwise."

Aaron's heart ached. "I want to believe that," he said. "Really, Dad, you have *no* idea how much." He shook his head, fighting back his pain. "But the truth is, if Kyran wanted to keep you away from Hadrian, he could have done it without hurting you.

He has the legacy of Air and Earth as well as Fire, but he chose to burn you. Kyran attacked you because he *wanted* to hurt you."

Pain filled Chris's expression, but he shook his head. "He's angry, and he has every right," he said. He swallowed heavily and his eyes glistened. "He thinks that we...we abandoned him. He's lived with that belief for fourteen years. I have to find him and tell him the truth. I need him to know that we didn't leave him behind. He has to understand that we felt the bond with him break. We felt him die. How it's possible for the bond to break when he's still alive, I don't know, but I will find out." Chris held Aaron's eyes. "Ben can attack me with all the fire in this earth's core, but I'm not backing down. He's my son, and I'm not giving up on him."

Aaron didn't say anything.

Behind Chris, Kate spoke up. "No one is stopping you," she said. "But he's my son too."

"It'd be dangerous for you," Chris said, swerving around to face her.

"No more than it is for you," she said.

"Kate." Chris reached out but Kate pulled back.

"I'm going with you," she said. "Argue all you like, but I'm going with you to find our son and bring him back home."

*** 

Aaron couldn't sleep. His mind refused to switch off. His mum and dad were set to leave as soon as possible, to find Kyran and explain themselves to him. It was a futile mission. Aaron knew it, but he couldn't convince his parents of it. Aaron kept his mind firmly away from Kyran. He had forced himself not to think about him. It had taken every ounce of his willpower not to delve into the last memory he had of his brother – the one where he was defending Hadrian, allowing the leader of the vamages to murder Neriah. It was Kyran's ring of fire that had prevented the mages from going to Neriah's aid after Hadrian had stabbed him. Kyran had purposefully held the mages back, allowing Hadrian to kill Neriah.

Aaron squeezed his eyes shut, trying not to remember Neriah in his last few moments, lying in the sand that had become wet with his blood, glaring through tear-filled eyes at Hadrian.

*You're forgetting something...nothing is more powerful than blood.*

That was the last thing Neriah had said – words aimed at Hadrian but his gaze had flickered to Kyran. He had said those words and a heartbeat later transferred his legacy to Aaron. Aaron may be young, but he wasn't naïve. Neriah had given Aaron the legacy with the belief that Kyran wouldn't be able to take it from Aaron because he was his brother, his blood. Neriah thought he was safeguarding the legacy by giving it to someone Kyran wouldn't be able to kill, or let Hadrian kill.

Once again, Neriah had placed his faith in the wrong person. Kyran may have been an Adams by blood, but it obviously meant nothing to him. Kyran had attacked his own biological father; burnt him with a wave of fire without a moment's hesitation. If he could do that to his dad for Hadrian, why wouldn't he hurt his brother to get from him what Hadrian wanted?

Even as that realisation played in his mind, Aaron's heart rejected it. Kyran had always protected him; sometimes going as far as stepping in front of him, facing the threat head on. But would Kyran allow him to be killed for the legacy? Aaron honestly didn't know what to think.

Eventually, Aaron gave up on sleep. He made his way outside, content to just stand at the front door, breathing in the fresh air.

It had stopped raining but the road was still wet and shiny under the moonlight. Shallow puddles reflected the floating lanterns in the sky. Aaron shivered as the cold wind ruffled his clothes, but he didn't go back indoors. Slowly, Aaron carried on down the road, heading to the secluded part of Salvador that held the remains of departed souls. A light drizzle of rain started, but Aaron kept walking. He wanted to go to Neriah's grave; now seemed like the perfect time. Everyone else was sleeping, or lying awake in their beds, contemplating the fate of their realm, but Aaron was the only one outside in the street.

Or so Aaron thought.

As he approached the graveyard, Aaron spotted the figure sitting at one of the graves. The large white tombstone with dark writing on it told Aaron, even in the limited light, that it was Neriah's grave. The three wavy lines – the symbol for the element of Water – was etched at the top, marking it as the grave of an Elemental.

Aaron came to a stop. The rain was getting heavier now, but it didn't seem to matter to the woman sitting at Neriah's grave. Aaron could see she was trembling, but it wasn't because of the cold or the rain. He could feel her tears as they slid out of her eyes. Her shaking shoulders, lowered head, and the way her hand wouldn't move from Neriah's name on the headstone, all exposed her grief. Aaron wanted to go over to her, to offer comfort even if she was a stranger. She was in obvious pain, heart-broken, and Aaron couldn't just walk away from someone like that.

He had taken a few steps when the woman raised her head, wiping at her cheeks. Aaron stilled. She wasn't a stranger. He had seen her before. He recalled seeing this very same woman at their door in Marwa. She had come to visit his mum. She was her friend, Jane...something.

"Don't worry." A voice came from behind Aaron. He turned around to find Ella walking towards him. "She'll be okay. She just needs to get all her pain out, cry as much as she can. Then she can start healing."

"I know her," Aaron mumbled. "She's my mum's friend."

"Jane Boyd," Ella said, coming to stand beside Aaron. "Or as I call her, Auntie Jane."

Aaron looked to her, but Ella's eyes were on the woman. "She never stopped loving him," she said quietly. "Even when he pushed her away, even after she got married to someone else; she was always going to be in love with him, I guess. That's why she's always been Auntie Jane to me."

*I had the usual plans — marry the girl I loved, have kids, set up a home...some things are not meant to be.*

Neriah's voice echoed in Aaron's head — the words he had spoken in response to Aaron's questions about not having any family other than Ella. He remembered the photos in his aunt Alaina's house, the ones that had group pictures. He had seen Jane in them, standing beside Neriah, but never thought much of it.

Aaron didn't know how to go to her side now, what to say to a woman who was broken after losing the man she once loved — still loved to this day. He didn't move towards her. He let Ella take his hand and lead him away, leaving Jane alone to mourn her lost love.

***

When breakfast was over the next morning, Chris and Kate got up to speak to Scott, while mages and Hunters tidied the dishes. Aaron stayed where he was, with his uncle Mike on one side and Sam and Rose on the other, but his eyes and ears were on his parents' conversation with Scott.

"I'm sorry for asking this of you, Scott, especially as you've just been discharged from the Empaths' care," Chris was saying. "I wouldn't bother you if it wasn't urgent."

"Don't worry," Scott said, waving a hand. "I'm fine. What can I do for you?"

Chris rubbed a hand at the nape of his neck, seemingly a little uncomfortable starting this conversation. "I know setting up portals without the Hub is difficult–"

"It's not difficult, it's impossible," Scott corrected.

"Not necessarily," Chris argued. "Hadrian used to do it all the time."

Scott's expression tightened. "Forgive me, but I'm not Hadrian," he said with a steely edge to his voice. "I can't set up a portal without my Hub."

Chris looked disappointed. "We need to find a way," he said. "We need to start evacuating Hunters from Salvador."

Aaron was surprised. He thought his dad was asking about portals because he wanted one set up so he could go and find Kyran.

Scott looked confused. "Why would we want to do that?" he asked.

"Hadrian has the Hub," Chris said. "He can set up Q-Zones to take out whichever zone he likes, as he demonstrated yesterday." He took in a breath. "No city is safe, not until we get the Hub back. And with so many Hunters gathered here, Salvador makes an attractive target. We need to spread out, take up residence in other cities, other zones, and set up defences. That way, if one zone is taken out–"

"We don't lose all our Hunters," Scott finished. He nodded. "I can't set up portals, but I can make arrangements to move Hunters to other cities."

"Thank you." Chris stepped closer to Scott. "I need you to arrange for Aaron and his friends to stay in Zone J-26. I have family there who can watch over them."

Aaron knew his dad meant Alaina; the woman who had been engaged to his uncle Alex. She may never have had the chance to marry him, but Chris and Kate still thought of her as family.

Scott nodded. "It will be done."

Chris shook his hand. "The sooner we can move Hunters, the better."

"No one's going anywhere," Skyler said, coming to stand before Chris and Scott. "Salvador is our home. We're not abandoning it."

The surrounding Hunters and mages stopped what they were doing, watching Skyler and Chris warily.

"No one is abandoning anything," Chris replied. "We just need to move, for our own safety."

Skyler let out a laugh. "Running to save yourself. Yeah, you would know a lot about that." He leant towards Chris, his blue eyes glinting with anger. "But we're not cowards."

Chris's expression showed his annoyance. "I'm not getting into this with you again," he said. "We're moving and that's all there is to it."

"I'm curious," Skyler said, cocking his head to the side. "What makes you think you can issue orders?"

Chris looked uneasy. With great difficulty, he met Skyler's eyes. A muscle twitched in his jaw but Chris held Skyler's icy stare. "I'm the only Elemental left of my generation," Chris said. "That makes me the leader."

Skyler smiled, like he had been hoping for that very answer. "Really?" he asked. "The leader?" He stepped closer. "You think you can run out on the rest of us, disappear from the realm for fourteen years, shirk your responsibilities as an Elemental and then return to become the leader?" His eyes grew cold. "Neriah is dead, and with him died his generation's leadership. You forfeited your right as an Elemental, as a *mage*, when you left the rest of us to die. You're not fit to lead anyone." He held his head up high. "It's our turn now."

Chris looked at him with disbelief. "You can't be serious."

"It's the way Elemental leadership works," Skyler reminded. "When no Elemental is left in one generation, the rule of the realm goes to the next generation. All Elementals rule the realm, but the eldest is the leader." He stood tall. "I am the eldest Elemental of my generation. By the laws of our realm, I am the new leader of the mages."

Aaron was too stunned to make a sound. He could only stare between his dad and Skyler.

Chris shook his head. "Skyler," he breathed. "You're still a kid."

"I stopped being a kid when I was eight," Skyler said. "I grew up the moment I saw my family butchered before my eyes."

Chris took a step towards him. "I'm not challenging your authority," he said gently. "You are the eldest Elemental of the next generation. You *will* be the leader, but not while the Elementals of this generation are still around."

Skyler smiled. "The Elementals of *this* generation?" he asked with derision. "Who are we talking about, Adams? The two Elementals left are Hadrian – the vamage that's trying to destroy this realm – and you – the Elemental who ran and left us to our fate." He squared his shoulders, his eyes full of fire. "No, Adams. Neither of you can lead us."

"Neither can you," Chris said. "You're not old enough. You need to be of age."

"And I will be in a few short months." Skyler said.

"Then until you do, I'll take on the responsibilities of a leader," Chris said.

Skyler chuckled. "You think anyone here is going to listen to you?" he asked. "No one wants you as their leader." He stood to his full height. "Nineteen or not, I am the leader of this realm. I am the one the mages will follow."

Chris didn't say anything but his eyes went to the crowd, as if silently asking confirmation to Skyler's challenge.

For a moment no one moved. Then Ella walked over to stand at Skyler's side. The Hunters went next, gathering behind Skyler. Even Bella quietly joined the crowd, despite always being at odds with Skyler. One by one, the rest of the mages followed the Hunters. Aaron watched as every mage joined Skyler's side. Even Mary, along with Alan and Ava, walked to stand behind the blond Elemental.

The entire time, Skyler didn't look away from Chris. Michael got up, and so did Aaron, and, along with Drake and Kate, went to stand by Chris's side.

"I'm sorry," Scott whispered, before walking to Skyler and standing behind him.

The smile that twisted Skyler's lips was full of triumph. He raised his head and held out both hands. "You got your answer," he said. "No one, other than your family and friends, wants you to lead them." His eyes glinted. "It's time for the new generation to take over," he called loudly, "and I'm the new leader."

# 4

## GUILT

It was a strange concept for Aaron to get his head around. Skyler was the leader of the mages, even though he couldn't *officially* take up the role until his nineteenth birthday. Aaron knew, though, that the rule to come of age before taking leadership was nothing more than a formality. One thing Aaron had been told since his early days in Salvador was that Skyler had the loyalty of the mages – something Christopher Adams did not. That's why they sided with Skyler, despite him being a brash, hot-headed jerk. Was it really a good idea to make him the leader of the realm?

"Hey." Aaron looked up to see Scott standing before him. He pointed to the step Aaron was sitting on. "Mind if I join you?"

Aaron shook his head and scooted to the side. Scott sat down. "Are your mum and dad still inside?" he asked, tilting his head to the cottage behind them.

"Yeah," Aaron replied. "They're just getting ready to leave."

Scott nodded. They lapsed into silence, watching the mages walk up and down the street, carrying various items to repair the wounded city. Aaron could feel Scott's body tense next to him, before he took in a deep breath.

"I came to apologise."

Aaron turned to look at him. "For what?" he asked.

"For taking Skyler's side," Scott explained. "Believe me, I have nothing but respect for Christopher Adams. He's an Elemental and that's enough for me to hold him in high esteem." Scott looked down at the ground. "But I had to choose Skyler–"

"Because you've known him for longer, I get it," Aaron interrupted. "It's fine, Scott."

"I do know Skyler," Scott said. "I know him very well and that's why I chose him, but not for the reason you think." He kept his eyes focused ahead of him, his hands clasped. "I chose Skyler so I could help keep him under control." He looked around at Aaron with dulled blue eyes. "Skyler can be a great leader. I know how passionate he is, how fierce his desire is to help this realm. And after what happened to Armana, I know how easy it is for Skyler to lose himself in this war. I don't want that." He took in a breath. "I can't lose Skyler too. This way, I can help guide him, hold him back when it's needed."

Aaron nodded. "That's a good idea," he said. "Something tells me you're going to have to hold Skyler back a lot."

"He's angry right now," Scott said. "He's lost what little he had. Neriah was just as much his family as he was Ella's. Losing Neriah so soon after Armana–" Scott paused for a moment, pressing his lips together. "It's going to make Skyler reckless and that's when he can get hurt."

"He won't," Aaron said. "You won't let him get hurt. None of us will."

Scott looked around at Aaron with a small smile. "Thank you, Aaron," he said. "You'll be a good ruler for this realm."

Aaron snorted. "Skyler's the leader. He'll be the one to rule the realm."

"No." Scott shook his head. "Skyler's the leader, but all of the Elementals rule the realm."

"I don't understand the difference," Aaron said. "I thought the leader was the ruler. Isn't that what Hadrian wants? To be the leader and rule this world?"

"What Hadrian wants is to be the one and *only* ruler," Scott explained. "But that's not the way it's supposed to be. All four Elemental families rule the realm. They make up the rules, they enforce them. They control what happens in the realm. The eldest Elemental may be called the leader but they all have to work *together* to rule the realm. The leader can't do anything the rest of the Elementals don't want."

"Somehow, I don't see Skyler caring about what I want," Aaron said.

"He has to," Scott said. "If he wants to be a successful leader, he has to respect your wishes, and Ella's." He took in a breath. "Unless he wants to make the same mistakes his family made, and have history repeat itself."

Aaron frowned. "What do you mean?"

Scott looked away. "Nothing."

"Scott–"

The roar of motorbikes interrupted him. Aaron looked to the street to see several Hunters, kitted out in their full hunting gear, riding their bikes towards the Gate.

"Where are they going?" Aaron asked.

"They're leaving," Scott said. "I've sent them to different cities." Aaron looked to him with surprise. "Your dad was right," Scott continued. "Having all our Hunters in the one place is far too dangerous. If Salvador is targeted, we'd lose all of our fighters."

"But I thought Skyler wanted everyone to stay here," Aaron said.

"I talked to him, made him see reason," Scott said. "He doesn't want any of Salvador's own Hunters leaving, though. They're staying here, but the rest of the Hunters are being moved back to their cities, except a few who have asked to stay in Salvador." He nodded in the direction of the red-haired Hunter, Bella – who was busy helping Mary and Alan clear out the debris from destroyed buildings.

Aaron smiled. "It's a good thing we have you," he said to Scott. "You're the only one Skyler listens to."

Scott chuckled.

The door behind them opened and Chris and Kate emerged, packed bags in their hands. Scott stood up and shook hands with both of them.

"I wish there was something I could do to help," Scott said.

"Just make sure Aaron and his friends are safely taken to Zone J-26," Kate said. "That would be the best thing you could do for us."

Scott nodded. "Of course."

Kate put down her rucksack and held Aaron from the shoulders. "Stay with Alaina," she instructed. "We'll keep in contact, I promise."

"I don't know why my previous letters didn't reach Drake," Chris said. "But this time I'll address the letters to you."

Aaron nodded. He had given up trying to talk them out of this. His parents were not going to back down. They were hoping to track Kyran's whereabouts in a bid to talk to him, to reason with him. Aaron could only imagine how that would go, and it made his insides churn with nervous energy.

He bid both his parents goodbye and watched them walk to the Gate. They turned once more to wave at him before the Gate opened and they left.

"It's going to take almost a full day to get you from here to J-26," Scott said to Aaron. "But I'll get started on the preparations."

Aaron turned to face him. "I'm not going anywhere, Scott."

Scott frowned. "But your mum and dad–"

"I know," Aaron interrupted. "But I'm not leaving Salvador – not now, anyway." He scanned the street, watching the mages hover the last remnants of debris away. "The city needs me," Aaron said. "I want to help rebuild Neriah's sanctuary."

Scott stared at him. "What about Michael?" he asked. "Your uncle will insist you follow your parents' wishes."

Aaron spotted Michael halfway across the street, helping the mages clear the pathway. He shook his head. "My uncle is nothing like my parents," he told Scott. "He knows what I want and he's not going to interfere."

An impossible smile crossed Scott's face. He clapped a hand to Aaron's shoulder, silently praising him for staying to help them. He walked away, and Aaron too headed to where Sam and Rose were helping the mages fix one of the cottages.

"Break's over?" Sam asked with a grin.

"Yeah," Aaron said. "Time to get back to work."

He rolled up his sleeves and held up his hands. The ground shuddered with his power, before the broken stone of the outer wall of the cottage smoothed over.

*** 

Salvador was slowly rebuilding itself. Aaron worked tirelessly with Sam and Rose, helping the mages from sunrise to sunset. Under a grey, overcast sky, they pieced the city back together. After five days, the cottages were restored, as was the Stove.

"We need furniture," Ryan said, standing with his hands on his hips, staring at the empty room of one newly finished cottage.

"And a table for outside," Ella said.

"And things like curtains and rugs for the rooms," Zhi-Jiya added.

"Okay." Ryan nodded. "I know most of these things would come from Lamont." After a moment he looked around at the rest. "Any idea how Jason got in contact with the Lamonts?"

No one had any answers. Jason Burns had been the caretaker of Salvador, but exactly how he liaised with the wealthy Lamont family to deliver things for the city, no one knew.

"Damn," Zhi-Jiya breathed. "Never thought we would lose Jason. He never stepped a foot out of Salvador."

"Because Salvador was always the safest city of the realm," Ella said.

"It was," Ryan said quietly. "Until the Gate was dropped."

Aaron tensed. He didn't want to hear again how Kyran was responsible. The mages blamed Kyran for dropping the Gate and giving vamages access to Salvador, but Aaron knew it wasn't him. Kyran could never do such a thing. He would never let vamages into Salvador. He just wouldn't.

Rose cleared her throat, and all eyes turned to her. "There might be something in Jason's cottage," she suggested. "We could have a look through his things, see if we find anything?"

Ella shrugged. "Worth a try."

They all headed outside, bracing themselves against the chill in the wind. Ella pulled her woolly hat over her head and stuck both hands into her jacket. They hadn't reached Jason's cottage when Aaron heard Scott calling his name. He turned to see the Controller hurrying towards him.

"There you are," he said. "I've been looking all over for you."

"Everything all right, Scott?" Aaron asked.

"Better than all right," Scott said, and a smile graced his face. "I've just had confirmation from the Lurkers. They've found it. It's back in its resting place."

"I'm sorry," Aaron said. "You've lost me. What have you found?"

"Neriah's sword," Scott said. "Well, your sword now, I guess."

Aaron's stomach flipped. The sword. One of the mighty Blades of Aric. Aaron had forgotten all about it. Only legacy holders could wield the Blades, and now that Aaron had Neriah's legacy, he could also take Neriah's sword.

"I'm making arrangements for you to leave tomorrow morning to retrieve it," Scott was saying. "You are going to have to learn how to use the Blade..."

But Aaron wasn't listening. He turned to look behind him and his eyes sought out Ella instantly. Her expression was one Aaron would never forget. Every inch of her was tensed, her lips pressed in a tight line, and her eyes glistening with hurt as she stared at Scott.

Aaron took a step towards her, shaking his head. "Ella–"

Ella turned and pushed her way past Ryan and Zhi-Jiya. She crossed the street and disappeared around the corner.

"Ella," Scott gasped. "I didn't notice her," he said, sounding mortified. "I'm so sorry, I didn't mean to say anything in front of her."

Aaron hurried after her, leaving the others behind in an awkward silence.

*** 

Aaron found Ella at the bank of the lake. The water had been whispering to him, calling him all day. He had picked up Ella's presence near the water, even before he spotted her sitting there, curled up, with her knees tucked under her chin, arms around her legs. Aaron walked over to sit beside her.

For long minutes, neither of them spoke. Aaron was trying to gather his thoughts, phrasing his apology the best he could, when Ella spoke.

"I always imagined myself holding that Blade," she said. "I would practise with a normal sword in the mirror, knowing that one day, that Blade of Afton was going to be mine." Her eyes were fixed on something in the far distance. "But now, when I think about the Blade, I think about Neriah." She paused. "He always insisted I call him by his name," she said. "I never understood why. I asked him once but he just smiled and said, 'Because we're not just family, we're best friends.' He was my friend, my uncle; the only family I had." She turned to look at Aaron with pained eyes. "Friends don't lie to each other," she said. "And neither should family. So *why* did he lie?"

Aaron didn't know what to say. He remembered what Hadrian had revealed to her, to all of them.

*Your uncle lied to you. Your mother wasn't killed by Lycans. I killed her. I held Lily, just like I'm holding you today, before snapping her neck.*

"Ella." Aaron shook his head. "I don't know why Neriah kept what happened to your mum a secret," he said. "But maybe, in his own way, he was trying to protect you."

Ella's lips quivered but she squeezed her eyes shut and dropped her head. She took in a deep breath and looked up, blinking back her pain. "He said it was the Lycans," she said. "He told me it was Raoul – that he led the Lycans to our house and set it on fire. He told me by the time he and the other Hunters arrived, the Lycans had killed my mother and left me to burn. I've lived my life believing that was true. I've tracked Raoul, killed Lycans, spent every minute of every day training to fight Lycans, so I could avenge my mother's death." She closed her eyes. "But it wasn't Raoul. It was Hadrian who was responsible."

"Raoul may not be responsible for the death of your mum," Aaron said, "but he's killed plenty of mages. He's out for

Elemental blood. The years you've spent learning how to fight him isn't a waste–"

"It *is* a waste," Ella cut across him, turning to look at him. Her voice shook and the tears she was fighting spilled out of her eyes. "Neriah stood back and watched me fight with everything I had to get to Raoul. How could he *do* that? Why lie to me about my mother's death? What was he hiding? And why would Hadrian go after my mother? What could she have done to him?"

"Nothing," Aaron said. "There's nothing that she could have done that justified Hadrian killing her."

Ella fell quiet. She looked down at the ground and took in a deep breath.

"You know the worst of this?" she asked in a quiet voice. "I'll never know the reason why my mother was killed, not unless Hadrian feels like gloating to me about it." She closed her eyes. "Neriah should have told me what happened to my mother. He owed me that much."

Aaron took a moment before saying, "That wasn't all Neriah owed you." He held her eyes when she turned to look at him with a furrowed brow. "I'm sorry, Ella," he said.

"For what?" Ella asked.

"For taking your legacy."

Ella's expression changed at once. She looked away from him, bloodshot grey eyes staring dead ahead, her jaw clenched. Aaron reached out and held on to her arm, afraid she was about to get up and leave.

"I'm sorry," he said. "This legacy was your birthright. I was never meant to get it."

Ella didn't move, but she didn't say anything either.

"If I could, I would give you the legacy in a heartbeat," Aaron said. "I don't want what I know is yours."

Ella still didn't respond.

"I can understand if you're angry with me," Aaron said.

"I *am* angry," Ella said. "I'm so angry you wouldn't believe it." She forced out a breath. "But I'm not angry at *you*," she said. "What happened wasn't your fault. It wasn't even Neriah's, to be honest." She paused for a moment. "It was the only way to save the legacy." She gave Aaron a weak impression of her usual smile. "And I'd rather you had my legacy than Hadrian."

Aaron smiled. "When you put it that way."

Ella chuckled, but it sounded awfully empty. She let out a sigh before getting up. "Come on," she said. "You should prepare for your trip tomorrow."

Aaron stood up. He couldn't even imagine how difficult this was for Ella, to stand back helplessly while someone else took what was hers. Even though Aaron didn't want the legacy for Water, or even its Blade, it didn't make Ella's pain any less.

"If there's any way I can get the legacy back to you–" he started.

"Aaron," Ella cut him off. "The only way for me to get the legacy from you doesn't bear thinking about." She gave Aaron a half-heartened punch in the arm. "Just...use it well." She turned to walk away, her hands tucked into the pockets of her jacket.

Aaron watched her go, feeling his heart grow heavy.

"Where is Ella going?"

Aaron turned to see Skyler walking up behind him. Aaron shrugged at him. "Not sure," he said.

Skyler stopped beside Aaron, his eyes on Ella's retreating form. "Did she find out about you going to get the Blade tomorrow?"

"You know about that?" he asked.

"I'm the leader, Aaron," Skyler said, facing him. "I know everything that happens in my cities now."

Aaron felt the urge to open his mouth and argue, to tell him he wasn't the leader yet, but he decided against it. One look at Skyler and Aaron could see he was still suffering from the loss of Armana, and possibly even Neriah. The dark circles under Skyler's eyes told of his sleepless nights. He looked thinner, like he hadn't been eating. Come to think of it, Aaron hadn't seen Skyler at any mealtime for days.

"Are you coming with me tomorrow?" Aaron asked, knowing the answer. There was no way Skyler was going to sit back while Aaron went to claim one of the Blades of Aric – the most powerful weapons of the realm.

"Of course," Skyler replied. "I wouldn't miss it." He grinned. "I wanted to show you something," he said and reached into his pocket. He pulled out a small, shiny, silver bullet.

Aaron looked at it and then at Skyler. "It's a bullet," he said. "Why are you showing me a bullet?"

"Look at it closely," Skyler prompted.

Aaron did and at first, he still didn't understand what it was he was supposed to be looking at, or why the ill-looking Skyler seemed so gleeful with it. Then Aaron spotted the thin, scrawling letters carved into the metal. Aaron leant in, his eyes struggling to make out the tiny letters. *B–E–N–*

Aaron's heart skipped a beat. He looked at Skyler in utter disbelief. *Benjamin Adams.* That was the name Skyler had carved into the bullet. The name of his brother; the name that Kyran had been born with.

"I've got another one," Skyler said, fishing out a second bullet with *Kyran Aedus* etched across it. "Just in case the first one doesn't work, what with him renouncing his family and everything."

Aaron couldn't speak. He could barely hear Skyler. Blood was pounding in his ears, his heart beating so fast it felt like he had been running for miles. Skyler had prepared the bullets, he had crafted them and then carved Kyran's names onto them – the only way one mage could take the life of another.

Weakly, Aaron shook his head. "Skyler," he managed. "What are you doing?"

Skyler held his eyes and smiled. "Why so surprised, Adams? I already told you: the day I find your brother, it will be his last." He looked at the bullets. "Now, I'm ready to meet him."

He pocketed both bullets and walked away, leaving Aaron to stare after him in horror.

# 5

## STRANGE ENCOUNTERS

Like Scott had promised, Aaron and his team of Hunters left the next morning, to retrieve the Blade of Afton. Aaron wasn't surprised to see Ella had held back, choosing not to accompany them. Aaron hadn't grown up in the mage realm with the knowledge that he was an Elemental, and awaiting the day he would wield one of the mighty Blades of Aric because he would become a legacy holder. Ella had. Aaron could only imagine how painful it must be to grow up with those dreams and then have them shattered before you. Ella had no choice but to tolerate Aaron taking her family's Blade, the sword that was supposed to be hers. Thinking about the injustice of it all had Aaron squirming on the back of Ryan's bike.

"You all right?" Ryan called, raising his voice over the roar of the bikes.

"Yeah," Aaron replied.

"Sit tight," Ryan said. "We've got a long way to go yet."

Aaron turned his head to glance at the Hunters riding along with them. Zhi-Jiya was almost matching Ryan's speed. Slightly behind her were Omar and Sarah. On Aaron's other side were Bella and Aaron's uncle Michael. At the front, leading all of them, was Skyler.

Skyler had been obnoxious to Aaron from their very first meeting, but over the past few months, things had started to change. Skyler had shown a softer side, one that Aaron could almost relate to. He'd even opened up about being rejected by his family's Blade, after the same had happened to Aaron. But Armana's death had affected Skyler badly, turning him vengeful, and his poisonous vitriol was directed at only one thing: Kyran.

Aaron didn't know how to behave with Skyler now that he knew there were two bullets with his brother's name on them sitting in Skyler's pocket.

"You okay?" Ryan's voice interrupted Aaron's thoughts.

"Yeah, why?" Aaron asked.

"You're holding on rather tight," Ryan said.

Aaron unclenched his fingers from around Ryan's shoulders.

"Sorry," he said quickly.

Aaron forced himself to think about something else, to steer his mind away from Skyler and Kyran. It had been briefly explained to him, but Aaron still didn't completely understand how the Blade that fell from Neriah's hand in the zone right next to theirs had magically ended up in another zone, hundreds of miles away. Scott said something about the Blades of Aric *seeking spots where their elements are the strongest,* so once Neriah's Blade was left untouched for a period of time, it got pulled to a location that had its element in abundance.

Aaron was thankful. At least the Blade wasn't in Hadrian's zone. Even though no one, other than Aaron, would be able to pick up and use the sword, it was a disturbing thought to have such a powerful weapon in the clutches of their enemy. Aaron purposefully didn't let his mind go to Kyran, who had three legacies and two of the Blades of Aric. His mind screamed that Kyran was – after all – an enemy, but his heart still refused to believe it.

They rode for hours. Aaron's body was soon stiff, not to mention cold, even under all his layers and thick jacket.

"Can we not stop for a break?" Aaron asked Ryan.

He could feel the older boy chuckle. "We've got an important mission at hand. Once you've got the Blade, we can rest," he replied.

Aaron sat back. He turned to meet Michael's eyes, who nodded at him, wordlessly asking if he was alright.

Aaron nodded back.

They rode along uneven paths, and through thick clusters of leafy overgrowth. The grey sky above them started sprinkling water, which only made the cold so much worse. But Aaron found it oddly comforting as the droplets clung to his face and neck, feeding him trickles of power.

He looked up at the sky. It must have been midday, but it was difficult to tell with the overcast clouds. The Hunters had slowed down, manoeuvring through a particularly dense forest.

It happened suddenly.

A sharp light hit them, so bright it blinded all of them. The Hunters lost control of their bikes, skidding and smashing into trees. Aaron and Ryan were thrown off, but thankfully landed on soft, moist ground. The light faded and Aaron found himself flat out on his back, under a tree, his head thumping from the impact. Blinking away spots, Aaron managed to make out the rest of the mages, sprawled out on the ground, groaning in pain and disorientation.

"Aaron," Michael called, a few steps away from him. "You okay?" His voice was breathless, winded from the accident.

"Yeah," Aaron replied. "What was that?"

Michael stood up, rubbing his elbow. He caught sight of something and stilled.

Several people stepped out from behind the trees, surrounding the dazed mages. Their hands were raised, as if holding invisible weapons, and aimed directly at the mages. Their expressions were hard, their stance undeniably hostile. They moved closer, tightening their circle around the fallen Hunters.

Aaron realised they were all fair-haired and light-eyed, with freckles on their faces and necks. Aaron knew these people. He had met their kind before.

"Pecosas," he breathed.

The first time Aaron had met Pecosas, it was on a futile mission to try to convince them to join forces with the mages and fight against Hadrian. Sam and Rose had been the ones to speak to them, and Aaron always thought Sam had almost convinced Grandor – the leader of the Pecosas. In the end, though, they refused to help, asking to be left out of the war. But the Pecosas had been somewhat amicable then; letting all of them stay the night in their city, so they didn't have to travel back in the dark.

Now, it seemed like a very different situation.

"Get up!" instructed a tall Pecosa with strawberry-blond hair.

The Hunters got to their feet.

"Drop your weapons," the same Pecosa said, his voice harsh and cold.

Aaron was surprised to see Skyler did so without argument. Taking his lead, the rest of them emptied their holsters and belts, piling their familiars onto the forest ground. Aaron followed suit, while confused to his core as to what was happening. Why were the Pecosas acting like this? But more than anything, Aaron was stunned that Skyler wasn't putting up a fight.

Slowly, Skyler raised his hands in surrender, further shocking Aaron.

"We are not your enemy," Skyler said, loud and clear for all the gathered Pecosas to hear. "You must've not recognised who we are. I am Skyler Avira–"

"We know who you are, Elemental," a new voice interrupted.

The Pecosas moved aside to reveal the woman who had spoken. She shared the same traits as the rest of the Pecosas – fair skin, light green eyes – but she wasn't all fair-haired. From her roots to her shoulders, her hair was a sun-kissed blond, but from there to the tips of her waist-length locks, her hair was as black as the feathers of a raven.

Skyler dropped his hands. "If you know who we are, then why did you attack us?"

The black-and-blond-haired Pecosa stepped forward, walking to the front of the crowd, her eyes on Skyler. "You entered our zone without permission," she replied. "We are within our right to stop you."

"Your zone?" Skyler asked derisively. "Since when?"

"Since we moved here," the woman replied.

"You can't just take over a zone and then claim it as yours," Skyler said.

"Why not?" the woman asked. "That's what the rest of this realm is doing."

"Listen here, Pecosa," Skyler said angrily, and stepped towards her. The surrounding Pecosas lifted their hands in warning and Skyler halted. He raised his hands again. "We're just passing through," he said slowly. "We have no business in this zone. We just need to cross it to get to our destination."

"That may be," the woman said, "but it's still trespassing."

Skyler lost the battle to stay calm, and his anger swirled through the air, dropping the already low temperature another few degrees.

"Trespassing? This is not *your* land," Skyler said. "You're taking it by force. We have already given you a safe zone."

"One that did us absolutely no good," the woman replied. Her words sparked something in the other Pecosas. They looked downright furious as they glared at the mages. "Turn back," the woman instructed Skyler. "Leave, and don't ever think to cross this zone again."

"This is hilarious," Skyler scoffed. "*You* are giving *me* orders? Where is Grandor? I'll sort this out with your leader."

"Grandor is dead," she replied.

The shock filtered through the mages, hitting Aaron. He had met Grandor, had seen him, spoken to him. He couldn't believe the leader of the Pecosas was dead, just like the leader of the mages.

Skyler didn't speak right away. "When?" he managed, his voice quieter now, the anger dulled from his tone.

"Two months ago," she replied. "When the *safe* zone you mages gave us failed to keep out the wolf demons. Grandor died protecting his people."

"Lycans," Skyler growled in realisation.

The mages shared angry looks, their pain clear to see. Aaron noticed even his uncle Michael looked infuriated. Lycans were perhaps the mages greatest enemies, along with Hadrian and his vamages.

Skyler closed his eyes and his head dipped as he struggled to reign in his anger at the thought of Lycans. He finally looked up at the woman. "I'm guessing you're the new leader?"

The woman raised her head with pride. "Rukhsana," she said, "successor to Grandor."

Skyler stepped forward. "And I'm Skyler, the leader of the mages."

Rukhsana nodded her head. "I know of Elemental Afton's passing," she said. "You have my condolences, but not my sympathy."

Skyler's expression hardened. "Good," he said. "'Cause I don't need your *sympathy*."

"You mages are losing the war," Rukhsana said. "But it's a war that was instigated by your own failings. You deserve whatever you get."

"You don't know the first thing about this war," Skyler said dismissively.

"But I know enough about you mages," Rukhsana said. "You were created for the sole purpose of eradicating demon kind, yet you have failed time and time again. You let demons roam these lands, picking off whomever they like. You can't even set up safe zones. Your Gates fall, and the innocent die."

Aaron found himself unable to look away from Skyler, whose hands had balled into fists at Rukhsana's words. Rukhsana was talking about the Gate falling in her zone and Lycans killing her kind, but it was clear she had reminded Skyler of Armana. She too was an innocent, killed by vamages when the Gate to Salvador fell.

"Grandor tried, but his good nature failed to keep you mages away," Rukhsana continued. She stood tall to match Skyler's height. "I won't make the same mistake. Pecosas will *not* tolerate mages, not any more."

"We are not the problem," Skyler said.

"Yes, you are," Rukhsana argued. "You bring chaos and death everywhere you go. You involve others in your conflict and then leave them to die. You even lie about your abilities. If you truly controlled the elements, the demons would be long gone by now."

"You have no idea how powerful we are," Skyler said.

"Clearly not powerful enough to save the innocent." She looked Skyler in the eye. "Leave our zone, and don't come back."

"We're not leaving," Skyler said. "We need to pass through to get to our destination."

"Find another route," Rukhsana said.

"Any other path will take us days to get there," Skyler said.

"So be it," Rukhsana replied.

Skyler had had enough. He stepped forward, ignoring the Pecosas standing ready to attack him. "Listen closely, *Pecosa*," he spat at Rukhsana. "This is not your zone. You have no jurisdiction here. I, on the other hand, am the leader of this *realm*. Every zone is *my* zone. No one will tell me where I can and can't go, and definitely not a Pecosa, who likes using the word *innocent* a lot, but is the furthest thing from it."

Rukhsana stared at him, her expression one of surprise.

Skyler smirked. "You think I don't know what this means," he asked, flicking the dark part of her hair with his finger. "You have seen the darkness. You were corrupted by it. Grandor must have brought you back, but for some time, you were one of them." He leant in, so he was looking into her eyes. "A filthy, low-life *demon*!"

Skyler had crossed the line, and everyone knew it. The mages tensed, their hands flexing to call on their powers. Aaron felt his uncle shift closer; a hand came very gently to rest on his arm, preparing to pull Aaron behind him.

Rukhsana smiled. "How very clever," she said. "You must feel so proud having deduced my past." She stepped back. "Let's see if you can predict your future."

She raised her hand, but no jolt of power came flying out at Skyler. No hidden weapon was fired. Instead, Aaron saw the tiny pinprick freckles on her face start to light up. The same was happening to the Pecosas surrounding them. Their freckles lightened, until each tiny one was a beaming light – a light so bright, no one could look directly at it. The air rapidly went from ice cold to a heat wave. Michael pulled Aaron down to the ground and covered him with his own body, shielding him from whatever the Pecosas were going to throw at them. The blinding light forced Aaron to close his eyes, so he had no idea what was happening, but he heard the clinking of metal as the mages snatched up their weapons from the ground.

A heartbeat later, the heat was gone. From behind closed eyes, Aaron felt the light fade and he opened his eyes. Some Hunters were kneeling, others standing, holding their guns and swords. Some had their hands outstretched, ready to use their powers. But the Pecosas were no longer aiming at them. They had all frozen where they stood, with their eyes wide and mouths open.

Skyler had his gun aimed at Rukhsana. "Why did you stop?" he asked. "We were just starting the fun."

"Quiet!" Rukhsana snapped. Her gaze was fixed above Skyler's head, far off into the distance. "No," she gasped, and horror filled her expression. "No, no, no!"

She turned at once and fled. The Pecosas ignored the mages and ran after their leader.

Skyler turned to look at his Hunters in bafflement. "Hey!" he called after Rukhsana. "Wait, where are you going?" he called as he ran after her.

Aaron and the others followed.

"Rukhsana! What's going on?" Skyler yelled.

The leader of the Pecosas came to a stop and whirled around to face him. "They're here! They just attacked our base."

"Who?" Skyler asked. "Who's here?"

Rukhsana's eyes grew fierce and her lips thinned around the word, "Lycans."

A hush fell over the crowd. Lycans were here. Lycans were attacking the Pecosa base.

Rukhsana waved a hand at Skyler. "Get out of here, Elemental," she said. "We have bigger problems than you."

"Wait," Skyler said, as Rukhsana turned to leave. "We can help."

"I don't need your help!" Rukhsana snapped. "You mages are the reason Lycans have started hunting Pecosas."

"I don't have the time to argue against your ludicrous accusations," Skyler said. "Fact is we hunt Lycans. We know how to fight them. You don't."

Rukhsana looked conflicted. She glanced to her Pecosas, who seemed just as uncertain as her. Rukhsana turned back to Skyler. "I don't trust you," she said bluntly. "How do I know you won't instigate the battle and then leave us to die?"

"We won't," Aaron said, unable to stay quiet at her question. "I promise we won't leave until the Lycans do."

Rukhsana looked over at Aaron and stilled. Her eyes widened and she staggered back a step. "Who – who are you?"

Aaron was taken back by her reaction. "My name's Aaron Adams," he said. "I'm an Elemental."

Rukhsana seemed rather alarmed by Aaron's presence. She kept staring at him, her mouth slightly open.

"Tick, tock," Skyler said, rousing her out of her shock.

Rukhsana looked to Skyler and then straightened up, before nodding. "Okay," she said. "But *you* follow *my* orders."

Skyler smirked. "Never going to happen."

# 6

# LEADER OF THE LYCANS

Rukhsana and her Pecosas led the mages through the forest and up a steep hill. "Our camp is on the other side," she explained in a tense, quiet voice.

"How many fighters down there?" Skyler asked.

"Another twenty," Rukhsana replied. "The others are here with me," she said with a gesture to the Pecosas behind her.

Skyler glanced through the crowd. "It's not enough," he said.

"It's all we have," Rukhsana returned. "The rest were killed with Grandor."

As they neared the top, they could make out the screaming coming from below. Rukhsana hurried forward, but Skyler grabbed her arm. "We need to sneak up on them," he said. "The element of surprise is what wins the battle with Lycans."

Rukhsana shrugged herself out of his hold, but she did slow down. All of them bent low to avoid detection, pressing their fronts into the moist dirt at the very top of the hill.

"Stay down," Michael warned Aaron.

"We can't let the Lycans see us – not yet," Ryan said.

Aaron nodded. He moved with the others, inching forward to peek over and witness the attack happening below.

What Aaron saw surprised him. He was preparing himself to witness a bloody, horrifying massacre. He had seen Lycans enough times to know what they were like: big, fearsome beasts, with dark fur on their backs. They stood on two legs instead of four, and had deadly claws and fangs. But when Aaron looked over the top of the hill, what he saw were the Pecosas, easily distinguished by their fair-hair, running and trying to get away from another crowd of men and women. There were no Lycans there, just average-looking people, chasing the Pecosas with menace; pushing and shoving them to gather in the middle of a clearing. The Pecosas were being rounded up, but Aaron couldn't figure out why.

It was easy to see that the Pecosas were greatly outnumbered. There seemed to be almost two hundred of the other group, and only fifty or so of the Pecosas, including children.

Skyler swore. "There's too many of them," he whispered. "We don't have enough Hunters."

"Then call for back up," Rukhsana said.

"It'll take them hours to get here," Skyler said, his frustration clear in his voice. "We don't have the Hub. Our Controller can't create any short-cuts."

Rukhsana stared at him, her expression growing cold. "So what is the plan?"

Skyler looked conflicted. He glanced at the Hunters on both sides of him before looking at the Pecosas behind Rukhsana. "Our numbers aren't enough. We can't engage in battle," he said.

"Skyler, we have to do *something*," Ryan said.

"We can create a diversion," Michael suggested. "Get as many Pecosas out as we can."

"Out where?" Skyler asked. "It's not like we can ask Scott to open a portal to get them into another zone."

"So what are you saying?" Rukhsana hissed at Skyler. "You're not going to help?" She shook her head. "I knew you wouldn't risk it, not for my people."

"I don't discriminate," Skyler answered back. "But fact is fact. We don't have the numbers. If we go in, all of us get killed."

Aaron was trying to pay attention to the argument, but all he could do was stare at the scene below. All the Pecosas stood huddled together, while the other group surrounded them. The crying and screaming had stopped…for now.

The crowd of people around the Pecosas stepped back, making way for someone. The Pecosas looked terrified as they clung to one another. Aaron pressed himself forward, his eyes narrowed at the man walking towards the Pecosas. He was tall, with long silvery-white hair that reached to the small of his back. Aaron couldn't see his face, not from this angle, but the way the Pecosas backed away from him, it was as if he had the face of a monster.

The man stood before the Pecosas for a long moment, then turned around to look at the people surrounding them. That's when Aaron caught a glimpse of his face. Sharp-featured, with a straight-edged nose and a large forehead, he was oddly handsome. He smiled and his brown eyes gleamed almost red in the daylight.

It took Aaron a moment to realise the arguing next to him had stopped. He looked over to see all of the mages were watching the white-haired man.

"Dammit," Ryan whispered. "We can't go in now, not with Raoul here."

Aaron's eyes locked back on to the man. "That's Raoul?" he asked.

"Yeah," Skyler replied, his voice low and guttural. "That's Raoul."

Aaron had met the leader of the Lycans, but it was when Raoul had been in his Lycan-form. It was Raoul who had attacked his dad when they crossed paths in search of the Blade of Adams. Raoul was the one who tore a four-year-old Ben away from his mother and threw him to the Lycans to be devoured. How Ben survived and lived to become Kyran,

Aaron still didn't know, but he would never forget how brutal Raoul's attack was on his pregnant mother and infant brother.

Aaron watched as Raoul faced the Pecosas. He must have said something, because a tremor of fear ran through them. They started shaking their heads, clutching their young close to them.

Raoul sauntered forward, leisurely looking through the crowd of Pecosas, taking his time choosing his victim. He stopped in front of a woman, hugging a Pecosa girl around Aaron's age to her chest. Aaron's breath quickened, his skin prickled with dread. Raoul reached out and grabbed the girl by her hair, yanking her out of her mother's arms.

The mages around Aaron bristled.

"I'm not letting him kill my people," Rukhsana seethed. "If you're not going to help, so be it!"

"Don't be stupid!" Skyler said. "You go in there, you're going to get killed too."

Aaron heard Rukhsana leading her Pecosas back the way they came, but he couldn't look away from the young girl in Raoul's grip. Even at a distance, Aaron could sense her tears, could *feel* them rolling down her face. Raoul dragged her away from the rest of the Pecosas by her blond hair. The Lycans moved towards the crowd, to stop them from trying to help the girl. The screaming mother of the girl was held back by other sobbing Pecosas as she begged Raoul to let her daughter go.

Aaron's heart was racing. He watched with morbid horror as Raoul held the crying girl, grinning at her, as she struggled in his grip.

"He's going to kill her," Aaron heard himself whisper. Raoul was going to murder the girl in front of her mother, just like he had tried to kill Ben in front of their mother. "We have to do something," he said. "We can't let him kill her."

"There're too many Lycans," Michael said. "We're outnumbered, even with the Pecosa fighters with us."

Aaron looked around at his uncle. "So we just let him kill her?" he asked incredulously.

"There are some battles we can't fight," Michael replied, and he looked like he hated himself for saying it. "This is one of them."

Disgusted, Aaron turned away from Michael. He saw Raoul let go of the girl, but she stood where she was, too scared to run. Raoul was saying something to her, but Aaron was too far away to hear his words. The girl was shaking but she nodded and closed her eyes. Raoul walked up to her and reached out gently, almost lovingly, to caress her tear-stained cheek. His hand trailed down to grip her around the neck.

Aaron knew what was coming. He took aim, ready to snatch the very ground from under Raoul's feet before he could snap the girl's neck. Before Aaron could do anything, the girl's mother broke away from the crowd and came at Raoul, screaming. The freckles on her face lit up and a glow began emitting from her. Raoul kept his grip on the girl, but turned and swiped a hand at the mother. She fell to the ground, a horrid gash across her neck and face.

Aaron didn't understand how that happened until he saw Raoul's arm from the elbow down had transformed into that of a Lycan's. His claws had sliced her flesh open. The mother's body convulsed in agony on the ground, as the Lycan venom entered her system. The girl, still in Raoul's clutches was crying out for her mother, but Raoul didn't let her go. He towered over the dying woman, before reaching out for her with his clawed hand.

Michael tugged Aaron down, so he didn't see what Raoul did to her, but Aaron already knew. The screams of the Pecosas told Aaron Raoul had plunged his claws into the woman's chest, taking her life.

The cries echoed in the air, surrounding Aaron, suffocating him. He was gasping for breath. He turned so he was lying on his back, but he couldn't fill his lungs with enough air, no matter how hard he tried. He could feel Michael's hands on him, could hear his voice calling his name, but he wasn't able to reply. Something was happening to him; he could feel his insides tightening – his core was taking over. The legacy was pulling its element with all the force it had.

Skyler suddenly grabbed him by the collars. "Adams, no!" he roared. "Stop it! We can't finish this fight if you start it."

But Aaron was far past the point where he could stop. His body was trembling, his core working like never before. The legacy inside him was gathering power from every source – and water was *everywhere*.

Skyler looked at something in the distance and swore. "Aaron," he growled. "Don't do this!"

The surrounding mages seemed just as unnerved as Skyler. They kept looking in front of them, and then at Aaron, wearing gob-smacked expressions. Aaron had no idea what his core was doing, but he knew he didn't want it to stop. He looked Skyler in the eyes and Skyler let go of him with a shove. "You're going to get all of us killed," he hissed.

Aaron didn't have the breath to talk back. He turned around, so he too could see what everyone was staring at. The sight was one Aaron would never forget.

A wave, tremendously big and deadly, was towering higher than the treetops. It looked like a wave seconds before it crashed, but the water simply stood where it was. It wouldn't collapse, not until Aaron commanded it to.

Raoul's attention had shifted from the Pecosas to the water that had appeared from nowhere, almost as tall as a mountain, directly above the Lycans and the trapped Pecosas. Raoul pushed the girl in his grip away and scanned his surroundings.

His searching gaze found the mages at the top of the hill and he stilled.

Skyler slowly straightened up. Following his lead, the mages all stood up. They had been spotted; there was no point in hiding now. Aaron got up too, all the while directing as much water from the grey skies to his monstrous wave, building it higher, feeding it power.

Raoul looked past Aaron, focusing on Skyler instead. Something inside Aaron snapped. Raoul was the reason Aaron didn't grow up with his brother. Raoul was the reason his parents thought their son had died. Raoul was the one who had ripped Kyran away from them. His Lycans had killed Alex. And yet, even after destroying his family, Raoul didn't even give Aaron a second look.

Aaron's hands lifted, shaking with anger, as he aimed at the leader of the Lycans. *Now!* Aaron commanded, and, with a boom like thunder, the wave came down on the Lycans.

No one was left on their feet. Lycans and Pecosas alike were hit and pulled under by the water. The trees swayed with the force of the water as it crashed against them. Many of them were uprooted, pulled clean out of the ground, and the Pecosas' tents and belongings washed away. The Pecosas resurfaced, clambering back to their feet, coughing and spluttering but there was no sign of the Lycans.

Then with a mighty growl, the Lycans leapt up, no longer looking human but the demonic beasts they really were. Raoul was easily recognisable with his blood-red fur, soaked through by the water. The Lycans stood on their legs and raised their heads to the sky, letting out angry howls.

Then they were racing up the hill, coming for the mages.

"Show time," Skyler said.

The mages attacked with everything they had: jolts of power, bullets and small blades. The Lycans leapt aside, dodging some of the strikes as they bolted up the hill. Skyler sent a hurricane ripping through the crowd, throwing the Lycans aside. Michael and Ryan were sending a stream of fireballs at them. Zhi-Jiya was fighting with her throwing stars, Sarah too. Omar and Bella were using a mix of their powers and guns. But no matter what they threw at the Lycans, how many they managed to hit and knock back, the Lycans kept coming at them, and were gaining ground.

Aaron gathered his power. He threw out his hand and the ripple that tore its way down the hill was so strong it shook the ground. It hit the crowd of Lycans, propelling them into the air. Raoul was thrown all the way back to the bottom of the hill as the ripple met him with full force. But Raoul just got up, gave himself a shake and started racing up the hill again.

There were too many Lycans and only a handful of mages. They couldn't keep them back for long. As the Lycans spilt over the top of the hill the mages backed away. Skyler's tornado blasted a large number back down the hill, as did Aaron's double ripple, but the Lycans just climbed back to the top.

The Hunters pulled out their swords, forced to battle in close combat now that the Lycans were upon them. Michael pulled Aaron behind him, throwing fire at any Lycan that tried to get close. Aaron caved the ground under the Lycans, throwing some into deep pits, but they weren't deep enough; the Lycans clawed their way out. Aaron's attacks were lacking power – his core was fast depleting having used too much power for the big wave. But he kept on fighting, not willing to give up.

The swarm of Lycans had surrounded the Hunters and were closing in. Aaron threw ripple after ripple, even used another gush of water to throw the beasts back, but for every one that was pushed back, another two came forward.

A sudden bright light halted everyone. The mages and Lycans stopped mid-battle. From both ends of the forest, Pecosas came charging at them. Their faces were hidden behind the blinding glow emitting from their freckles. Michael pulled Aaron to the ground and covered him with his body. Aaron caught a glimpse of the other mages doing the same; crouching on the ground with their hands over their heads.

A blast of heat erupted, searing through everyone. Aaron heard his uncle hiss in pain above him, but he didn't move, keeping Aaron protected from the Pecosas' attack. The Lycans howled in agony, but the light was too bright for Aaron to see what was happening to them. The stench of burnt flesh and fur filled the air.

Then the light was gone, and so was the heat. Aaron opened his eyes, but Michael was still covering him. Slowly, with pained movements, Michael uncurled his arms and pulled back. Aaron looked over to catch a glimpse of the Lycans scampering into the forest. Aaron couldn't believe it; they had done it, they had defeated the Lycans. Well, they and the Pecosas.

Aaron turned to his uncle, to see the grimace on his face. "Uncle Mike, you okay?" he asked.

Michael nodded stiffly. "I will be," he said. "Fire is my element. I can take a few blisters."

Aaron was confused, until he looked behind Michael and saw the few Lycans that didn't survive the Pecosas' attack. They were charred black, burnt from the inside and out. Aaron looked away from the grotesque sight. He stood up, before helping Michael straighten up. The rest of the Hunters were picking themselves up too, examining the blistered and reddened skin of their hands and arms.

Rukhsana and her Pecosas walked over to them.

"You could've given us a better warning that you were about to have a barbecue," Skyler said, sporting a rather nasty-looking burn across his hand.

Rukhsana didn't look apologetic in the least. "Be thankful all you got were second-degree burns," she said. "We didn't have to spare you."

"So why did you?" Skyler asked.

"Because you were a good distraction for the Lycans. It gave us the opportunity to gather all our fighters and come in for a surprise attack," she replied.

She turned to find Aaron and walked towards him. Michael stepped in front of Aaron, shielding him. But Rukhsana only gave Michael a single glance before looking past him to Aaron.

"It was you, wasn't it?" she said. "You're the one who brought that wave of water. You started the fight."

Aaron didn't hesitate to answer. "Yes," he said. "I'm sorry about your people being hit too. I didn't mean to hurt them–"

"Hurt them?" Rukhsana said, her pale green eyes wide. "You *saved* them. Your fellow Elemental was happy to leave them to their fate." She turned to give Skyler a scathing look. "But you, Elemental Adams–" she turned back to Aaron, "you acted to help my people. You endangered yourself to stop Raoul and his Lycans from massacring what was left of my kind." She smiled. "You, Elemental Adams, have our respect and gratitude," she said. She turned to look one more time at Skyler before turning back again to Aaron. "And from today, you – and *only* you – have our allegiance."

*** 

That night, the Pecosas held a celebration in Aaron's honour. Various dishes derived from food that Aaron had never seen or tasted before were served in abundance, along with drinks made from all kinds of fruit. A huge fire pit was lit to ward off the cold, and the mages were happy sitting around it, enjoying the satiety of dinner.

Aaron was at the other side, away from the fire pit and the crowds of Pecosas and mages. He was leaning against a tree, staring out at the dark forest that lay before him. At his right, in the distance, was the girl who lost her mother today. She sat at the mouth of her tent, tears in her eyes. Many of her fellow Pecosas came to her, urging her to eat, but she just sat in silence, crying. Aaron's heart broke at the thought of her loss.

"Not feeling the celebrations?"

Aaron turned to see Rukhsana smiling at him. "I just needed some quiet to sort out my thoughts," he explained.

"Anything I can help with?"

Aaron shook his head.

Rukhsana stared at him for a long moment. "When you arrived this afternoon, I admit I was distracted," she said. "I knew there was more than one Elemental in the midst of the mages, but I was too busy quarrelling with Elemental Avira to fully notice you."

Aaron waved a hand at her. "It's okay. It's near enough impossible for anyone to be noticed when Skyler's around."

Rukhsana chuckled softly. She stared at Aaron for a long moment before asking, "Are you well versed in the nature of Pecosas, Elemental Adams?"

"I'm not well versed in anything belonging to this realm," Aaron admitted.

"Pecosas have many abilities," she started. "We have our defensive powers, which you witnessed today, but there is another talent we possess, which is just as powerful." She stepped up to Aaron, looking into his eyes. "We can sense auras. We can tell who are mages, who are Elementals, and who are demons."

Aaron was impressed. "That's pretty cool."

Rukhsana nodded. "It is," she said. "We know who stands before us, regardless of their disguise."

Aaron felt his skin prickle. "What do you mean?" he asked.

Rukhsana didn't speak right away. "Your aura confused me," she said in a quiet voice. "When you spoke up about defending us from the Lycans, I looked over at you and I was struck by your aura. I knew you were an Elemental, the only one present other than Elemental Avira, but you also hold a power that doesn't belong to you."

Aaron understood she meant the legacy for Water that was residing within him. Guilt made him lower his head, looking away from her.

"I've only ever seen that in one other individual," Rukhsana said.

Aaron snapped his head up. His heart kicked at his insides. "You have?" he asked, knowing exactly who she was talking about. It couldn't be anyone else.

A haunted look came in Rukhsana's eyes as she uttered, "The Scorcher."

Hearing Kyran's alias spoken with such fear made Aaron's stomach turn. Aaron held her eyes. "Have you met him?" he asked.

Rukhsana took a moment to slowly nod. "Many times," she said. "He used to come with the mages to see Grandor. We always knew who he was, but we couldn't expose him, not when his vamages had so many of our people." She paused for a moment. "But I first saw him when I had attended a meeting Machado had arranged. The Scorcher came at the end, not to speak to us, but to Machado. He looked like any other mage, but his aura–" She stopped and closed her eyes, visibly gathering herself. "It was like nothing I had ever seen. I knew he was an Elemental but he too possessed power that wasn't his."

The legacies. Kyran had three legacies: Earth, Fire and Air. Only Earth truly belonged to him.

"When I saw you today, it reminded me of *him* – of the Scorcher," Rukhsana said. "That's why I asked who you were."

Aaron had to force himself to speak. "Neriah," he started. "He gave me his legacy before he died, to save it from Hadrian."

The lines on Rukhsana's forehead disappeared. "That makes sense," she said. "That's why you have that power."

Aaron nodded. He didn't need to tell her, but he felt he should explain his relationship with the Scorcher. "There's something else," he started. "The Scorcher..." He faltered, but then pushed on. "The reason why you felt a similarity in our auras—"

"I never said that," Rukhsana cut him off. "Your auras are not similar, not at all. Don't ever say that. Your aura is beautiful; it shimmers gold with purity. But the Scorcher's aura is tainted black."

Aaron's heart twisted in his chest. "What do you mean?" he asked.

Rukhsana took a moment to speak. "There's a darkness in him," she said. "It's a part of him – a shadow he cannot escape. Its influence weighs down on him, interfering with everything he does." She paused to take in a shaky breath. "I have seen all sorts of creatures, good and evil. I have battled my own darkness, but never have I seen anyone with an aura as burdened as that of the Scorcher's."

***

Aaron was caught in a whirlwind of tormenting thoughts. He couldn't get Rukhsana's words out of his head. He had already been conflicted about his brother, but now he didn't know what to think. Aaron had no idea where he was going, but he took off into the dark forest the moment Rukhsana returned to the celebrations.

He had walked so deep into the forest that even the moonlight couldn't penetrate the tight canopy of trees over his head. Aaron had to rely on his elemental instinct to keep himself from bumping into tree trunks. All he could think about was Rukhsana's words...

*There's a darkness in him...a shadow he cannot escape...never have I seen anyone with an aura as burdened as that of the Scorcher's...*

Aaron caught a sudden flash of light. He came to a standstill. Peering into the darkness, he could see nothing. Aaron shook his head. He must have imagined it. He took another few steps, only to stop when it happened again. Aaron narrowed his eyes. What *was* that?

He walked in the direction it had appeared. Another flash. It looked like a spiral – the symbol for the element of Air. It glowed for a moment and then disappeared. As Aaron neared, another symbol blinked brightly: an inverted V – the symbol for Fire. Aaron's heart skipped a beat. What was going on?

Aaron reached the spot the symbols had flashed before disappearing. He stood, waiting, but nothing happened. Then a little flicker of light started forming a circle in mid-air, directly in front of Aaron. As a baffled Aaron watched, symbols appeared inside the circle. An inverted V, three wavy lines and a spiral. They slid into place inside the circle to make Aric's mark – the symbols for the four elements.

The glowing Aric's mark grew bigger, until it was half Aaron's height. It suddenly occurred to Aaron what this was. A portal.

Aaron's stomach flipped. He had to run back and warn the Pecosas and Hunters that Hadrian had opened a portal, and vamages were coming for them. But before he could take a single step back, a hand shot out of the portal and grabbed

Aaron from the front of his jacket. Aaron's shocked cry didn't make it out in time, as he was yanked into the portal and out of the forest.

# 7

## SURPRISES

Aaron stumbled forward, momentarily blinded by the bright light of the portal he had just been dragged through. The hand that had pulled him in was still holding him, the grip tight and secure. Aaron used both hands to fight it, to break free, before a familiar chuckle halted him.

"Easy, Ace."

Aaron blinked furiously. His vision cleared and he saw Kyran before him. They were in a dark alley. A solid brick wall behind Kyran showed it was a dead end. Not a single other person was around. Kyran let go of Aaron, standing back to look at him from head to toe. He smiled.

"Like the haircut," he remarked. "It's not in keeping with the usual Hunter style," he said, raking a hand through his own tousled hair, "but I guess that's a good thing, right?"

Aaron didn't say anything. Over the past few weeks he had tried so hard to keep himself from thinking about Kyran. Mostly because he didn't know *what* to think of him now. Yes, he was his big brother, but he had attacked their dad. Kyran was a mage, yet he let Hadrian kill their leader. Kyran was Ben Adams, but he identified himself as only Kyran Aedus. So what did that leave Aaron with? A brother who wasn't family any more?

Aaron believed with every fibre of his being that Kyran hadn't dropped the Gate to Salvador. But Hadrian had the Hub now, so Kyran must know that he had attacked Salvador to get it. Did Kyran not care? The glow of the portal behind him answered that question. Kyran wasn't bothered in the least, which was why he was freely using the portals created by the stolen Hub.

The anger that had settled in Aaron ever since he saw his dad set aflame by Kyran rose up inside him. His hands curled into fists and before Aaron could stop himself, he pulled back and punched Kyran, square in the jaw.

Kyran staggered back. He shook his head before looking at Aaron with a grin.

"You've got a mean right hook," he said. "So glad I taught you that."

"Left's not bad either," Aaron growled. "You want a demonstration?"

Kyran held up both hands with a laugh. "I believe you."

Aaron glared at him. "Why did you bring me here?"

Kyran dropped his hands, and his smile fell away too. "To talk."

"About what?" Aaron asked.

"You know what," Kyran replied. He paused for a moment. "What Neriah did–"

"He did what he had to," Aaron interrupted. "To save his legacy."

Kyran's eyes narrowed. "Do you have any idea what that means for you?"

"I do," Aaron said. "But I don't see why *you're* bothered by it."

Kyran looked taken aback. He pulled in a breath. "All right," he said. "I get that you're mad at me–"

"Mad at you?" Aaron asked. "*Mad* at you? Kyran, you attacked my dad! You set him on *fire!*"

Kyran's expression hardened. "He had that coming."

Aaron had to remember to breathe. "I swear to God," Aaron seethed, shaking his head, "I'm going to deck you again."

Kyran smirked. "Go for it. I let you get one in – doesn't mean it'll happen again."

Aaron didn't even care if Kyran did fight back. He was so angry he was ready to launch himself at the Scorcher – the one the rest of the realm was so terrified of. But instead, Aaron said the thing that had been tormenting him for weeks.

"You let him kill Neriah." As hard as Aaron tried, he couldn't stop his voice breaking. "How could you do that, Kyran?"

This time a flicker of something akin to regret flashed on Kyran's face, but he was quick to hide it.

"Hadrian didn't go into Neriah's zone and kill him," he said. "Neriah invaded *our* zone. He attacked my father. Hadrian was just defending himself."

"Defending himself?" Aaron asked. "Hadrian laid a trap! He knew Neriah would come looking for the Hub. He lured Neriah there so he could kill him!"

Kyran's brow furrowed. "Wait, wait," he said. "The Hub? What are you talking about?"

"Oh, come on, Kyran!" Aaron snapped. "Drop the act, okay? I may not know that much about how this realm works, but I've learnt enough to know that you can't make a portal without the Hub." He gestured to the glowing Aric's mark behind him.

Kyran's gaze flickered to the portal and back to Aaron. He stepped closer. "Portals can be made without the Hub," he said quickly. "Not to everywhere and not by everyone, but it *can* be done." He pushed on. "Why did you say Neriah came looking for the Hub?"

Aaron held his confused stare. "Because Hadrian's vamages stole it from Salvador."

Kyran's eyes widened and the look of shock and disbelief in them couldn't be faked. Aaron realised, in that moment, that Kyran hadn't been aware of what Hadrian had done.

It took Kyran a moment but he finally asked, "When?"

"Around the same time you came to see me on the Gateway, when I called for you," Aaron replied.

It was as if Aaron had struck Kyran again. He staggered back, in utter disbelief. Aaron pushed on, "After you left and I went back, the Gate had already been dropped. The vamages had entered the city."

Kyran was breathing hard, his chest heaving. His hands raked through his hair. He looked at Aaron and for a moment he couldn't speak. Then, in a small voice, he asked, "How many?"

Aaron understood Kyran wasn't asking for the number of vamages that had attacked Salvador. The slight tremor in his voice indicated he was asking how many casualties Salvador had suffered. Aaron had to swallow hard, to get his voice past the growing lump at the back of his throat.

"Too many," he said. "Jason, Danielle, Jean..." His heart ached. "Armana."

Kyran closed his eyes, clenching them shut. He turned his back to Aaron, leaning on the brick wall with both hands, his head dipped. He stayed like that for a moment. Then one hand formed a fist. Kyran pulled back and punched the wall. He spun round and stormed past Aaron.

"Go," he growled at him, before heading down the dark alley.

Aaron didn't move. He watched Kyran until he disappeared into the shadows. Then Aaron stepped back into the portal to reappear in the forest, a short distance away from the celebrating Pecosas and mages.

***

The doors to the manor slammed open as Kyran entered. He hurried to his father's private chambers, only to find them empty. He tried various meeting rooms, but Hadrian wasn't there. Kyran checked room after room, but found neither his father nor the Hub.

Kyran knew Aaron wouldn't lie, not about the Hub being stolen, or Salvador being attacked, but he couldn't bring himself to believe his father had done such a thing behind his back. But with every empty room he found, Kyran's conviction wavered. Aaron must have been mistaken. Maybe the Hub was taken by other dark forces and the blame – as per usual – was put on Hadrian. But even Kyran knew no other being could control the Hub; it would only operate under a chosen mage's hand – or one particular vamage's.

Kyran searched the manor with desperation, but he didn't find anything out of the ordinary. He was about to collapse against the wall with relief, when he remembered the small, rarely used upper left wing of the manor. He hadn't checked there yet. He took three steps at a time to race to the forgotten part of the manor, and ran smack into someone at the top of the stairs.

"Oh my." Layla grinned, showing her perfect set of teeth. "I enjoyed that. We should bump into each other more often."

Kyran pushed her aside. "Get out of my way." He hurried forward to check the rooms.

Layla followed after him. "What are you doing in this part of the manor?"

"I could ask you the same," Kyran said and opened the door to the first room. There was nothing in there but old furniture.

"I like it here," Layla said. "It's nice and secluded. My own little world. No one here but me." She looked at Kyran. "Well, usually."

"You're the only one of your kind," Kyran reminded, checking more rooms. "The only vampire left in existence. Isn't that lonely enough?"

Layla giggled. "Look who's talking." She leant against the wall as Kyran opened another door. "You're the only mage living amongst vamages. Until your little undercover mission in Salvador, you hadn't even *seen* another one of your kind for over a decade."

Kyran glared at her before walking away, checking the other rooms.

"What are you looking for?" Layla asked.

"The mouth of hell," Kyran replied. "So I can push you through it."

Layla smiled. "Oh, Kyran," she sighed. "When are you going to see it? We're already in hell."

Kyran ignored her. He headed to the furthest room and opened the door. He stopped short. There, sitting in the middle of the room, was the round white table – the Hub. Kyran felt something inside him break. He had been so sure, so convinced Aaron had it wrong; that the Hub had been taken by another foe. But Aaron was right. It had been Hadrian, and the proof was right there in front of him.

"Oh," Layla gasped, peeking into the room from behind Kyran. "Is...Is that what I think it is?"

Kyran's eyes darkened. He turned and stormed past Layla, racing down the stairs. He reached the main atrium in time to find a group of vamages returning from one of their hunts. Machado, Hadrian's right-hand vamage, was one of them. Kyran's hands balled into fists and he darted towards him. Machado halted mid-step, his satisfied smile replaced with a confused frown at the sight of Kyran coming at him with such fury.

"Whoa, wait–" The rest of Machado's words didn't make it out as Kyran grabbed him with both hands and threw him against the wall.

The other vamages backed away, knowing better than to interfere with an angry Scorcher.

"You just couldn't help yourself, could you?" Kyran raged.

Kyran's arm was pressed against Machado's throat, but the vamage still managed to croak out, "What are you...talking about?"

"The attack on Salvador," Kyran said. "I told you straight up Salvador was to remain untouched, but you went behind my back and attacked it anyway."

Machado's eyes were fast turning red. His fangs started to slide out. "Let me go," he warned.

Kyran was only too happy to oblige. He pulled back his arm and threw Machado to the ground. The vamage sat up like a wounded animal, his fangs bared.

Kyran's eyes had darkened. The four lines on the back of his hand started to glow. The watching vamages turned tail and ran out of the manor. Machado's fangs slid back, and his eyes returned to their glittery blue, but now widened with fear.

"No," he gasped and fell back in his haste to get away. "Kyran! No!"

Kyran moved towards him, but something hit him, knocking him bodily to the floor. It was Layla. She sat on top of him, pinning him to the ground.

"Na-ah." She waved a finger in front of his face. "About to bleed out Hadrian's favourite little pet?" she tutted. "Daddy won't be happy."

"Get off me," Kyran growled.

"First promise you'll play nice," Layla said.

Kyran was too angry for Layla's games. He pushed her off, using a little help from the element of Air to send her spinning across the atrium. Layla landed on all fours, like a cat, grinning. "That was fun," she said. "Let's do it again."

But Kyran wasn't interested. He had eyes only for Machado, who had picked himself up from the floor but hadn't run. Kyran started towards him.

"Kyran!"

Kyran stopped at his father's call. He turned to see Hadrian at the door, having just returned to the manor. He was looking at Kyran with surprise. More accurately, he was looking at the glowing light coming from his hand and chest.

"What is going on?" he demanded, coming towards Kyran.

The light in Kyran's hand and chest dulled before going out completely. Kyran stared at his father. It was easier to go after Machado, to blame him for Salvador's attack, but Kyran knew the truth: it wouldn't have happened if his father hadn't authorised it.

"Kyran?" Hadrian's voice was cold and authoritative. "I asked you something."

"And I had asked you to leave Salvador alone," Kyran said quietly.

Understanding dawned on Hadrian and his annoyance melted at once. He straightened up and looked over at Layla. "You can go," he instructed.

Layla nodded. She gave Kyran a big smile as she passed him. "Until next time." She winked and headed towards her designated wing.

"Machado, leave," Hadrian said.

With a hateful glower directed at Kyran, Machado turned and walked away. Only Hadrian and Kyran were left. Hadrian gestured to his room.

"We should sit and discuss this."

"What's left to discuss?" Kyran asked with ire. "You attacked Salvador for the Hub. You sent your rabid dogs into the city to attack the innocent–"

"I would hardly call Hunters innocent," Hadrian interjected.

Kyran's hands were curled so tight his nails were cutting into his skin. "They sought out and attacked those who couldn't fight back. You sent your men to Salvador for the Hub. Their job was to get it and get out, not murder the blind Empaths or defenceless humans."

"I wasn't aware of that," Hadrian said. "You know how much I despise unnecessary bloodshed." He stepped up to Kyran and put a hand on his shoulder. "But I didn't send them to Salvador," he lied easily. "An opportunity arose and Machado made an executive decision to take it. They got into Salvador and managed to take the Hub." He smiled. "This is a victory for us, Kyran."

"Then why did you hide it from me?" Kyran asked.

"Who said I was hiding it?" Hadrian asked with a chuckle.

"You chose the most secluded location in the whole manor to house the Hub."

"Because I wanted to keep it safe," Hadrian said.

"Why didn't you tell me?" Kyran asked.

"I had every intention of telling you," Hadrian said. "But it's been rather difficult to speak to you these days. This is the first time in weeks that I've seen you longer than ten seconds."

Kyran closed up at once, clicking his mouth shut.

Hadrian took in a deep breath. "I know that you've been...distracted lately, and I understand why. It can't be easy, preparing for what you have to do, to secure the last legacy."

Kyran dropped his gaze. He felt his father's hand squeeze his shoulder.

"Kyran," Hadrian called gently. "Take all the time you need. I won't rush you. I know this is complicated for you, but just remember he's an Adams and you are an Aedus." Hadrian smiled. "You are *my* son. The Adams are not your family, so that boy means nothing to you."

Kyran didn't say anything but gave Hadrian a small nod.

If only that were true, it would make his life so much easier.

# 8

# THE BLADE OF AFTON

Skyler had the mages up at daybreak, which meant most only had a few hours of sleep.

"Shouldn't have been up partying all night," Skyler said to the bleary-eyed Hunters, who were strapping their weapons belts clumsily onto their torsos.

Aaron hadn't had much sleep either, but it had nothing to do with the party. He had spent the night going over his meeting with Kyran. Every time his eyes closed, he recalled Kyran's shocked reaction to finding out about the attack on Salvador. It couldn't have been pretence. It had been as genuine as it comes.

"You're just bitter 'cause you weren't invited to the celebration," Ryan said to Skyler.

"That's why it was so much fun last night," Bella said with a grin. "Because Skyler was sent to his tent, and not allowed to come to the party."

Skyler didn't so much as look at Bella. He simply walked away, heading to the other tents.

Ryan shared a surprised look with her. "That's the first time I've ever seen Skyler not take the bait from you."

"I know," Bella said.

"He's taken Armana's death pretty hard," Ryan said quietly. "He's still not recovered from it."

Bella nodded, her sea-green eyes on Skyler as he rounded the rest of the mages out of their tents. "Somehow, I don't think he ever will," she said. "Not completely."

Aaron looked at Skyler too. The blond-haired Elemental held Kyran responsible for Armana's death, blaming him for dropping the Gate to give the vamages access to the city. But if Skyler had seen Kyran last night, if he had witnessed how angry Kyran had got after learning what happened, even Skyler would have been convinced of Kyran's innocence. Aaron scoffed at his own thoughts. Who was he kidding? If Skyler had seen Kyran last night, he would have used the two bullets he was carrying in his pocket, no questions asked.

Gradually, all the Hunters were awake, and after a quick breakfast of exotic fruit, that tasted just as sweet as it did bitter, they were ready for the rest of the journey. Aaron had just got up from the table when Skyler appeared at his side.

"Adams, a word." He held Aaron by the elbow and steered him to one side.

"What is it?" Aaron asked, pulling himself out of Skyler's grip.

"Just a word of warning," Skyler said. "We still have a long trip ahead, and chances are we might run into more demonic scum." His icy blue eyes narrowed. "I don't need to remind you that I'm the leader now. That means that you listen to me and follow my instructions."

"You're right," Aaron said. "You don't need to remind me." He made to walk away.

"Hey," Skyler snapped, and his hand slammed against Aaron's chest, halting him. "You need to cut out the cheek and listen to me. You almost got all of us *killed* yesterday. If you pull that kind of crap again, I'll—"

"You'll what?" Aaron interrupted. "You'll make a bullet with my name on it too?"

Skyler stilled. Aaron pushed against Skyler's hand and walked away. Skyler watched him go, but didn't follow.

Pecosa children had gathered around the Hunters to look at the motorbikes with awe and fervour. Despite his agitated mood, Aaron couldn't help but smile at the sight. They reminded him of Sam. He'd been just as excited when he first saw the Hunters' bikes.

As the mages mounted their bikes, Rukhsana and some of her Pecosas came to bid them goodbye. Rukhsana shook everyone's hand, even Skyler's, but she held Aaron's hand the longest.

"Thank you, once again, Elemental Adams," she said. "You will always have our gratitude and our loyalty."

"Thank you," Aaron said. "That means a lot." He knew Scott was still trying to get the Pecosas to join the fight against Hadrian. There may only be a small number of them left, but their allegiance meant a win for the mages, and Aaron was more than happy to take it. They needed it, after losing the Hub and Neriah.

Rukhsana smiled at him before leaning in to whisper in his ear, "Keep that aura shining, Elemental Adams. Never let it fade."

*\*\**

The day was as grey and miserable as they come. A fine spray of rain had all of the Hunters drenched after a few hours of riding their bikes. Aaron sought comfort from it, but the rest had the opposite reaction.

"I hate this weather!" Bella grouched, when they all stopped for a quick break. She looked up at the sky and said, "If you're going to rain, just pour already. What's up with this sprinkling crap?"

As if hearing her, the rain got heavier. Zhi-Jiya muttered a few choice words as she hoisted the hood of her top over her head. "You had to ask!" she snapped at Bella.

Aaron held out his hand to catch the thick droplets. Water pooled in his hand, before streaming down to his wrist and encircling it. Aaron watched it with fascination.

"We need to keep moving," he heard Skyler say. "We want to get to the Blade before nightfall."

The Hunters finished stretching their legs and went back to their bikes. Aaron let the watery bracelet fall from his wrist before climbing on behind Ryan.

They rode for hours, passing acres and acres of grassland. The rain was pelting down on them but the Hunters didn't stop to find refuge. They shook their heads to throw water out of their soaked hair and kept going, following on after Skyler. Gradually, the rain stopped and the Hunters paused briefly, long enough for Michael and Ryan to use their powers of Fire to dry all of them.

The landscape changed as they continued their journey. The trees began to thin, as did the grass on the ground. Soon they were driving with nothing around them but open air and hardened, rocky ground. Far off into the distance, Aaron could see craggy mountains. The air was getting colder.

Aaron felt it miles before he saw the first glimpse of blue on the horizon. Water – *a lot* of water – was waiting for them ahead. Skyler slowed down to a stop. He got off his bike and the Hunters followed his example.

"We need to go on foot from here on," Skyler said.

Aaron quickly saw why. The ground ahead was no longer straight and smooth. It was hilly, with rocks jutting out at odd angles; it looked like the ground was made out of slabs of rough stone, thrown carelessly together. Aaron followed the others, climbing up a steep hill. His foot slipped a few times on the uneven ground, forcing Aaron to slow down, but he managed not to fall too far behind. Michael stayed with him, adjusting to his pace.

His core was telling him there was water all around him, so when Aaron reached the top of the hill, he wasn't surprised to see the vast pool stretched before him. All of the Hunters came to a standstill, taking in the sight. The water was a rich blue, surrounded by mountains in the distance, forming a perfect semi-circle. In the middle of the pool, was an enormous glacial block of ice.

Aaron stepped forward, not believing his eyes. Sitting inside the glacier was the Blade of Afton.

"You have got to be kidding me," Aaron muttered.

Bella came to stand next to Aaron, grinning from ear to ear.

"Well, Adams." She gestured to the mountain of ice, through which the magnificent sword was visible. "Go get her."

Aaron turned his head to look at her. "Nice try," he said. "But I'm starting to catch on to this whole being a mage thing."

Bella raised her eyebrows. "Yeah?" she said. "Let's see it, then."

Aaron made his way down the hill. Some mages followed him, like Michael. Others stayed at the top of the hill, like Skyler. Aaron left everyone behind and walked across the shore, stopping at the edge of the spit of land jutting into the lake. The feeling of fatigue overwhelmed him, but Aaron knew it was only because he was near one of Aric's blades. The water began lapping at the edges, trying to get to him. Aaron breathed out. His eyes were fixed on the sword, the Blade of Afton, one of Aric's legendary swords. He had seen it in Neriah's hand. He had also watched it fall from his hand when Hadrian killed him.

Shaking his head, Aaron dispelled that image. He couldn't think about that now. Raising his hand, Aaron aimed at the glacier holding the sword. The mages behind him were deathly silent, watching him.

*Give me the sword,* Aaron commanded the water of the glacier.

Cracks formed in the glacier at once, but then stilled. The sword remained where it was. Aaron frowned.

*Give me the sword, now!*

The glacier rocked from side to side, but the sword remained firmly inside it.

Aaron could feel everyone's eyes on him.

*Give me the Blade of Afton!*

A few more cracks in the glacier but the sword stayed put.

Aaron dropped his hand, before realising what he was doing wrong. Licking his lips, Aaron tried again. His hand extended forward.

*Come,* Aaron called, but he was talking to the Blade this time, not the water.

In the blink of an eye, the sword smashed through the icy wall of the glacier, splintering the front like glass. The sword zoomed through the air and straight to Aaron's hand.

The moment Aaron's fingers closed around the hilt of the mighty Blade, a burst of power rushed through him, stealing his very breath. It was like nothing Aaron had ever felt before. A sense of bliss settled through him, taking away every worry, every concern. Aaron looked at the sword, at the strange engravings along the shiny silver. Under his hand, on the hilt, there were tiny white stones set in Aric's mark. It was truly magnificent, in every sense of the word.

It took Aaron a moment to realise the Hunters behind him were cheering. He turned around with the sword in hand, to see the Hunters on top of the hill and on the shore clapping and whistling. The only exception was Skyler, who was looking at the sword with a pained expression. Aaron understood why. The sword he was holding was never supposed to be in his hands. It was destined for Ella; Skyler's best friend. But there was a flash of hunger in Skyler's expression, and Aaron understood that too. Aaron was holding the one thing Skyler desperately wanted for himself but couldn't have. Kyran had his legacy, without which Skyler couldn't wield his family's Blade, couldn't use one of the most powerful weapons of the realm.

*** 

It took the mages another day to return to the city of Salvador. The moment the Gate opened and Aaron rode into the city on the back of Ryan's bike, the residents stopped to stare at them. Aaron found every eye turning to him, scanning him, searching for the sword. Skyler had already told Scott via his Hunter pendant that they had succeeded in retrieving the Blade of Afton, but Aaron figured the mages wanted to see it to believe it.

Aaron made it easier for them. He lifted the sword out of its protective sheath and held it up as Ryan rode down the street. The blade gleamed, even in the limited evening light; its dark engravings shimmered, before a tinge of blue ran through it. The mages of Salvador laughed with relief, and some even started clapping.

Aaron spotted Sam and Rose in the crowd, staring at him in surprised awe. Aaron couldn't help it, the jubilation around him forced a smile to cross his face. He thrust the sword higher into the air, and the mages cheered loudly, clapping with earnest.

The bike came to a stop and Aaron climbed off. He saw Ryan grinning at him.

"Feels good to have a win after so long," he said.

Aaron couldn't agree more. He turned around and in the midst of the excited, applauding crowd, Aaron spotted Ella. She wasn't clapping. She wasn't cheering. She was standing there, staring at Aaron, at the sword in his hand. Aaron stilled. The euphoria from moments before drained out of him. Ella met his eyes, and for moment they just stood locked in the other's gaze.

Then Ella stepped back, turned around and pushed her way past the crowd, disappearing from view.

All of a sudden, the Blade felt too heavy in Aaron's hand.

Scott made his way over to Aaron, wearing a proud smile. "I'm so relieved you've all made it back safely," Scott said. "Lurkers reported Raoul and his Lycans were circling the area, searching for the sword."

"Well, they failed," Bella said, coming to Aaron's side with a wide grin. "We got to it first."

Scott looked to the Blade before his eyes moved to Aaron. He gave him a tight smile. "I wish you were holding the Blade of Adams," he confessed. "This must be so confusing for you. Your power is Earth, but you hold the legacy for Water. Using the Blade won't come easy to you. It'll take time and lots of practice."

Aaron nodded. He had already figured that much. Kyran had taught him how to wield a sword, but using a Blade of Aric was going to require more than basic fighting skills.

"Who will teach me?" Aaron asked.

Scott's face dropped. He didn't answer right away. The truth was, the only people who knew how to use the Blades of Aric were the Elementals who held the legacy for their element. Aaron had one legacy, and Kyran had the other three.

"We'll figure something out," Scott said. "Right now, we need to decide how to store the Blade," he said. "As a general rule, Blades of Aric are kept in their own locations, a spot that has their element in abundance, so the Blade can feed off it. Elementals usually go to the Blade to train with it." He let out a sigh. "But with the Hub gone, we don't have that option. I can't make portals for you to go to the Blade, which is why I asked you to bring the Blade here."

"But if you store the Blade in Salvador, it's going to drain the powers from everyone here," Bella said.

"Not if we store it at a good distance," Ryan said. "The Blade is going to need its own space, but it has to be in Salvador."

"I know the perfect spot," Aaron said.

\*\*\*

Aaron stood at the bank of the lake, the Blade in his hand. The chilly air nipped at his face. He could feel the moisture in it. The clouds were sitting heavily, on the verge of showering them with rain again. Aaron looked down at the sword in his grip. It was one of the most powerful weapons of this realm, but it was useless in his hands. He didn't know how to fight with it. He had no idea how to unleash it's strength, how to use it to their advantage in this war. The only one who could teach him was Kyran; the very person the mages wanted the Blade to fight against.

Aaron pulled back his hand, raising the sword high above his head. With all his might, he threw the Blade. It spun in the air before hitting the water. The moment it broke the surface of the lake, the water shimmered an impossible blue before thick ripples ran across it.

Aaron raised a hand and closed his eyes. His core found the sword, sinking to the bottom of the lake. Aaron breathed out, gathered his strength, and started manipulating the bed of the lake. He forced the ground the sword was sitting on to sink lower, effectively making a well under the lake. The sword rested deep inside the well. Aaron opened his eyes to see the water swirling in a vortex at the spot in the lake, exactly above the sword.

Aaron stepped back. The Blade of Afton would be happy in its new spot, with plenty of water feeding it, and the vortex would remind the mages not to get too close, or the sword would drain them of their powers.

Aaron turned to go, and saw Ella. She had evidently been watching him. She looked at him for long, silent moments before clearing her throat. "Skyler told me about the Lycans and Pecosas, and what you did."

Aaron could only imagine how Skyler must have told the story. "It wasn't as bad as he made it out to be," he said defensively. "It was an instinctual reaction. I didn't plan it. I don't even know *how* to plan something like that," he said. "But I couldn't just stand back and let those Lycans kill the Pecosas."

"I know," Ella said. "Neriah wouldn't have held back either."

Aaron fell quiet.

Ella looked to the lake, at the swirling vortex, and a small, sad smile came to her face. "You have great control over an element that wasn't yours to begin with," she said. "You've proven you deserve to hold the Blade of Afton."

Aaron fidgeted. "I'm not too sure about that," he said. It was true that he could manipulate the element of Water with much more ease than before. It was slowly becoming a part of his instinct, a natural power. It didn't, however, mean he had any right to Ella's legacy or her Blade.

Ella dropped her gaze. "Just because I can't find it in myself to accept that you have my family's legacy, doesn't mean that you get to doubt yourself." She shook her head when Aaron opened his mouth to speak. "I don't want to hear that you're sorry," she said. "I know that you are, and *you* know that it wasn't your fault."

"It wasn't Neriah's fault either," Aaron said. "He wanted you to have his legacy."

Ella's face tightened with pain. "I know," she said quietly. "But it didn't happen, and there's nothing you or I can do about that."

Aaron stared at her, and a thought began to surface in his mind. She was right. He couldn't do anything about it, and neither could she. But maybe there was someone else who could. Maybe, just maybe, he could find a way to put things right, and get Ella her legacy back.

# 9

# THE BIRTH OF KYRAN AEDUS

Aaron took in the sight before him. Lanterns floating in the dark sky, giving light to the street. The rich mahogany table was groaning under the weight of the countless dishes that were spread across it. Gathered around the table were the habitants of Marwa, including the Elementals who once ruled the realm.

Aaron knew he was dreaming. Or, more accurately, he was receiving his Inheritance, – a series of visions from the present, past and possible future linked to his bloodline.

At the head of the table, there was James Avira, the leader who had been murdered by Hadrian. A few seats down sat, Joseph Avira; Skyler's father. Aaron assumed the woman next to him, caressing her baby bump, was Skyler's mother. Both of them had been killed by Lycans. Then there was the beautiful Lily Afton, filling glasses with water by nothing but a twitch of her fingers. She was Ella's mother, killed at Hadrian's hands too. Aaron's heart skipped a beat when he found Alex Adams; his uncle, killed in the Lycan attack that took Aaron's brother from him. He was the carbon copy of Kyran, from his green eyes to his dark tousled hair. He even looked to be around Kyran's age in this memory.

And then there was Neriah. Aaron found he couldn't look away from the sight of Neriah sitting happily next to Hadrian, chatting animatedly with him. It was a little over a month before that Aaron had watched Hadrian kill Neriah in cold blood. Yet here they were, eating together at the table, grinning at each other like adolescent teenagers sharing a joke. There was a sense of ease about them, the kind that showed they had been friends for a very long time. Their camaraderie reminded Aaron strongly of him and Sam, and that realisation chilled Aaron to his very bones.

"Oh, come on, Alex," Aaron heard his dad's voice. He looked over to see a youthful Chris talking to his younger brother. "You wouldn't even have her if it wasn't for me."

"And I don't want to lose her to you either," Alex replied. Aaron felt a tingle of unease run down his spine. Even his voice was *so* much like Kyran's.

Chris grinned. "We're talking about your bike, not your first-ever girlfriend," he said.

"Sod off," Alex said.

Chris was laughing. "Hey, is it my fault little Jessica liked your stronger, older, sexier brother more than you?"

Alex put down his fork and pointed a finger at Chris. "First of all, she wasn't my girlfriend – we were nine," he said. "And the only reason she liked you was because you used to show off your powers all the time."

"No, I didn't," Chris said.

"Yeah, you did," Joseph said, joining the conversation.

"All the time," Hadrian added, lifting his glass to take a sip.

"It was really annoying," Neriah said.

Chris frowned. "It's not like you lot were any better at sixteen," he said. "Hadrian *still* shows off the first chance he gets."

Everyone around the table laughed, and Hadrian smiled widely, nodding his head in agreement.

Aaron watched the scene with a sense of disbelief. He had been told time and time again that Hadrian used to be one of them – one of the mages, the Elementals – and that all of the Elementals used to live together, working as one to protect the realm. But seeing them interacting like this, laughing and joking, was such a stark contrast to what Aaron had seen and experienced of Hadrian.

"Showing off is a right of passage," Neriah said. "Everyone does it before they turn nineteen and their full powers come in. But after that, you are supposed to mature and act *responsibly*." He stressed the last word, giving Hadrian a pointed look.

Hadrian shrugged. "I must have missed that lesson in etiquette-for-the-mundane," he said with a smirk.

There were more snorts of laughter, while Neriah gave Hadrian a mock glare, shaking his head at him.

"Alexander," James called from the head of the table, cutting through the laughter. Aaron turned his head to look to the leader of the mages. "As I understand it," James started, "it's been a month since you last came to Marwa. Is that correct?"

Aaron blinked with surprise. He had been told all the Elementals lived together, in the City of Marwa. So where was his uncle Alex staying if not in Marwa? He sought out his uncle to see Alex looking a little startled at the question.

"Um, yeah, I think so," Alex replied.

"And the month before last, you were only in Marwa for a few days," James said. "And if I remember correctly, you didn't spend more than a week of the month before that here in the city."

Aaron saw Alex give a one-shouldered shrug. "Yeah," he said.

"And this entire time, you've been staying in the City of Halia with your friend?" James asked.

"With Alaina," Alex corrected. "And I think we all know she's more than my friend."

Aaron knew Alaina had been his uncle Alex's fiancée, but it seemed they weren't engaged at this point in time.

Disapproval was etched in every line of James's face. "I have told you this before, Alexander," he started. "It is customary for the Elementals to live together, in one city."

"Customary, yes, but not mandatory." It was Hadrian who spoke, interrupting the conversation. Aaron could see the coldness in Hadrian's eyes as he looked at James. "Alex can stay wherever he wants."

"I believe Alexander is more than capable of answering my questions," James said, and there was a slight bite to his tone. "There is no need for you to jump to his defence, Hadrian."

"There is no need to be defensive at all," Chris said. "Alex is free to stay with Alaina or come home to Marwa whenever he wants. It's not a big deal."

Aaron was stunned. Since when was his dad the laid-back type? If anything, Aaron would have thought his dad would be the one to have a problem if his brother was away from home for weeks on end.

James's blue eyes moved from Chris to rest on Alex. "I would like to see you return to Marwa every night, Alexander."

"James," Joseph started. "Come on—"

"You're being unreasonable, James," Neriah said.

"You do whatever you want, Alex," Hadrian called loudly, glaring at James. "Stay wherever you like."

Aaron could feel the tension thicken the air. He looked from Hadrian to James. Both looked just as annoyed as the other.

"I am only asking Alexander to adhere to the rules," James said.

"Oh, so it's a rule now, is it?" Hadrian asked, his eyes slitted with annoyance. "A minute ago it was only customary. Now it's another rule the great James Avira decided to make up on the spot."

The flames of the bonfires around the table crackled, and Aaron jumped with surprise.

"Hadrian, don't," Alex said quickly, looking nervously at him.

"I enforce the rules, I don't make them up," James said, and Aaron could tell he was trying to remain level-headed in the fast approaching argument.

"Yeah, right," Hadrian scoffed and the flames jumped, becoming twice as tall.

James's cold blue eyes hardened and a wind swept across the table, rattling the dishes.

"Will both of you calm down?" Alex said, his voice raised. "I've not moved out of Marwa. I've just been really busy with training, so only get to see Alaina if I stay with her, which is why I've not been in Marwa." He looked over at James and Aaron saw the resignation in him. "But I'll make sure I'm back here every night from now on."

"Alex–" Hadrian started.

"It's cool," Alex said turning to him. "Really, Hadrian, it's fine."

It was obvious to Aaron that it wasn't fine, but Alex seemed to be more concerned with diffusing the fight between Hadrian and James than getting what he wanted.

What was it his mum had told him? *Alex was always the one to give in, always trying to keep the peace.*

Hadrian gave James a fierce glare and turned his head, looking in the other direction. Neriah leant in to whisper to him, "Take it easy, Hadrian. It's not worth getting into it with James."

"Yeah," Hadrian muttered, with his eyes still blazing and hands clenched into fists. "It never is, is it?"

Aaron woke up abruptly. He blinked in the darkness, staring at his ceiling. He had never had this type of Inheritance dream before, not with all the Elementals present. He knew he had witnessed it because his dad and uncle Alex were a part of it, but he couldn't help but focus on Hadrian and James.

He knew that Hadrian had killed the eldest Elemental, but he hadn't ever given their relationship prior to Hadrian turning much thought. After witnessing this moment, it was clear that both Hadrian and James had very little tolerance for each other. It seemed it wouldn't take much for them to start a fight. But try as he might, Aaron found he couldn't blame Hadrian for this particular argument. He was only standing up for Alex. It was unfair what James was demanding. Why couldn't Alex stay where he wanted? If Chris, who was Alex's only family, didn't have a problem with him staying with Alaina, why did James?

Aaron could only surmise that James Avira had been a strict, stick-to-the-rules, no-questions-asked type of leader. He remembered what Kyran had taunted to Skyler once, about Hadrian killing James.

*Because my father had enough of James Avira's tyranny? Or because my father decided to do what everyone else wanted but couldn't muster up the courage to do themselves?*

After his dream, Aaron couldn't help but wonder if James had been a tyrant after all. But had the others really wanted James dead? Had Neriah?

*You used me to take out James, then locked my powers.*

Aaron had to sit up. Hadrian's words spun in his head, making it ache. He couldn't let himself think like that. He didn't want to disrespect Neriah's memory by accusing him of something so heinous as orchestrating one Elemental's death at the hands of another. It was simple. Hadrian had to be lying. But even as Aaron soothed himself with that thought, a niggle of doubt irritated him. Would he ever find out the truth? Or were Neriah's secrets buried with him?

***

"Are you sure about this?"

Aaron took in a breath. "Yeah."

Amber, the head Empath after Armana's passing, nodded her head and held out a small vial for Aaron to take. Her unseeing eyes stared past Aaron.

"Drink it all and then lie down," she instructed. "Take my hand and I will guide you there and back. Remember, time moves differently where you're going."

"Yeah, I remember." It wasn't that long ago that Aaron had gone to this very same place, under Neriah's instructions. Now he was doing it of his own accord.

"Whenever you are ready," Amber said.

Aaron looked at the vial, uncorked it and drank the clear liquid in one go. He lay down on the bed and took Amber's hand. His eyes closed and Aaron easily slipped from one plane of existence to another.

Aaron found himself outside, shading his eyes from the sun. It was a warm summer day, with a clear blue sky above him, and crisp green grass under him. He was in a park. Surrounding it were lines and lines of trees, their branches ruffling in the soft breeze. Aaron could make out a children's playground in the distance, with swings, slides and a climbing frame. He thought it was the sort of place a child as young as Naina would like to play, but the playground was empty.

Across from Aaron was a single tree with a full head of leaves. Standing under the tree, tending to its branches was a young woman. She was the only one Aaron could see in the park.

"Excuse me," he called.

The woman turned to look at him and Aaron was momentarily stunned by how pretty she was. Her blond hair sat in thick curls around her shoulders, and her eyes were a sparkling blue. She had delicate features: a small forehead, straight-edged nose and thin lips. Aaron had to give himself a mental shake to stop staring at her.

"I'm looking for someone," he said, walking towards her. "A little girl, about five or six years old. Her name is Naina."

The woman smiled. "Hello, Aaron," she said. "It's nice to see you again."

Aaron paused. His eyes widened. "Naina?" he asked, recognising the little girl in the older woman's features. He had met Naina no more than a month ago and she was barely older than six. Now she looked like she was in her early twenties.

"Man," Aaron breathed. "I was told time moved differently here but this is just insane."

Naina laughed. The sound reminded Aaron of wind chimes.

"It's got nothing to do with time, Aaron," she said. "You came to me for wisdom, and wisdom comes with age."

"You've aged this much because of me?" Aaron asked, feeling oddly guilty.

Naina nodded.

"Well, I hope you have enough wisdom for what I'm about to ask you," Aaron said.

"I know what you've come to ask me," Naina said. "You want to know if there is a way for you to give the legacy you hold to Ella Afton, without dying in the process."

"It's her legacy," Aaron said. "I'm not supposed to have it. It belongs to her."

"But it was given to you," Naina said. "Neriah made that choice."

"Only because he was forced to," Aaron said. "He was trying to save it from Hadrian, and he thought by giving it to me he would be protecting it, that Kyran wouldn't let Hadrian hurt me for the legacy." He paused. "I know Neriah wanted Ella to have his legacy. He told me that himself." Aaron paused and slowly shook his head. "I can't stand seeing Ella hurting like this. When she catches me using the power of Water, or holding the Blade of Afton, it's like a part of her dies. I can feel it – her pain, her anger, her heartbreak." He held Naina's eyes. "Please, help me find a way to give Ella back her legacy."

Naina didn't speak right away. She looked like she was struggling to find the right words. "You already know how to give Ella the legacy," she said quietly. "You have to will it to her when you are taking your last breath." She shook her head at Aaron. "I'm sorry, Aaron. For you, there is no other way."

Aaron's disappointment was difficult to hide. His shoulders sagged and his head bowed. He closed his eyes, trying to quell the rush of anger that came at the injustice of it all. He had come to Naina with so much hope, but she had told him what he desperately didn't want to hear. Then it occurred to Aaron what she had *actually* said.

"Wait." He lifted his head to look at her. "What do you mean, for *me* there is no other way?" he asked. "As in, it *is* possible to give your legacy without dying, but just not for me?"

Naina was watching Aaron closely. "No one can give away their legacy and survive," she said. "Unless they possess a higher power."

Aaron's heart skipped a beat. "What kind of a higher power?" he asked. "How do I get it?"

"You don't," Naina said. "It's a power that surpasses elements and legacies. It's a power that only a select few are chosen to possess. A power they are born with."

Aaron's hopes came crashing down again. "But this isn't fair," he said. "I was never supposed to have this legacy."

"You're wrong," Naina said. "I told you that the day you figured out where your loyalties lay, your core would find its strength and the legacy would come to you," she reminded him. "When Neriah fell and you ran to his side, you showed him great loyalty. That's why the legacy came to you. It was *always* going to come to you, Aaron. This power was meant for you."

"But it's Ella's birthright," he said. "How could it be meant for me?"

"Not everyone gets what is rightfully theirs," Naina said. "It may be unfair, but it is what it is. You got the legacy after showing your loyalty, just like I said you would."

Aaron remembered his last conversation with her; he could recall every word of it. "You said something else that day," he started. "And it's been bothering me ever since." He paused, wondering if he wanted the honest answer or not. He told himself he had to know, especially now, when the situation was much more complicated than he had first realised. "You showed me a memory," he started. "Of Kyran."

Naina nodded. "I asked you why you were fighting for him."

"And I said it was because he was my friend." Aaron swallowed. "You told me he wasn't my friend."

"Because he isn't." Naina smiled. "He's your brother."

Aaron felt like a huge weight had been lifted from him. He closed his eyes, dropping his head as a choked breath of relief escaped him. "That's why you said that?" he asked, looking up at her. "I thought you meant Kyran was my enemy."

Naina's smile saddened. "Kyran is not your enemy," she said. "But you can become his."

Aaron felt his blood run cold. "Why would you say that?"

"It's your choice, Aaron," she said. "You could just as easily decide to save him instead."

"Kyran doesn't need saving," Aaron said. "He's the one that usually does the saving."

Naina stared at Aaron for a long moment before turning to the tree she had been tending to.

"Did you know that trees are symbolic?" she asked. "They can represent a lot of things. To some, trees mean life, to others it's nature. But for some, it's a physical manifestation of family." Her hand caressed the tree. "The trunk, leading down to the roots, reminds us that at our very core, we are one. We began as one," she continued. "The branches are the sprawling families, reaching out in every which way, expanding to a distance, but never leaving their roots. The leaves are the individual beings, kept together by the branches. But should a leaf get ripped from its branch–" she plucked a leaf off and held it in her hand – "it's forever broken. It can't go back; it can't be reattached to its branch. Whichever way the cruel wind blows, the leaf has no choice but to go." She let go of the leaf and it fluttered up in the breeze. "It will inevitably be forced far away from its tree, from the place it truly belongs." She looked at Aaron. "But if high up on the treetop there happens to be a web–" she looked pointedly at Aaron – "a small but deceptively strong web, that traps the leaf as it flies past, it can save the leaf from being lost forever."

Aaron remembered Naina had called him a web before. He'd had no idea what she meant, until now.

"That web holds on to that leaf," Naina continued, "and no matter how strong the wind blows or how much it howls, the web will *never* let go. The leaf may never be a part of its branch again, but the web keeps it from being lost in the wind. The web keeps the leaf close to where it belongs." She stepped towards Aaron. "You are the web that can hold on to Kyran, before he's dragged away by Hadrian," she said. "I told you that you have another battle to fight, one that is much harder than this war. This is it, Aaron. And if you lose, you will not only lose your brother, you will lose everything dear to you."

Aaron had to force his voice past the growing lump in his throat. "I've already lost," he said. "Kyran is gone. He's with Hadrian, and there's nothing I can do to bring him back."

"That's not true," Naina said. "You have a very unique bond with your brother. Your family bond is very strong."

Aaron's heart twisted at her words. "If that's true, then why can't my parents feel Kyran?" he asked.

"Because they felt him die," Naina replied.

Aaron stilled, gaping at her. "How is that possible if Kyran is alive?"

Naina didn't reply. She tilted her head upwards and Aaron followed her to see a hologram appear at the head of the tree, just like the one Naina had showed Aaron inside the doll's house the last time they'd met.

Aaron was frozen when he saw images of the Lycan attack flash in the hologram. He had seen the memory from his mum, and he didn't ever want to see it again. But try as he might, Aaron couldn't look away as Naina showed him a four-year-old Ben being ripped out of his mum's arms and thrown to the hungry Lycans.

"Ben survived that attack," Naina said. "Why your parents felt him die when he in actual fact survived, I can't tell you."

"Why?" Aaron asked, still watching the hologram.

"Because it's not your question to ask."

Aaron looked at her. "He's my brother," he said. "I have a right to know what broke my family apart."

"Until the one who matters asks the question, it can't be answered," Naina said.

"Kyran," Aaron muttered in realisation. He needed to be the one to ask. Aaron turned to Naina. "Kyran doesn't believe my parents. He thinks they're lying. He thinks they ran away and didn't bother to come back for him."

Naina's blue eyes were glistening. "Do you blame him?" she asked.

She glanced up and Aaron raised his head to see that the memory of the attack had ended, and now the hologram was showing four-year-old Ben standing on rocky ground, staring at something in the distance. The small cuts and bruises on his face told Aaron it was shortly after the Lycan attack on the city of Marwa.

Aaron stepped closer, his eyes glued to the hologram. Ben was just standing there, his blue eyes tired and pained, with dark circles under them. The wind was ruffling his hair, the sun was on his face, but Ben didn't move. He just stood, waiting for something.

The memory faded and another took its place. Ben, on the same rocky ground, but this time he was sitting. His clothes were different, his hair slightly longer, but his eyes were a deep blue – the exact shade of their mum's eyes.

"He waited for them to return," Naina said. "For years, he came to the mountain at the Gateway of Marwa, and he watched the tear, waiting for his parents to come back from the human realm for him."

Aaron watched the memories of Ben, waiting day after day, as they played across the hologram. In some Ben would be sitting. Others showed him standing, or pacing as he watched the tear with great longing. In each and every memory, Aaron noticed that Ben's gaze never wavered from the tear. He watched that tear with the belief that his parents were coming for him. But as the memories progressed, that light slowly started to fade from his eyes. He was losing hope.

In one memory, Aaron's breath caught with surprise when he saw none other than Hadrian come to sit next to Ben. He didn't speak, his expression wistful, but his hand extended to caress Ben's hair. Ben didn't move. He sat with his knees against his chest, his arms around his legs, and saddened eyes fixed to the tear.

More memories flashed before Aaron, with Ben waiting, and sometimes Hadrian was by his side. In one, Aaron saw Ben had fallen asleep as night came but his parents didn't. Hadrian lifted the small boy with great care and carried him away, with Ben's head resting on Hadrian's shoulder.

Aaron couldn't look away from the hologram, as it continued to show Ben's childhood spent waiting for those who never came for him. Then a memory played where Ben was not looking much older than six, maybe seven, years old. He was picking up stones from the ground and throwing them at the tear. Aaron couldn't hear it, but he saw Ben was shouting, screaming something. Then Ben slid to his knees. His face wet with tears, his shoulders shaking as sobs racked through him. Aaron could see the pain, raw and exposed on his brother and it made his heart ache.

Then the memory changed and Aaron felt a jolt of surprise when the hologram showed not Ben, but him – Aaron – as a young baby, sleeping in his room in the human realm. He watched in surprise as his two-year-old self cried in his sleep, with tears rolling down his face.

"You may not have known about Ben's existence until recently," Naina said. "But you've felt his presence all your life." Naina looked to the hologram. "Every time Ben cried out, no one but you heard him. You felt his pain but you were too young to understand." She smiled sadly at Aaron. "That's the reason why your bond is so exceptional. You have always been connected to him through his pain, through the cries only you could hear." She met Aaron's eyes. "His tears dried on your lashes."

Aaron didn't know what to say. The memory shifted from Aaron back to Ben, and Aaron saw that he was no longer on top of the mountain. Ben was walking down a deserted street. He looked slightly older than the last hologram, maybe around eight years old. He walked with a purpose, his gaze fixed ahead of him. Tears lingered in his eyes, which were now the strangest shade – not blue but not quite green either. Aaron had no idea what was happening, until Ben came to stop in front of a house. Aaron's heart sunk. Ben was standing in front of their house in the city of Marwa. For a moment, Ben did nothing but stand there, staring at the house with red-rimmed eyes.

Then Ben's hands curled into fists. Out from the ground, long vines started to grow and wrap themselves around the house. Aaron's breath choked out of him. He watched as Ben encased the house completely with the vines, locking it. The anger in him, the venom with which he was staring at the house, even while tears fell from them, told of Ben's anguish, as well as his rage.

"When he finally gave up, Ben accepted the truth," Naina said, "that his parents had left him and they weren't coming back."

Aaron couldn't speak. He watched as Ben turned around and walked away, leaving his home wrapped in vines. It was exactly how they'd found the house, some ten years later. He remembered how his dad had struggled to loosen the vines' hold. *Damn, they were angry when they did this.*

That's what his dad had said, thinking the vines were from neighbours, a reaction to their disappearance. Little did he know it was his own heartbroken son that had done it to their house.

How Ben had managed to use his powers at such a young age, Aaron didn't know, but he didn't have it in him to ask. He watched the hologram show Ben crossing a hallway in a large house Aaron didn't recognise. He wrenched open a set of double doors to find Hadrian inside. Hadrian looked up from his desk to see a tearful and upset Ben. He stood up at once, hurrying around his desk, looking concerned. Aaron watched as Ben strode up to Hadrian, and without a word, he fell to his knees in front of him. Hadrian didn't say anything, but was staring at Ben with surprise. Slowly, Ben lowered his head. Hadrian reached out and placed a hand on top of Ben's head, and Ben closed his eyes, allowing the last of his tears to fall.

"That's the day Benjamin Adams died," Naina said quietly. "And Kyran Aedus was born."

# 10

## MIDNIGHT MEETINGS

It had to be a pub, Aaron thought, as he surveyed the tightly packed room with men and women sitting around tables and along the bar, drinks in hand. It was loud, with a lot of swearing hanging in the stuffy, smelly air. Aaron stood to the side, watching it all with a frown. How did he get here? Where was here, exactly? He had no idea. The last thing he remembered was leaving the Empath Huts after returning from Naina's plane of existence and going to his room, wanting to be alone. So how did he get to this pub? His gaze stopped on the young boy standing by the door, looking around the room with nervous eyes.

Aaron felt his breath hitch. He knew who it was – he could recognise Kyran anywhere, even though he looked less like Kyran and more like Ben at this particular moment. His eyes were still more blue than green, and his face resembled Aaron when he was around seven.

Aaron watched as Kyran stood awkwardly next to the front door, the only child amongst adults so inebriated they didn't even notice him. Until one finally did. A man, easily in his forties, staggered over to where Kyran was, leering at him in a very creepy way.

"Well, hello, lad," he said. "What are you doing here?"

Kyran looked at the man and recoiled slightly, probably because of the stench of alcohol on his breath.

"I'm looking for someone," Kyran mumbled.

"Aww, did you lose your mummy and daddy?" the man snickered.

Kyran gave him an angry look, but didn't say anything.

"Come on, come with me. I'll help you find them," the man said.

Kyran, Aaron was glad to see, had the sense to back away from his hands.

"No," Kyran said.

"Oh, come on, don't be shy," the man said. "I don't bite." He grinned to show his fangs. "Okay, I do, but it'll be over before you know it."

Aaron bolted forward instinctively, but found someone had stepped in the way, blocking Kyran from the vampire.

"Leave him alone, Fergus," Hadrian said, looking at the vampire with barely concealed revulsion.

"Aww, come on, Hadrian," the vampire – Fergus – said with a pout. "Let a man have some fun."

"Find it elsewhere," Hadrian said.

"What's your problem?" Fergus said, his amusement changing to annoyance. He gestured to Kyran. "It's only a kid."

"Yeah, only a kid," Hadrian said. His eyes gleamed a strange golden shade as he stepped closer to the vampire. "*My* kid."

Fergus looked stunned. He glanced to Kyran and then back to Hadrian. "I didn't know…" He started shaking his head. "I thought…I-I'm sorry," he stammered before hurrying away.

Hadrian was glaring at him, but he didn't go after Fergus. He turned and walked past Kyran, opening the door. He held it until Kyran walked out, before following after him. Aaron was brought out of the pub and found himself in the street, watching as Hadrian made his way over to a parked SUV, with Kyran tottering after him.

"Did I not tell you to stay in the car?" Hadrian asked, and Aaron could hear the anger in his voice. "What were you thinking coming in after me?"

"You said you'd be back in five minutes," Kyran said.

"So?" Hadrian asked.

"It's been an hour," Kyran said.

Hadrian shook his head. "If I'm running late, it doesn't mean you have to come looking for me," he said. "You have any idea how dangerous those people are? If I hadn't spotted you when I did–" He broke off, unable to complete his sentence. His hands balled into fists as he walked.

"Why'd you lie to that man?" Kyran asked. "I'm *not* your kid, and you're not my dad. My dad is coming for me."

Hadrian kept walking, but Aaron saw the way his steps faltered, like what Kyran had said had affected him, almost like it...hurt him.

"I know that," Hadrian said quietly. "I said it to make that vampire back off."

They reached the car. Kyran opened the passenger door, but didn't climb in yet. "You didn't have to lie," he said to Hadrian, who was walking to the driver's side. "You could have told him to back off without saying I was your son–"

"Ben," Hadrian cut him off, talking over the top of the car. "I've had a *really* rough day, okay. The last thing I need is more cheek from you. So get in the car and *shut up*."

Kyran didn't move. His jaw clenched and he slammed the door he had opened shut. He moved to the door behind and opened that, throwing himself angrily into the back of the SUV instead. Hadrian looked up to the skies, as if silently asking for help, before opening the door and settling into the driver's seat. The SUV's engine roared to life and the headlights blinded Aaron.

Aaron blinked and found he wasn't in the car park any more. He was in his room, on his bed. For the first few moments he stayed as he was, sprawled out on his front, his pillow askew and his arm dangling off the edge of the bed. Then he turned himself over and lay staring at the ceiling.

He wondered what it was he had just experienced. Was it another Inheritance moment, or was it something his mind had come up with after seeing glimpses of Kyran's childhood in Naina's hologram? As heartbreaking as it was to see Kyran on top of that mountain, waiting for his parents to return, the thing that astounded Aaron was seeing Hadrian with Kyran. Aaron had never thought Hadrian would be a part of Kyran's wait for his parents. He hadn't given Hadrian's role in Kyran's childhood much thought, if he was honest.

As much as Aaron hated Hadrian for being the enemy this realm was fighting, for killing Neriah, for waging war against magekind, he couldn't help but feel a small twinge of gratitude towards him. If what he'd seen was in fact a real memory, then Hadrian had protected Kyran, even when all he got in return was Kyran's ire. He'd waited with Kyran on top of that mountain for the Adams to return. He'd picked up Kyran's sleeping form when he had passed out from the exhaustion of waiting. As loath as Aaron was to admit it, Hadrian had been there for Kyran when his parents hadn't.

A strange sensation was taking over Aaron. His heart started beating faster, and his hands felt clammy. He needed some air. Aaron pulled the covers aside and slipped out of bed. He was careful not to wake Sam and Rose, who were back to sharing a room with him.

Aaron picked up his shoes and coat, and quietly went downstairs. He opened the front door and stood outside in the cold, taking deep breaths. The feeling didn't subside; if anything, it got stronger. There was a knot in his stomach, and a jitter in his bones that he couldn't get rid of. He started walking, hoping to shake the feeling away.

He found himself in front of Salvador's Gate. Something told him to go outside – a feeling so strong it compelled Aaron to do just that. Aaron walked into the eternal sunshine that bathed the Gateway beyond. His feet led him into the forest there and Aaron went on, listening to his gut. He walked deep into the woods, heading to where he had stood and spoken to Kyran while the city of Salvador was being ravaged by vamages.

Aaron shivered, but it wasn't so much due to June's chilly night air as the memory of speaking to Kyran, after learning that he was his brother. The pain he had seen in Kyran at being abandoned was something Aaron could never forget. And now that Naina had showed him glimpses of Kyran waiting and watching the Gateway for his parents' return, Aaron could understand, could feel maybe a fraction of the pain Kyran had lived through.

A chill ran down Aaron's spine. The first time he'd met Naina, the five year old had called him a web, and Aaron hadn't understood what that meant. Now he did, but he wasn't sure he was strong enough to hold on to Kyran. In her analogy, Naina had made Aaron the web, Kyran the stranded leaf, and Hadrian the air, determined to take Kyran away from the family he belonged to. But Hadrian wasn't a gust of air, he was a tornado – a force not everyone survived. What could a measly web do against a power like that?

His skin prickled and Aaron's breath caught when he heard familiar footsteps behind him.

"I was hoping you'd come."

Aaron turned at Kyran's voice, to see him appear out of the shadows. Kyran stopped, roughly where he had the last time they'd met. A tired smile crossed Kyran's face as his vivid green eyes rested on Aaron.

"Guess the bond works both ways."

Aaron swallowed heavily. That's what that sensation was; his core reacting to Kyran. His subconscious led him there, because his brother had been calling to him.

"What are you doing here?" Aaron asked. "You shouldn't be anywhere near Salvador." The thought of Skyler finding them, finding Kyran, panicked Aaron. He had no doubt Skyler would use those personalised bullets in a heartbeat.

"I had to talk to you," Kyran replied. He stepped closer. "I didn't know about the Hub, or the attack on Salvador. I found out when you told me. I swear, Ace."

Aaron believed him. He could see the sincerity in Kyran. But there was one thing he didn't understand.

"If you didn't use the Hub, how did you make a portal?" Aaron asked.

"I told you, portals can be made without the Hub."

"Scott can't do it," Aaron said. "And he's the Controller."

"Well, then, I guess Hadrian's ten times the Controller Scott is," Kyran said. "Because he's the one who taught me."

Aaron didn't know why the statement shocked him. Hadrian had brought Kyran up. There must be countless things he trained Kyran in; making portals without the Hub was probably just one of them.

Aaron pushed his unease aside. "How do you make them?" he asked.

Kyran looked at Aaron, as if figuring out if he was asking due to curiosity, or because he wanted Kyran to prove he knew how to make them without the Hub. Giving in, Kyran let out a sigh.

"Portals are usually created and set up in one particular location," he started. "Like the one that used to sit here, for Salvador Hunters to use." He gestured to the trees behind him. "Every city has its usual portal location. When portals are created in one spot time and time again, they leave behind a mark, an indentation if you like. After considerable time, it's possible to create a portal in those exact locations, without the help of the Hub. You have to use an incredible amount of energy, and it's not easy to find these indentations on your own." Kyran shrugged. "But it's not impossible. Hadrian taught me how to pick up on the signs and create portals when I need them."

Aaron nodded. "It's probably not a challenge for you, what with having three legacies and everything," he said. "You have more than enough energy to make portals."

Kyran's eyes narrowed. "It's got nothing to do with being a legacy holder," he said. "It's all about knowing how to manipulate your core."

Aaron stared at him. "How do you do it, Kyran?" he asked. "How do you not feel guilty for taking legacies that don't belong to you? How can you look Skyler in the eye and taunt him, when you have what is rightfully his?"

"I didn't take anything from Skyler," Kyran said defensively. "I got the legacies by accident."

"So did I," Aaron said. "But it's still tearing me up from the inside. I can't face Ella without feeling crushed by guilt."

Kyran's eyes darkened, and his jaw set. "You getting the legacy was no accident," he said. "Neriah did that on purpose. He *forced* the legacy on you, to mess with all of us!"

"He gave me the legacy to protect it from Hadrian," Aaron said.

"He should have just *let* Hadrian take it!" Kyran snapped. "He shouldn't have involved you in this fight. He died and left you with this — this *curse*. Neriah gave you the legacy so you would become Hadrian's last victim!"

Aaron tried to calm his erratically beating heart. He already knew this, knew that he would be on Hadrian's radar now that he had the legacy. But aside from his own panic, Aaron could sense Kyran's fear, his complete and utter terror at the situation Neriah had left Aaron in.

"You weren't of any concern to Hadrian," Kyran was saying. "He would have been happy to just let you be, as long as you didn't get in his way. But because of Neriah, you're his target now. Hadrian wants the legacies, *all* of the legacies, and there's nothing I can do to change that."

The ire Aaron had for Kyran completely melted as he witnessed how worried his brother was for him. Aaron took a step towards him.

"We'll figure something out," he said, knowing how empty that sounded. "Hadrian can't get to me."

Kyran shook his head. "You don't get it, Ace," he said. "I have three legacies. I could have taken the fourth too, but Hadrian wanted to be the one to take Neriah's legacy from him. But now that you have the legacy, the burden falls back on me."

Aaron stilled, his blood running cold. "He wants you to take the legacy from me."

"He wants the legacy, and the only way that can happen now is with you dead." Kyran faltered for a moment, but then pushed on. "He won't do it himself. He won't come for you, but he's expecting me to do it."

Aaron's heart pounded in his chest. "How can you?" he asked. "You're not a vamage."

Hadrian could drink the blood of a legacy holder, taking their life and their legacy, but what could Kyran do? Killing a legacy holder meant the legacy would go to the next elemental in its bloodline, not be transferred to the murderer.

Kyran's eyes darkened. "Don't ask me how I can do it," he said. "Just trust me when I say that I can."

Aaron wanted to probe further, to ask questions until Kyran explained, but Kyran's next words wiped everything from his mind.

"He's not asked me yet," he said. "But he will. He will tell me to come for you, and return to him with the legacy." He held Aaron's gaze with tortured eyes. "I swore to obey him, Ace. I have always done what he's asked, and sooner or later, he will ask me to kill you."

Aaron's body tensed, his heart raced and he could taste fear on his tongue. Steeling himself the best he could, he forced out the words, "So what are you going to do?"

Kyran pulled in a breath, his head lowered. After a moment's contemplation, he looked up at Aaron.

"What I have to," he replied. "I have to kill you."

# 11

## PLANS

Aaron felt numb with disbelief. He had seen this moment – when Kyran told him he was going to kill him, in one of his Inheritance visions, but the shock of it still knocked the breath out of him.

"It's the only way," Kyran was saying. "And it has to be a spectacle, with plenty of witnesses."

Aaron couldn't believe his ears. Was Kyran really discussing his murder with him?

"Kyran," Aaron started. "I don't–"

"It can't be that difficult to pull off," Kyran was saying, seemingly talking to himself now. "Hadrian will believe it, and it'll buy us some time to figure out a way to get that legacy out of you."

Now Aaron was just confused. "What?"

Kyran started pacing, and it reminded Aaron strongly of their dad. "I don't care what everyone says, there *has* to be a way to get that legacy out without it killing you," Kyran said. "And I'll find it, I just need time to figure it out. If Hadrian thinks you're dead and I have your legacy, he will be satisfied. Then we can work on getting the legacy out of you in peace."

Aaron finally caught on. "You're planning on faking my death?" he asked.

Kyran stopped to look at him. "I can just kill you if you prefer," he said, his trademark sarcasm seeping into his tone. He shook his head at Aaron and continued pacing. "We just have to make it believable."

"Kyran, wait," Aaron said, stepping forward. "This is ridiculous. We're not going to fake my death."

"Why not?" Kyran asked. "It's the perfect plan."

"It's anything but perfect," Aaron said. "No one is going to believe you killed me."

"They will if we put on a show," Kyran said. "Trust me, everyone who sees it will believe you're dead."

"Mum and dad won't," Aaron said. "They'll know I'm still alive."

Kyran's expression hardened. "Don't be so sure about that," he said. "They seem to have difficulty sensing bonds."

"Kyran," Aaron started, but Kyran shook his head.

"It doesn't matter," he said quietly. "Even if they do sense you're alive, it won't make a difference."

"How?" Aaron asked.

Kyran glared at him. "Are they going to go running to Hadrian to tell him you're still alive?"

"No, of course not–"

"Then we don't have a problem," Kyran cut him off. "The plan will still work. Hadrian will think you're dead and I have all four legacies–"

"What if he wants proof?" Aaron interrupted. "How are you going to prove you have all *four* legacies, when you only have three?"

"He won't ask for proof," Kyran said.

"But what if he does?" Aaron insisted. "What if he wants you to take the Blade of Afton? You can't touch that sword if you don't have its legacy."

"You let me worry about that," Kyran said. "All you have to do is play along and then go into hiding." He took in a breath.

"I was thinking you could go back to the human realm. You've lived there all your life, you'll adapt with no problem."

"Kyran," Aaron started. "I'm not leaving this realm."

"Fine," Kyran said. "There's a small town in Zone B-25. It's got a tiny population – ten, maybe twelve residents at the most. It's a little run down, but everyone keeps to themselves. You can stay there–"

"Kyran, stop," Aaron said. "I'm not letting people think I'm dead. Mum and Dad will know the truth, but what about Sam and Rose? And the friends I've made in this realm?"

Kyran's expression softened a little at the mention of Rose, but he shook his head. "You have to make sacrifices, Ace."

"This isn't one I'm willing to make," Aaron said. "I can't let my best friends believe I'm dead. I'm not putting them through that."

Kyran heaved out a frustrated breath. "Then what, Ace?" he asked, annoyed. "What do you suggest we do?"

Aaron smiled at him. "*We?*" he questioned. "You don't have to be a part of this mess, Kyran," he said. "I'm the one stuck with the legacy. It's my problem, not yours."

"It is my problem," Kyran said. "And I'm going to find a solution, no matter what it takes."

"Then I'm helping you find that solution," Aaron said.

Kyran looked surprised. "I don't need your help."

"Tough," Aaron replied with a smile. "Because you're getting it."

*** 

It didn't take long for Aaron to get used to the feeling of Kyran calling to him. It always made his heart race – that was one of the first signs. Then his palms would become clammy.

There was something deep in the pit of his stomach, a sense that told him Kyran was outside the Gate, waiting for him.

Kyran always came after nightfall, so sneaking out wasn't an issue. Aaron would sometimes wake up with the effects of the call weighing down on him. He felt an unbearable urge to rush out of the city and go running to his brother. But Aaron forced himself to take his time, making sure he didn't wake Sam or Rose in his haste to leave the cottage.

The flash that lit up the city every time the Gate slid open and closed worried Aaron at first, but no one ever came out to investigate. After a while, Aaron stopped fretting over it.

Kyran came as many as three times a week, sometimes even more. They met deep in the woods that lined the Gateway to Salvador. But Aaron was growing paranoid that eventually someone would follow him out and catch Kyran.

"Who is going to follow you out of the city at two in the morning?" Kyran asked.

"Anyone who sees me leaving," Aaron said. "And knowing my luck, it'll be Skyler."

"Why are you so scared of Skyler?" Kyran asked with a chuckle.

"Because he carries two bullets around with your name on them," Aaron said.

Kyran didn't look the least bit concerned. "So?" he asked. "He could carry around ten bullets, doesn't mean he'll get the chance to shoot me."

"How can you be so calm about this?" Aaron asked. "Skyler has what he needs to *kill* you."

"Anyone can carve a name into a bullet, Ace," he said. "But to actually go through with it is a different story. Skyler's a jerk, but he's not capable of an execution."

Aaron shook his head. "You've not seen what he's like now," he said. "He's changed, ever since Armana—" He faltered and his heart skipped a beat at the memory of the kind-hearted Empath. He took in a breath and continued, "Don't underestimate him, Kyran. If he gets a chance, he'll do it, I know he will."

But Kyran just laughed and dismissed Aaron's worry with a shake of his head. "Come on," he said, and he started leading Aaron through the forest.

"Where are we going?" Aaron asked, as he fell into step with him.

"If you're going to be paranoid, we won't stay here," Kyran said. "We'll go somewhere else."

Aaron saw the portal sitting proudly where it used to before Kyran destroyed it in a bid to escape the Hunters, after he stole the key from Neriah to unlock Hadrian's powers. Aaron didn't question where they were going, but followed Kyran into the glowing Aric's mark, walking through the centre of the spiral.

The brightness of the portal blinded Aaron, but his vision returned with a few blinks. He found himself on a deserted street. Tall buildings stood on either side of the cobbled road, which was littered with debris from a past attack. There were no lanterns in the sky; only the moon's glow gave them its light.

"Where are we?" Aaron asked.

"Where we need to be," Kyran replied.

He led Aaron down the street. Aaron glanced at the four-storey-high buildings with darkened windows. Aaron knew not many people would be awake at this hour, but somehow he knew the street was empty. No one lived here.

Kyran turned to go into a building, pushing the door open. Aaron followed him into a dank and dark lobby. There was a set of stairs leading the way up to the apartments on the next floor, but Kyran went to the door on the right, opening it without a key.

Aaron entered the flat warily, looking around the dark hallway. Kyran closed the door, and with a wave of his fingers he lit the lanterns hanging from the ceiling. The place had been abandoned in a hurry, that much was apparent. There was plenty of furniture left in the flat – table and chairs, a bed in one room and most of the kitchen appliances – but it was devoid of any personal belongings. Aaron did find a broken frame with a photo of a young couple, smiling in each other's embrace.

"Whose house are we in?" Aaron asked.

Kyran shrugged. "Don't know," he said. "There's no one left in this city. It's a ghost town after the Lycan attack three years ago."

Aaron had been right. It wasn't just the street but the entire city that had been vacated. Aaron found himself wondering how many had perished in the attack. It must have been a significant number, to scare the surviving residents away from their homes and not have anyone return in three years.

Kyran took off his jacket and threw it over the back of a chair sitting in one corner of the hallway, before heading to the kitchen. Aaron frowned. Kyran had certainly made himself at home here. He followed behind him, but stopped at the door. His eyes widened, taking in the mess of books on the kitchen table – over fifty tomes at least.

"They must have been big readers," Aaron said.

Kyran shook his head, flicking through the pages of a thick volume. "These are mine," he said.

"Yours?" Aaron asked. "How long have you been living here?"

"I'm not living here. But I come here to study these," Kyran said.

"Why can't you study them at home?" Aaron asked, picking up a book with a faded title scrawled in frayed golden thread.

"Because," Kyran took the book from him, setting it back down, "I don't want anyone knowing what I'm researching."

"What are you researching?" Aaron asked.

Kyran let out a sigh and pinched the bridge of his nose. "Take a wild guess, Ace," he said.

Aaron looked at the stacks of books with disbelief. "You can't be serious," he said. "You're looking for a way to transfer the legacy out of me in these books?" he asked.

"Yes," Kyran said. "That's exactly what I'm doing. Look, I have the book titled, 'The Way To Get The Legacy Out Of Aaron Adams' right here," he said, waving the book in his hand. He glared at Aaron and shook his head, as if to say *idiot*.

Aaron sulked. "What are you looking for then?" he asked.

"Information on how legacies work," Kyran said. "As well as something else, something that can probably solve all our problems if only I can find a way to get to it."

Aaron felt the first stirring of hope. "Really?" he asked. "What is it?"

Kyran didn't meet his eyes. "I'll tell you once I find a way to get to it."

Aaron wanted more of an explanation, but he knew Kyran wouldn't give him it. He glanced to the books. He shrugged off his jacket and put it behind a chair, before sitting down. "Which one shall I look through?" he asked.

Kyran seemed surprised that he wanted to help, but he didn't push him away. Instead, he picked up a book titled, 'A Theoretical Study Of The Core,' and handed it to him. "Here," he said. "Start with that." He pushed a pad of paper and a pen towards him. "Take notes about legacies and how they work with the core."

Aaron glanced to his brother as he sat down too, already lost in the pages of his book. Aaron flipped the pad open to see Kyran's writing had taken over the first thirty pages. He had evidently been working hard on this. It seemed Kyran had started working on finding a way to get the legacy out of Aaron the moment Neriah had transferred it to him.

\*\*\*

Kyran escorted Aaron back to the Gateway of Salvador. It was just a little after five in the morning, but the sun didn't rise until eight. Aaron had a few hours to catch up on sleep.

"I'll see you the day after tomorrow," Aaron said.

Kyran nodded, but didn't say anything. He walked back to the portal, disappearing through it. The moment he left, the portal shut down and faded from sight.

Aaron couldn't help but feel saddened. He wished with all his might that Kyran didn't have to leave, that things were different – drastically different – so his brother could live in the same city as him. If the Lycan attack on Marwa had never happened, or if his parents had taken Ben with them, or if they had come back for him – if any of these scenarios had happened, their small family would have been complete. How different would life have been?

Aaron walked past the Gate of Salvador and made his way down the street, lost in his thoughts. He wondered if Kyran would have been just as cocky if he had grown up with them, and not Hadrian. He wouldn't have three legacies, that was for sure. Would that have made him less arrogant? Somehow, Aaron couldn't imagine Kyran without his brazen attitude. He wouldn't be Kyran, if he didn't have his confidence.

*That's right,* a voice said in his head. *He wouldn't be Kyran at all. He would have been Ben.*

Aaron shook his head to stop these thoughts. He couldn't dwell on what-ifs. It would bring him nothing but heartache.

He opened the door to his cottage as quietly as he could. He took off his shoes so as not to make any noise and crept upstairs. He would just sneak back into bed and Sam and Rose would never know he was missing. He opened the door to the bedroom and froze.

"It's about time," Sam said, sitting at the foot of his bed.

Rose was standing by the window. "Where were you?" she asked.

Aaron let the moment of shock pass before he walked in with as much nonchalance as he could muster.

"I went for a walk," he said.

"At five in the morning?" Sam asked.

Aaron shrugged. "I couldn't sleep."

"You left Salvador," Rose said. "I saw you walk in just now."

Aaron took off his jacket. "I just went to the woods at the Gateway," he said. "I needed some time with my element."

"'Cause Salvador doesn't have any trees," Sam mocked. "There's a whole orchard full of your *element*."

"What's with the third degree?" Aaron asked. "You're acting like I committed a crime." He ignored the fact that meeting and conversing with the Scorcher was most likely a punishable felony under mage law.

Sam's brown eyes were full of suspicion as he stared at his best friend. "You're up to something," he said. "I thought I heard you leave in the middle of the night last week too, but I wasn't sure. But this time I know you've been out of the city for at least an hour."

Aaron was thankful Sam had only woken up an hour before. If he'd known Aaron had left at two in the morning, there was no way he would believe Aaron was out walking for three hours in the freezing cold.

"I'm not up to anything," Aaron lied, climbing back into his bed. "I had to clear my head. I went out. It's not a big deal." He pulled the covers up and lay down, his back to Sam.

He could feel the twins staring at him. He stayed as he was, willing his friends to either go back to sleep, or leave the room. At long last, Rose shuffled back to her bed and Sam lay back in his. Aaron closed his eyes and let out a slow breath, willing his racing heart to slow down. He had to be more careful. He couldn't risk Sam or Rose catching him meeting Kyran. They might be his best friends, but neither of them would understand. They already thought Aaron was blind when it came to Kyran. They wouldn't take his word that Kyran was innocent; that he hadn't dropped the Gate to Salvador and allowed the vamages into the city. Truth was, Sam and Rose hated Kyran just as much as the rest of the mages.

*** 

Over the next two weeks, Aaron met up with Kyran a handful of times. He didn't stay long though, keeping the visits under two hours at a time. That way, should Sam and Rose notice him missing during the night, he could pick an excuse:

"I went for a walk."

"I felt sick so went to see an Empath."

"The Blade of Afton was calling to me."

"I had a bad dream so went out for some air."

But so far, Sam and Rose hadn't caught him out of bed again.

Kyran always came to the forest to wait for Aaron, and then led him through the portal to the abandoned city. They went back to the same flat, sat around the table full of books, and carried on their study of the legacies. Aaron still had no idea what the other thing was that Kyran was searching for. He wouldn't tell him, no matter how many times Aaron asked.

"Just give me a clue," Aaron said, "I'll figure the rest out."

Kyran didn't look up from his book. "Sure, Ace," he said. "You can't work out which end to hold a sword, but this you'll figure out."

"That happened one time," Aaron said defensively. "And only because the hilt was broken. Both ends were long and pointy."

Kyran looked up at him and grinned. "Yeah, okay," he teased. "Whatever you say, Ace."

Aaron ignored him and picked up his pen, going back to taking notes. He had learnt a lot about legacies over the month he'd been meeting up with Kyran. He now understood the basic principles of how legacies worked, how they connected with the core, and what happened when they were transferred.

If the legacy went from a parent to their child, it was a simple case of reassignment. Once the child's core awakened, or in some rare cases, when the child came of age, the legacy detached from the core of the parent, and sought out the holder in the next generation. Aaron read that it was the core that called out for the legacy, and the stronger the core, the quicker the legacy went to it.

Aaron's eyes flitted to Kyran. He had three legacies. Earth came from their dad, Christopher Adams. Kyran must have received that when he turned thirteen. Fire was from Hadrian. Air was the legacy belonging to the Avira family, but Hadrian had taken the legacy from James Avira when he killed him. How Fire and Air passed to Kyran was a mystery to Aaron. He wondered if Kyran's core happened to be so strong, it pulled the legacies from Hadrian? Was that even possible? Aaron didn't know, and Kyran wasn't big on sharing.

"Take a picture, Ace," Kyran said, his eyes on the book.

Aaron quickly looked away. "Don't flatter yourself," he said. "I was just looking at what you were reading."

"Uh-huh," Kyran replied.

Aaron went back to reading his notes. If for whatever reason the legacy didn't pass to the next generation, it had to be handed over by the legacy holder. But since the legacy was attached to the core of a mage, it couldn't be given without the core being damaged. That's why a manual transference of a legacy resulted in the death of the legacy holder, because the legacy was essentially ripped out of the core and given away. That's what Neriah had done; he had given his legacy to Aaron, and possibly tiny fragments of his core, still embedded in the legacy. That's what would happen to Aaron, if he chose to give the legacy to Ella. It would tear his core, and he would die, unless they found a way to detach the legacy first and then transfer it.

Aaron put down his pen and rubbed a hand across his face. He was tired – too tired to take any more notes that night. He looked out of the window; the sky was still dark with flashes of lightning every few minutes. The rain was heavy against the glass. Aaron used to be terrified of lightning. He would run into his parents' room every time it struck in a thunderstorm. His heart skipped a beat at the thought of his parents. He hadn't heard anything from them since they left. He gave Kyran a sideways glance.

"I've been meaning to tell you something," Aaron started.

"Hmm," was all the reply Kyran gave, head lowered over the book, reading intently.

Aaron picked at the corner of the paper pad before him. "Mum and Dad are out looking for you."

Kyran didn't so much as lift his head, but his voice was quieter when he asked, "They are?"

"Yeah," Aaron said. "They're trying to find you."

Kyran shifted his shoulders, sitting up a little, but he still didn't look away from his book, even though Aaron could tell he was no longer reading it.

"Fourteen years too late," Kyran said.

Aaron's heart jolted with pain. "Kyran," he started, his tone pleading.

"We're not talking about this," Kyran cut him off.

"But if you would just agree to meet them—"

"Aaron." Kyran finally looked at him, and the intensity in his eyes made Aaron stop. "I said, we're not talking about this," he repeated. "We're here to read, so just read, or go back to Salvador." Kyran turned back to his book.

Aaron nodded. There was no point in fighting it. Kyran wasn't willing to discuss their parents.

"Until the one who matters asks the question, it can't be answered," Aaron murmured, mirroring what Naina had said to him.

"When you don't get answers, you'll eventually stop asking questions too," Kyran said.

Aaron didn't say anything. He had seen glimpses of Kyran – of Ben – waiting on top of that hill for his parents to come back for him. He must have had so many questions, but after four years, he gave up and stopped waiting, stopped asking why his parents never came back for him.

Aaron pulled the book he had been reading closer and picked up where he had left off. A sudden thought occurred to him and Aaron lowered the book, turning to look around at his brother again.

"Suppose we find a way to transfer the legacy out of me," he started. "Can we choose who the legacy goes to?"

"You've obviously not been reading enough," Kyran said, flicking through the pages of his book. "If the legacy isn't specifically transferred to another, like Neriah did with you, it will find the strongest Elemental from the bloodline it belongs to."

"So if it ever left me, it will automatically go to Ella?" Aaron asked.

"Yeah," Kyran replied. "She's the only Afton. The legacy has no one else to go to."

"What happens then?" Aaron asked.

Kyran stopped reading, but he didn't meet Aaron's eyes.

"Once Ella has her legacy, won't Hadrian go after her?" Aaron said.

Kyran gave him a quick nod. "Yeah, he probably will."

Aaron stared at him. "And you're going to let him?"

Kyran finally looked over to meet Aaron's eyes. "He wants the legacies. I told you, there's nothing I can do to stop him."

"So you're just going to stand back and let Hadrian kill Ella for the legacy?" Aaron asked.

"Yes," Kyran replied.

Aaron's heart jumped. He didn't expect that. "Kyran!" he snapped. "You're *not* going to let her die!"

"I can't stop him," Kyran said.

"So you're doing all this, finding a way to transfer the legacy, just so you can get Hadrian off my back and onto Ella's?" Aaron asked, outraged.

"I don't want Ella hurt either," Kyran started, "but there's nothing I can do for her. She was going to get this legacy from Neriah, and she was going to be targeted by Hadrian because of it. But you were never meant to be a part of this mess. My priority is saving *you*. That's all I care about." His eyes darkened. "The others can go to hell, for all I care."

Aaron didn't speak right away. He took in a breath.

"Understand this, Kyran," he said. "I'm not letting anyone hurt Ella, or any of the mages for that matter. I want this legacy to go to Ella because it's her birthright." Aaron fixed Kyran with a hard look. "And I will fight to my last breath to keep Hadrian from taking it."

# 12

## LETTERS

The start of July brought a drop in the temperature and more rain. It felt as if there were grey clouds suspended over Salvador indefinitely, splattering them with fat raindrops one day, and then a light drizzle the next. Aaron didn't mind it. He'd never had a problem with rain, even when he was living in the human realm, oblivious to mages, vamages and legacies. Now that Aaron had the legacy of Water, he found he enjoyed the rain even more than he used to. The rest of Salvador, however, didn't feel the same way.

Although the restoration of Salvador was almost complete, the mages still had to work outside in the rain and cold. They complained about it, levitated umbrellas over their heads as they worked, and the ones with an affinity to the element of Fire tried to keep everyone happy by drying the droplets of water on them, but it was a never-ending cycle.

The cottages had been fixed and the Stove rebuilt, but there was the orchard to repair, as well as the workshops, not to mention the glass building that once held the Hub.

The mages had checked the cottage belonging to Jason Burns, but all they'd found of interest was a binder with checklists documenting each and every item that had ever been brought to Salvador and other cities in the safe zones of the realm. The binder had numbers and scrawling notes that no one could decipher, but no clues as to how to actually *get* the items.

As a result, the city was still without a communal table, as well as vital furniture for some cottages, like beds and sofas. So it came as a surprise to everyone when they saw the Gate flash open one day, and several trucks drove in, with large canopies covering the loads, protecting them from the rain. Aaron and Sam stopped in their tracks, the baskets of debris they were clearing from the workshops forgotten in their hands. The rest of the mages gathered around in confusion, watching the trucks slowly drive in. The trucks stopped in the middle of the street. The door to one opened and Bella jumped out. She grinned at the mages.

"What are you waiting for?" she asked. "Come on. We've got a lot to unpack."

The mages hurried forward, calling for others to help. Aaron and Sam dropped their heavy baskets and ran to the trucks. The canopies were pulled aside to reveal beds, chairs and sofas. Two of the four trucks had nothing but tables and chairs.

"What is this?" Ella asked, looking at Bella with surprise. "Where did you get all this from?"

"I contacted some of the chiefs of other cities," Bella said. "They all got together to donate what they could." Bella smiled. "Salvador's been a home to most of us at some point in our lives. We couldn't let it suffer."

The overjoyed mages unloaded the trucks, not bothered in the least now to be working in the rain. They used the power of Air to help lift the heavy items and settle them safely on the ground. Aaron, Sam and Rose helped carry beds and sofas into various cottages.

Then came the individual tables. They were rectangular in shape, and big enough to seat six at least. There were some thirty tables, made of pine, some oak, others mahogany, and various other types of wood.

"Sorry they don't match," Bella said, as the mages lined the tables end to end in the middle of the street. "Everyone gave up one of their tables. It's all they could give."

Mary shook her head, looking as if she were struggling to keep her eyes dry. "It's perfect," she said. "Now when Salvador sits together, we'll be reminded of all the cities that came together as one for us."

Aaron had to admit it was a powerful moment to see the mismatched tables form the communal table. Every city was represented by one section of their table, and when it came together it was enough to fill the street of Salvador again.

The mages were laughing now as they carried the chairs to the table to complete it. The air was full of jubilation; something Aaron hadn't witnessed for a while.

"We have to start preparing dinner," Mary was saying to her kitchen staff. "This is a cause for celebration."

As Mary and her helpers started preparing for the feast, Ella and the other Hunters started erecting an enormous tent that would cover the length of the table. Ryan and Michael were doing a good job drying the table and chairs so everyone could sit and enjoy their dinner.

Salvador had come alive with excited energy. The mages were bustling around, either helping prepare dinner, or setting the canopy of the tent over the table. Rose ran off to help in the Stove and Sam needed no excuse to be close to Ella.

Grinning, Aaron followed behind Sam.

"Aaron."

Aaron turned at the call, and his eyes widened with surprise. "Aunt Alaina," he breathed.

Making her way towards him was his uncle Alex's fiancée. Aaron hurried over to her.

"What are you doing here?" he asked.

Alaina smiled. "Hello, Aaron. It's nice to see you too," she said.

Aaron grinned, abashed. "Sorry," he said. "It's just I wasn't expecting to see you here."

Alaina scanned her surroundings. "I've never been to the City of Salvador before," she said. "It wasn't easy finding it. It took me almost a full day to get here."

"Is everything okay?" Aaron asked. He couldn't think of a reason why his would-have-been-aunt needed to come to Salvador. Mages only came there if they lost their homes to an attack. His stomach twisted at the thought. Alaina had already lost the love of her life, she didn't deserve to have anything else taken away from her.

But Alaina gave him a smile. "Everything is fine," she said. "I came to see you."

Aaron frowned. "Me?" he asked. "Why?"

Alaina reached into her pocket and pulled out several envelopes. "To give you these."

Aaron had no idea what they were. He took them from her and saw his own name sprawled on the front of the envelopes in very familiar handwriting. Suddenly, it came to him. His dad had said he would send him letters, to keep him informed about their progress in tracking Kyran.

"They're from my dad," he said.

Alaina nodded. "I could tell that much," she said. "I can recognise Chris's handwriting. It's very similar to Alex's."

Aaron's heart gave a painful lurch. Fourteen years since his death, but Alaina still remembered what Alex's handwriting used to be like.

"What I couldn't figure out was why Chris was sending letters to *my* house." She smiled at Aaron in a way that told him she knew exactly why, and was only asking to tease him. "Mind explaining?"

Aaron ran a hand through his rain-damp hair. "I was kind of supposed to be staying with you," he admitted.

"Any reason you're not?" Alaina asked.

"I wanted to help here," Aaron explained. "Salvador was left broken by the attack. I couldn't just leave it like that and walk away."

Alaina nodded. She gave the city another glance. "Looks like you've been working hard," she said. "Maybe once you're done you could come live with me, like your mum and dad asked?" She held Aaron's gaze. "I lost my parents when I was very young," she said quietly. "The Adams have always felt like family. Despite what happened – with Chris and Kate leaving–" She faltered for a moment but then pushed on. "They never stopped being my family." She smiled at Aaron. "And it would be really nice to get to know you, finally, after fourteen years."

Aaron found himself nodding. "Yeah," he said. "I'd like that."

Alaina looked relieved, like she had been anticipating Aaron to refuse for some reason. She looked to the ground for a moment. "Your parents told me about Ben," she said. She met Aaron's eyes. "He's alive?"

Aaron was surprised. He wasn't expecting her to bring up Kyran. He nodded to answer her.

"He's...the Scorcher?" she asked.

Aaron's heart missed a beat. He didn't want to say the words out loud, so he nodded again.

Alaina looked heartbroken. She gathered herself before asking in a small voice, "Does he really resemble Alex?"

Now Aaron couldn't even nod his head. He didn't know what to tell her. Both answers would probably hurt her. If he told her the truth, that the realm's most feared and hated Scorcher looked exactly like the man she still loved to this day, how would that bring her any joy? But if he lied and said no, then that small spark of hope he could see in her eyes would go out. She had spent fourteen years waiting to see Alex's echo. Seeing Kyran would possibly bring her some sort of peace, wouldn't it?

Aaron's lack of answer made Alaina shake her head. "You know what, don't answer that," she said. "I don't know which answer would hurt less."

Aaron wanted to tell her that Kyran wasn't evil, like the mages believed. But he couldn't do it here, like this, in the middle of the street, with other mages close by.

Alaina looked around the city once more before hugging her coat closer to herself. "I should go," she said. "It's a long way back." She gave Aaron a small pat on the cheek and turned to go.

"Aunt Alaina?" Aaron called.

Alaina turned, looking both surprised and a little touched at being called 'aunt' by Aaron.

"You should stay," he said. "It's going to get dark soon. Have dinner with us, and then you can leave tomorrow morning." That way, he could take her aside and explain everything concerning Kyran.

Alaina's smile spoke volumes of her joy at being invited to dinner, but she shook her head. "I have to get back," she said. "I can't be away from home."

She walked away, leaving Aaron staring after her, clutching his dad's letters.

***

Dinner had been an event. Ella and her team of mages – and Sam – had set up a magnificent tent over the complete length of the table. They had then made a tunnel leading from it to the entrance of the Stove, so Mary and her helpers could bring food to the table without facing the rain. Colourful lanterns hung in mid-air, casting multi-coloured glows against the walls of the tent. The pitter-patter of the rain falling on the canopy was oddly soothing as they sat under it.

Aaron enjoyed the ambiance and the laughs around the table. It felt like the dinners Aaron used to have in Salvador, before Kyran was revealed as the Scorcher. In a few short hours, Mary had somehow managed to prepare a mouth-watering feast: roast chicken with potatoes and steamed vegetables, grilled chops served on platters of rice, and juicy rump steaks with chips and crispy salad. For dessert, she served treacle tarts and ice cream.

Late that night, after everyone had gone to bed with full bellies and satisfied smiles, Aaron stayed up to read the letters his dad had sent. He sneaked downstairs to use the lit lantern to read. There were six letters, and in each one, his dad started off by assuring him they were okay. He told Aaron they were staying away from Hadrian's zones. His mum and dad were trying to catch Kyran in a safe zone – one of Neriah's zones – and according to their research, Kyran visited a lot of safe zones. Exactly why Kyran was going to these zones, they didn't know, but they hoped to find him so they could talk.

Aaron read each letter with a growing sense of guilt. His mum and dad had left Salvador to look for Kyran, but Kyran was coming to Salvador every other night to meet with him. His parents were trying so hard to find their son, and Aaron had a way for them to reach Kyran, but was keeping it to himself. Aaron could tell how desperate his dad was to speak with Kyran – he could feel it resonate from the words his dad had written. For a fleeting moment, Aaron considered finding a way to contact his parents to tell them to return to Salvador, and then tricking Kyran into meeting them. Would that help his mum and dad get their eldest son back, or would he just end up losing Kyran too? Aaron gave himself a shake. He couldn't do that. He couldn't betray Kyran's trust. He looked down at the letters on the coffee table. But he couldn't leave his parents wandering around the realm, searching for someone who wasn't there either.

Aaron felt the pull of Kyran's call. He stood up and gathered the letters, shoving them into the pocket of his coat. As quietly as he could, Aaron opened the front door and stepped out. The rain had finally stopped. Aaron hurried towards the Gate, slipping out quickly. He made his way into the forest, to their usual meeting spot. He saw Kyran was waiting for him next to the portal, with a backpack slung over his shoulder.

Aaron frowned at him. "What's with the bag?" he asked.

Kyran smirked but didn't answer. He tilted his head towards the portal and said, "Hurry up," before walking into the glowing Aric's mark.

Aaron went in after him. He walked through the blinding light, only to end up in another forest. Aaron blinked at his surroundings.

"Where are we?" he asked. Usually, the portal brought them to the street outside the flat they used to do their research.

"No reading today," Kyran said. "We're going on a field trip instead."

A thrill of excitement went through Aaron. "Where?" he asked as they started making their way through the forest.

"You'll see," Kyran replied.

The chilly nip in the night's air had Aaron bury his hands into his pockets to keep them warm. His fingers touched the edges of his dad's letters. "Kyran," he started. "I need to talk to you about someth—"

A twig snapped behind them.

Both Aaron and Kyran turned at the same time.

Aaron gaped in shock, his heart skipping several beats.

"Rose?" he breathed.

Rose was standing there, staring at Aaron and Kyran with utter disbelief. The portal glowed behind her. Rose's wide eyes went from Aaron to Kyran one more time, before she took a stumbling step back.

Aaron realised what she was about to do, and it made his stomach turn with panic. "Rose, wait–!"

Rose turned and ran for the portal, so she could go back to Salvador.

"Rose, no!" Aaron darted after her.

Kyran clenched his fist and the portal collapsed, just before Rose could pass through it.

Rose whirled around to face them, her eyes slitted with fury.

Aaron held out his hands. "Please, don't freak out–" he started.

"Don't *freak out?*" Rose asked incredulously. "What is wrong with you?" she demanded. "What are you doing, Aaron? What are you doing with *him?*"

Aaron tried to hold on to her, to calm her, but Rose pulled away. "Don't touch me!" she snapped.

"Rose, please," Aaron begged.

"I knew you were up to something," Rose said, "but this? This I didn't expect, Aaron."

Aaron glanced behind him, but Kyran hadn't moved. He was staring at Rose, but he didn't say a word.

"I know what you think," Aaron said to Rose, "but it's not like that. Kyran's helping me."

"Helping you?" Rose seethed. "He's not helping you, Aaron. He's helping Hadrian, just like he helped him *kill* Neriah!" She was so angry she was shaking. "He's the one who dropped the Gate! He's the reason Salvador was attacked!"

"No," Aaron shook his head. "No, he didn't."

"Take me back," Rose said. "Now! I want to go back to Salvador right now."

Aaron was breaking into a sweat, despite the cold wind whipping at his face and neck. "Rose, you can't tell anyone–"

"I'm telling *everyone*," Rose said. "I knew you were sneaking out of Salvador but I didn't think it was to meet him," she said. "I followed you tonight and caught you walking through that portal. To think I was actually *worried* about you, scared that you were going out into the realm on your own–"

"We're trying to find a way to get the legacy out of me," Aaron explained. "If you tell anyone, all it's going to do is get me in trouble, and Kyran won't be able to help me."

"Good," Rose said icily. "You should get in trouble." Her eyes moved to rest on Kyran. "And he should stay the hell away from us."

"Rose, come on," Aaron pleaded. "Don't you want Ella to get her legacy back? If we can figure out a way to get the legacy out of me and back to Ella, isn't that worth it?"

Rose didn't answer him, folding her arms across her chest.

"Take me back," she said.

"Not until you promise you'll keep my secret," Aaron said.

"Or what?" Rose challenged. "What are you going to do?"

Aaron stared at her. "You're my best friend," he said. "I'm asking you, *please* don't tell anyone."

Rose looked away from him. "Open that portal thing so I can go back," she said.

Aaron didn't know what else he could say to her. He turned to look at Kyran. "You want to weigh in here?" he asked.

Kyran took a moment before letting out a breath and walking towards them. But he passed them by, without looking at Rose. He came to a stop where the portal had been and raised his hands. Aaron hurried forward.

"What are you doing?" he asked, coming to Kyran's side.

"She wants to go back," Kyran said quietly.

"If she goes back, she's going to tell everyone about us meeting up," Aaron pointed out.

"Let her."

"What?" Aaron exclaimed.

"She's only doing what she thinks is right," Kyran said, and Aaron could hear the hurt in his voice.

"You could try denying it," Aaron said.

Kyran looked at him. "How can I do that?" he asked, glancing at Rose. "From where she's standing, I'm nothing but the enemy."

Aaron didn't know what to say. Unhappily, he stood back as Kyran worked to open the portal again.

For a few minutes nothing happened. Then small sparks started to sizzle in the air. A dull glow started making shapes: a circle, then the inverted V, but before the last two symbols could take form, the circle and V vanished. Aaron frowned. Kyran gave his hands a shake and then started again. A few more minutes passed but nothing happened.

Kyran cursed, dropping his hands.

"What is it?" Aaron asked. "What's happening?"

"I can't open the portal," Kyran said. "I closed it too fast. It needs time to regenerate before it can reopen."

Aaron looked from the empty spot where the portal should be to Kyran. "So, you're saying we're stuck here?"

Rose turned at that.

"Yeah," Kyran replied. "For a few hours, anyway."

"Oh, please," Rose scoffed. "You expect me to believe that?"

"Rose," Aaron started. "We can't get back to Salvador without the portal. We're just going to have to wait it out."

"No," Rose said. "We can walk." She headed off through the woods.

"Rose," Aaron yelled behind her. "We can't walk back to Salvador. God knows how far we are."

"Six zones," Kyran offered quietly.

"Rose!" Aaron cupped his hands around his mouth so his voice carried. "It's going to take us days to get back on foot. Just wait a few hours for the portal."

"I'm not staying here!" Rose called back to him. "You coming with me or not?"

"Rose!" Aaron tried again, but she didn't stop. "Dammit." He chased after her.

Silently, Kyran followed after them.

# 13

## TRUE LOVE NEVER DID RUN SMOOTH

"Rose?" Aaron called to her as she trailed through the woods ahead of him.

Rose kept on walking.

"Rose, come on, this is crazy," Aaron said. "Just wait for the portal to regenerate. Then Kyran can open it."

Rose turned to glare at him. "He can open it now, he just doesn't want to."

"You saw for yourself the portal wasn't working," Aaron said.

"I don't think much effort was put into it," Rose countered.

Kyran, who was walking behind them, came to a stop. "Rose?" he called.

She almost tripped, but Rose stubbornly kept on walking.

"Rose," Kyran called again. "Rose."

She whipped around, full of fury. "What?" she snapped.

"We've come full circle," Kyran said.

Rose glanced around and found to her horror that they were back where they had started. She recognised the spot where the portal had been before Kyran collapsed it. The small sparks were still flying in the air, trying to ignite the portal.

"We'll try this way, then," she said, heading off in another direction.

Kyran and Aaron shared a look but followed after her.

They must have stumbled around the dark woods for an hour at least, before Rose finally admitted defeat. She took refuge under a tree, to get out of the cold wind that had turned her hands, cheeks, and nose pink.

"The minute that portal is ready, we're leaving," she told Aaron.

"Yeah, okay," Aaron said. He looked at Kyran, who had taken off his backpack, resting under a tree at a little distance from them. Aaron went to Rose and sat down next to her. "Rose—" he started.

"I'm not interested," she said. "The minute we get back to Salvador, I'm telling everyone what you're up to." She turned to look at Aaron with fierce eyes. "Unless you *swear* to me, that after today, you'll never meet him again."

Aaron couldn't promise her that. "Rose," he pleaded.

But Rose didn't want to listen. She gave Aaron a disappointed shake of her head and got up to sit under another tree. Aaron let out a difficult sigh and closed his eyes. He didn't know what to do, how to convince her to keep his secret. Aaron wasn't too bothered about the rest of Salvador, but if Skyler found out he had been meeting Kyran...Aaron suppressed the shudder. He didn't even want to imagine what the unofficial leader of the mages would do to get to Kyran.

***

Rose was freezing. Sitting in the shelter of a tree did nothing to protect her from the icy grip of the cold wind. The thin jacket she was wearing was useless in keeping her warm. Nevertheless, she hugged it tight across her body, rocking to generate some sort of heat.

She threw Aaron an angry glare. She was stuck in this situation because of him. A little voice in her head told her, *He never asked you to follow him out. You did that on your own.* Rose told that voice to go to hell. She saw Aaron had dozed off while still sitting up, leaning against the tree, his head at an angle as he slept. Rose found herself fighting the urge to go and straighten Aaron up, so he'd be comfortable and not wake up with a painful crick in his neck. She suppressed it. She was mad at him; she wasn't going to mother him.

Rose kept her eyes firmly away from where Kyran was sitting. He was still awake, her peripheral vision told her that much. But she was damned if she was going to look at him. She had been so confused about Kyran, ever since finding out that he was the Scorcher. She didn't know if he had truly felt anything for her during his stay in Salvador, or if it had been nothing but an act. Even at the revelation that Kyran had a vampire girlfriend, Rose continued to feel *something* for him; an emotion that she couldn't name or understand.

But that day, when the mages returned to Salvador with an injured Christopher Adams and an unconscious Aaron, Rose had finally understood. When she had watched a broken and sobbing Ella help levitate the dead body of Neriah Afton into Salvador, the reality came crashing down on her. After learning how Kyran had helped Hadrian kill Neriah by trapping them in a ring of fire, Rose had decided at that very moment that Kyran was nothing but an enemy. She promised herself that she would feel nothing but anger for him.

It had worked, up until today. It was so much easier to hate Kyran when he wasn't around. But the moment Rose had met Kyran's eyes, her resolve weakened. She had been fighting to keep her anger going. She kept reminding herself of who Kyran really was, of what he was capable. Rose glanced to Aaron. He was just as naïve as she had been. He still trusted Kyran, but she knew better now.

Her teeth began chattering and Rose couldn't take the cold any more. She got up, peering through the darkness to find twigs and sticks. She dumped what she found next to the tree and then went looking for dry leaves. That was a mission, seeing as the rain had made everything damp. She found a handful at the base of a tree, sheltered by a large rock. She brought the leaves and sticks to a clearing, away from the trees and their overhanging branches. She made a loose pile, reminding herself to keep space between the sticks, to allow plenty of air to flow.

With that done, she went back to searching in the dark, feeling the ground for rocks or big stones she could use to make a spark. Finding two rocks, Rose sat down before the pile of sticks and dry leaves. It was all theoretical. She had never used rocks to light a fire before. She always had matches on her camping trips. She hit the rocks together. Once, twice, three times. Nothing happened. Rose scratched the rocks against each other, and tiny sparks flew, but they weren't enough to light the fire. Not one to give up, Rose kept at it, banging the rocks together. It was so frustrating. Rose pushed the loose strands of her hair out of her face and tried again, hitting the rocks harder, banging them with vigour.

"I can help with that."

Rose paused, startled with surprise. She had been so focused on the fire, she hadn't seen Kyran come to stand across from her. She straightened up and continued to hit the rocks together, keeping her eyes firmly away from him. "No, thanks," she said stiffly.

Kyran took a step closer. "You're not going to get a fire started like that," he said.

"I've been camping since I was six," Rose said, still smacking the rocks together. "I know how to make a campfire."

"Really, Rose." Kyran knelt to be on the same level as her. "It'll take me less than a second—"

"I know that!" Rose spat, finally raising her head to glare at him. "I know it won't take more than a twitch of your finger to start the fire, but I don't want you to," she said. "This is *my* fire, I built it, *I'll* be the one to light it, not you. I don't want you anywhere near it!"

"Rose," Kyran started softly. "I'm only trying to help."

"I don't *want* your help!" Rose seethed. "I don't want you to make the fire, I don't want *anything* from you!" She was panting as if she had been running. Anger and pain thrummed inside her, aching to get out in the form of tears, but Rose furiously kept them back.

Kyran didn't say anything. He nodded and got up, silently walking away.

Rose let out a shaky breath, creating mist in the air. She went back to hitting the rocks, trying to get the fire started. She hit them again and again, but it wasn't happening.

She cried out when she accidentally caught her finger with the other rock. "Dammit!" she hissed and threw the rock across the clearing as hard as she could, followed by the other. She dropped her head into her hands. She felt numb with cold, except that one finger she had hurt, which was throbbing. Could things possibly get any worse?

Droplets of rain fell onto her head.

Rose groaned and lifted her gaze to the sky. "Really?" she asked under her breath.

With a sigh, she picked herself up and hurried back to her tree, taking refuge against the rain. She was now wet, cold and utterly miserable. Shivering, Rose hugged her useless jacket to herself and lay down, eventually falling into an exhausted sleep.

\*\*\*

The sun had just begun to rise when Rose awoke. She was curled up under the tree. The rain had stopped at some point in the night, but it had made the air crisp and fresh. Cold air blew loose strands of hair away from Rose's face. Oddly enough, she didn't feel very cold. She sat up to find a heavy jacket draped over her. Rose stared at it in surprise. She ran her fingers over it, as if checking it was really there. She looked to Aaron, in time to see him stirring, blinking sleep from his eyes. He was still wearing his jacket.

Rose turned to stare ahead, to the spot Kyran had taken. She saw him lying at the foot of the tree. Even in the limited light, she could see his blue zipped top and dark jeans. Rose looked down at the jacket again. She spotted her failed campfire. Kyran hadn't lit the fire, but he had given his jacket to keep her warm during the night.

Rose didn't know how to react. Should she get angry? No, that didn't feel right. Why should she be angry? If anything she should be thankful to Kyran for keeping her warm on such a cold night. He had braced the cold himself but protected her from it. But she couldn't be grateful to him – he was the enemy; he had helped kill Neriah, he had dropped the Gate to Salvador that resulted in so many deaths. He could have stopped vamages from killing her parents. Rose squeezed her eyes shut. Last night had been tough enough. She didn't want to go through all that anger again.

She got up, holding the jacket firmly in her hands. She walked across the clearing. He was fast asleep, an arm over his eyes, so only the bottom half of his face was visible. Rose couldn't help but stare at his lips. She still remembered their kiss; the one and only time she had felt his lips on hers. It was a memory that filled her with remorse, knowing she kissed the Scorcher responsible for so much misery and death. But no matter how much she fought it, or denied it, there was a part of her that held on to the memory of that kiss with fierce passion. It was enough to undo her, this feeling deep inside that told her his kiss *must* have meant something.

Rose was about to drop the jacket next to him, when she noticed something on the arm Kyran had draped over his eyes. Her breath caught as she stared at Kyran's wrist – at the black thread tied around it.

Rose couldn't believe it. Kyran still had the thread that she had fastened around his wrist, just before they shared their kiss. So much had happened since then, but Kyran hadn't taken it off. It was still there, half hidden under the sleeve of his top.

Aaron wandered up to her, stifling a yawn. "What's wrong?" he asked.

Rose shook her head. "Nothing," she said. She lowered the jacket gently next to Kyran, her eyes darting back to the black thread. "Nothing at all."

***

Kyran led Aaron and Rose through the woods and back to the spot the portal had been. It didn't take long for Kyran to set up the portal, since it had taken the night to regenerate itself. The glowing mark of Aric formed in the space of a heartbeat. Kyran opened the portal and then stepped back. His eyes met Rose's.

"There you go," he said. "A portal back to the Gateway of Salvador."

Rose didn't say anything but moved towards it. Aaron followed after her. He paused next to Kyran.

"Kyran–" he started.

"It's okay," Kyran said. "I'm going to keep looking for a way. I have a lead we were going to chase up last night." He paused for a moment before going on. "But I'll do it on my own. It's okay. You just do what you need to, follow whatever rules they force on you."

"I wanted to help you," Aaron said.

Kyran smiled. "I know."

Rose didn't say anything but took Aaron's hand. She walked into the portal, bringing Aaron with her. The moment they appeared in their familiar forest, Rose let go of Aaron's hand and started making her way to the Gate.

"Rose," Aaron called, hurrying after her. "Please, I'm asking you one last time: don't tell anyone about me meeting Kyran."

Rose didn't say anything.

"Hadrian wants Kyran to kill me," Aaron said.

Rose stopped and turned to look at Aaron with wide, horrified eyes.

"He wants the last legacy," Aaron went on. "If Kyran was really as bad as you think he is, he would have done as Hadrian wants, and I would be dead by now." He held Rose's eyes. "But he's going against everything to help me. Kyran's working day and night to find a way to get the legacy out without it killing me. He's doing it for me, so how can I leave him to do it all on his own?" He stepped closer. "If we succeed, I'll be able to give Ella back what is rightfully hers. You might think what I'm doing is wrong, but it's for all the right reasons."

Rose didn't speak. She gave Aaron a long stare before turning around and walking away.

"Rose?" Aaron called after her, but she didn't stop.

Aaron considered for a moment running back to Kyran, leaving Salvador for good and just staying with his brother. Then he remembered who Kyran lived with and that idea was crushed. He was sure Hadrian would just love for Aaron to walk into his home. It would make killing him and taking the legacy so much easier.

With a frustrated sigh, Aaron started after Rose. They reached the Gate and Rose put her hand to the bright white door. The Gate slid open, and Aaron and Rose walked inside.

"There you two are."

Aaron heard Ella's voice and spotted her walking up to them wearing a big smile. Sam was behind her. A few other mages were in the street, getting breakfast ready.

"Where did you go?" Ella asked in an exaggerated annoyed tone, her hands on her hips. "Sammy here was losing his bananas looking for you two." She grinned. "Quite literally. He knocked over several baskets of bananas while running through the orchard, yelling your names."

"I did not," Sam grumbled as he passed by her to come to Rose and Aaron's side. "What the hell, guys?" he said. "I woke up and you two were gone. I looked everywhere, searched the whole damn city."

Aaron didn't speak. He looked to Rose, who was just standing there, her expression hard to read. Aaron saw Skyler appear out of his cottage and he felt his heart drop.

"Rose?" Sam reached out to his twin. "What is it? What's wrong?"

Ella's smile slid away as she too stared at Rose with narrowed eyes. "What's the matter, Rose?" she asked.

Sam looked to Aaron, brown eyes wide and confused. "What happened?" he asked Aaron. Then he frowned, as if he just realised something. "Why were you two on the other side of the Gate?"

Aaron didn't say anything. He was so panicked, he didn't think he was capable of speaking.

"Aaron?" Ella came up to him. "What's going on? You're freaking us out." She looked to Rose. "What happened?"

Rose pulled in a breath. "Nothing," she replied. "Nothing's wrong."

Aaron hid his surprise the best he could, but he couldn't stop himself from turning to look at Rose.

"I couldn't sleep last night," Rose said. "Aaron was awake too. We started talking and after a while we decided to go out for a walk. I just felt...suffocated. Like I needed to get out. So we did just that, and went outside."

"You went out of the city to go for a walk?" Sam asked.

"Yes," Rose replied.

"Because Salvador is clearly not big enough," Ella mocked.

"I needed a change of scenery," Rose said. "I wanted to go deep into the woods. Aaron went with me and we had a nice, long, heart-to-heart." She glanced to Aaron. "We both needed it."

Aaron dropped his gaze to the ground.

"You could have woken me up," Sam grouched. "Or at least left a note."

"We didn't plan to go for so long," Rose said. "We lost track of time."

"Well, next time, don't," Skyler said, coming to stand by Ella's side, having eavesdropped on their conversation. His harsh blue eyes were on Rose. "We don't know what kind of demons roam outside," he said. "You are only safe on *this* side of the Gate. So next time you feel like going for a walk amongst trees, take a trip to the orchard." He looked to Ella. "We need to talk." Without another word, he led Ella away.

Sam watched him go. "Git," he muttered under his breath. He looked back to his sister. "You feeling better now?" he asked.

"Yeah," she said.

"Good." Sam smiled. "'Cause I can't find my boots."

"So?" Rose frowned.

"So you can find them for me."

"What do you think I am, a bloodhound?" Rose asked.

"Well, yeah," Sam said. "Either that, or your keen sense of smell is a superpower."

Rose whacked him on the arm.

Sam chuckled. "Do me a favour and find me those boots; I need to help Drake in the orchard."

"Find them yourself," Rose said.

"Come on," Sam whined. "I'll owe you one. Please?"

Rose sighed. "Fine. They're probably under the sofa, stinking up the place."

Sam grinned. "See? Using that sharp nose of yours all the way from here. Who's a good girl?"

Rose moved towards him with a raised fist but Sam took off, laughing.

Aaron was left alone with Rose. "Thank you," he managed, his relief making his voice a low whisper. "What made you change your mind?"

Rose took a minute to answer. "If getting rid of that legacy helps to keep you safe from Hadrian, then I don't care who you have to meet up with."

Aaron smiled.

"Hey, Aaron!" Sam called, halfway down the street, wearing the boots he had been looking for. "Come on! Drake's waiting."

Aaron nodded. He leant in and kissed Rose on the cheek. "Thank you," he said again and left her side, racing Sam to the orchard.

***

Once again Kyran found, to his annoyance, Layla waiting for him outside his bedroom door.

"Don't you have anything better to do?" he asked as he walked towards her.

Layla grinned. "You know you're my only source of entertainment, Kyran," she said, moving to give him access to his room. "And you're so good, why would I look for anything else?"

Kyran turned his back to her as he opened his door.

Layla's smile faltered. She stepped closer to him and took a deep inhale. "That's a strange aroma," she said. "Not warlocks or shifters this time." She stared at Kyran's back, all hints of amusement gone. "Where were you?" she asked. "Who were you with?"

Kyran walked into his room. "How is it any of your concern?" he asked.

Layla lingered in his doorway. "You know, refusing to tell me where you were only makes me all the more curious."

Kyran took off his jacket and threw it over the back of his chair. "Good," he said. "'Cause curiosity doesn't only kill cats." He turned to give her a glare as he unzipped his top and pulled it off. Heading to his en-suite, he started unbuttoning his shirt. "You can get the hell out now," he called to her before closing the door.

Layla stayed where she was. She waited until she heard the shower turn on before hurrying into Kyran's room. She went straight to the chair and picked up his jacket. She brought it to her nose and took a good, long sniff. There was no mistaking that scent. It was human. A female.

Layla lowered the jacket, but her fingers refused to uncurl from it. Her pale blue eyes were burning at the thought of a human clinging to Kyran, being so close to him that her scent was all over his clothes, his jacket. There was only one human Kyran would allow to get that close to him, and Layla knew exactly who she was.

# 14

# Jealous Vampires

"So where exactly do you go?" Rose asked, walking along the street with Aaron.

"It's a small flat," Aaron replied. "The lead he had didn't pan out. So we're back to researching. He got a dozen new books, so we're going to work through them."

"No, I meant, *where* do you go? What city? Do you know what zone it's in?" Rose asked.

Aaron shrugged. "No idea."

"Don't you think that's risky?" Rose asked, sounding concerned. "You should know where he's taking you."

"Why?" Aaron asked, with a laugh. "He wouldn't take me anywhere dangerous."

Rose turned her head to look at Aaron. "You trust him." It was more of a statement than a question.

"Of course I do," Aaron said. "He's my brother."

Rose didn't say anything in return. They reached the Gate. Aaron looked around the empty street. Everyone was either in the Stove, preparing dinner, or in the cottages, resting after another hard day of rebuilding the city.

"Are you sure you don't want me to come with you?" Aaron asked.

Rose shifted her weight from one foot to the other. "I want to speak to him alone."

Aaron nodded. "Okay. I've called him. He'll be here. You know where to go?"

"Yeah," Rose said. The Gate began to slide open. "I'll be back soon," Rose said and quickly slipped outside.

She made her way into the woods, heading to the spot she had seen Aaron disappear into the glowing portal. That's where Aaron said Kyran usually waited for him. Rose felt nervous and excited at the same time. She told herself it was because she was sneaking out of the city; it had absolutely *nothing* to do with seeing Kyran. She locked that notion tightly away, refusing to let it run free and create more havoc on her heart and mind.

She spotted him from a distance. He was wearing that same jacket – the one she had woken up under, warm and protected from the cold. Rose gave herself a mental shake. She had to keep her wits about her if she was going to do what she came to do.

The green of Kyran's eyes brightened with surprise as she neared him. He smiled and Rose almost stopped in her tracks. She pushed herself to keep going, berating herself for being so easily disarmed by his simplest of gestures.

"Hi," he said.

"Hi," Rose replied quietly.

A moment of silence fell between them.

"I was expecting Aaron," said Kyran.

"I asked him to call you," Rose explained.

At once, his smile vanished. His brow creased with concern. "What's wrong? Is everything okay?"

Rose didn't really know how to answer that. Everything was wrong, and nothing would ever be okay again.

"I wanted to talk to you," she said. "About Aaron."

"What about him?" Kyran asked.

"He told me about…about Hadrian wanting you to…kill him," Rose started awkwardly.

Kyran didn't speak, but the confusion left his expression. Rose pushed on.

"He told me that you're helping him, that you're trying to find a way to get that legacy thing out of him without it hurting him."

Kyran nodded.

Rose took a step closer to Kyran.

"Aaron is my best friend," she said. "Actually, he's more than that. He's like my little brother. Sam and I have always protected him, and we always will." A small, bitter smile came to Rose. "I know you're powerful. You have abilities that I can't even understand, but that doesn't mean I can't fight you."

Kyran didn't speak, just continued to stare at her.

"If you're pretending to help him, just so you can win his trust so you can later crush it," Rose continued, "or if you're planning on handing him over to Hadrian so he can take the legacy for himself, I swear I *will* kill you." She held his eyes. "I hesitated once to shoot you. Don't think that'll happen again."

Rose braced herself for his response. She had practised this conversation so many times in her head, with Kyran reacting differently every time. She had prepared for his anger, his disgust, his brazen arrogance at the notion that she could hurt him; she had thought of every possible reaction, but was left dazed with surprise when Kyran did nothing but smile.

Nodding his head, he said, "Understood." He looked intently at Rose. "Is that all you came to say?"

"Yes," Rose replied.

Kyran nodded again. "Well, then, I guess I better be going." He turned to walk away.

Rose let out a breath. That had gone better than she had imagined. In fact, it went so well, she was left somewhat underwhelmed.

"Rose?"

She looked up to find Kyran had stopped to speak to her, the portal shimmering in the distance ahead. "Aaron may be *like* your little brother," he said, "but he happens to *be* mine." He smiled again, but this time Rose saw a glimmer of pain behind it. "I won't let anyone hurt him," he said. "Myself included."

He walked to the portal and disappeared through it.

Rose turned and slowly made her way back to the Gate. Kyran's departing words rang in her head. He wouldn't let anyone hurt Aaron, including himself. That meant he wouldn't let Hadrian hurt him either. Was he lying? As much as Rose mistrusted him, she couldn't argue that his words hadn't seemed sincere. She desperately wanted to believe him, to have that comforting reassurance that Aaron would be safe.

She was reaching the edge of the forest when she heard something – a faint ruffling of leaves. Rose turned to glance behind her. Everything was quiet and still. Feeling a chill settle over her, Rose crossed her arms to keep in some heat, and hurried away. She had the strangest feeling, a sense that told her she was being watched. Rose shook it off. Her mind was just playing tricks on her because she was in the woods on her own. The path leading to the Gate was just a little way ahead. She would be in Salvador in no time.

A twig snapped, closer, loud and unmistakable. Rose stilled mid-step. Her heart was pounding, her skin prickling with dread. Skyler's words came back to her.

*We don't know what kind of demons roam outside. You are only safe on* this *side of the Gate.*

Rose turned to look behind her, her eyes searching from tree to tree. She couldn't spot any demons, or even wild animals lurking. She let out a slow breath, telling herself to calm down. There was nothing here.

She turned around and met the pale blue eyes of a smirking vampire.

"Hi," Layla said. She tilted her head. "Rose, isn't it?"

In her shock, all Rose could do was stare at her.

"We've got some serious girl-talk to get through," Layla said. She grinned and her fangs glistened. "Let's get right to it."

Rose didn't see the strike coming. One minute she was standing before the vampire, the next she found herself flat out on her back on the forest floor, her cheek smarting from the blow. It left her momentarily disoriented.

"I have to say," Layla murmured, sauntering over to her, "I never imagined he would be interested in humans."

She bent low and gripped Rose by the throat. Rose's breath caught, her airway compressed by Layla's hold as she was lifted up, her feet dangled above the ground.

"I can't understand why," Layla said, wrinkling her nose at Rose as she surveyed her from head to foot. "What is it about your boring, mundane existence that interests him?"

The pain of being held by her throat didn't even register. Her whole being was fighting for air – that was all Rose could concentrate on. Her fingers scratched at Layla's hands, trying to break free, and her legs kicked out, trying to find the ground.

Layla laughed in response. "So pathetic," she whispered. She threw Rose to the floor. Rose lay there, gasping and wheezing for breath.

Layla circled her leisurely. "You know, I always figured he would go for a strong woman, someone who could rival his status. He has three of the four legacies, after all. His power outmatches most of his kind. There's very little he can't do, or so he likes to tell me, anyway." She looked down at Rose with a feral grin. "But even he can't reverse death."

Rose panted, her eyes wide and fixed on Layla. She moved so fast, Rose didn't see her coming. In the space of a heartbeat, Layla was sitting on top of Rose, fangs bared. Rose's scream didn't make it out. Pain blossomed in her shoulder, cutting her cry short. She couldn't move. All she could think was that she had been bitten. A vampire had sunk her teeth into her shoulder, and now she was going to die. It was only when Layla chuckled that Rose was brought out of her fear-induced daze, and she realised it wasn't Layla's fangs but her claw-like nails that had pierced her flesh and dug into her shoulder.

"Tsk tsk," Layla said. "I'm not going to end the game just yet. We have so much more to talk about."

She dug her razor-sharp nails deeper into Rose's shoulder, making her yowl in agony.

"What – what do you want?" Rose managed to force out.

For the first time since she arrived, Layla's smile vanished. Her pale blue eyes grew furious. She leant in and hissed, "To know why he chose *you*."

Rose, petrified and in so much pain, still managed to hold the vampire's gaze.

"What is it about you that he finds so attractive?" Layla asked. "All I see is the same weak, easy-to-snap-in-two, miserable kind of human as the rest of your kind. What makes you so damn special?"

Rose was fast losing herself in a haze of pain. Her shoulder was bleeding badly. Layla had her pinned in place, her nails piercing deep into her flesh. The smallest of movements sent waves of agony through Rose. But the will to survive made Rose use her free hand to search the forest floor, to reach for something, anything, that could help her.

"It's not what you – you think," Rose said. "Kyran–"

Layla grabbed her by the face, squeezing hard. "Don't," she warned. "Don't you dare say his name."

She let go and Rose had to take a moment to regain herself.

"I'm not…He's not interested in me," Rose tried again. "You don't have to…to do this. You're still his girlfriend."

Layla looked momentarily surprised before she started laughing. "Oh, sweetie," she said. "I was never his girlfriend. I just made that up so the damn Hunters wouldn't torture me."

Rose stared at her, shocked. Her attack started to make sense. She wasn't Kyran's girlfriend but she wanted to be, and she thought Rose was standing in her way. Rose's searching fingers found a fallen branch that felt heavy and thick in her hand.

"Let me go," Rose said.

"Oh, I will," Layla said. "When I've had my fun, I'll leave your mangled corpse before that Gate of theirs." She looked up and let out a sigh. "I wonder how long it will take for Kyran to find out what happened to you." Her wide smile stretched from ear to ear. "I wonder if your death is what will finally break him."

Rose was confused; she thought Layla liked Kyran, but it sounded like she wanted to hurt him. She didn't get the chance to ponder over it. The vampire dug her claws back into Rose's flesh and twisted her fingers deeper. Rose screamed.

"That's it," Layla encouraged. "Scream as loud as you can." She grinned. "There's no one to hear you. No one is coming to save you."

Rose's voice was guttural with pain. She glared at Layla and said, "Who said I need saving?"

She gritted her teeth and swung her free arm, smacking Layla across the face with the branch. Layla was thrown off, and went tumbling to the side, freeing Rose at last. Clutching a hand to her bleeding shoulder, Rose clambered to her feet and blindly started running. Her legs wobbled under her as fear and pain clouded her senses. Stumbling, and not daring to look behind her, Rose managed to reach the pathway that led to the Gate.

She ran as fast as she could. The Gate was right there. Once she got past it and into Salvador, she would be safe.

In the blink of an eye, Layla was before her, standing between her and the Gate. Rose came to a halt, out of breath and utterly terrified.

Layla grinned to flash her fangs. "Vampire speed," she said. "You can't outrun me, *human.*"

Rose stared desperately at the Gate. She couldn't come this far and not make it. She refused to accept that.

Layla pulled down her shoulders, her murderous gaze fixed on Rose. It suddenly clicked with Rose what Layla was about to do: she was going to pounce on Rose again. Rose knew she wouldn't be able to see Layla coming; she was too fast. So she just went for it.

She ran *towards* her.

Layla stilled, confused, and it was that moment of hesitation in trying to figure out what Rose was doing that gave Rose her chance. Just as Layla started to move, to catch Rose as she came for her, Rose ducked to the side, escaping Layla's clutches by mere inches. Layla turned around, but it was too late. Rose had thrown herself at the Gate, and her fingers just managed to touch the glistening mass of white.

The Gate slid open and Rose tumbled inside.

Aaron hadn't left the street, but had been joined by Sam and Ella. They all turned when the Gate opened with a flash – they all saw an injured Rose, covered in blood and bruises, fall past the threshold.

"Rose?" Sam started with disbelief. "Rose!"

He ran towards her, with Aaron, Ella and a few other mages at his heels. Sam fell to his sister's side, picking her up, holding her in his arms. Aaron saw – just as the Gate was sliding shut –

the red-haired vampire Layla standing there, staring at them with a vindictive smirk.

The Gate closed and although the surrounding mages had grabbed their weapons and darted towards the Gate to open it again, Aaron knew there was no point. Layla was long gone.

*** 

Ella supported Rose as they walked out of the Empath's room. Sam and Aaron, who had been pacing outside, hurried over to them. Aaron could see part of the bandage covering Rose's shoulder from the neckline of her ripped top.

"You okay?" Sam asked Rose. "What did Amber give you?"

"I'm fine," Rose said, sounding exhausted. "She gave me a healing balm. Ella helped put it on and then she bandaged it."

"The cuts are pretty deep," Ella said, guiding Rose to sit down on one of the chairs. "It'll take time to heal, but Amber said the balm should help fight any infections."

Sam turned to his sister. "What were you thinking?" he asked.

"Sammy." Rose gingerly held up a hand. "Not now."

"Now seems like a perfect time to ask that question."

They turned to see Skyler had arrived at the Empath hut. His cold blue eyes went straight to Rose and narrowed at her. "Did I, or did I not, tell you to stay inside the city?" he asked, walking up to her. "I told you it wasn't safe."

"Sky, come on," Ella started. "She's been through enough."

"She wouldn't have gone through any of it if she had *listened* to me," Skyler said. He turned to Rose. "You have any idea how lucky you are to have walked away from a vampire attack?"

"Yes," Rose replied quietly.

"Then explain what the *hell* was going through that head of yours?" Skyler said.

Rose didn't speak.

"Hey, I'm asking you something!" Skyler raised his voice. "Do you know how close you came to dying today?"

"What do *you* care?" Rose said, glaring up at him.

Skyler stared at her. "I do care," he said. "I care more than you can imagine." He stood still, staring at Rose but everyone could tell he was seeing someone else. "No more innocent blood," he said in a quiet voice that almost quivered. "No more, not as long as I'm in charge."

Everyone fell silent.

Ella slowly shook her head. "I don't get it," she said. "What was Layla doing on our Gateway?"

"Maybe she was staking out the place, preparing for another attack," Skyler said.

"Hadrian doesn't tend to use her for spying," Ella pointed out.

"Doesn't mean he can't," Skyler argued.

Ella's eyes fell on Rose, on the bruise on Rose's check and neck. She shook her head. "By the look of your injuries, it seems as if Layla's attack was personal."

Rose shifted but didn't say anything.

"Why would a vampire attack Rose?" Sam asked. "What could Layla possibly hold against Rose?"

"Nothing," Skyler said. "Layla attacked Rose because she's the only one dumb enough to go for a walk on the Gateway."

"Back off, Skyler," Sam said. "That's my sister you're insulting."

"What you gonna do, *Sammy*?" Skyler taunted.

"That's enough," Ella said, breaking it up before Skyler and Sam got too into it.

While they bickered with one another, Aaron knelt next to Rose, and took her hand. "I'm so sorry," he whispered. "I should have gone with you."

Rose shook her head. She glanced up at the arguing trio before looking to Aaron. "She came for me," she said quietly.

Aaron frowned. "What? Why?" he asked.

"She attacked me, but I think her real target was someone else; someone *she* thinks will be affected by me getting hurt."

Aaron got it right away: Layla had attacked Rose to hurt Kyran. He nodded at Rose, to show her he understood. He didn't want to say his brother's name in Skyler's presence.

Aaron was already mentally calling out to Kyran, his core yelling for his brother, so he could tell him what had happened, what Layla had done to Rose. He didn't know how Kyran would react, but he hoped whatever he did, it would be enough to keep Layla away from Rose for good.

# 15

## Playing Dangerous Tricks

The doors to Layla's wing blew off their hinges as Kyran stormed inside. His green eyes had darkened, his face taut with anger. He spotted the red-haired vampire, sitting at the table with Machado and a few other vamages, tall glasses in their hands and lingering smiles on their faces.

Kyran swiped a hand and Layla was thrown off her seat. She skidded along the floor and hit the wall with a loud *thwack*.

Machado and the other four vamages leapt to their feet, but Kyran pushed them back with a twist of his hands, sending all five sprawling in the air. They too hit the walls but Kyran was only interested in Layla. He went for her, grabbing her by the throat and hauling her up. He threw her back against the wall and held her there.

"I warned you," he growled, his voice guttural with rage. "I told you if you went anywhere near her, I would bleed you out, drop by drop."

Layla couldn't speak, couldn't get out a single whimper because of Kyran's tight grip. Her eyes widened when she saw the round beam of light on Kyran's chest shine through his clothes. She scrambled to get free, her hands trying to break the hold against her throat, as the four lines on the back of Kyran's right hand started to light up.

Machado threw an arm around Kyran's neck and the other four vamages grabbed Kyran by both arms, pulling him back, freeing Layla. She collapsed to the floor. Catching her breath on all fours, Layla looked up at Machado.

"Thanks," she wheezed.

"Returning the favour," Machado replied.

Clenching his jaw with fury, Kyran closed his eyes and dropped his head. The vamages let go of him with yelps of pain at the burns on their hands. Kyran went for Layla again. He pulled her up by the arm and shoved her against the wall. He was about to grab her with his right hand with the four glowing white lines, when a shout boomed across the room.

"KYRAN, NO!"

Kyran halted at Hadrian's command. His hand was less than an inch away from Layla's throat. Kyran was shaking, the urge to kill Layla was battling furiously with his need to obey his father. Layla watched Kyran, mesmerised by his struggle.

Hadrian reached them and pushed Kyran away from Layla, before standing before her. The gold specks in his hazel eyes were fast coming alive, and the air began to smell like smoke.

"What the *hell* is going on?" he demanded.

Kyran was breathing fast, the rage in him was too fierce to allow him to speak.

"First Machado and now Layla?" Hadrian asked. "What has got into you? Why are you trying to bleed out your own?"

"They are *not* my own!" Kyran said at once.

"But they are mine," Hadrian said. "And I want an explanation as to why you were about to kill the very person I told you to always protect."

Kyran didn't say anything.

Layla stepped out from behind Hadrian. "Are you going to tell him, Kyran?" she asked. "Or should I?"

That's when it hit Kyran what she had done. He couldn't believe it. She had played him and he'd fallen for it.

"Tell me what?" Hadrian asked, turning to Layla.

It was apparent how much Layla was enjoying this, as she faced Hadrian with bright eyes full of glee and a smile on her lips.

"Kyran tried to kill me because I attacked someone he cares about." She shot Kyran a look. "Cares a *lot* about, actually. So much so, I may even go as far to say that he...loves her."

Hadrian turned to Kyran in surprise. "What?" he asked. "Who is she?"

"She's lovely," Layla said with clear mockery. "Dull brown hair, boring dark eyes, pale complexion, and, oh, the best part?" She smirked as she locked eyes with Kyran. "She's a human."

Kyran didn't speak. He watched with a sinking heart as Hadrian turned from Layla to look at him with shock and disappointment. He stared at Kyran for a long moment, then he straightened up, turned and walked away. He gestured to Machado and the other vamages to follow him out.

Kyran watched him go. He knew this wasn't the end of it. His father was going to make him talk, and what Kyran had to say he knew his father wasn't going to like.

"Tut tut. Oh dear," Layla said. "Looks like father and son are about to get into a fight neither of them can win."

Kyran glared at her. "You did this on purpose," he said.

"I did," Layla admitted.

"You're sick," Kyran said with disgust. "You tried to kill Rose just to out me to my father?"

Layla laughed. "Oh, honey," she said. "If I wanted to kill her, she would be dead." She sauntered up to Kyran. "I just wanted Hadrian to find out about your... extracurricular activities." She tilted her head as she stared at Kyran. "You staying out all night to be with her...her scent all over you and your clothes." Her eyes grew fierce. "It all stops. Now that Hadrian knows about it, he will order you to stay away from her, and that's a good thing.

That way, she gets to live." Her eyes sharpened. "If I find a hint of her scent anywhere near you again, make no mistake, Kyran, I *will* kill her."

Kyran's jaw was clenched so hard it made speaking almost impossible, but he leant in towards her and said, "Touch her again and I will kill you, regardless of what Father says."

Layla studied him. "I guess we'll see who kills whom first." She winked and walked away, flicking her hair behind her as she went.

Kyran stood for a moment with curled fists. Then his furious jolt of power upturned the table, smashing the bottles and glasses into millions of tiny shards.

***

Aaron slipped past the Gate that night and found Kyran standing by the trees, not deep in the forest like usual.

"I can't talk for long," Aaron said, hurrying towards him. "Skyler is going berserk about security. No one is supposed to leave the city–"

"I know, I'm sorry," Kyran said. "I just...I had to know – is she okay?"

Aaron paused, momentarily stunned by how worried Kyran was. He nodded. "She's okay. She's shaken up a little, obviously. She's got some bruising on her neck and cheek, and really nasty cuts on her shoulder, but the Empaths said she'll be fine in a few days."

Kyran looked heartbroken.

Aaron observed his brother for a long minute before saying, "I know you have...feelings for Rose," he started. "Is that why that vampire attacked her? Because she's jealous?"

Rose had told Aaron in private everything about Layla's attack, including that she wasn't in fact Kyran's girlfriend.

Kyran shook his head. "She's not jealous. She's psychotic."

Aaron looked back at the Gate. It was three in the morning, the whole of Salvador was asleep, but Aaron was terrified the flash of the Gate opening was going to rouse someone from their slumber – especially if that someone was Skyler.

"I have to get back," he said.

"Go." Kyran nodded. "Lay low for a while. I'll call for you when I have a lead."

"I want to help you find that lead," Aaron said.

"I can't risk it," Kyran said. "Layla followed me here. I can't have Machado or some other vamage doing the same. Layla saw me with Rose and jumped to the wrong conclusion. If she had seen you with me–" He paused, unable to go on. "It's just safer this way, Ace."

"I don't care," Aaron said. "I'm not leaving you to find a way out of this mess on your own. I'm staying with you, throughout the whole thing."

"You can't do anything if I stop coming to see you," Kyran pointed out. "I decide whether or not I'm opening a portal to come here, not you."

Aaron smiled. "I won't leave you on your own, Kyran. If you stop coming to see me, then I'll find some way to get to you."

Kyran fell quiet. Aaron's words struck him hard. *I won't leave you on your own.* Aaron had no idea how powerful his words were, or what effect that kind of a promise had on Kyran.

***

Early next morning, Kyran lifted a hand to knock on his father's door. He wasn't looking forward to this conversation, but he knew the quicker he had it, the better. His father's ire was only going to increase the longer Kyran made him wait. He pushed past his hesitation and knocked once, before opening the door and striding inside.

Hadrian was at his desk, a large paper map rolled out across the impressive length of it. Kyran silently marvelled at his father's dedication. They hadn't had breakfast yet, but here he was already working on his plans to take over the realm.

"Glad you could join me," Hadrian said, his head still bowed, eyes on the map.

"I wasn't sure if you were awake yet," Kyran said. He glanced to the large arch windows at the lightening blue sky. "It's only a little after sunrise."

Hadrian looked at Kyran. "I didn't sleep much last night. Had too much on my mind."

Kyran didn't say anything.

Hadrian walked around his desk and leant against it, hazel eyes fixed on Kyran.

"Are you going to explain yourself, or should I take what Layla said as the whole truth?" he asked.

Kyran snorted. "Since when has Layla ever told anyone the truth?" he asked, his anger spiking through his words.

"So you don't have feelings for a Shattered?" Hadrian asked.

Kyran clicked his mouth shut and didn't answer.

Hadrian closed his eyes and ran a hand over his forehead, as if soothing a headache. "Kyran," he groaned.

"You don't have to worry," Kyran started.

"Of course I do," Hadrian snapped, looking at Kyran with great annoyance. "A *Shattered?* You ignored all the mages in this realm and chose a Shattered?"

"Human," Kyran corrected quietly, because he knew how much Rose hated that term. "And it's not like that," he said. "It's...complicated."

"Kyran." Hadrian pulled himself away from the desk he was leaning against to walk towards him. "We are on the cusp of winning this war. The last thing you need is a distraction."

"She's not a distraction," Kyran lied.

"What is she, then?" Hadrian asked, coming to stand before him. "Was she not the reason you almost bled out Layla yesterday?" The gold in his eyes was gleaming, turning them from hazel to amber, warning Kyran that he was close to losing his temper. "You were ready to kill the one being in the realm I asked you *specifically* to protect."

"I warned Layla to stay away from her or I would bleed her out," Kyran replied. With a smirk he added, "You raised me to be a man of my word."

"I raised you to be *obedient*," Hadrian said, annoyed.

Kyran held his eyes. "No," he said. "I gave you that freely. I obey you because that's what I owe you."

Hadrian closed his eyes and shook his head. "How many times do I need to say it? You don't owe me anything." With a sigh, he stepped back and ran a hand through his hair. "I shouldn't have to repeat this, but seeing what happened yesterday, I think I need to." He fixed Kyran with an intense look. "You will ensure that no harm comes to Layla," he said. "You will protect her at all costs, and under no circumstances are you permitted to bleed her out. Is that understood?"

"Yes, sir," Kyran ground out. "But you have to warn her—"

"She won't go anywhere near your Shattered." Hadrian dismissed him with a wave of his hand.

Kyran felt better. Layla wouldn't go against Hadrian's instructions. She obeyed him just as fiercely as Kyran did.

"And neither will you," Hadrian added.

Kyran's heart dropped.

"You know very well that I don't have any problem with you having fun," Hadrian said. "But humans are a subpar species. A mage should never associate themselves with such weaklings as humans."

"Aric did," Kyran said before he could help it.

Hadrian looked momentarily surprised, almost as if he had forgotten their forefather had taken a human girl as his partner for life. He smirked at Kyran.

"You're not Aric," he said. "You're Kyran Aedus, and Kyran Aedus will not consort with humans." He looked Kyran right in the eyes and asked, "Is that understood?"

Kyran had to use all the willpower he possessed to nod his head and give the all too familiar reply, "Yes, Father."

\*\*\*

The tavern was busy. The cold and battering rain outside encouraged many to seek refuge inside the dry, warm bar. The drinks helped chase away the icy nip of the weather. At a table at the very back of the pub, Chris and Kate sat with their drinks.

"Are you sure this is the place?" Kate asked.

"Yeah," Chris replied, tired green eyes trained on the door. "This is it."

Kate turned her head to give the place another glance. Almost two decades had passed, but Kate still remembered how to map a room from her days of being a Lurker.

"There are four in the right corner," she told her husband, raising her cup and speaking behind it. "Another three at the far left and one at the bar."

Chris gave a slight nod. "A half hour ago, there were only three."

"They're gathering here," Kate said. "But for what?"

"Right now, I don't even care," Chris said, his gaze lingering on the door. "I just want him to walk in."

Kate's heart gave a little jump at the thought of finally, after weeks and weeks of searching, meeting her eldest son. It hadn't been easy, but they had narrowed it down to this tavern. Apparently, the Scorcher frequently visited this place to run errands for his so-called father.

"It might get complicated," Kate said, voicing her fears. "With the vamages here."

"Complications I can deal with," Chris said. "But I don't think I can handle another failed attempt to find him."

Kate reached out to take his hand. She smiled, but Chris could see her pain behind it. He put his other hand on top of hers, trapping it in a comforting grip.

The door opened and Chris's gaze darted to the newcomer. His breath rushed out of him, as the very being he was so desperately waiting for, walked inside. Kyran paused at the door, scanning the tavern. Chris lowered his hat and dipped his head, so he wouldn't be seen. Kate kept her back to the door, but her breathing had picked up. Chris couldn't keep his eyes away from his long lost son. He raised his head only enough to sneakily chance a look.

He saw Kyran stride over to the bar. The mages in his way cleared a path for him, recognising the Scorcher, but no one dared to confront him. Kyran reached the bar and gestured to the keeper to come close. The elderly mage inched nearer, looking rather fearful. Kyran pulled a pouch out of his pocket and was saying something to him, but the keeper looked conflicted, as if he didn't want to do whatever it was Kyran was saying.

A nod of Kyran's head towards the waiting vamages in the corners of the tavern had the keeper quickly agree. He held out his hands and Kyran dropped the pouch into them.

The keeper muttered something and walked away. Kyran turned and signalled something to the vamages. Chris's hand went to the gun and blade holstered to his belt, but the vamages only nodded back and returned to their drinking. Having completed whatever his mission was, Kyran walked to the door, leaving the tavern.

This was it; the opportunity Chris and Kate had been waiting for.

They both got up. Chris kept his head low and his hat lower as he and Kate made their way out of the tavern. The cold air hit them the minute they stepped outside. The rain was still heavy and it was a few hours after sunset; it was impossible to see where Kyran had gone.

"You go this way," Chris said to Kate, pointing to the left. "I'll go the other way. If you find him—"

"Call you, yeah, I know," Kate said. She was already halfway down the street. "You do the same."

Chris hurried along the street. He couldn't miss this chance. He had to get to his son, before he lost him all over again. Thunder clapped overhead and forks of lightning lit up the street. The rain was coming down heavier than ever. Chris was blinking it out of his eyes as he turned the corner, and came to a dead stop.

Kyran was waiting for him, with a gun in his hand, raised and aimed at Chris's chest. Chris was so surprised, he didn't even register the fact that his son was holding a gun to him. He also didn't realise that four of the eight vamages inside the tavern were now standing behind him, trapping him. All Chris could focus on, was his son before him.

"Ben," Chris breathed.

Kyran smiled. "Hi, Dad," he said.

And then pulled the trigger.

# 16

## TESTING LOYALTIES

Chris opened his eyes to find himself in a dark cell. There was a single torch hanging from the wall, but it didn't give enough light for him to see his surroundings. He knew he was lying on cold, hard concrete. His head and back could vouch for that. Chris tried to sit up, but his chest burned the moment he moved. His hands were cuffed, but Chris brought them up, pressing to the bloody wound just above his heart.

It all came back to him.

He had been shot.

By his own son.

Chris bit down on his lip and dragged himself to sit up, leaning against the wall. The ache in his chest had him panting. He looked at his wrists to see steel bands around them, etched with strange markings. Inhibitor cuffs. He wouldn't be able to use his powers. He was completely defenceless. Chris's chest throbbed but he knew he had to get the bullet out or he would continue to bleed. He wouldn't die, since it had been a mage who shot him, but if he lost too much blood he would be left weak and defenceless. Once the bullet came out, the wound would gradually heal. He had no option but to try to dig the bullet out with his fingers. He lifted his trembling hands to his chest.

"Relax," a voice called out, startling Chris. "I've removed the bullet."

Chris peered into the darkness and his heart jumped with surprise.

His eldest son was in the cell with him, sitting on the edge of a chair, evidently waiting for Chris to wake up. Chris wondered how he had managed to miss him. The cell was dark, but surely he should have noticed someone else was in the cell with him. He should have *felt* his son's presence.

"Ben," Chris said, his voice rough with pain. He caught the way his son bristled at the name.

"It's Kyran," he corrected.

Chris shifted, trying to sit up straighter, but had to stop when the gunshot wound ached, seizing his whole body. He took in quick breaths, easing the pain away.

"I've been looking for you," Chris said, ignoring the fact that, given where they were and how they had got there, that his words were probably going to fall on deaf ears. He had to talk, he had to tell Ben everything; he had to make him understand.

Kyran smiled. "I noticed," he said. "Did you really think you could go around asking questions about the Scorcher and it wouldn't come back to me?" he asked. "My father has contacts in every zone, be it his or Neriah's." He smirked. "You were set up at the tavern. The bar keeper reported your arrival the moment you sat down at that table."

"I figured that much," Chris said, realising the pouch Kyran had handed to the keeper was most probably something valuable, as payment for turning him in. "But I don't care. I had to meet you."

His eyes, which were no longer blue like Chris remembered, narrowed at him. "Oh?" he said. "And why is that, Adams?"

Chris felt his eyes sting. "Don't do that," he said, shaking his head. "Don't alienate yourself. You're an Adams too."

"I stopped being an Adams a long time ago," he said.

"No," Chris said. "You can never change who you truly are. You are Benjamin Adams; you're my son."

The green eyes glistened and a bitter smile came to his face. "Your son?" he asked. "So tell me, why didn't you hear *your son* crying out for you?"

Chris felt a sharp jolt of pain in his chest, and it had nothing to do with the gunshot wound.

"Ben," he breathed. "I felt you–"

"Die, yeah, I heard," he said. His fierce eyes never moved from Chris. "You couldn't come up with anything else? Did you not think such a blatant lie would be easy to pick apart?"

"I'm not lying," Chris said. "Everyone felt you die – me, your mum, Alex–"

He sucked in a hissing breath, and Chris paused. Kyran's eyes were blazing. "Don't involve Alex in this," he warned.

"Your uncle Michael felt it too," Chris pushed on. "Why would we lie, Ben?"

"To make yourselves feel better about abandoning your son," he replied.

"We could never abandon you," Chris said. "You have to know that. Deep down, you *have* to know that we would *never* leave you on purpose."

"That's what I told myself for years," Kyran said. "I held on to the belief that you would come back. That you wouldn't leave me. You couldn't." He straightened up. "But after four years of waiting – four years of doing nothing but sitting and watching that tear, willing you to appear out of it – I finally admitted the truth. You were never coming back for me, and I had to find a way to live with that. So I stopped caring. Told myself it didn't matter. That *you* didn't matter to me any more, just like I obviously didn't matter to you."

Chris felt like he couldn't breathe. Kyran's words were like splinters of glass being pushed under his skin, searing his body and soul with agony. "No," he protested, shaking his head.

"You do matter. I've lived the last fourteen years with a hole in my heart, a gap in my bloodline that shouldn't have been there! I've mourned you every day and every night for fourteen years!" he said, choking back his tears. "I felt you die, Ben."

"Ben did die," Kyran said. "The day I gave up on you was the last day Ben Adams lived. I'm Kyran now, the son of Hadrian Aedus." He stood up. "And unfortunately for you, Kyran Aedus doesn't care what happens to you."

He walked to the door of the cell and waved it open, slamming it shut behind him. Chris watched him go. A moan sounded from somewhere in the chamber.

"Chris?"

Chris felt bile rise to his throat when he recognised the voice.

"Kate?" Chris scrambled forward, heedless to the way his chest throbbed at the movement. He grasped the bars to the cell with his bound hands. "Kate!" He couldn't see the cell next to his, but he heard his wife's voice.

"Chris? Are you okay?"

"Are *you* okay?" Chris asked. He had thought Kate had got away, that it was only him who had been captured.

"I'm fine," Kate replied. "I–" she paused. "Ben?" she whispered. "Ben!" she called, raising her voice.

Chris turned to see Kyran had paused mid-step at Kate's call. The chamber was dully lit, but Chris still saw the conflicted emotions flit across his face when he turned to look at her.

"Ben," Chris called, drawing his attention. "Let her go," he begged. "Do whatever you want to me, but please let her go – *please.*"

"I'm not the one who's going to do anything to you," he replied. "You're Hadrian's prisoners."

Chris's stomach turned. "You can't let him hurt her."

"It's got nothing to do with me," he replied.

Chris slammed his hands against the bars, making the metal cuffs ring in the chamber. "Dammit, Ben!" he cried. "She's your mother!"

"She's no one to me."

Chris couldn't see her, but he knew how much those words must have hurt Kate.

"You can say what you want, it doesn't change the truth," Chris said desperately. "She *is* your mother and I will *always* be your father. And you are willing to stand back and let your parents die?"

Kyran looked over at him. "Why not?" he asked. "You did the same to me."

Chris fell silent, at a loss as to how to convince him that wasn't true, that it was the furthest thing from the truth.

"Ben, please–" Kate started.

"Don't," he cut her off but his eyes stayed on Chris, refusing to look at her. "Don't ask me to help you. Don't ask me for anything. You don't have the right."

\*\*\*

The vamages came for Chris and Kate a few hours after Kyran left. Chris was hauled out of the cell by two vamages, who took great pleasure in kicking his legs out from under him so they could drag him across the chamber. Chris twisted around to see vamages bring Kate out of her cell, none too gently either. One of them had grabbed her by her hair. Her hands were cuffed, and there wasn't a thing she could do to protect herself.

Chris struggled against the vamages. "Leave her alone!" he growled. He fought against them, to free himself and go help his wife, but his efforts were in vain. The vamages' grip was iron, and all his struggling got him were several kicks to his solar plexus.

The vamages brought Chris and Kate out of the chamber and down a set of corridors. Chris would have memorised it, but he knew they weren't going to be coming back to the cells. They were being led to their deaths.

The doors opened and Chris was pushed out into the open, cold air. He was in a courtyard – a big square-shaped, paved area that was built on top of a cliff. Chris could see the vast landscape surrounding them. Lined along the four edges of the courtyard were vamages, eagerly awaiting them.

The wind was cold, the sky a miserable grey, and a light drizzle was settling on Chris, clinging to his hair and skin. Kate was pushed out too and Chris turned to catch her with his cuffed hands. Kate gasped at the wound on his chest. Chris whispered a quick assurance as they huddled close to one another in the midst of smirking vamages. Chris glared at the men and women who stood waiting to see them tortured and then killed. His eyes stopped on Kyran at the other side of the courtyard, standing at the front, rows of vamages behind him. That's when Chris's bravado cracked. He was here too? His own son wanted to witness their deaths?

It was only when the dark-haired vamage next to Kyran took a step forward that Chris looked away from his son, to notice Hadrian. The mage who had once stood by Chris's side, called him his 'Elemental brother', was walking towards him with a twisted smile and a hunger to kill.

He came to a stop before Chris and Kate, his eyes going from one to the other. He let out a sigh. "I really had hoped it wouldn't come to this," he said.

Chris glared at him. "You wanted all the Elementals dead," he said. "I'm sure you had something exactly like this planned for us."

Hadrian chuckled. "You know what, Chris? I never liked you," he said. "Your tantrums were entertaining but after a while they began to get on my nerves. I only tolerated you because you were Alex's older brother."

Chris bristled at Alex's name.

Hadrian looked over at Kate. "But you, you I actually liked, Kate. You were like my sister. We used to be close."

"I thought of you as my brother too," Kate said, hurt shining in her eyes, "before you started killing your own kind."

Hadrian shook his head slowly. "So self-righteous," he said. He stepped closer. "Tell me, do you even realise what it is *you've* done? I may have killed another mage, an Elemental, but what you both did is so much worse than killing." He turned to glance behind him, to Kyran, before turning back to Chris and Kate with blazing eyes. "You left your own son to die."

Kate gasped, as if Hadrian had physically struck her. "You know that's not true," she said. "Ben might be mistaken, but *you* know we could never leave our son. You grew up with Chris. You know us, you know we would rather have died than leave Ben behind."

"Then why didn't you come back for him?" Hadrian asked. "He called for you every day and every night for *years*. Why did you ignore your own flesh and blood?" His eyes hardened. "You weren't here, but I was. I saw him break every time his call went unanswered. I watched that boy die a little every day, until nothing was left." His eyes gleamed gold. "You killed your own son," he said. "And then you dare to come back to this realm, fourteen years later, and try to take *my* son from me?" He glared at Chris. "If you hadn't tracked down my Scorcher, you wouldn't be here facing death. This is not my doing. Remember that. You've brought this on yourself. You should have stayed away from my son." He turned to walk away.

"Hadrian," Chris called.

Hadrian stopped to look at him. Chris's burning green eyes met his. "He's *my* son," he said.

The gold of Hadrian's eyes glowed and sparks ignited in the air. "No," he growled. "He's mine. And I won't let you take him from me."

He nodded at the vamages and turned to walk away. He strode across the courtyard to stand by Kyran's side. The vamages stationed behind Chris came forward and grabbed him and Kate.

"No!" Kate gasped as she was ripped away from her husband.

"Let her go!" Chris yelled, but the vamages dragged them both to the middle of the courtyard, ready to start their execution.

***

Hadrian could feel the tension in Kyran's body as he stood rigidly by his side, darkened green eyes watching the vamages bring Christopher and Kate Adams to the centre of the courtyard to be killed. Every eye was on the two mages, but Hadrian's gaze was fixed on Kyran. He was struggling; Hadrian could see it, feel it like a sixth sense. Both of Kyran's hands were curled into fists so tight, Hadrian wouldn't be surprised if his nails had drawn blood. But it was the pain in his eyes that unsettled Hadrian. He knew Kyran hated the Adams for leaving him, but did that mean he wanted them to die? Hadrian knew Kyran's obedience knew no limits, but this was perhaps the hardest test Hadrian had demanded from him: to stand back and watch his birth parents being killed.

Like so many times before, Hadrian felt his ice-cold resolve crack because of his son. His hand closed on Kyran's arm. "Go," he said quietly. "You don't have to see this."

Kyran swallowed hard, but his eyes never moved from Chris and Kate. "I do," he said, just as quietly.

Hadrian pulled his hand back but his focus remained on Kyran.

Chris and Kate were manhandled to the centre of the courtyard. Both husband and wife were struggling to free themselves from the vamages' hold, but it was useless. They couldn't fight them off, and as long as the Inhibitors were around their wrists, they couldn't use their powers to defend themselves either.

The vamages kicked Chris's legs out from under him and he fell to the hard ground. Hadrian noted the way Kyran's eyes darkened to a poison green at the sight. But when the vamages did the same to Kate, and the woman fell to her knees with a pained gasp, Kyran's self-resolve broke. He jolted forward, as if to go to her, but then stopped.

Hadrian's heart sank. The look on Kyran's face…Hadrian hadn't seen such heartbreak on him since he was eight years old and had finally accepted his parents' abandonment. Hadrian remembered how the boy had collapsed in front of him, with tears in his eyes, completely broken. Hadrian had placed his hand on the child's head and vowed to always look after him, to take care of him, to be his father. And from that day forth, Hadrian had made damn sure his son never looked so completely defeated again. And he hadn't – until today.

Hadrian watched as, slowly, Kyran pulled himself back, forcing himself in place. Hadrian let out a breath of relief. Kyran had come to his senses. He wasn't going to try to help the Adams.

The vamages started to make their way over to their victims, eager to taste the blood of an Elemental. Chris would be the first to die; Kate would follow.

Hadrian noticed the four lines at the back of Kyran's hand had started to glow. Kyran was still trying his best to hold back. He had gripped his right wrist, his hand curled again into a tight fist, but the light continued to grow brighter. Kyran's eyes were so dark, there was hardly any green left as he watched the vamages crowd around Chris and Kate.

Machado was the first to go in for the kill. With his fangs bared, he lunged towards Chris, aiming for his neck. Chris grabbed Machado with cuffed hands and threw him to the ground, holding him there. Kate went for the sword resting in the sheath clipped to Machado's belt. With her hands still bound, Kate swung the sword in an arc, catching the closest vamages. They fell back, sporting cuts across their arms and torsos. Kate managed to floor one vamage. She disarmed the fallen vamage and turned to throw the sword to Chris, who caught it with his shackled hands.

Kyran moved forward but Hadrian grabbed his arm. "My men can handle it," he said. "Don't get involved."

Kyran nodded, but his darkened gaze stayed on Chris and Kate as they stood back to back, their swords at the ready, since they were still cuffed with the Inhibitors and couldn't use their powers. The vamages, however, could. As Hadrian and Kyran watched, the vamages threw everything from fire to ice at the pair. Kate and Chris were forced to dodge the strikes or use the swords to knock back what they could.

They backed away, nearing the edge of the courtyard, but staying close to one another as they battled the vamages and the elements they were throwing at them. They stepped onto the rocky ground of the cliff, still by each other's side, fighting back where they could. Then a mighty jolt of air caught them, they lost their footing, and both Chris and Kate tumbled over the edge of the cliff.

Hadrian couldn't hold him back this time. Kyran went running, racing to the edge of the cliff, Hadrian right at his heels. The vamages gathered in a crowd, staring over the edge, looking baffled and confused.

"They disappeared," Machado said, as Kyran and Hadrian reached them.

"What?" Kyran exclaimed, his voice cracking. "How can they disappear?"

He shoved his way to the edge and looked for himself. It was at least a forty-metre drop to jagged rocks below. But Machado was right. Christopher and Kate's bodies were nowhere to be seen.

"Where could they go?" Machado asked. "It doesn't make any sense."

"Kyran?" Hadrian called. "Can you feel them?"

Kyran turned to him, stoically playing a poker face, but it could never fool Hadrian. He could see the relief in Kyran's vivid green eyes. "They're still alive," he said. "They couldn't have gone far. They're close by."

Hadrian turned to the vamages. "What are you waiting for?" he asked with a growl. "Go after them! Find them and bring them back alive." The sparks in his eyes grew brighter as he glanced to Kyran. "This time, I'll be the one to kill them."

# 17

## FALLING APART

Aaron could only describe his surroundings as some sort of a cellar. It was a vast room, with high ceilings and no windows. The torches hanging from the wall allowed Aaron to see the baskets full of fruit, lined in neat rows against the wall. There were barrels of what Aaron assumed was ale of some kind, against the other wall. Between the baskets and the barrels were three men and a woman. The first was Aaron's dad, Christopher, looking rather pale and a little sickly. The second was Alex, who was sitting hunched over on top of one of the barrels, looking not much better than his brother. The last was Neriah, standing with his head bowed and his back curved, with his sister, Lily, by his side.

No one spoke. They stood in silence, until long minutes ticked by. Aaron was beginning to wonder what the point of this Inheritance moment was, when Alex asked in a small voice, "What are we going to do?"

Neriah didn't give a reply but he looked over at Alex and Aaron felt his heart jolt at how bloodshot his eyes were.

"We have to do something," Lily said. "We can't just keep him locked up forever."

"We have no other choice," Chris started. He swallowed hard. "We have to execute him."

Neriah snapped his head up, looking thunderstruck.

"Chris," Alex said with a breath of indignation.

Chris swerved around to face him. "He *killed* James!" Chris cried. "He went to a *vampire* and asked to be turned. He's not a mage any more, he's a demon!"

"Chris, it's *Hadrian*," Alex said, and his voice quivered with the effort to keep back his emotions. "He may have become part demon, but he's still part mage. He's still our Hadrian. We can't execute him."

"We don't have a choice," Chris said. "If we don't get a handle on this now, we run the risk of him escaping. He's always been powerful, even for an Elemental and a legacy holder." He turned and gave Neriah a dirty glare. "But now he has James's legacy for Air too. God only knows what powers he has from being part-vampire." He pulled in a breath and slowly nodded his head, as if convincing himself. "We need to kill him. He's too dangerous."

"We're not killing him," Alex said.

"Alex—" Chris started.

"No!" Alex stood up, glistening green eyes fixed on his brother. "We're not doing this again, Chris. I can't go through another execution, and definitely not *Hadrian's*."

"Then what do you suggest we do?" Chris asked, taking a step closer to his brother. "What other solution do we have?"

Alex didn't say anything. He turned away, running his hands through his hair.

Chris turned to look at Neriah and Lily. "Please," he said. "Someone give me another way out of this mess. I'm willing to try anything."

Lily didn't speak, but dropped her head, having nothing to suggest.

"Neriah?" Chris called.

Neriah finally spoke. "We're not killing him."

Chris closed his eyes. "Neriah—"

"We're *not* killing him," Neriah said with a note of finality. "Aside from everything else, Hadrian has no heir. If he's killed, his legacy will die with him."

Chris fell quiet. After a moment or two he gathered himself and asked, "So what do we do?"

Neriah was quiet for a moment. "I know what Hadrian's done is unforgivable," he started. "But I'm not giving up on him. He's still Hadrian. He's in there somewhere and I'm going to get him back."

Chris shook his head. "You're fooling yourself," he said. "Hadrian would *never* have hurt another mage. As much as he and James fought, Hadrian would've given his life to protect James, we all know that." He pointed a finger at the door at the very end of the cellar. "That *thing* in there is not Hadrian, not any more. It's a monster and we need to put it down."

"Say whatever you like," Neriah started, "but after James, I'm the next in line. I'm the leader now, and I'm telling you, Chris, Hadrian will *never* be executed."

"Chris is right, Neriah," Lily started quietly. "He's not Hadrian any more."

"Yes, he is," Neriah argued. "He's still Hadrian and I'm not giving up on him. I *will* fix him, I just need time to figure out how." He faltered for a moment, a look of unease flashed on his features, before he pulled out a small purple gem from his pocket. "Until then, this is our only solution." He held the gem up for the rest of the Elementals to see.

Aaron recognised it: it was the key that Neriah used to wear around his neck, the one that Kyran had come to Salvador to steal.

Both Chris and Alex seemed taken aback. Lily gasped, looking horror-stricken.

"No," she whispered. "Neriah, you can't–"

"I have to," Neriah cut her off. "There is no other choice."

"Where did you get that?" Chris asked, deathly quiet.

Neriah didn't answer right away. "I got it from the same source that gave me and Hadrian the truth about what Aric did with our powers: how he split them on purpose so his children would stay together." He looked at the gem pressed between his thumb and finger. "This will give me the time I need to help Hadrian. He won't be able to hurt anyone while I find a cure."

"Neriah," Alex breathed, shaking his head. "Don't do this," he pleaded. "That's...that's torture."

"It's better than killing him," Neriah said.

"Is it?" Chris asked. "Having your core locked, your powers gone. That's worse than death."

"Is there a cure?" Alex asked. "Because if not, all you're going to do is make Hadrian suffer in agony, just to end up having to execute him."

"There must be a way to get rid of that vampiric virus inside of him," Neriah said. "And I'm going to find it. I'm not forsaking Hadrian to this darkness."

"Neriah," Chris started.

"I'm going to pull him back," Neriah said, holding Chris's gaze with glistening eyes. "I'm not giving up on him."

Aaron snapped awake to see a worried Rose by his side, her hand on his shoulder, gently rousing him awake.

"Aaron, you okay?" she asked. "You looked like you were having a nightmare."

Aaron wasn't sure why he was shaking. His dream was intense, but not exactly a nightmare, but his heart was racing and his breath was laboured. He could feel sweat at the back of his neck and across his forehead. He looked around his room in a daze, not remembering how he came to be in his bed, fully dressed, at what seemed like the middle of the day.

"What time is it?" he asked, sitting up and rubbing a hand across his eyes. His fingers felt moist from the perspiration clinging to his skin.

"Almost three," Rose said. She sat down beside him, looking concerned. "You alright?" she asked.

Aaron nodded, even though it was a lie. He was far, far away from alright.

Two days ago, his mum and dad had staggered their way into Salvador, injured and exhausted, their hands bound by Inhibitor cuffs. Since then, Aaron had spent every waking moment with them. He was with them when they were taken to the Empaths to be healed. He had stood by their side while Skyler, Scott and Ella questioned them about their injuries, but they didn't say much, just that they had been attacked by vamages.

"You haven't had anything to eat," Rose said, pulling Aaron out of his thoughts. "I saved you a plate. It's downstairs."

Aaron shook his head. "I'm not hungry."

"I know that's not true," Rose said. "You hardly touched anything at breakfast. You must be starving."

Aaron didn't say anything. Rose reached out and took his hand, then gasped. "You're burning up," she said. She moved her hand to touch Aaron's face. "It's not the day of the full moon, is it?"

Aaron shifted, just enough to move out of Rose's hold. "No," he said.

Rose looked out of the window and then back at Aaron, her brow furrowed with suspicion. "It's because of him," she said. "He's still calling you?"

Aaron rubbed at his head. "He never stopped."

"And because you're ignoring his calls, it's making you ill," Rose deduced. She went quiet for a moment and then said, "Maybe you should hear Kyran out, see what he has to say."

Aaron turned to glare at her. "What *could* he say?" he asked.

"You've been rejecting his calls for two days now," Rose said. "You're so exhausted you fell asleep in the middle of the day." She held his eyes. "I know you're angry with him—"

"Angry doesn't even begin to cover it," Aaron cut her off. He looked away, and dropped his head, taking in a breath to try to not fall apart. "He *shot* my dad," he said, and despite his best efforts, his voice still shook. "I saw it, Rose. The flesh memory opened up the minute I touched the wound on Dad's chest. I saw Kyran shoot him – no hesitation, no remorse." He sat up, squaring his shoulders. "It's over. I'm done with him. He's not my brother, not if he can hurt my dad like that."

"Aaron—" Rose started.

"He was going to let the vamages kill them," he said. "No matter how much Mum and Dad try to hide it from Skyler and Scott, and even me, I heard them tell Uncle Mike. Kyran stood there, and did *nothing* to help them when they were being attacked by vamages."

"You don't have to tell me what that feels like, Aaron," Rose said quietly. "I get it. I'm probably the only one who understands just how much that hurts."

Aaron wished he could take back what he had said. He didn't mean to remind Rose of her pain. He looked away, staring at his hands. Rose moved closer and hugged him, wrapping her arms around his shoulders and resting her head against the side of his. They sat like that for long minutes, not speaking a word, but taking quiet comfort from each other.

\*\*\*

Rose finally managed to coax Aaron outside around dinner time. The cold air felt good against his fevered body.

Aaron looked to the Gate and then turned his eyes away. Kyran could stand outside and call to him as long as he liked; Aaron was never going to answer him.

Aaron noticed that the tent over the table had been removed. The sky was overcast with thick grey clouds, but not a drop of rain had fallen for a few days. Another roll of thunder clapped loudly but Aaron had learnt to ignore it. They had been experiencing dry thunderstorms on and off for the last few days now. Apparently this was normal weather for the month of July.

Many of Salvador's residents were gathered around the table, ready to eat, including Chris and Michael. Aaron went to sit next to his dad.

"You enjoy your nap?" Chris asked with a teasing smile, but Aaron noticed it didn't quite reach his eyes. "I came up to get you when it was time for lunch, but you were knocked out." He looked at Aaron with concern. "You okay?"

"Fine, just a little tired. Didn't sleep much last night," Aaron said.

"Why is that?" Chris asked.

*Because my brother won't stop calling me and by ignoring him I feel like I'm being torn in half.* Aaron shrugged, "Dunno," he lied.

"I reckon he's getting lazy," Michael chipped in with a smirk. "Got to get you working again, building a few more cottages." He winked. "That'll tire you out and you'll be sleeping like a log."

Aaron gave him a weak smile.

"Michael was just telling me about all the work you did to help rebuild Salvador," Chris said. "Even though I had asked you to go stay with Alaina."

"I'm sorry," Aaron said. "But I couldn't just walk away. Salvador needed me."

Chris didn't speak but his gaze softened and he smiled. He clapped a hand on Aaron's back. "You did a good job," he said. He scanned the street. "The city looks as good as new."

Aaron blinked in surprise. "Seriously?" he asked. "That's it? You're not mad?"

"I was, at first," Chris said, "but then I realised something: you did what I probably would've done if in your place." He shrugged. "You're like your old man. I can't hold that against you."

Aaron smiled. "So what you're saying is, it's *your* fault that I don't listen to you, 'cause I'm just like you?"

"No, no, that's not what I said," Chris said quickly.

"That's what I heard," Aaron said.

"Me too," Michael added.

Chris turned to Michael. "Stay out of this, troublemaker."

Michael grinned and winked at Aaron again.

"Where's Mum?" Aaron asked with a relaxed smile.

"She's talking to Mary–" Chris paused, his eyes narrowed and he frowned at something in the distance.

Aaron followed his dad's gaze to see Scott hurrying down the street. One of his hands was gripped around the silver pendant formed by four separate symbols coming together to make Aric's mark. His brow was furrowed and glistening with sweat, his eyes wide and fixed to the mages sitting at the table. He looked utterly petrified.

Chris rose from the table, followed by Aaron and Michael. Other mages around the table spotted the Controller and leapt to their feet, running towards him. In under a minute, Scott was surrounded by his Hunters and mages.

"What happened?" Skyler demanded.

"Scott, what's wrong?" Chris asked.

Scott let go of the pendant and looked to Chris. "I received distress calls," he said. His eyes clouded with pain. "Hadrian just wiped out three of our cities."

A jolt of horror went through the crowd.

"He trapped them," Scott said, looking dazed, as if he couldn't believe what he was saying. "The entire cities were mapped into the Q-Zones. He hid the walls, so no one realised until it was too late." Scott's voice choked and he shook his head, trying to remain composed.

Aaron felt numb. The shock, terror, the pain, it was still to come. For now, all he could feel was a deep sense of disbelief. Three cities full of innocent mages, killed for absolutely no reason.

"Any survivors?" Skyler asked.

"A handful from each city," Scott said. "It was all the Hunters managed to get out, when the walls became visible a few minutes before the Q-Zones collapsed. They're the ones who contacted me." His hand went up to the pendant around his neck. "They're too afraid to stay in their cities in case Hadrian targets them with Q-Zones again. They're asking where they should go." He looked to Skyler and then Chris. "What should I tell them?" he asked. His eyes were still wide, hurt and pain glistening in them. "Which city is safe? Hadrian could target anywhere in this realm with the Hub under his control. Where do I send them?"

No one had an answer. Skyler looked lost. He turned to meet Ella's eyes, but she dropped her head too, not knowing what to say. The Hub could be used to map any city, even full zones at a time, with deadly Q-Zones. Forty minutes was all you had to get out before the Q-Zone collapsed and obliterated every living thing inside it. Forty minutes to leave everything behind and run from your homes, run out of your city, but Hadrian wasn't even allowing that small mercy. He was hiding the walls of the Q-Zone, only revealing them when the forty minutes were almost over.

"Tell them to make their way here," Skyler said. "We can figure out the rest later."

"We need to find a way to safeguard ourselves from Q-Zones," Ella said.

"We can't," Scott said. "There's nothing that can be done to protect against Q-Zones."

"Which cities did he target?" Chris asked.

"Wever, Tanfor and Sakon," Scott replied.

"Why them?" Aaron asked. "What's so special about them? What was Hadrian after?"

"I'm thinking death and destruction," Zhi-Jiya said.

"Those cities were popular places to settle down. They had big populations," Scott said distractedly. "I'm guessing Hadrian wants to target large numbers."

"We can look for motives later," Ella said. "We need to come up with a strategy. We all knew this was coming when the Hub was taken." She looked to Scott. "Hadrian won't stop destroying cities and Q-Zones are perfect for that." She took in a breath. "We need to figure out how to survive this."

"And how do we do that?" Ryan asked. "What *can* we do?"

An image came to Aaron: desolate streets with littered debris, houses left unoccupied, entire cities left empty and no one living there – like the place he went to with Kyran, to study about legacies.

"Abandoned cities," he muttered.

A few heads turned towards him.

"What was that?" Ella asked.

But Aaron ignored her, turning to Scott instead. "The realm has cities that have been abandoned – complete ghost-towns," he said. "What if we moved people there? If Hadrian's targeting cities that have large populations, he's not going to bother with empty ones. So if we move people into abandoned cities, they'll be safe there. Unless–" his moment of euphoria died – "the Hub will give us away."

He remembered the little green dots on the white table during the very first Q-Zone hunt he had witnessed. Scott could see exactly how many Hunters were in the Q-Zone. Would mages show up like that on the map of the realm?

"No, the Hub shows only those who wear a pendant," Scott explained, reaching up to touch his own. "And the only ones who wear them are the Hunters," he said. "Or me."

Aaron met his eyes with a spark of hope. "So if we move everyone into the cities Hadrian thinks are empty–"

"We stand a chance of survival," Scott said.

"But wait," Zhi-Jiya said, "that means we can't wear our pendants, and neither can you. No one can contact you."

"It's a small price to pay," Scott said. "Ryan, Ella, you two come with me," he instructed. "We need to locate the nearest abandoned city to transfer the survivors of Wever, Tanfor and Sakon. Help me replicate the map."

Ella began drawing on the ground with streams of water, twisting and turning them to take shape of zones. Ryan used fire to make amendments, as Scott corrected them both.

Skyler came to Aaron's side. "That was impressive," he said. "Thinking about using the ghost-towns. But I'm curious." His eyes narrowed with suspicion. "How did you know the realm has empty cities?"

"Neriah mentioned it once," Aaron lied.

Skyler's eyes remained on Aaron for longer than Aaron was comfortable with, but finally, he gave a nod and stepped back. "Good work," he said, clapping a hand to Aaron's shoulder.

"I need a team to escort Empaths to heal the survivors," Scott said to Skyler, as Ella and Ryan worked on the map. "Start making the preparations. We need–"

The rest of his words were drowned out by a loud clanging sound. Aaron and the others turned to see shimmering white walls appear out of nowhere, surrounding the entire street on both sides. Grey bars had fallen from the top to the bottom, criss-crossing the whole length of the walls that towered from the ground to the sky.

Aaron felt all the breath leave him. He gaped at the sight, his mind refusing to take it in.

"What is it?" Sam asked Aaron, unnerved by the horror-stricken mages around him. "What's wrong?" He and Rose, being human, were the only ones who couldn't see the walls.

"Q-Zone," Aaron managed to choke out. "We're inside a Q-Zone."

# 18

## TRAPPED

Hadrian had trapped the City of Salvador inside a Q-Zone, one that could collapse at any minute, taking all of them with it. A moment of complete panic swept through the crowd before Chris, Scott, Skyler and Ella snapped into action, calming the hysteria and taking control.

"Get the bikes and SUVs," Scott instructed the Hunters. "We need to evacuate the city."

"Leave everything and move towards the Gate," Chris said to the rest of the mages.

"Come on, move, move, move!" Skyler barked.

There was no way of knowing how long they had before the Q-Zone collapsed, killing whoever was still inside. Hadrian had given the other cities mere minutes. How long did Salvador have?

Aaron grabbed hold of Sam and Rose before they were swept up in the rush as everyone raced towards the Gate. Alan and Ava ran to the cottages, banging on the doors to make sure everyone was out and aware of the evacuation. Aaron, Sam and Rose did the same.

Scott raised a hand to the sky and a beam of light shot upwards, exploding with a bang to form Aric's mark – the distress signal, to notify the whole city.

Aaron spotted his mum running out of the Stove with Mary and her kitchen staff. Drake came with a group of orchard workers. They all formed tight circles, waiting before the Gate. Quicker than Aaron thought possible, the Hunters arrived on their bikes, followed by four SUVs. The residents of Salvador climbed behind the Hunters on motorbikes or piled into the cars. Aaron made sure Sam and Rose were safely with Zhi-Jiya and Ryan, and Chris and Kate ensured Aaron was with Ella, before they hurried to the SUVs with Michael and Drake. Aaron saw the Hunters had grabbed weapons, most probably from the artillery next to the garage with the bikes and cars.

A sudden thought struck Aaron and he jumped off Ella's bike.

"Wait," he said to her. "I'll be right back."

"Where are you going?" Ella cried.

"I need to get something," Aaron said and started running down the street.

"Aaron!" Ella yelled. "Have you lost your mind?"

But Aaron didn't turn back. He pelted down the street, heading to the lake. He had almost forgotten about the priceless weapon he had hidden there. He couldn't leave it behind. Aaron had no idea what the Q-Zone collapse would do to one of the Blades of Aric; if it would damage it, or even destroy the mighty sword, but he didn't want to risk it.

He was nowhere near the bank of the lake when he felt the draining effects of the Blade of Afton hit him. He was already fatigued from Kyran's constant calling, and for a moment he feared he would collapse with exhaustion. But Aaron held out a hand, fear and the desperation to survive giving him the strength to stay standing.

*Come!* Aaron commanded, and from deep below the lake, the Blade stirred.

From the centre of the swirling vortex, the sword shot upwards into the sky, gleaming a beautiful silver, dripping with its element. It zoomed straight to Aaron and he caught its hilt. A wave of power swept through him. His mild fever and fatigue vanished, leaving Aaron feeling rejuvenated.

He turned to run back, but Ella had followed him on her bike. She looked downright furious, but one glance at the Blade and understanding filled her expression.

"Hurry up," she said, and Aaron ran to climb on behind her, the sword in his hand.

They rode back to see the Gate had opened, and the bikes and cars were racing out of the city.

Skyler was on his bike but he wasn't leaving. He was next to the Gate, guiding the others out. Ella soared across the street and out the Gate. Aaron twisted around to see the last SUV full of Salvador's residents leave the city and Skyler finally exited behind them.

But Aaron's already racing heart kicked up a further notch when he saw the white walls of the Q-Zone extended past the Gate of Salvador. Even the Gateway was Q-Zoned.

The bikes roared and cars screeched as the Hunters sped into the woods, trying to find the way out of the Q-Zone. They had no idea if they had forty minutes, or forty seconds before the Q-Zone collapsed. The smell of rubber burning filled the air, as the bikes and cars screeched across the ground, their engines screaming as they sped down the Gateway.

Aaron worried if they were even going in the right direction. There was no way to determine which wall Hadrian had kept open. He suddenly had a terrible thought. "What if all the walls are locked?" he asked Ella, having to yell next to her ear so she could hear him over the roar of the bikes and cars.

"You can only lock three," Ella replied. "It's not possible to lock all four walls of a Q-Zone."

Aaron thought he would feel better, but if anything, his anxiousness and panic worsened. What if they didn't get to the open wall before the Q-Zone collapsed? How much time did they have? What if they were going the wrong way and the open wall was somewhere in Salvador? What if he died? What if *all* of them died – his parents, Sam, Rose, Ella? His grip tightened on the Blade. He couldn't die yet. He had to find a way to give Ella back her legacy first. He wondered what would happen if he and Ella both died? Who would the legacy go to then? Would it be lost too? According to what he'd read, then all mages that shared an affinity to the element of water would lose their powers and start dying...He gave himself a shake; he couldn't think like that. They were going to survive this. They had to.

The Hunters rode through the woods, while the SUVs were forced to stay on the wider path, but the walls of the Q-Zone refused to come to an end. They stretched as far as the eye could see. Aaron felt sick with fear. What if the Q-Zone was so big it was impossible to cross in under forty minutes – if they even had that long? Was that what Hadrian had planned? To kill them while they desperately tried to escape the Q-Zone? Would Salvador have any survivors?

Then, like a glowing ray of hope, the unlocked wall of the Q-Zone loomed before them. The shimmering white wall was devoid of bars but it was still impossible to see what lay beyond it. Aaron was certain it was more of the forest.

The bikes and cars picked up even more speed, the Hunters desperate to get out of the death trap before it was too late. Aaron mentally willed Ella to go faster. The cars and bikes ahead of them reached the wall and passed through.

Relief swelled in Aaron. They'd got out; some of them had made it. Salvador *would* have survivors. Ella revved her bike, pushing it to its absolute maximum speed and bolted towards the exit. The white wall was coming closer. Aaron could see the faint outline of the other cars and bikes parked beyond the wall. They had come to a stop, waiting for the others to escape the Q-Zone as well.

The wall came closer and closer. Aaron closed his eyes. They were riding so fast, it felt like they were flying. They passed through the wall and came out on the other side. Aaron opened his eyes as they left the Q-Zone, gasping with relief. They had done it! They were out. They were safe.

Ella came to a screeching halt that almost threw Aaron off the bike. He smacked into her back, but she didn't turn around to scold him. She didn't turn to face him at all. She was sitting rigid, her shoulders tensed. Aaron looked up and lost his breath.

Hadrian was standing with his army of vamages, waiting for all of the mages and Hunters to pass through the wall of the Q-Zone.

The last to arrive was Skyler, who came to a sudden stop, like everyone else.

Hadrian smiled. "You all made it," he said. "And with only a few minutes to go. I'm impressed."

Aaron couldn't believe it. They had escaped the Q-Zone, but they were still trapped. His gaze darted through the crowd of dark-clothed men and women standing behind Hadrian with gleeful smiles and hungry eyes. Aaron's thudding heart almost came to a stop when he spotted Kyran, standing to Hadrian's right.

If Aaron had felt ill these last few days, Kyran looked it. His eyes were bloodshot with dark circles under them – as if he hadn't slept in a long time. He seemed paler. His usual smirk was missing, as was the confidence in his stance and the arrogant glint in his eyes.

Kyran held Aaron's gaze with great unease, until finally looking away.

Hadrian scanned the crowd of mages. "I know what you have been told about me," he started. "And most of it is probably true." He smirked. "But contrary to popular belief, I don't enjoy killing mages, especially if it can be avoided." He raised his head to stand tall. "Join me," he said, "and you will be spared. Oppose me and you will die. It's that simple."

No one moved; every eye was on Hadrian, staring at him with defiance.

"If you make the right decision, you'll be ending the war," Hadrian said. "I can be the leader you all need. I'm an Elemental, I have three of the legacies under my control." His wandering gaze found Aaron and stopped on him. Surprise flitted across his features. Then he smiled and the gold in his eyes shimmered. "And it seems today I'll have the fourth and last legacy too."

Aaron looked to Kyran, but he had his eyes stubbornly fixed to the ground.

Hadrian scanned the crowd once again. "Give me your allegiance," he said. "Or give me your life."

No one said anything. From one of the SUVs, Chris, Kate, Michael and Drake jumped out. They strode forward, coming to stand in front of the mages, facing Hadrian with their weapons drawn.

Hadrian smiled broadly at Chris. "I was wondering where you were," he said. "I have to say you impressed me with your daring escape." His eyes narrowed slightly. "How *did* you get away?" he asked. When Chris didn't answer, Hadrian glanced to Aaron. "I'd have thought you would do a better job of hiding your son," he said, looking back to Chris. "I was prepared to search to the very ends of this realm to find him, and all along he was simply in Salvador."

"You're *not* taking my son," Chris said. A moment of pain flickered across his face as his eyes went to Kyran. "Not again."

Hadrian's smile fell. He took a step forward. "I didn't *take* him," he said. "You *left* him – alone and dying. He found me."

Aaron looked to Kyran with a frown, but Kyran's head remained lowered, eyes diverted from everyone.

Skyler walked over to stand next to Drake, his sword in hand, blue eyes cold and hard. "If you want to fight, then get on with it," he said to Hadrian. "No one here is going to join you."

Scott, Ryan, Zhi-Jiya and Omar came to stand next to Skyler. The rest of the Hunters followed, along with Alan, Mary and even Ava. Ella didn't move, but only because she didn't want to leave Aaron exposed and unprotected.

The whole of Salvador stood before Hadrian, their weapons drawn. Hadrian surveyed them, looking like he had expected nothing less. He nodded.

"Fight it is, then," he said. His head tilted to the side and he called out with great pride, "Kyran."

Kyran finally raised his head. He lifted a hand and fire erupted from the very ground, spreading in a wide circle, surrounding all of them – the mages and vamages – keeping them inside a fighting ring.

Hadrian's eyes glinted with joy as he looked to the mages. "I'm still giving you a chance," he said. "Fight or surrender." His gaze landed on Aaron. "Either way, I'm leaving with the last legacy."

The Q-Zone behind them collapsed with a bang, and the battle started.

The mages, as one, ran towards the vamages with their weapons raised. Ella swerved the bike around and rode in the opposite direction.

"What are you doing?" Aaron asked.

"Getting you out of here," Ella said. "He's not getting you or the legacy!"

She raced towards the line of fire and lifted a hand. Her element came alive from thin air. Twisting like a serpent, a torrent of water slithered across the ground and extinguished enough of the fire to allow Ella to ride through the circle of flames. Ella barrelled her way forward, not looking back.

A ball of fire flew over their heads, singeing the tips of Aaron's hair. In a tremendous blast, it exploded in front of them, building a wall of flames. Ella screeched to a halt, turning her bike to the side to avoid a head on collision.

She cursed and turned to see Hadrian smirking at her in the distance. He wasn't going to let Aaron escape. Ella and Aaron saw the battle raging around Hadrian. The mages were horribly outnumbered. Out of the population of mages, only a third were actually Hunters. The rest knew how to fight, but not against such large numbers of vamages. Ella turned to Aaron with clouded grey eyes, glancing once to the mighty blade in his hand, before looking at him. Aaron knew the dilemma she was trapped in: protect him, or lead him in the fight, armed with one of Aric's Blades.

Aaron nodded. "I can help," he said.

Ella didn't get the chance to reply. White smoke surrounded them before a group of vamages stepped out of the cloud, swords raised and fangs ready. Ella and Aaron leapt off the bike and straight into action. Ella threw out both hands, impaling two vamages with ice daggers. Aaron lifted the heavy sword and swung it at the nearest vamage, who jumped out of the way and snickered.

"You don't even know how to use it," he said, his yellow eyes gleaming with hunger. "What good is the legacy to you?"

Aaron held out a hand and threw a ripple at the vamage. The ground cracked in a line of semi-circles, all the way to the vamage, hitting him so hard he was propelled through the air and smacked into a tree. Aaron ducked to avoid the blade of another vamage, before lifting his sword to awkwardly block the next strike. He pushed the vamage back and then sent another ripple at him.

Aaron didn't understand what was happening. He had the legacy for the element of water, and he was wielding the Blade of Afton – the sword meant for the Elemental holding the legacy. So why wasn't the Blade unleashing its power? It was supposed to be a lethal weapon, but all it was doing right now was slowing Aaron down. It was too heavy for him to use in battle as an actual sword.

"Aaron!" Ella yelled. When he met her eyes, she held up her own sword. "Twist the hilt and swing!" She demonstrated by striking a vamage across the chest with her own sword.

Aaron rested the tip of the sword against the ground and gripped the hilt tight. He turned his hand and the hilt rotated before clicking. The engravings on the sword lit up an electric blue, and at the same time, Aaron felt a tremendous pull deep in his core. His stomach lurched, like he had plummeted from a great height.

Aaron pulled in a breath, lifted the blade and arched it up and over his head. It was as if Aaron had sliced open an invisible barrier that was holding back a sea of water. A wave came crashing out from the arch Aaron had drawn in the air. The water didn't touch Aaron but rushed outwards, knocking countless vamages to the ground.

Aaron looked at the Blade with wonder. He met Ella's eyes and she nodded at him, as if to say, *Well done.*

They turned to the fierce battle just a little way ahead of them. Ella started running, Aaron close behind her. Aaron directed a wave of water to the ring of fire Kyran had made, putting out the flames. The moment Aaron and Ella stepped past the scorched ground however, the fire came back to life with a roar. It encircled them, trapping them with the rest of the fighting crowd of vamages and mages.

Aaron's gaze darted this way and that, trying to locate Sam and Rose. He couldn't see them anywhere in the chaos. Aaron couldn't spot Kyran either.

There was just a sea of dark-clothed vamages, battling against the mages. Swords clanged against one another, bullets pierced the air, and jolts of power flew in every direction. In one place, trees were being uprooted and thrown towards vamages. *Dad,* Aaron thought. He spotted Skyler, using a sword in one hand, and his gun in the other. Every mage, Hunter or not, was fighting. Alan, Ava, Mary, the boys who helped Drake pick fruit in the orchard – absolutely everyone was fighting with blades, bullets or the elements.

The roar of an engine sounded behind him. Aaron turned to see Sam driving an SUV, Rose seated next to him, knocking down a group of vamages that had surrounded Alan. Sam reversed the car, put it into gear and drove off, towards another group of vamages. That was Sam and Rose added to the list of fighters, then.

All of a sudden, Aaron caught sight of Hadrian, who had raised a hand to form a ball of fire. He sent it flying, straight at Sam's SUV. Aaron twisted the hilt of his sword and swung. A rush of water cascaded from the tip of his blade. His wave extinguished the fireball before it could go anywhere near Sam's car, but it also knocked over the vamages and mages in its path. Ryan and Omar spluttered as they picked themselves back up from the pooled water, drenched from head to foot.

"Damn it, Aaron!" Ryan said. "Don't take out your own side!"

Aaron held up a hand in apology. He couldn't help it. He had never practised using the Blade of Aric. He didn't know how to control the immense power of the sword, or the element it was conjuring.

Hadrian's gaze found Aaron and locked on him. Aaron gripped the sword tight. Hadrian didn't do anything at first, just stared at Aaron. Then his hand lifted and Aaron panicked. Before Hadrian could send anything his way, Aaron swung his blade and a mighty gush of water raced towards Hadrian.

It never reached him.

Kyran stepped in front of Hadrian, the Blade of Aedus in his hand. He blocked the water with his sword, using the power of Fire to evaporate the water until not a drop was left. The wave Aaron had sent was gone.

Something inside Aaron snapped. Kyran was protecting Hadrian, the one person who was ready to kill all of them – kill him, Aaron, and *still* Kyran was on his side. Kyran had silently watched as Hadrian set up Q-Zones to kill entire cities full of mages. He did nothing to stop Salvador being Q-Zoned. He came with Hadrian to trap them here, to force them to give Hadrian their allegiance or lives.

He had stood back and let the vamages try to kill his parents.

The rage Aaron had been battling for the last few days finally won, and Aaron's grip tightened on the Blade of Afton. He lifted it up, twisting the hilt with all the strength he had. With a thunderous sound, a great wave of water rushed out from the end of the sword, shaking it in Aaron's hand. The wave swept across the ground and hit Kyran, pulling him under.

Kyran didn't stay down long. He got back up, soaking from head to foot, flames killing the water circling around him. He strode forward, his clothes and hair drying as he did so. He swung his blade, and with a roar a blast of fire came straight at Aaron.

Aaron blocked it easily with a wall of water, extinguishing the flames. He swung his hand this time and Kyran was hit by the branch of the tree closest to him. Kyran recovered and threw a jolt of air, which Aaron narrowly avoided.

Aaron used the Blade to direct another wave of water at Kyran, who managed to block it. In retaliation, Kyran sent a stream of fireballs at him. Aaron's defence wasn't as good as Kyran's, and he was struck by one, burning his shoulder. He fell back with a cry, the sword almost slipping from his grip. Aaron swung it, sending a wave of water at Kyran, but this time commanded it to spin around him, build tall as a tower and then fall on him, crushing him under its weight.

It did just that and for the second time that day, Kyran was pulled under the water. Rage thrummed inside Aaron, blinding him, taking over him, and he instructed the water to hold on to Kyran, to not let him go – to let him *drown*.

But Kyran came back up like a hurricane. The blast of air rippled out and threw Aaron on his back. Aaron picked himself up. He lifted the sword over his head and ran towards Kyran, about to swing it down with all his might. Kyran stood his ground, dripping wet, his sword gripped tight. Waiting.

A single leaf fell from a tree, floating in the space between Aaron and Kyran. Aaron came to a sudden stop, the sword still raised high, but his eyes were on the leaf, watching it slowly fall to the ground. He stared at it, breathing hard.

*"...should a leaf get ripped from its branch, it's forever broken."* Naina's words rang in his head. *"...a small but deceptively strong web...it can save the leaf from being lost forever..."*

Aaron looked up at Kyran, staring at him with bloodshot eyes, coming out of the haze of anger to remember who Kyran was: his brother, his family – his blood. Aaron lowered his sword. Kyran's brow furrowed as he looked at Aaron with confusion. Aaron held his stare and dropped the Blade. The mighty weapon fell to the ground with a hard clang.

Kyran's eyes widened. "What are you doing?" he asked, panic in his voice. "Pick up your sword."

Aaron shook his head. "No," he said. "I won't fight you."

"Aaron." Kyran stepped towards him. *"Pick* it up!"

But Aaron stood with his hands curled into fists and resolutely shook his head. "I'm not fighting you," he said. "I won't turn against my own brother." He held Kyran's eyes. "I won't give up on you."

Kyran shook his head, his eyes full of desperation. "Ace—"

"Kyran." Hadrian appeared behind him, a satisfied smile on his face, and hazel eyes on Aaron's Blade lying on the ground. "He has surrendered." He smirked and his eyes flashed golden as they moved to Aaron. "Now kill him."

# 19

## CHOICES

Kyran turned to Hadrian with wide eyes. Hadrian had done it – done what Kyran had feared the most. He'd told him to kill Aaron. It didn't matter that Kyran had known this day would come, it still didn't prepare him for the gut-wrenching pain that came with the order to kill his brother.

Hadrian held Kyran's eyes with ruthless authority and nodded. "Bleed him out."

Kyran looked to Aaron, his expression full of horror. Aaron was just standing there, staring back at him. For the first few moments, neither Kyran nor Aaron moved. Hadrian's command hung in the air as the battle raged all around them, the rest of the mages oblivious to what was happening between the two brothers.

"Kyran," Hadrian called, and the note of impatience in his voice had Kyran stagger forward a step. Then another and another, until he was standing before Aaron.

Kyran didn't speak. He couldn't, even if he'd tried.

"Go ahead." Aaron nodded. "Do what he says. Bleed me out." He held Kyran's tortured gaze with blazing eyes. "Bleed out your own blood."

Kyran's pounding heart was breaking. He took in a breath and reached out a trembling hand – but he didn't rest it on Aaron's chest to steal his life and the legacy. He grabbed Aaron by the arm instead. The next moment, he was running, dragging Aaron behind him.

The moment of dizzying confusion passed, and Aaron reached out to his Blade on the ground. The sword zoomed straight to his hand at his unspoken command.

Kyran didn't let go of Aaron, and neither did he look back at Hadrian, as he raced across the battlefield. The ground had been cracked and scorched, trees uprooted and thrown across the forest, and ice daggers melted into puddles.

Kyran headed to the spot where the Hunters had abandoned their bikes. He grabbed the first one he came across. Both boys quickly climbed on and, with a roar, they set off.

Out of nowhere, Skyler stepped into their path, bloodshot eyes on Kyran, aiming a gun at him. Kyran gripped the bars of the bike tight, preparing to dodge the bullets, but found he didn't have to. Aaron leant over his shoulder and directed a powerful ripple at Skyler. The ground cracked as the jolt raced along it and hit Skyler, knocking him aside. The sound of his gun going off echoed in the forest as Kyran raced past his fallen form.

Kyran raised a hand, and the fire trapping the mages went out like a candle in the wind. He rode into the woods, taking Aaron away from the battle, disappearing into the thick cluster of trees. He zipped this way and that through the forest, trying to find a pathway.

Kyran saw the spark a little way ahead, the one he had been searching for. He held out a hand and pulled the last dregs of power from his exhausted core, commanding the portal to take form. It burst into existence, springing open moments before Kyran passed through it, taking Aaron with him into another zone.

\*\*\*

At the speed they were going, it was a miracle they didn't break anything when they passed through the portal and fell off the bike. Aaron put it down to the thick, soft snow they landed in. Aaron panted as he lay where he had fallen, flat out on his back, the Blade of Afton still clutched in his hand. The sky was dark, with glittering stars. Snow was falling; flakes of ice no bigger than dewdrops settled on the leaves of trees and the ground. Aaron could sense them, like tiny pinpricks all over his body.

Hands grabbed him from the front of his clothes and hauled him upright. Aaron met his brother's furious green eyes.

"Have you lost your mind?" Kyran yelled. "What were you *thinking* dropping your sword?"

Aaron didn't say anything, but let the moment of déjà vu pass over him. Kyran had grabbed him like this before, yelled at him with just as much fury, when Aaron had jumped into a collapsing Q-Zone. The only difference was that time Aaron had been trying to save Sam; today he was trying to save his brother.

"Why didn't you keep fighting?" Kyran asked, jostling Aaron. "You were *supposed* to keep fighting! I would have thrown the fight, and you would have defeated me and escaped." He let Aaron go and pulled back, sitting on his knees. He ran both hands through his hair, dropping his head. "Oh God," he groaned. "You have any idea what you've done?"

Kyran wasn't looking for an answer, but Aaron swallowed hard and nodded. "Yes," he said quietly. "I made you choose."

Kyran looked up at him, vivid green eyes pained with surprise. It seemed he hadn't – until this very moment – fully realised what his actions had meant. Kyran leant against a tree, as if he didn't have the energy to hold himself up any more, and closed his eyes.

For long moments, neither spoke or even moved. Aaron stayed where he was, sitting in the snow, letting the moisture seep into his skin and feed his spent core.

"I've never disobeyed him before," Kyran said, breaking the silence. He was staring ahead, past the trees, into the dark forest. He pulled in a breath. "I never thought I could."

"Why do you *have* to do everything he says?" Aaron asked.

Kyran tilted his head towards Aaron. "I don't have to," he replied. "I *want* to. It's my choice."

"Why?" Aaron asked.

Kyran didn't say anything.

"I know that he brought you up," Aaron said. "You think of him like a dad." The flashes of memories Naina had showed him, as well as the moments his Inheritance had revealed of Kyran's childhood, came back to Aaron: Hadrian with little Ben, waiting with him at the top of the mountain, carrying an exhausted Ben as he slept, putting up with Ben's tantrums, placing his hand on Ben's head – accepting him as his own. "He was there for you," Aaron said, realising it himself in a moment of clarity. "You feel that you owe him something–"

Kyran's dark chuckle cut him off. "Owe him *something?*" he asked. "I owe him *everything*, Ace. He took me in when my own parents left me to die. Hadrian looked after me, brought me up, taught me everything I know. I wouldn't be who I am if it wasn't for him."

"I don't believe that," Aaron said. "You are who you are because of your heart, and your choices. You chose not to kill me today, when Hadrian wanted you to."

"Only because he wants your legacy," Kyran said. "He's not interested in killing for no reason."

"Really?" Aaron asked. "Because chasing a whole city out of their homes with the threat of a Q-Zone, only to attack them while they are unprepared, doesn't fit with that idea." He held Kyran's eyes. "He Q-Zoned three cities today – four if you count Salvador."

Kyran dropped his head. He gave a small nod. "I know."

Aaron's hands curled around fistfuls of snow. "You know he's killing innocent mages. He's destroying this realm, and still you're on his side?"

"He asked for their allegiance," Kyran said. "When they didn't give it, he attacked them."

"Stop defending him!" Aaron cried. "He's killing anyone who won't accept him as a leader."

"This is war, Aaron," Kyran said. "What do you expect? Both sides are fighting for power, and the killing isn't going to stop until one side wins."

"Hadrian's not fighting a war," Aaron said. "He's orchestrating a massacre. It's an unfair fight: he's got the Hub, you have three of the legacies, and vamages can use the mage part of them to protect themselves against our attacks." He looked at Kyran. "What do we have?"

"The choice to submit to Hadrian," Kyran said.

The snow in Aaron's fists turned hard as rock. "He's not fit to rule this realm."

"And Neriah and James were?" Kyran asked.

"They never killed an innocent!" Aaron cried, and the snow around him swirled up in into a storm.

Kyran didn't as much as flinch. He kept his eyes on Aaron. "Don't be so sure," he said.

The storm died, leaving flakes of snow to float back to the ground. Aaron's stared at him in shock. "What does that mean?"

For a long moment Kyran didn't speak. Then he looked away from Aaron. "Nothing," he said.

"No, tell me," Aaron pushed.

"Forget it, Ace," Kyran said.

Aaron fell quiet, staring at him. "Tell yourself all you want that James and Neriah were just as bad as Hadrian," he said. "But you know, deep down, that's not true." He leant towards him. "I know you don't agree with Hadrian's killings," he said. "You don't want mages dying any more than I do." He felt his eyes prick. "Please, Kyran, walk away from him. Just leave."

Kyran shook his head, closing his eyes. "I can't."

"Yes, you can," Aaron said. "And you should."

"You don't get it, Ace," Kyran said, looking at him. "It doesn't matter that I don't agree with what he's doing. I can't turn my back on him."

"Why not?" Aaron demanded.

"I won't abandon someone who never abandoned me."

Aaron fell quiet.

"He didn't have to do what he did for me," Kyran said. "I wasn't his responsibility, but he looked after me, even when I didn't want him to. I gave him nothing but grief, but he still didn't walk away from me. He made sure I never went hungry, and that I had clothes on my back. When I had nightmares, he sat by my bed so I wouldn't wake up terrified and alone. He taught me to read and write, trained me to use my powers, taught me how to fight, how to defend myself. He did everything a father would do." He held Aaron's eyes. "So how can I not be his son? How can I not obey his every command?"

Aaron didn't have an answer to that.

"I may not agree with how Hadrian is fighting this war," Kyran said, "but I will *never* leave his side. I won't walk away from the father that brought me up."

Aaron didn't say anything. He looked away, not able to hold Kyran's eyes. They lapsed back into silence, just sitting in the freezing cold, letting snow fall in their hair, dusting it white.

"What do we do now?" Aaron asked finally.

Kyran didn't answer right away. He rested his head against the tree and closed his eyes. "We wait," he said. "Then I take you back home."

\*\*\*

Kyran slowed down to a stop at the exact spot he usually met Aaron at in the woods outside Salvador's Gateway. They had driven back to Salvador using a longer route, but Kyran had insisted it was safer than going back the way they had come through the portal. Aaron had wanted to see what state the battlefield was in, but Kyran didn't want to ride through it.

Aaron had no idea what had happened after they left. Had Hadrian won? Did the mages run back to Salvador after Kyran extinguished the ring of fire? Was anyone willing to stay in Salvador after the Q-Zone threat? What if Scott had taken up Aaron's suggestion and moved the residents of Salvador to an abandoned city, to keep safe from further attacks by Hadrian? Where would Aaron go? How would he find them? But he knew if that happened, he wouldn't be alone. Kyran would find a way to get him back to his parents. If only Aaron could figure out a way to do the same for him.

Kyran cut off the bike's engine and Aaron came out of his thoughts. He pulled himself off and stood up, but didn't make a move to walk away.

"What are you going to do?" Aaron asked.

Kyran pulled in a breath. "Go home," he said, "and deal with the consequences."

Aaron's heart missed a beat. "What will he do?" he asked with worry. "What will Hadrian do to you for disobeying him? He's not – I mean – he won't...like...kill you, or anything, right?"

Kyran looked surprised at first, and then he started laughing, shaking his head at Aaron. "No," he said, chuckling. "He won't *kill* me."

Aaron could feel a strange sensation creep over him, a sense of foreboding he couldn't understand. "Then why am I not reassured?" he asked.

Kyran stared at him, a smile still on his lips. "He's not a monster, Ace," he said. "He'll be angry, furious even, I bet, but he's still my father. He's not going to hurt me."

Aaron's whole being tensed when Kyran so casually referred to Hadrian as his father. He understood it now to some extent, but he still couldn't help feel upset that Kyran thought of Hadrian that way but not his actual dad. He looked down at the ground, his grip around the Blade of Afton growing tighter.

"Okay." He nodded. "I guess I better go." He started to walk away.

"Aaron?"

Aaron stopped at his call and turned back.

Kyran paused before asking, "Why didn't you answer my calls?" His eyes searched Aaron's for an answer. "I called to you for two days straight," he said, "to warn you about the attack, to tell you to evacuate Salvador before it was Q-Zoned." His mask slipped, exposing the pain at being ignored by his blood yet once again. "Why didn't you answer?" he asked.

Aaron held his eyes. "Because you shot Dad." He saw Kyran tense. "And you did nothing to help him and mum when they were about to be killed by vamages."

Kyran didn't say anything. His eyes hardened and he nodded, looking to the ground.

"I was ready to never speak to you again," Aaron said.

Kyran lifted his head and smirked. "Yeah?" he asked coldly. "What changed?"

"I remembered that you were my brother," Aaron said simply. "You may be capable of putting a bullet in Dad, but I can't hurt you." He watched as Kyran's irate expression slipped away. "Your actions don't define mine," he said. "You're my brother, and I won't give up on you." He thought about the leaf analogy Naina had used. "I'm holding on to you; I won't let the wind blow you away."

Kyran frowned. "Did you knock something loose when you fell off the bike?" he asked. "What are you on about?"

Aaron smiled and shook his head. "You won't get it," he said.

Kyran gave him a look. "Not sure I want to."

Aaron chuckled.

A twig snapped behind him and Aaron spun around, the Blade of Afton raised and ready. He stopped, lowering the weapon.

"Rose?" Aaron whispered.

Rose had paused mid-step when Aaron turned towards her with a sword. Her eyes darted from Aaron to Kyran but she didn't say anything. Behind her, Chris and Kate appeared. Aaron's relief welled up at seeing his parents alive and unhurt. Chris darted around Rose and enveloped Aaron in a tight hug.

"You're okay," he breathed. "Thank God, you're okay."

Aaron returned the embrace, equally grateful that his parents had survived the battle.

Chris looked up to find Kyran on the bike, watching their reunion with a quiet intensity.

Chris let Aaron step out of his arms as he locked eyes with his estranged son. "Ben," he started.

Kyran looked away and started up the bike.

"No wait!" Chris said quickly. "Please, don't go."

Kate hurried to Aaron and embraced him, but both mother and son's attention snapped back to Kyran.

Kyran didn't say anything, but kicked his bike into gear.

"Please," Chris said, braving a step closer. "Just give me one minute, that's all I'm asking."

Kyran paused. He didn't cut the engine, but he didn't leave either. He stayed where he was, his hands clutched around the handlebars, but he held back to give Chris his one minute.

"I was hoping to find you here," Chris said. "Rose told us about you and Aaron meeting on the Gateway."

Aaron met Rose's eyes and she looked apologetically at him. "They were in a bad state," she whispered in explanation. "I had to tell them Kyran had a way to bring you back to Salvador, to calm them down."

"I wasn't sure if you would take the risk and come to Salvador," Chris was saying to Kyran. "But I'm glad that you did."

Kyran turned then to look at Chris. "I'm not the one who's afraid of taking risks," he said.

Chris fell quiet. His pain showed in his expression.

Kate moved forward. "Ben," she called.

Kyran bristled, and Aaron could see the tension in his body, across his stiff shoulders and straight back.

"Please," Kate said. "Believe us, we didn't know–"

"I'm not interested," Kyran said. "I'm not looking for answers to why you did what you did. I don't care any more."

"That's not true," Chris said. "If you didn't care, you wouldn't be this angry with us."

Kyran turned to glare at him. "Believe me, you haven't seen my anger yet."

Chris stared at him. "Why are you holding back?" he asked. "Go for it."

"Dad," Aaron called out worriedly, but Chris ignored him, keeping his eyes on Kyran.

But Kyran didn't do anything.

"You do care," Chris said to him. "You care about your family, your blood. That's why you took your brother away today, to protect him."

"Just because I helped Aaron doesn't mean I'll ever do the same for you," Kyran said. He twisted the handle, ready to kick off and disappear in a burst of speed.

"You already have."

Kyran halted. He turned to look at Chris with a frown.

Chris smiled. "I know it was you," he said. "When we got to Salvador, everyone asked how we escaped. We didn't know what to say, because we had no idea what had happened. All we remembered was being knocked over the edge of the cliff and a bright flash later, we hit the forest ground that surrounds the Gateway to Salvador. I couldn't figure out how we managed to fall off a cliff in one zone and land in another," Chris said. "That is, until Rose mentioned you could open portals."

Aaron felt his breath hitch in his chest. His eyes darted to Kyran. He was staring at Chris, his expression unreadable.

"You opened a portal under us as we fell," Chris continued. "And I'm assuming by Hadrian's confusion at our escape, you closed it before anyone saw." Chris stared at Kyran. "You saved our lives."

"I didn't do it for you," Kyran said. He glanced once to Aaron, and then dropped his head.

Aaron felt shame well up inside him. He had blamed Kyran for not helping his parents when he'd been the very one responsible for their escape.

"Regardless of why you did it, the point is that you did," Chris said. "You helped us, so let us help you."

Kyran was mildly intrigued, Aaron could see it in his expression. "Help me?" he asked.

"Rose told us why you've been meeting up with Aaron," Chris said.

Kyran gave Rose a single glance, but she was too busy avoiding his eyes.

"Don't worry, we're the only ones she told," Chris said. "No one else knows, and that's how it'll stay," he promised. "I can help you find a way to get the legacy safely out of Aaron."

"Do you know a way?" Kyran asked.

Chris faltered before shaking his head. "No, but I can help you in your research."

Kyran had lost interest. "I don't need your help," he said.

"Ben, please," Chris said. "After what happened today, you shouldn't go back to Hadrian," he said. "We could all go to the human realm, live there until we find a way to get the legacy out of Aaron."

"That's a good idea," Kyran said, his eyes blazing. "You should do that: run and hide. It's all you're good for."

Chris paused, pain filling his eyes. "I'm not going to stop fighting for you, Ben," he said. "Not until I earn your forgiveness." His eyes gleamed. "Not until I bring you back home."

Kyran smirked, but it did nothing to change the anger and hurt in his eyes. "I already have a home," he said. "You try to follow me again, Adams, I'll kill you myself."

The threat drove a dagger into Aaron's heart. He watched, blinking back the pain as his dad simply smiled.

"You do that," he said. "But I'm not giving up on you, son."

Kyran didn't say anything. He turned his head, tearing his angry gaze away from Chris and sped off, leaving his parents staring after him.

\*\*\*

Aaron walked into Salvador with his parents and Rose by his side. The bright flash of the Gate lit up the street, but it fell back into darkness quickly after. The City of Salvador looked just as peaceful and beautiful as it always did. There was no sign of the Q-Zone having collapsed here. Aaron knew that's how Q-Zones worked though. They were temporary zones, created as a trap, but they never left behind any sign of destruction after they collapsed.

The sun had set an hour before, but Aaron knew most of Salvador was still awake, probably reliving the attack. He had meant to ask if there had been any casualties on their side, how many mages were in need of Empath care, but he didn't have the heart to ask. A part of him didn't want to know.

"You go on ahead," Chris said, breaking away from their small crowd. "I just need a quick word with Scott about the plan for tomorrow."

Aaron spotted the Controller in front of one of the cottages, speaking with Ella. "What plan?" he asked.

"After the Q-Zone today, it's been agreed that Salvador should be evacuated," Chris said. "We're going to move to one of the abandoned cities."

So Aaron had been right. Scott had acted on his suggestion. It was a safe move; Hadrian had attacked Salvador once, he could do it again as long as he controlled the Hub. But the idea of Salvador lying empty and bare made Aaron's heart ache. They had worked so hard to restore Neriah's sanctuary, to rebuild the city that protected mages and humans from demons. But now they had to leave it and go start over somewhere else.

Chris went to speak to Scott, and Aaron quickly headed to his cottage before Scott or Ella spotted him. He didn't want to speak to anyone, didn't want to answer their questions. He was exhausted, mentally and physically. All he wanted was his bed.

Kate opened the door to their cottage and Aaron walked in with Rose. Aaron went for the stairs before Kate or Rose could say a word. He opened his door, expecting Sam to be inside, waiting for him. That he didn't mind so much. Sam was the only one Aaron could talk to, no matter how tired he was.

But it wasn't Sam who was waiting for him. Aaron walked into his room and stopped, surprised at the boy sitting at the foot of his bed.

"About time, Adams," Skyler drawled.

# 20

## PROTECTING YOUR OWN

Aaron slammed the door shut behind him. "I'm really not in the mood, Skyler," he said.

Skyler acted like he hadn't heard him. He bowed his head, his hands clasped before him. "You made a big mistake today," he said.

Aaron sighed. "I'm tired, can we do this tomorrow?"

Skyler looked up at him. "You wasted one of my bullets," he said. "Do you know how difficult it is to carve names into tiny bullets?"

Aaron turned to glare at him. "Get out, Skyler," he said. "Before I throw you out."

The old Skyler would have laughed at him, challenged him to try it. But this new Skyler just stared at him with cold blue eyes. "You protected him," he said. "You knocked me out of the way so you could save him."

"Save my brother? Yeah, I did," Aaron snapped. "And I'd do it again. I'm not going to let you *kill* him."

Skyler's eyes gleamed. "Yes, you are," he said as he stood up. "In fact, you're going to help me."

Aaron gave him a disgusted look. "You really have lost your mind," he scoffed.

"He's your brother," Skyler said, taking a step closer to him. "Your family, your blood. Which means he can hear you if you call out to him."

"Obviously," Aaron said. "So?"

"So." Skyler stood before Aaron, staring down at him. "Call him."

Aaron held his ground. "Or what?"

Skyler didn't say anything. Slowly, he pulled out his gun and held it to Aaron's chest. Aaron's body tensed with panic but his eyes stayed fixed on Skyler. There was a glint of madness in his eyes, determination in the tight clench of his jaw, but even that did nothing to break Aaron's resolve. Skyler's shot wouldn't kill Aaron, not unless the bullet had Aaron's name on it, but that didn't mean being shot wasn't going to hurt.

"Call him," Skyler repeated, his voice quiet but a little shaky. "Or I swear you'll spend the rest of tonight in agony, digging bullets out of your body." His eyes gleamed with anger. "Call him."

Aaron smirked. "Never going to happen, Skyler."

A small knock sounded on the door before it opened and Kate appeared. "Aaron, Rose has gone to the Stove to help Sam—" She stopped dead in her tracks, her eyes widening at the sight of Skyler holding Aaron at gunpoint.

"What are you doing?" she exclaimed. "Get away from him!"

"Not until he calls his brother," Skyler said. "Kyran dies tonight."

Aaron didn't do or say anything. Skyler cocked his gun and Kate cried out in panic. She ran and pushed Aaron back, stepping in front of him, shielding him from Skyler's gun.

"Get out!" Kate said to Skyler. "Leave, now!"

"Not until I persuade your son to do the right thing," Skyler said.

Aaron moved from his mum's protective stance, coming to stand in front of her. "I'm not tricking Kyran into coming here and meeting your bullet," Aaron said. "So if you're going to shoot me, then go ahead and do it." His calm green eyes met angry blue. "Or go home. You're not going to win this one."

Skyler didn't move. He was glaring at Aaron, the gun in his usually steady hand shook before he dropped his arm. He stepped forward, to get right in Aaron's face. "You mark my words, Adams," he hissed. "I *will* kill Kyran, and there's not a thing you can do to stop me."

Aaron felt his throat close up with fear. He glared at Skyler, who held his eyes with just as much ferocity.

"You won't touch either of my sons," Kate said, her voice shaking with the strain of holding back her anger. "Now, get out!" A gust of air accentuated her threat.

Skyler gave her an irritated look. Threatening an Elemental with his own power didn't hold much weight, but Skyler turned anyway, storming out of the room and downstairs, slamming the front door shut behind him. He had taken no more than two steps when he spotted Sam and Rose making their way out of the Stove with the rest of Mary's helpers, having finished packing the food for the next day's evacuation.

Skyler stilled, his eyes narrowed at the twins. Then his expression changed from anger to a forced calm, and he started walking towards them.

***

Coming home was something Kyran usually cherished. After long weeks of completing assignments and running errands, Kyran looked forward to returning to the manor and spending a little time with his father. But for the first time in his life, Kyran felt trepidation as he climbed the stairs to reach his father's wing. He knew his father had a temper – Hadrian was more suited to his element than most mages – but very rarely was his anger directed at Kyran. Today, however, Kyran knew it was all going to be for him.

The double doors were firmly closed and Kyran paused in front of them, taking in a breath to settle his nerves. He raised a hand and knocked, before twisting the doorknob to open one of the doors. He paused at the threshold. The room had been trashed. The walls scorched black. Furniture was lying broken and in disarray across the length of the room. Standing at the arched window, with his head bowed and hands on the glass panes, stood Hadrian.

Kyran stepped in and closed the door. Hadrian raised his head at the sound, but didn't turn around. Kyran walked to the middle of the wrecked room, but he didn't speak.

Minutes ticked by, but neither Hadrian nor Kyran moved. Eventually, Hadrian pulled his hands back and stood tall. "I'm surprised you came back," he said.

Kyran bowed his head. "Father–"

"There's no need to call me that," Hadrian said, turning to look at him. "Don't bother with titles that mean nothing to you."

Kyran let the angry words roll off him. "You know that's not true," he said. "You are my father."

Hadrian walked towards him. "Do me a favour, Kyran," he said. "Just leave. I know now that you're eventually going to walk out on me, so just do it today. Get it over with."

Kyran didn't move.

"Go!" Hadrian bellowed. "Get out!" He shoved Kyran hard in the chest, making him stagger back a step. But Kyran only straightened up again, his head still bowed and eyes on the ground. "Leave!" Hadrian yelled. "Go back to *them*, back to the family that *abandoned* you." His eyes were a liquid gold, glistening in the soft light. "I was a fool to think I meant anything to you. I should have known better. I should have known that it wouldn't matter that I brought you up, that I became your *father*, you could never truly be my son."

"Don't say that," Kyran pleaded, raising his head at last to look at him. "I *am* your son."

"Then why did you go against me?" Hadrian asked.

Kyran held Hadrian's angry gaze and shook his head. "I can't kill him," he said. "He's my brother."

Hadrian fell quiet. Then he stepped closer to him. "What was it that I said to you the day you agreed to become my son?" He asked in a quiet voice. "Before you became *Kyran Aedus*, I asked only one thing from you. What was it?"

"Father," Kyran started.

"*What* was it?" Hadrian demanded.

Kyran looked at him, but couldn't hold his angry eyes. He dropped his gaze to the ground again. "A promise," he replied. "To always be your son, even if the Adams came back."

Hadrian nodded. "I asked that from you because I didn't want to become your father and bring you up, care for you, look out for you, *love* you, only for you to leave me if they came back." He stared at Kyran with blazing eyes, full of anger and pain. "I asked you to make a decision: to become Kyran Aedus and cut all ties with the Adams forever, or to remain as Ben Adams and wait for their return." He pointed a finger at Kyran. "*You* made that choice. It was completely up to you, no one forced you."

"I know that," Kyran said.

"Then why are you blurring the lines?" he asked. "You're not Ben Adams, you're Kyran Aedus. You are *my* son. You are *not* that boy's brother!" he seethed. "He shouldn't mean anything to you."

"But he does," Kyran said.

Hadrian stilled. He was breathing hard, his eyes glinting gold as he stared at Kyran with shocked disappointment. "Stamp it out," he said. "Whatever compassion you've foolishly allowed yourself to feel for him, get rid of it."

"I can't," Kyran said.

"Find a way," Hadrian instructed. "I swear it, Kyran, I don't care what I have to do, I'm not losing you to any of the Adams!"

"I care about Aaron," Kyran cut across him, "but that doesn't mean I want anything to do with the other Adams," he explained. "You're not losing me. I am, and always will be, *your* son. I'm loyal to you."

"Then prove it," Hadrian said. He kept his eyes on Kyran. "Bring me the last legacy," he said, "along with the legacy holder's head."

Kyran stilled. His eyes grew impossibly wide. He shook his head slowly. "You can't ask that of me," he said in a breathless whisper.

"Why not?" Hadrian asked. "When you bleed the legacy out of him, it's going to kill him anyway."

"There is another way to get the legacy out of Aaron without it killing him," Kyran said, "and I'm close to finding it. I just need a little more time." Kyran held Hadrian's hard gaze. "I will get you that legacy, Father, I swear."

"It's not enough, not any more," Hadrian said. "I want the boy dead as well."

"Why?" Kyran demanded. "You have no quarrel with him."

"I do now," Hadrian said. "He's the reason you disobeyed me. I want to see you kill him."

"Father," Kyran started, "you're not thinking straight. You're letting your anger speak for you. You want the legacy, you don't *need* Aaron dead–"

"I may not need it, but I want it," Hadrian said.

Kyran's jaw clenched and desperate green eyes started to darken with anger. "No," he said.

Hadrian stepped closer. "No?" he asked. "Now you're talking back to me?"

"If you're going to make unreasonable demands, then yes, I'll talk back," Kyran said.

"You're testing my tolerance, Kyran!" Hadrian warned.

"And you're testing my obedience," hissed Kyran.

Hadrian stilled, staring at Kyran, as if he didn't recognise him.

"I have done everything you have ever asked of me," Kyran continued, a fierce look in his eyes. "I have fought for you, bled for you, bled out *others* for you. And I have done it all without a single complaint." His eyes glistened with fury. "But I will not kill an innocent just to satisfy your insecurities."

"This is far beyond insecurity," Hadrian said. "You're rebelling against me, and you're doing it for an *Adams*. Then you claim that your loyalty is to me?"

The fire in Kyran went out. "I would rather die than rebel against you," he said. "My loyalty will always be to you, Father. If I'm protecting others, it doesn't mean I'm turning my back on you. You are the only one I will fight for."

Hadrian didn't say anything, but Kyran's words soothed his anger a little.

"All I'm asking for is a little time," Kyran said. "I *will* work out a way to get that legacy without it killing Aaron."

"And if you can't?" Hadrian asked.

Kyran paused. He swallowed hard before meeting his eyes. "You will have your legacy, that I swear to you," he said. "No matter what I have to do. But let me at least *try* to save his life first."

Hadrian stared at him. Slowly, he straightened up and gave a reluctant, tight nod. "One month," he said. "You have thirty days to waste. On the thirty-first day, you better be standing before me with the last legacy."

Kyran nodded. "Thank you, Father."

Hadrian didn't say anything. He had given his son what he'd asked for, but he didn't like it. He didn't like it one bit.

***

Aaron wrapped the thick coat tightly around him as he trudged through the ankle-deep snow. He couldn't stop shivering. It wasn't so much because of the sub-zero temperature mid-July brought, but the draining effect of the full moon that made Aaron tremble and yearn for his warm bed. He had spent the majority of the day resting, as had the other mages, but at the first sign of Kyran's call, Aaron forced himself to get up and go out into the freezing cold. He hadn't seen or spoken to Kyran since the day Salvador was Q-Zoned.

Aaron kept his eyes on the ground as he walked. He didn't want to look around at his desolate surroundings. They had moved to the City of Ailsa, which had evidently been left empty for decades. Pretty much everything needed restoring: the houses, the farmland, orchard – absolutely everything. In the two weeks that the residents of Salvador had moved there, they had managed to clean the houses and make them habitable. Aaron and his dad had helped get rid of the overgrown vegetation, as well as revitalise the orchard, which Drake took over. Mary and her helpers worked with what food they had brought from Salvador, which was mostly fruit and vegetables. The livestock had been killed in the Q-Zone collapse.

They were all working hard to revive the dead city. But no matter what they did, however hard they worked, the city could never become like Salvador. Aaron was surprised by how much he missed it. It was the first city he had seen of this realm, the place he had met his brother, where he had trained to use his powers – the city he now thought of as his home. Even Sam and Rose seemed depressed having to leave Salvador.

The sun still had a few hours to set, but the sky was already dark with grey clouds. Aaron cast a quick glance around the street when he reached the Gate. Not a soul was anywhere in sight. Everyone was in bed, recovering from the full moon, and Sam and Rose – the only humans in the city – had taken the day off to rest and recuperate too from the hard work of restoring a whole city.

Aaron opened the Gate, hoping no one would notice the flash that swept through the street, and stepped out. Kyran was waiting for him on the Gateway – a bricked path that had trees lined on either side. Aaron hurried to him.

"Hey," he greeted him, his eyes darting all over Kyran, to check if he was okay. Even though Kyran had laughed at the notion of Hadrian hurting him, Aaron had worried endlessly about it. And it didn't help that Kyran hadn't contacted him for weeks, leaving Aaron to fret and wonder what had happened to him. "You okay?" Aaron asked.

Kyran nodded, but Aaron could see it wasn't completely true. The dark circles under his eyes had Aaron wonder if Kyran had slept at all since he last saw him.

"Come on." Kyran gestured for Aaron to follow him. "We need to go."

"Go?" Aaron frowned. "Go where?"

Kyran didn't say anything, but moved into the shadows of the trees, beckoning Aaron to follow.

"Kyran?" Aaron called, trailing after him. "It's the day of the full moon–"

"Which is why I've come today," Kyran said, as he made his way through the forest. "It's the only day it will work."

"What will work?" Aaron asked.

"I'll explain on the way."

"On the way to where?" Aaron said, coming to a stop. "I can barely stand, Kyran. I'm not walking miles–"

"I brought a car," Kyran said. "It's parked in a clearing, next to the portal. All you have to do is sit in it."

Aaron knew there was no way Kyran could have ridden here on Lexi. The snow was too thick. But he couldn't figure out where Kyran wanted to go. "What's going on?" he asked.

There was a spark in Kyran's eyes as a small smile crossed his face. "I found it, Ace," he said. "I finally found it."

Aaron's heart skipped a beat. "Wait. You found a way to get the legacy out?"

Kyran shook his head. "No, I found the stage before it."

Aaron frowned. "What does that mean?"

"I found what I was looking for: a way to reach the force that can help us get that legacy out of you without it killing you."

A rush of relief swept through Aaron, strong enough to make his legs almost give out under him. He reached to steady himself against a tree. This must be the something else Kyran had been looking for that he'd refused to tell Aaron about, claiming he would reveal all once he found a way to get to it. It seemed today was that day.

"Kyran," Aaron started, "that's brilliant." He grinned. "So what is it?"

Kyran didn't answer him. "We need to move," he said. "I want to get there before sunset. Come on."

Aaron narrowed his eyes. "Kyran, what is this 'force' that you've found a way to get to?"

"You won't understand it," Kyran said. "It's complicated."

"Try me," Aaron said.

Kyran shook his head. "Ace…" he started.

"Tell me what this force is," Aaron said, crossing his arms. "And how exactly is it going to help us?"

Kyran let out a sigh of resignation. "If I tell you, do you promise to trust me?"

"I already trust you," Aaron said.

An emotion flickered over Kyran, making him smile. He nodded. "It's something that mages as a whole don't like talking about," he started. "But it's the only thing that can help us, Ace. It's not easy to get to, which is why it took me so long to find a way." He paused and held Aaron's eyes. "It's something called the Influence."

# 21

## A NECESSARY EVIL

Aaron couldn't believe what he just heard. He gaped at Kyran as if he had grown two heads.

"I'm sorry," Aaron started. "Did you say the Influence?"

Kyran grimaced. "So you've heard of it?"

"Yes, I've heard of it!" Aaron snapped. "Have you lost your *mind*, Kyran? We can't go to the Influence for help."

"Why not?" Kyran asked.

"Because who knows what it might ask for in return," Aaron said. "It gave Empaths the ability to heal others, but took their sight in exchange," he said, repeating what Armana had once told him.

"The Influence has the answer to our problem," Kyran said. "If it wants something in return then so be it."

"But if it helps me with something as important as the legacy, it's going to ask for something just as vital in return," Aaron said. "What if I can't afford to give it what it wants?"

"I'm the one making the deal," Kyran said. "Whatever the price is, I'll pay it."

Aaron fell quiet, stunned into silence.

"If the Influence gives us a way to get that legacy safely out of you, I'll give it whatever the hell it wants," Kyran said.

Aaron shook his head in protest. "You can't do that," he said. "I won't let you."

"Ace–" Kyran started.

"It's my problem," Aaron cut him off. "I'll be the one to make the deal with the Influence."

A crooked smile crossed Kyran's face. "Do you have any idea how to make contact with it?" he asked. "Where to even start trying to summon it?"

Aaron shifted from one foot to the other. "Well, no—"

"Then shut up and let me handle it," Kyran said. He gestured for him to follow and started walking.

Aaron fell into step with him. "Where exactly are we going?" he asked.

"The Influence only makes itself known if it can't be harmed," Kyran explained. "Everything I've researched seems to suggest the Influence will come when summoned, but only if the circumstances meet its requirements."

"Which are what exactly?" Aaron asked.

"That's the difficult part," Kyran said. "The thing is, the Influence has been banned by the Elementals for so long, no one knows much about it any more. Books have documented facts about it, as well as case studies of when mages used it, but nothing about the summoning of it, or what the ideal circumstances should be. So I've been...asking around." He shifted uncomfortably. He didn't want Aaron to know he'd been bleeding out demons to get his information. "Turns out, the Influence is wary of mages, just as much as mages are wary of it, I suppose," he said. "Since mages control the elements, it makes every street, every city, every *zone* of this realm unsuitable – except the places where even mages are left vulnerable."

Aaron got it right away. "The spots that hold the Blades of Aric," he said.

Kyran nodded. "That lead I told you I had?" he reminded. "That was to go to the Blade of Avira and try summoning the Influence."

"But then Rose found us and we didn't go," Aaron remembered out loud.

Kyran didn't say anything, but his expression tightened. It wasn't long after that day that Rose was attacked by Layla.

"You said that lead didn't pan out," Aaron said.

"Because it didn't," Kyran said. "I tried summoning it, but it didn't happen. Turns out, the Influence needs more assurance. I've wielded the Blade of Avira, it's connected with me, so the Influence didn't deem it safe to come, in case I attack it using the sword, I guess. I thought about the Blade of Afton, but you've used it now, so it's no use trying that." He didn't look at Aaron, as he walked on. "So we're going to have to go to the one Blade neither of us have wielded."

Aaron's heart gave a little jump. "The Blade of Adams," he said in realisation. "That's where we're going."

"Being in the proximity of a sheathed Blade of Aric drains mages of their powers temporarily," Kyran said. "Which is why it's the perfect spot to contact the Influence. And during the full moon, mages are further weakened. So I figured this is our best shot. Summoning the Influence under the full moon, in the presence of the only unclaimed Blade of Aric, means the Influence doesn't have anything to worry about. It should come to us."

"But you have the legacy for Earth," Aaron said. "You *can* wield the Blade of Adams."

"Yeah, but the Influence doesn't know that," Kyran said, smirking.

Aaron fell silent. Kyran had really put a lot of thought into this plan. He glanced to his brother, understanding the circles under his eyes now. He had been working so hard to find the best way to contact the Influence, he had sacrificed his sleep, his peace, until he'd found it. It felt as though Kyran was more worried about getting the legacy out of Aaron, than Aaron was himself.

"By the way, where are you keeping the Blade of Afton?" Kyran asked.

"In Salvador," Aaron replied. "I couldn't bring it with me here, there's no place in this city to store it without it draining everyone. Scott said it would be safe in the lake in Salvador. Q-Zone collapses apparently don't damage weapons."

"Not Blades of Aric, that's for sure," Kyran said.

"Where's your car?" Aaron asked, feeling his legs tremble under him.

"Just a little further," Kyran said.

Aaron looked at Kyran with narrowed eyes. He looked tired, but not necessarily ill. "How come you're not struggling with the drain?" he asked. "I can barely stay upright."

Kyran chuckled. "I told you, I'm stronger than you. You're just a little baby."

A smile came to Aaron at the memory of the first time Kyran has said that to him; he had been mimicking Sam, who thought Aaron's sudden falling ill was due to staying in wet clothes the day before. That was the day Aaron had learnt about the full moon and its effects on magekind. And just like everything else in this realm, it had been his big brother who'd taught him.

Something rustled behind them, and both Aaron and Kyran came to a stop. They turned around as one, Kyran with his semi-automatic pistol, while Aaron was empty-handed. Kyran lowered his gun at once, as Rose came into view, pushing her way past branches and leaves.

Aaron couldn't believe she had followed them again. Had she taken an oath to never let him sneak off on his own? "Rose," he called. "What are you doing?"

Rose came to a stop. Her eyes flickered to Kyran once before darting back to Aaron. "I saw you leaving," she said. "I waited at the Gate for you, but you didn't come back." She shifted nervously. "So I...I came looking for you." She stared at Aaron with clear panic. "Where are you going?"

"I can't explain right now," Aaron said. "I need to go, but I'll tell you everything afterwards, I promise," he said. "Go." He nodded in the direction Rose had come from. "I'll be back soon."

Rose didn't leave. Instead, she turned to look at Kyran. "Can we talk?"

Kyran was thrown. He was clearly expecting to be ignored by her.

"About what?" he asked.

Rose didn't answer right away. She took in a long breath. "Everything."

Kyran looked torn. He glanced to Aaron, before turning back to her. "Rose," he started, "I want to talk things out too, but now isn't the time. We really need to leave, before we miss our chance to get the legacy out."

Rose went quiet for a minute. "Then take me with you."

Both Kyran and Aaron stared at her with surprise.

"I don't think that's a good idea," Aaron started.

"Why not?" she asked.

"Rose," Kyran said, breathing her name in a whisper. "Where we're going, it's not safe."

"I'll be with you," Rose said. She stopped, her eyes widening, like she hadn't meant to say those words out loud. She ducked her head. "And Aaron," she added, in an attempt to cover her slip. "I'm sure I'll be fine."

Kyran shook his head. "Rose, I can't–"

"Please," she said, meeting Kyran's gaze. "I'm sick of this. I feel so confused about...about us, about everything that's happened." She paused, before pulling in a breath. "We need to talk," she said. "I need answers – now – and I want them from you – only you."

Kyran didn't say anything. He stepped forward and held out his hand.

Rose seemed surprised, as if she hadn't expected Kyran to give in so easily. She lowered her gaze to his offered hand and caught sight of the black thread around his wrist. She reached out and took his hand.

***

Aaron was falling asleep, curled up on the passenger seat of the SUV. Rose was in the back, sitting in silence, as Kyran drove them through a gleaming portal and into another zone. Aaron's body ached with fever, but he didn't complain. He glanced at Kyran; he was probably just as ill, but was putting on a brave face. Aaron could do the same.

They drove through the thick snow, sticking to the wide path leading through the forest. The sun was setting. The overcast sky had started to darken. Aaron pressed his fevered brow against the cold window and stared out. From the beam of the car's headlights, Aaron could see the trees were getting closer together, the path ahead narrowing; soon the forest would get so dense, they would have to give up the car and walk the rest of the way. Just the thought of getting to his feet made his legs ache in protest. He closed his eyes. He wanted to sleep. Just even for five minutes...

"Aaron?"

Aaron opened his eyes to find Kyran gently shaking him by the shoulder. "Wake up, we're here."

"I wasn't sleeping," Aaron said groggily, sitting up.

"Sure," Kyran said. "You were just *resting your eyes*," he said. "And drooling in my car."

Aaron wiped at his mouth, before realising Kyran was only teasing.

"Sod off," he grumbled.

As Kyran chuckled, Aaron braced himself for the long journey ahead, and opened the door. The cold hit him like a punch in the gut. Aaron sucked in a breath and hugged his coat tighter around him. He was already shivering, he didn't want to imagine how much more he was going to suffer when in the presence of one of the Blades of Aric. Rose came to his side, her hands in the pockets of her coat, shoulders hunched against the cold.

"Ready?" Kyran asked. He had a backpack slung over one shoulder. "Let's go."

The three of them set off, Kyran slightly ahead, leading the way. Aaron and Rose followed after him, huddled close to one another. Kyran must have noticed how cold they were, because he lifted a hand and a ball of fire formed in thin air, floating before him. Kyran waved his hand and the fireball hovered over Aaron and Rose's heads, radiating heat down onto them. It also gave some light, so they could see where they were going. So thick was this forest, there were patches on the ground where the snow hadn't managed to reach. The trees were capped, though, with glittery white snow.

To Aaron's relief, they didn't have to walk long before they found the shimmering Gate that guarded the Blade of Adams. He remembered the first time he had gone there with Neriah. It had felt like he had walked for hours that time. Kyran must have used another route, bringing them closer to the Gate so Aaron didn't have far to walk.

Kyran gestured to Aaron to come forward. Pushing himself on shaky legs, Aaron walked to Kyran's side and the two brothers held their hands against the Gate. The towering mass of glistening white lit up with all sorts of symbols and numbers. Then a circle – the sign for the element of Earth flashed, along with other signs and numbers, and the Gate slid open.

The three of them walked in, and the effects of the Blade weighed down on Kyran and Aaron almost instantly. The ball of fire Kyran had conjured disappeared. Despite the cold, Aaron started sweating. His breathing, already laboured, began to get heavier. He stumbled but Rose and Kyran were quick to catch him.

"What's wrong?" Rose asked, sounding worried. "You okay?"

Aaron nodded. "It's just the...the Blade," he explained. "I'm fine."

He looked to see Kyran was in a similar state, with beads of perspiration on his forehead, his breathing quick and strained, but his vivid green eyes narrowed with concern, fixed on him.

Aaron straightened up, nodding at both Kyran and Rose. "I'm okay," he assured them. "Come on, let's go."

They walked through the dark forest, taking care not to slip on the frost-covered ground. Aaron could sense a stream nearby that had frozen over; the same one at which he'd spotted a Banshee on his first visit.

This time, nothing came their way. The woods were quiet and still, with only the wind ruffling through the snow-covered trees, shaking some flakes free. They found the cave in which they knew the Blade of Adams was resting, lodged into the rocky ground.

They stopped a few steps before the entrance. Kyran turned to Rose. "It's probably not a good idea for you to come in," he said.

Rose looked into the dark mouth of the cave and shuddered. "Yeah, I'm good out here."

Kyran cast a quick glance around, then met Rose's eyes. "You should be safe," he said. "Nothing can get past the Gate, but just in case..." He pulled out his gun and offered it to her.

Rose quickly shook her head. "I don't know how to use it."

"I'm sure you can figure it out," Kyran said. "You look pretty confident holding it."

Rose fell quiet and diverted her eyes. Aaron looked between the two of them, wondering when Rose had pulled a gun on Kyran.

Kyran took out a short dagger from his pocket and offered that to Rose too. She took them both, avoiding his eyes.

Kyran turned to Aaron. "I think I know the answer, but I'll ask anyway. You have any weapons on you?"

Aaron shook his head, shivering.

Kyran gave him a look. "How many times have I told you to not leave the house without your familiars?" He pulled out his second gun.

"I was asleep when you called," Aaron said.

"So?" Kyran asked, bringing out the rest of his daggers.

"So I don't sleep with an artillery in my pockets," Aaron said. "And how was I supposed to know we were going to be coming here?"

Kyran shook his head at him, as he dumped his weapons on the ground. "If you have anything on you that resembles a weapon, leave it here," he said. "The Influence won't come if it detects any weapons on us."

Aaron checked. "I don't have anything," he said.

"Except a knack for getting into trouble," Kyran teased.

He looked up into the sky. The full moon was visible, just for a second or two, before clouds moved in front of it. Kyran let out a breath, betraying his nerves, as he turned to the cave. "Come on," he said to Aaron. "Let's do this."

With a last look at Rose, both boys walked into the cave.

\*\*\*

"I can't see anything," Aaron said.

"That's what happens when it's dark and there's no light," Kyran said.

Aaron blindly aimed a punch, hitting Kyran's arm. "Shut it," he said, "and look for a torch."

"Where do you expect me to get a torch from?" Kyran asked.

"Neriah found one," Aaron said, recalling the leader of the mages running his hands across the walls. "It should be hanging on the wall somewhere," he said.

"I've got a better idea," Kyran said.

Aaron heard the rustle of the bag, before a zip opened. Kyran rummaged through it for a moment, before a small click sounded. A beam of light came from Kyran's hand. Aaron stared in surprise.

"Is that–?"

"A flashlight," Kyran said.

"You got that from the human realm?" Aaron asked.

"These things have always fascinated me," Kyran said. "It's not fire, but it gives light." He held the long, thin torch in his hand, turning it this way and that, making the beam of light dance around the cave. "I wonder how they work."

"It's a light bulb," Aaron said, "an electric circuit and batteries."

Kyran turned his head, but Aaron couldn't see his expression. "Batteries?"

Aaron shook his head. "Never mind," he said. "What else is in that bag?"

"Everything I need to summon the Influence," Kyran said. He hoisted the bag onto his shoulder and set forward, using the flashlight to see where they were going. Aaron stayed by his side.

Aaron didn't need to see that they were nearing the sword. He could feel the effects of the drain worsen with every step he took. His body began shaking, his stomach clenching with pain. He felt faint, like he was going to collapse to the ground. Still Aaron pushed on, blinking moisture out of his tired eyes. The beam of light caught the sword, just a little way ahead of them, and Aaron's heart skipped a beat. He had forgotten how magnificent the Blade of Adams was.

It sat with great pride, wedged in the ground. The light hit the white stones set on the black hilt, illuminating Aric's mark in the darkness. Aaron could feel the pull of the Blade. It was demanding all the elemental energy he had, and it left Aaron feeling light-headed. He doubled over and put his hands to his knees, taking in several breaths, trying to ride out the wave of dizziness.

"You okay, Ace?"

Kyran sounded just as breathless as Aaron felt. Aaron forced himself to stand and nod. His body felt flushed with fever, his skin clammy with sweat. He turned to look at his brother. "We're here," he said. "Next to the sword. What happens now?"

"Now, we summon the Influence," Kyran said. He crouched to the ground, bringing his backpack in front of him. Kyran held out the flashlight to Aaron. "Hold this."

Aaron took it, directing the beam of light to Kyran's bag. Kyran unzipped it and, using both hands, he pulled out a rectangular box. It looked like an ordinary wooden box. The only interesting thing about it was the engraving on the lid: a large circle with a series of smaller circles, all linked together inside it.

Kyran placed the box carefully onto the ground. Kneeling before it, he gently lifted the lid, and Aaron found himself holding his breath. But the only thing inside was a strange, silver dagger. Aaron stared at it in amazement. It was like nothing Aaron had seen before. The end was definitely made of razor-sharp steel but the handle looked like it was made from a mix of liquid and gas, encased by glass. There were tiny silver specks, liquid in form, swimming inside the cloud, glittering against the glass. Kyran reached in and picked it up.

Aaron's stomach was turning with nerves, his heart racing. "What is that?" he asked.

Kyran stood up, looking at the dagger. "The key," he said, "You need to offer the Influence something, before it'll come to you."

Kyran held out a hand, palm open and brought the dagger to it.

"Kyran." Aaron grabbed his arm, stopping him from making the cut. "I'm not sure about this."

"It's the only way," Kyran said. "The Influence is the only thing that can help us."

Fighting against his better judgement, Aaron forced himself to drop his hand.

Kyran took in a breath, and sliced the dagger across his palm. The cut dripped blood into the open box. The dagger in Kyran's hand evaporated, before a blast of air shook the cave. The torches hanging from the walls lit by their own accord, and a whistling sound filled the air.

Aaron dropped the flashlight in his surprise, watching as a silver mist lifted out from the box and twisted in the air. He didn't need Kyran to confirm what it was. He knew this was what they had come for.

The Influence had arrived.

## 22

# THE INFLUENCE

In a matter of seconds, the cave was filled with the silvery mist. Aaron and Kyran watched in stunned silence as the mist started taking the shape and form of tall, thin beings. Heads formed, as well as arms and abnormally long-fingered hands, but they had no legs, just silvery white torsos flaring at the ends – almost as though they were dressed in floor-length robes. Though their shape was of strange-looking humans, they remained nothing more than smoke. They had no faces, just dark shadows where the eyes, nose and mouth should be. Long, thin strands of mist poured from the top of their heads, mimicking hair.

Aaron couldn't look away from the wispy beings floating before him. There were at least fifty of them, standing wall to wall in front of them. One of them glided forward, coming closer to Aaron and Kyran. The dark-shadowed line representing its mouth turned up at the ends, resembling a smile.

"What is this?" The voice was feminine and soft, and although it was the one that had stepped forward who had spoken, the words echoed around the cave as if all fifty of them had spoken at the same time. "We have not been summoned by your kind in a long time," it said.

"Probably for good reason," Kyran said. "But I'm always up for taking risks."

"That much, we can tell," the Influence said. Its head tilted as it seemed to observe Kyran with dark lines for eyes. "What do you want from us?"

"I want to make a deal," Kyran said. "I want you to find me a way to remove a legacy without it killing the holder."

Aaron held his breath, waiting for the answer. The Influence didn't speak. It seemed to be studying Kyran.

"You already have a way to do that," it said. "It is only a matter of time before you can give away your legacies without it harming you."

Aaron looked to Kyran with stunned surprise.

But Kyran's eyes were on the Influence. He shook his head. "It's not for me," he said. "I'm not worried about my legacies."

The ghost-like form turned its head towards Aaron. "Ah," it said, echoing the word around the cave. "So it is for him." It extended one of its long arms out towards Aaron.

Aaron backed away on instinct, and found Kyran standing in front of him in a heartbeat.

"I didn't say you could touch him," Kyran said in a low, threatening voice.

The Influence pulled back its hand. "We meant no harm," it said. "We only wanted to see his aura."

"See with your eyes, not your hands," Kyran. "Or, whatever your equivalent is for eyes."

"Oh?" It floated closer to Kyran. "Or what?"

Kyran smirked. "You don't want to know," he said. "You must be aware of what mages are capable of. That's why you don't come to them unless you feel safe."

"Self-preservation," the Influence replied. "All forms of life have it."

"Well, if you want to *preserve* your life, you'll stay the hell away from Aaron, and tell me how to get the legacy out of him," Kyran said.

The Influence floated closer, looming over Kyran. "What is it you threaten us with, if we do not adhere to your command?" it asked.

Kyran smirked and gave a pointed look to the sword, wedged in the ground. "I told you, you don't want to know."

A high-pitched laugh echoed around the cave. "You used your blood to summon us," it said. "We know you hold the legacy that will allow you to wield that Blade."

Kyran wasn't expecting that. His surprise was mirrored by Aaron, who came to stand by his brother's side.

"Then why did you come?" Aaron asked, unable to stop himself.

"Because we know we are in no danger," it said. "We know that you will never claim that Blade," it told Kyran, "since you refuse to accept that lineage as truly yours."

Aaron looked to Kyran, to see his expression grow uneasy.

"We're veering off topic," Kyran said. "Are you going to make a deal or not?"

The Influence stayed silent for a moment. "What do you offer in return?" it asked.

"Anything," Kyran replied. Aaron looked at him with panic, but Kyran's intense green eyes were fixed on the Influence. "You give me a way to get the legacy out of him, without it harming him in any way, and I'll give you whatever you want."

The Influence turned its head to Aaron and then back to Kyran. "A tempting offer," it said. "But there can be no deal made. The only way for him to get rid of the legacy, is to give it along with his life."

Aaron's hammering heart sunk. He had believed Kyran when he said the Influence would give them a way out of this mess. But it had only repeated what everyone else had said. There was no way he could give the legacy to another without dying in the process.

Kyran stepped forward. "No," he said. "I don't accept that. There must be another way."

"You are repeating what your kind has already asked," the Influence said. "So we will repeat the answer. Legacies cannot be transferred without killing the holder," it said. "Given freely or seized by force, legacies will take with them the life source of the holder."

"I know that's not true," Kyran said. "I have a way of giving up my legacies without dying in the process. If there's a way for me, there must be one for him too."

The Influence tilted its head at Kyran. "He does not possess the power you do."

Kyran's fists were curled tight, his jaw clenched. "Thank God for that," he hissed.

The Influence started floating back towards its crowd. "You cannot save him," it said. "You know it as well as we do."

Kyran swore. The profanity rang loud in the cave. "You're not going anywhere!" he snarled. "You *will* give me a way, or you will die – it's that simple!"

Aaron felt his stomach coil tightly. Those words were too similar to what Hadrian had said to them, demanding their submission to his rule. He pushed it to the back of his mind. He couldn't dwell on how alike his brother was to their enemy right now. He grabbed Kyran by the arm.

"Kyran, don't," he said in a shaky voice. "Just leave it."

"No!" Kyran freed himself from Aaron's grip. "I didn't do all of this just to return empty-handed."

The Influence turned back to Kyran. "You have no other choice."

"I'm getting what I came for," Kyran said. "Or I'm ending your kind today. That sword is not the only way for me to kill you."

"And are you aware of what we can do to you?" the Influence asked.

Kyran snorted with derision. "Bring it on," he said. "You have no idea who you're messing with."

The Influence hovered in the air, before floating towards Kyran, lowering itself to be at his eye-level. "Such arrogance," it said, hissing the words. "You may show great confidence in your abilities, hold your head up high and behave as if you are mightier than the rest, but we see you as you *truly* see yourself."

Kyran smirked, looking into its featureless face. "Yeah?" he challenged. "And what's that?"

The wispy form moved even closer and whispered, "Worthless."

Kyran's smirk fell.

"You hide behind this façade of self-assurance, but every moment of every day, you battle with your past," the Influence continued. "It is what you struggle with, even after all these years. You were abandoned by your parents, left to die by those who should have died saving you. And deep down, you know the reason why." It moved even closer, speaking right into Kyran's face. "Because you were not worth the effort to save."

Aaron felt sick. He caught the haunted look in Kyran's eyes, as he stared at the wispy figure hovering before him.

"We are the Influence; we are everywhere," it said. "We can see not only what is around you, but inside of you." It reached out with a long-fingered hand to ghost over Kyran's chest. "We can feel the jagged pieces beneath your skin, sense the ache in the wounds no one can see." It paused. "So you can act as though you are invincible, but we know how *broken* you really are."

Kyran didn't speak. Aaron willed him to say something, to threaten the Influence with some cocky warning, to prove that the Influence didn't know what it was talking about, but Kyran remained silent. Aaron had never thought he would see Kyran look so...defeated. His brother was a fighter, but it seemed as if the Influence had hit him on his Achilles heel.

"You cannot scare us," the Influence said softly. "Not when we can see all your insecurities."

The Influence pulled away and floated back up. The fifty or so smoke-like beings began to gather closer, merging into the one that had been speaking to them. The Influence was getting ready to leave.

"Wait," Kyran finally spoke, but his voice was quieter, devoid of its usual authority. "Please," he said, casting aside his pride. "You have to help me. Give me a way to get the legacy out–"

"You already know what choices you have," the Influence said. "You know you cannot win this; there is no way to save him." It hovered in the air, looking down at Kyran. "You know this and yet, you keep fighting anyway."

"I won't ever stop fighting," Kyran said, "not for him."

The Influence paused, before whispering, "We know."

With a whooshing sound, the wispy figure turned back to a shapeless mist and zoomed straight back into the box it had come from. The torches in the cave went out, plunging Kyran and Aaron into darkness.

\*\*\*

"What was that all about?" Aaron asked, hurrying after Kyran as he headed out of the cave. "What did the Influence mean by you knowing what choices you have?"

"Nothing," Kyran spat, storming his way back through the cave.

"That wasn't nothing, Kyran," he said. "What was the Influence on about?" Aaron asked, running to catch up with Kyran's long strides.

"Just drop it, Aaron," Kyran warned. His hands were still curled into balls. He swore again. "This was a waste of time!"

"Kyran – wait." Aaron chased after him.

They walked out of the cave, with Kyran in front and Aaron behind him. "Kyran, come on," Aaron called.

Kyran came to a sudden stop. His head turned to the side, his eyes wide. "Rose?" he breathed.

Aaron looked to the spot they had left her but no one was there, just the weapons Kyran had dumped on the ground – and the two he had handed to Rose.

"Rose?" Aaron called, panic welling inside him. "Rose! Where are you?"

Kyran's gaze darted all around him, searching desperately. "Rose?" he yelled.

"K-Kyran!" came her terrified voice.

Both boys turned to see a group of men walk out from under a cluster of trees. One of them was holding Rose - by her throat. Aaron and Kyran stilled, green eyes sharpening in recognition of the man with sleek white hair and brown eyes that gleamed oddly red, even in the moonlight.

It was Raoul, the leader of the Lycans.

Aaron met Rose's frightened eyes. He nodded at her, trying to assure her she would be okay. He wasn't going to let anything happen to her, and he knew for sure Kyran wasn't going to either.

Raoul walked towards Kyran and Aaron, holding Rose in front of him like a shield.

"I knew I could smell mages," he said, giving a pointed look to Kyran's bleeding hand.

His voice surprised Aaron. He was expecting a low, growling tone – something befitting a wolf's persona. But his voice was smooth, his tone elegant and charming.

Kyran's eyes were dark as he glared at Raoul. His whole body tensed, like a spring that could snap at any moment. His hands curled, one of them dripping blood.

"Let her go," Kyran said, his voice quiet but full of threat. "She's not of any concern to you."

Rose's pained gasp was cut short as Raoul's grip tightened. "On the contrary," he said. "Do you know how long it's been since I've tasted human blood?" he asked. "It's funny, we came searching for one of the Blades of Aric, but found a nice treat along with it," he said, jostling Rose.

Kyran shot a quick glance to his guns and daggers, lying out of reach.

Raoul chuckled. "Don't even think about it," he warned.

Kyran didn't move, his eyes darting to Rose, who was struggling to breathe in Raoul's iron grip. Being close to the Blade of Adams meant Kyran and Aaron couldn't use their powers, otherwise Kyran could have used the element of air to bring his weapons to him, or even use his powers directly to fight the Lycans.

Raoul gestured four of his men to move towards Kyran and Aaron. Kyran held up his hands in surrender, but his fierce gaze never left Raoul. Two Lycans grabbed Kyran by his arms and twisted them behind his back. They pushed him onto his knees and held him there as the same was done to Aaron. Raoul threw Rose to one of his men, who held her by the arms. Rose could barely stand; she was coughing and gasping so hard, trying to get her breath back.

Raoul sauntered up to his captives. He pointed a finger at Aaron. "You, I recognise," he said. "You're the one who was on top of that hill at the Pecosa camp." His smile widened into a feral grin. "You tried to drown us."

Aaron didn't say anything, but glared up at him.

Raoul turned. "But you," he went to stand in front of Kyran, "you I don't know, even though your blood smells very familiar."

Kyran gave him a cold smirk, but there was fire in his eyes. "Think a little harder," he said in a low voice. "It'll come back to you."

Raoul's eyes narrowed as he studied Kyran. He crouched down, to look at him intently. "It's so odd. It's like I've seen your face before, but I can't remember where or when." Then he shrugged and stood up, running a hand down his long coat. "Ah well, why linger on the past, when you can enjoy the future?" He turned around and the Lycan holding Rose strode forward.

Both Kyran and Aaron struggled, fighting against the Lycans' hold, but neither could get free. Helpless, they watched as Rose was shoved towards Raoul.

"Leave her alone!" Aaron shouted, his heart hammering at his insides, his stomach tight with fear, as Rose stood shaking before the leader of the Lycans. "Don't touch her!"

Raoul grabbed Rose by her hair and roughly pulled her forward, so he could stare into her face.

Kyran lunged forward, fighting against the Lycans' hold, his jaw clenched tight and eyes so dark there was hardly any green left in them.

Rose was panting with pain. Both of her hands were in her hair, failing to loosen the Lycan's cruel hold.

Raoul took a moment to study Rose, twisting her hair to force her to stay still. "She is pretty," he said, looking to Aaron and then to Kyran. "Which one of you does she belong to?"

"Leave her," Kyran growled, so angry his voice shook.

Raoul smiled. "That answers my question," he said. He looked to Rose with hungry eyes. "I'm going to enjoy this. Not just the kill, but doing it in front of loved ones." His eyes glinted red as he looked to Kyran. "It's so much fun to put on a show with a sensitive audience."

Aaron thrashed wildly but couldn't get free. Desperately, he looked to Kyran, who was holding Raoul's gleeful gaze. Kyran was on his knees, arms wrenched painfully behind him, but if looks could kill, Raoul would already have been dead on the ground.

In the dark night, the small glow coming from Kyran's chest was instantly noticeable. Aaron stopped struggling, staring in surprise at the small, circular white light coming from his brother, exactly where he knew Kyran's birthmark was. Raoul saw it too, and it wiped the smirk clean off his face. He stared at the light for a moment, before his eyes moved to Kyran's face.

"No," he breathed in disbelief.

Another source of light came from somewhere behind Kyran – again visible because of the darkness of the night – and one of the Lycans holding Kyran let out a cry before arching his back, as if he had been stabbed. He fell to the ground, dead.

Kyran twisted around, leaping to his feet at the same time and grabbed the second Lycan that had been holding him. Aaron saw it clearly this time – Kyran's hand was glowing too – no, it wasn't his hand but the four lines across the back of his hand that had lit up in blinding white. Kyran grabbed the Lycan across the throat with his glowing hand, and the Lycan stiffened. Black lines seeped into Kyran's hand, racing up and under his sleeve, and this Lycan too fell to the ground, dead.

Kyran turned to face Raoul, breathing hard. His hand and chest were glowing but his eyes were a dark, dark green. Raoul let go of Rose and stepped back, his eyes on Kyran. His mouth opened and the word 'Scorcher' formed at his lips, but his voice didn't carry.

It seemed the other Lycans recognised the Scorcher now too. They turned tail and ran, scampering away as fast as they could. The ones that were holding Aaron almost fell over one another in their haste to get away. Raoul took off close behind them, but not before giving Kyran a dark look – one full of a promise of retribution.

The Lycans ran through the woods, leaping over the stump that was left of the Gate, and disappeared into the darkness. Aaron and Rose were still on the ground, staring at Kyran with shock, confusion, and a little fear.

\*\*\*

Aaron looked up as Kyran walked into the cave. Aaron cleared his throat and asked, "Is it done?"

Kyran nodded. He didn't look at Aaron, who was sitting against one wall with Rose. "The Gate's back up," Kyran said quietly, sitting down just at the mouth of the cave. "I've warded it against Lycans." He looked at the dagger in his hand, stained with Lycan blood. "The rest of the wards are going to have to wait." He threw the dagger out into the snow, no longer having any use for it.

Aaron remembered the small vials, containing different demon bloods, that Ella and Skyler had used to build a Gate. Kyran didn't have any of those, but he used his dagger to draw blood from the dead Lycans to keep Raoul and his men away.

"I could have helped set it up," Aaron said.

"You're ready to collapse," Kyran said, glancing at him. "It would have taken too much out of you. I handled it." He forced out a frustrated breath. "I don't get it, how could that Gate have fallen?"

"Maybe Raoul did something to it," Aaron suggested.

"Only mages can control the Gates," Kyran explained. "And Gates are warded against demons, especially Lycans. They can't touch them, let alone destroy them."

Aaron didn't say anything. He knew Lycans sometimes found a way into safe zones, while the Gates still stood. Kyran and Neriah both had suggested Raoul had found another way to enter the zones, a back door of some sort. But this time, the Gate that protected the Blade of Adams had been brought down.

How the Gate was dropped, Aaron didn't know, but he figured this new Gate Kyran just put up would be much stronger, as it was set up by an Elemental holding three legacies. He turned his head to check on Rose, who hadn't stopped shaking since the Lycans left.

"You okay?" he asked again, as he wrapped an arm around her. Physically, she was unhurt, save for faint bruises on her neck, but emotionally she seemed wrecked.

Rose nodded. "I'm fine. I just…need a minute."

"Why don't you lie down?" Aaron suggested.

Rose didn't object. She curled up on the floor of the cave immediately, hugging her coat around her and rested her head on Aaron's lap. Small tremors ran through her body but she closed her eyes, breathing out to try to calm herself.

Aaron noted Kyran's eyes were on her, watching her with a pained expression. It was clear he wanted to come to Rose's side and comfort her, but he was forcing himself to stay put at the mouth of the cave, away from her.

A few minutes later, Rose was asleep. Her trauma and shock had pulled her into an exhausted rest. Aaron turned to his brother, waiting for him to speak, but Kyran remained silent.

"Are you going to explain what happened?" Aaron asked at last.

Kyran took in a breath. "Can't we just pretend it was nothing?" he asked.

Aaron's eyes bulged out in shock. "Nothing?" he repeated. "Kyran, I saw you – I don't even know what I saw!" he exclaimed. "What *was* that?"

Kyran leant his head back to rest against the wall. "That was a part of me I had hoped you would never see."

Aaron paused. "You can tell me," he said. His gaze dropped to the four silvery lines at the back of Kyran's hand. "Those aren't tattoos, are they?" he asked.

Kyran closed his eyes. "No," he admitted quietly. "They're not tattoos."

Aaron didn't push for more. He waited in silence until finally Kyran sat up, visibly gathering himself.

"When I woke up after the Lycan attack," he started, "I was...I was in a bad state. I had lost a lot of blood, chunks of my flesh had been ripped out–"

Aaron tensed when he realised what Kyran was referring to. Kyran was revealing the aftermath of the Lycan attack on Marwa, the time he was only four years old. The incident that had separated him from his family.

"I was left badly scarred," Kyran continued. "With time, my wounds healed. My body recovered – regrowing flesh where it was needed, mending broken bones and torn ligaments." He paused, dropping his head to stare at his hands in his lap. "All my scars faded." He lightly traced the four thin silvery lines. "All but these."

# 23

## SCARS

Aaron's eyes snapped up to Kyran's face. "Those...those are scars?"

Mages didn't scar, that's what Aaron had always been told. He had seen it first hand: mages getting hurt and then healed without a scratch left on them. How did Kyran have scars?

"I still don't understand it," Kyran said. "Why these never faded like the rest, or why they were silver from the very start." His hand dropped from tracing the four lines and he sighed. "But I learnt to ignore them, until I realised what they could do."

Aaron was staring at Kyran, barely breathing. "What?" he prompted, when Kyran didn't speak.

"I was seven," Kyran started, "and still delusional. I had wasted another day waiting at the top of that mountain. But on my way back, I was attacked by a group of Ichis." A faint smile crossed Kyran's face, thinking of the snake-demons. "They didn't know I wasn't alone. Hadrian took care of them."

Aaron could hear the pride in his voice.

"That was the first time he really lost it with me," Kyran said. "I was supposed to tell him whenever I left, but I had sneaked out...again. If Hadrian hadn't come looking for me, I would have been dinner for the Ichis." His expression was full of guilt. "We started arguing. He was only trying to get me into the car, because he was afraid there might be other demons lurking around the abandoned city of Marwa, but I didn't want to go with him. I told him the same crap as before – I didn't want to stay with him, he was nothing to me, I wanted my dad and not him." He went quiet. "He grabbed me, probably to force me into the car, and I just reacted. No one had touched me like that since – since the attack and I...I was angry, and scared and...just really scared." He paused. "I pushed him back, but the minute I touched him, the lines on the back of my hand lit up." He shook his head, his eyes haunted. "I still remember the look in his eyes. He was dying. I was killing him. I pulled my hand back, and both of us fell to the ground." Kyran closed his eyes. "I'll never forget that pain. I've never felt anything like that, and I've had Lycans throw me around like a chew toy."

Aaron didn't have any words to say. He sat in silence, listening to his brother's horror-filled story.

"Both of us were left weakened and in agony for weeks," Kyran said. "It took a month before we fully recovered, but the moment we did, Hadrian started researching, trying to figure out what had happened, what it was that I had unintentionally done." Kyran faltered, as if saying the next words were physically painful. "Turns out, I have the power to drain life."

Aaron's already racing heart sped up a further notch. He couldn't speak, couldn't ask questions. He just sat and listened as Kyran bared his soul.

"When Raoul and his Lycans attacked me, something – something went wrong," Kyran said. "I should have died. The venom from the Lycans should have killed me. But I survived, and Hadrian thinks it's because of this." He held up his hand, to show Aaron the silvery lines. "The Lycans gave me this by mistake. They are creatures that get their power from the moon and by some accident, they passed that power onto me, making me immune to their venom. But I'm not a Lycan, so that power manifested into something else, mixing with my core and giving me the ability to drain life as easily as the moon drains powers out of a mage."

Aaron held Kyran's tormented eyes, and he felt like he couldn't breathe. There was so much pain, so much self-hatred in his eyes, it was suffocating to witness.

"I tried everything to get rid of this...this *power*." Kyran spat the word. "Hadrian worked tirelessly to find a solution, but there was nothing that could be done. I'm stuck with this darkness, this power to drain life, to *bleed out* others." He touched his chest, at the spot Aaron knew his birthmark was. "It's become a part of me, no matter how much I fought it." He looked at his hand as if it were an enemy. "They did this to me," he said quietly. "They may not have meant to, but Raoul and his Lycans gave me a little of their darkness and made me a monster that can kill with a touch."

Aaron remembered the leader of the Pecosas, Rukhsana, had told him the same thing – that the Scorcher had a *darkness* in him.

Everything Aaron had heard about the Scorcher and the phrase 'bleed out' made sense now. It didn't mean to physically bleed someone out by wounding them, like Aaron had first thought, but rather to drain the life source – to *bleed* their life out of them.

"That's how you killed those Lycans," Aaron said. "You bled them out, drained their life."

"I had to," Kyran started defensively.

"I'm not saying you shouldn't have," Aaron cut across him. "I get it. You had no other choice. You did what you had to and I'm thankful for it." His hand brushed lightly over Rose's hair. "We would have lost Rose otherwise."

Kyran fell quiet. His eyes lingered on Rose for a moment before he looked away, breathing out a heavy sigh. "To think, I almost did the same to Hadrian that day." He closed his eyes and shook his head. "Thank God I pulled away in time. If I hadn't–" He stopped and rubbed at his eyes. "I still took a little of his life source, though," he said, sounding regretful. "The half-bleed caused a tiny fragment of his core to transfer to me." He paused. "Along with his legacies."

Aaron stilled. So *that's* how Kyran had Hadrian's legacies. It was through the accidental half-bleed that Kyran got the legacies of Fire and Air from Hadrian. It had been driving Aaron mad, trying to figure out how Kyran got what only a direct descendant could receive from Hadrian.

"Machado came looking for Hadrian a few hours later," Kyran continued. "He took the both of us back home. Machado had very recently changed to a vamage, so still had a little decency in him back then." A small smile came to his face. "Hadrian used to joke that we were lucky it was Machado and not Neriah who found us in that state. It would have been over for both of us." He looked over at Aaron. "The half-bleed connected our life sources for a short period of time. If one of us was killed, the other would die too. It didn't last long. The connection broke once we recovered."

Aaron didn't say anything. He wanted to point out that if Neriah had found them that day, he wouldn't have hurt either of them. Neriah had confided in Aaron that he struggled to harm Hadrian. Unfortunately, Hadrian had no problems killing him.

A thought came to Aaron and he sat up straight. "Wait a minute." He stared at Kyran. "I can't believe it."

"What?" Kyran asked, frowning.

"Kyran, you've had a way to get the legacy out of me all along," Aaron said with an excited smile. "You did a half-bleed on Hadrian and got the legacies from him. You can do the same to me. At least that would get Hadrian off my back. The legacy would be safe with you until we figure out a way to get it back to Ella."

Kyran's eyes darkened. He shook his head. "It's not that simple."

"Why not?" Aaron asked.

"I can't risk it," Kyran said. "A full bleed, I can do no problems. But the only time I did a half-bleed was with Hadrian, and it almost killed us both."

"That's because it was accidental," Aaron said. "This time you'd know what you're doing."

"That still might not be enough," Kyran said. "For all I know, Ace, the only reason Hadrian survived the half-bleed was because he's a vamage. You're a mage who's not even come of age yet. Your core hasn't matured. If I try to bleed out your legacy, your core might come with it. I'll end up killing you."

Aaron went quiet for a moment. "It's worth a try."

"What is *wrong* with you?" Kyran asked. "I tell you that I have a dark power that allows me to kill with a touch, and instead of being disgusted, you want me to try it out on you?"

"You thought I'd be disgusted?" Aaron asked.

"Yes!" Kyran exclaimed. "That's the *normal* reaction."

"But why would I be disgusted with you?" Aaron asked. "You never asked for this. It's not your fault this happened to you."

Kyran looked surprised, like he'd never heard those words spoken to him before. He looked away, lapsing into silence.

No one spoke for long minutes. Then Kyran quietly said, "You should get some rest. When Rose wakes up, I'll take you both back."

Aaron didn't fight the suggestion. He felt like he needed to lie down. As carefully as he could, he lifted Rose's head from his lap and gently laid her down. Rose curled tighter, putting an arm under her head, but slept on. Aaron lay down, while Kyran stayed where he was, looking out at the dark forest.

Aaron stared at Kyran while his mind replayed the last few minutes of their meeting with the Influence, and the heart-wrenchingly painful things it had said to his brother.

"Kyran?" he called.

"Hmm," came his reply, as he scanned the forest.

Aaron steadied himself. "What the Influence said, about how you see yourself – you don't really think that, do you?"

Kyran didn't say anything. He didn't even turn his head to look at Aaron.

A voice in Aaron's head told him he shouldn't be surprised. Like the Influence had said, Kyran was abandoned by his parents, left to die. It didn't matter if it was true or not, it's what Kyran grew up believing: that he wasn't *worth the effort to save.*

"Kyran," Aaron said softly. Kyran still had his back to him. "You know that you're not worthless, right?" he asked. "No one is worthless. Everyone has someone that cares about them." He paused. "And you have an entire family who loves you. You know that, right?"

Kyran took a moment, then turned to look at Aaron with a carefully guarded expression. "Get some rest, Ace," he said.

Aaron held his eyes, but he could see Kyran wasn't ready to listen to him. But then again, there was fourteen years of damage to fix. It couldn't be done in one night.

Somewhere out in the woods, Lycans howled at the full moon. Aaron sat up, his heart almost in his mouth. Kyran held out a hand, to stop him from jumping to his feet.

"It's okay," he said. "They can't get across the Gate. And if they somehow find a way to drop it again, they won't get past me."

Aaron's sore body protested to his sudden movement, urging him to lie back down. Aaron did, but his eyes stayed on his brother. "You need to rest too," he pointed out. "The moon is affecting you as well."

Kyran's lips lifted in a half smile. "The silver lining to this very dark cloud is that the full moon doesn't affect me quite as much as the rest of the mages," he revealed. "I guess having some power related to the moon leaves me immune to the draining."

"Your powers don't get drained?" Aaron asked with surprise.

"Not completely," Kyran said. "And I don't get as fatigued. That's why I left Salvador on the day and night of the full moon, so no one picked up on my lack of weakness." He smirked. "Plus, I got to kick some demon ass when they least expected it."

Aaron felt himself smile. "You really *are* stronger than me."

Kyran chuckled.

The Lycans let out another series of howls, making Aaron's skin crawl. Kyran looked to the dark forest, sharp green eyes scanning the area, making out the towering Gate in the distance, still standing. He turned back to Aaron.

"Sleep," he encouraged. "I'm right here."

Aaron couldn't fight it any longer. His tired eyes shut and almost at once, he slipped into a peaceful and deep slumber.

***

It was just as the sun was rising that Aaron and Rose woke up. Both of them looked around the cave with bleary eyes, confused initially as to where they were. Kyran hadn't moved from his spot next to the mouth of the cave. He turned to both of them with a small smile.

"Morning," he greeted them. "That was a longer than expected nap."

Aaron sat up, stretching. "Yeah, well, it was a rougher than expected night."

Kyran's smile fell, as if he had just remembered Raoul's attack. His stare went to Rose. "How you feeling?" he asked.

Rose nodded. "Fine," she said quietly, tucking her hair behind her ears.

Kyran stood up. "We should get going. If we leave now, I can get you both back before anyone realises you've been missing all night."

"Oi, hold on," Aaron said. "At least get us breakfast first."

Kyran looked at him. "Do you see a kitchen anywhere?"

"I see trees with fruit," Aaron said. "And I'm starving."

Kyran's eyes, once again, darted to Rose, as if realising that she must be hungry too. He nodded. "Okay, I'll see what I can get."

"Thank you," Aaron said, and lay back down. The day and night of the full moon was over, but it always left him feeling ravaged with hunger.

Kyran turned to go, but paused, looking over at Rose. "I know you came here so we could talk," he said. "I haven't forgotten. Once I get back, we'll talk."

Rose didn't meet his eyes, but she nodded.

"See if you can find pineapples," Aaron said.

Kyran frowned at him. "Why?"

"Because I like pineapples," Aaron replied.

Kyran sighed, his hands on his waist. "Anything else, your highness?"

"I could go for some bacon and eggs," Aaron said.

"Sorry, the 'bacon and eggs' tree is all tapped out," Kyran replied, turning to walk out of the cave.

"Make sure you bring lots of oranges," Aaron teased. "I have to have freshly squeezed juice in the morning."

"I'll squeeze you into a juice," Kyran yelled back.

He was smiling at his younger brother's antics when something hit him, right in his shoulder, and a searing pain exploded across it, shooting down his arm. Kyran stumbled back a step, hissing in surprise as well as pain. His hand shot up to his shoulder to find the handle of a dagger sticking out of it.

"Kyran!" Aaron yelled, seeing him take the hit.

Kyran didn't look at Aaron. Instead, his sharp gaze darted around his surroundings, trying to find the attacker. It wasn't Raoul – Lycans didn't use blades and bullets when they had fangs and claws.

Kyran caught sight of the figure at the top of the hill, directly across from him. Skyler made no attempt to hide. In fact, he brazenly stepped forward, staring down at Kyran with a twisted smirk. Kyran held his eyes and pulled the dagger out of his shoulder. He let the stained blade fall from his hand to the snowy ground.

Aaron reached Kyran, his face flushed with panic, but his eyes quickly found Skyler. As both brothers watched, Hunters began revealing themselves on top of the hill, standing up from their hiding positions. There were easily twenty of them, lined on either side of Skyler, guns and blades in their hands, all aimed at Kyran.

Kyran was outnumbered. Being in the close proximity of a Blade of Aric meant none of them could use their powers, but the Hunters had their familiars. Then again, so did Kyran.

Kyran reached for his twin handguns. "Get back inside the cave," he instructed Aaron.

Aaron didn't move from his side.

Kyran took aim, targeting Skyler with both guns. He pulled the triggers, but nothing happened. Kyran paused, surprised. He tried again, but the guns clicked. Kyran slipped the magazine out of one gun to find it empty.

A moment of confusion swept over him, before he stilled. Slowly, he turned around, to find Rose standing at the mouth of the cave. She hadn't come running to him, like Aaron had. She didn't even look surprised at the appearance of the Hunters. She just stood there, staring at Kyran with glistening eyes. Without a word, she put her hand into her coat pocket and pulled out a handful of something. For a moment, she kept her fist closed. Then, holding Kyran's eyes, she unfurled her fingers to reveal silver bullets.

Kyran's gaze lingered on his bullets, until Rose tipped her hand and they fell, burying deep into the snow at her feet. Kyran lifted his head to look at Rose, who held his eyes with wavering emotion.

Cold realisation made its way through both Kyran and Aaron. Rose had tricked them. She had taken the bullets out of Kyran's guns, so he couldn't fight the Hunters she knew were coming. She didn't come with them last night to talk things out with Kyran; she came as part of a plan to ambush him.

A bullet from a Hunter's gun buried into the back of Kyran's leg, bringing him to his knees. One hit his back, and another struck his shoulder.

"NO!" Aaron screamed, and stood in front of Kyran, shielding him from the Hunters who were making their way towards them, shooting at him. "Stop!" he cried, holding out his hands. "Stop it! Drop your guns."

But the Hunters were going to do no such thing, Kyran knew that much. Steeling himself, Kyran sucked in a breath and leapt to his feet. He dropped his useless guns and pushed Aaron out of the way with one hand, and spun a dagger through the air with his other, catching one of the Hunters in the chest. The rest of the Hunters fired as one, and a rain of bullets hit Kyran's chest, making him stagger back.

Rose looked on in complete horror. Her legs trembled under her, and she silently collapsed to the ground, her body shaking as she cried, watching Kyran take bullet after bullet.

Stumbling and falling, still catching bullets, Kyran headed as fast as he could into the thick cluster of trees, the same one Raoul and his men had appeared out of the previous night. The bullets and blades followed after him, striking his back. Small daggers buried into his flesh – arms, legs, one even pierced into the side of his neck – but Kyran kept going, running deeper into the cover of the trees. He pulled the daggers out as he ran, throwing them behind him in an effort to slow down those chasing him.

The rational side of Kyran knew it was no good; he wasn't going to make it very far, not with so many gunshot wounds slowing him down. But the Hunters didn't seem to want Kyran's surrender. They were attacking him regardless.

Another bullet grazed his shoulder as he ran. One struck him on his lower back and another buried between his shoulder blades. It was that last shot that threw Kyran to the ground. Panting and hissing, Kyran got up onto his hands and knees, trying to work past the agony. He told himself to just breathe, to focus only on pulling air into his battered body and ignore the excruciating pain. It didn't work.

From the corner of his eye, he saw something move. Kyran looked over to see a Lurker, dressed all in white, crouching on the ground a few steps before him. The Lurker turned his head towards Kyran, but his face was hidden beneath the hood. The Lurker didn't say anything but turned and jumped over an edge, disappearing from view. Kyran hadn't even realised he was on top of a hill.

Crawling on all fours, Kyran dragged himself to the edge. The Lurker was gone, but Kyran wasn't looking for him right now. He was judging the drop. It was a long way down, with trees and thick vegetation making it impossible to find a path. A click behind his head stilled him.

With great effort, Kyran turned to see Skyler pointing a gun at his head. He was breathing hard, and his cold blue eyes were narrowed at Kyran. The gun in his hand was shaking. "It's over, Scorcher," he said. He steadied his gun with both hands, aiming for the spot between Kyran's eyes.

Aaron knocked into him and the gun went off, the bullet bearing Kyran's name hitting a tree. Aaron wrestled with Skyler, throwing him against the closest tree, knocking the gun out of his hand. Kyran closed his eyes, sucked in a breath and threw himself over the edge of the hill. He rolled all the way down the steep slope, smacking into several tree stumps, until he hit the ground with a thump, completely winded. The soft snow cushioned his fall a little, but Kyran was barely aware of it. Pain was all he knew. It originated from the gunshot wounds and cuts all over his body. The glistening white snow under him was quickly turning red.

Gasping for breath, Kyran tried to pull himself up, but couldn't. The adrenaline that had kept him going until now was fast depleting. He had been shot plenty of times before, but the very most he'd had to bear were three bullets at once. Today he had countless bullets buried in him.

So lost was Kyran in his haze of red-hot agony, he didn't hear the hurried footsteps approach from the parked SUV a short distance away. He only realised someone was standing there when he saw the pair of legs before him.

Kyran lifted his head, and to his surprise, saw Sam shakily pointing a semi-automatic gun at him.

"Sam," Kyran croaked.

"Shut up!" Sam snapped, and the gun he was holding shook so badly Sam had to hold it with both hands to steady it.

Kyran didn't have much breath left in him to speak, so he obediently fell quiet. He didn't want Sam to panic and shoot him. If Sam – a human, not a mage – shot him in the head or chest, it would kill him.

But even though Kyran stilled, Sam stepped closer and straightened his arms, aiming directly at Kyran's head.

"Sam!"

Aaron came running, having found a track down the hill. Aaron's eyes were wide, Skyler's gun gripped in his hand but pointing to the ground. He stared at Sam with disbelief. "Sam, what are you *doing?*"

"Go away, Aaron," Sam said, tears thick in his voice. He wasn't looking at Aaron, his focus was solely on keeping his gun steady and aimed at Kyran's head.

"Sam." Aaron stepped closer cautiously, holding out a hand. "If you shoot him, you'll kill him."

"I know," Sam said. "That's the plan."

"Sam?" Aaron gasped with horror.

That's when Sam lifted his tearful gaze to look at Aaron. "He deserves to die, Aaron," he said. "You don't know what he's done."

"He hasn't done anything," Aaron defended. "Please, put the gun down."

"He killed my parents!" Sam cried, one hand falling from his gun.

"No, he didn't," Aaron said. "He doesn't control the vamages–"

"No, Aaron, *he* killed my parents!" Sam spat. "He put a gun to their heads and killed them!"

SCARS

Aaron's shock was mirrored by Kyran.

"They died at his hand," Sam said, and tears fell from his furious eyes. "He shot them. He deserves to die the same way." He took aim again with both hands.

"Sam, no," Aaron cried, darting towards him.

"Stay where you are," Sam warned. "Don't come any closer, Aaron."

Aaron halted. "You've got it all wrong," he said. "Please, Sam, just listen to me."

"Sam," Kyran tried, but his breath had become so laboured, he could barely get his voice out.

Sam slid back the hammer, his finger on the trigger, and barrel aimed at Kyran's head,

"Sam, no!" Aaron yelled and raised his arm, pointing Skyler's gun at him.

Sam paused, looking at Aaron with bloodshot eyes.

"Put the gun down," Aaron ordered.

Sam stared at him. "Or what?" he asked. "You're going to shoot me?" he asked in disbelief. "You're going to shoot *me?*" He glared down at Kyran. "For him? You're choosing him over me?"

"Sam, come on," Aaron begged, his hand and voice trembling. "He's my brother."

Sam stared at him with glistening eyes. "I've been more your brother than he will *ever* be!"

"Sammy," Aaron implored, fighting the stinging in his eyes. "Don't, please. Lower your gun. You don't want to do this."

"Do what? Avenge my parents?" Sam asked. He straightened up, his eyes growing colder. "Sorry, Aaron, but I'm not walking away today without killing my parents' murderer." He turned his attention back to Kyran, taking aim once more.

"Sam! Sam no!" Aaron cried.

Sam's finger pulled the trigger – and so did Aaron's.

"SAM!" Aaron yelled as he fired a shot, delivering a bullet straight into Sam's chest.

# 24

## LOSING FRIENDS

The force of being shot pushed Sam bodily aside, knocking his aim off target. His fired bullet missed Kyran, soaring over his head instead of burying into it. Sam staggered back a few steps before collapsing to the ground. He didn't move.

Aaron stood where he was, shaking, the sound of the gunshot still ringing in his ears. A sense he wasn't even aware of using told him there were others coming; feet were pounding across the ground, heading this way. Aaron lowered his gun and started forward. But he didn't go to Sam, he ran to Kyran's side, his stomach turning violently at the sight of the crimson blood mixed into the snow where his brother lay.

"Kyran." Aaron's voice shook, and his vision blurred as he dropped to his knees next to Kyran. He turned Kyran onto his back, choking out a cry at the sight of his brother's chest, drenched in blood.

Kyran was struggling to breathe. He clutched at the front of Aaron's coat. "What — what did you do?" he asked, his voice barely above a whisper, but full of horror.

"He was going to kill you," Aaron said, his words barely making it past his tight throat.

Kyran was clenching his teeth, hissing in pain, writhing on the ground, but he pushed Aaron in Sam's direction. "Go…check on him," he said. "See that he's — he's okay."

"Kyran," Aaron started, turning his head to spot the crowd of Hunters fast approaching.

"Go," Kyran urged. He was fighting to stay conscious, Aaron could see that. There was no way he was going to get back up. They couldn't escape the Hunters, not now.

Aaron looked to where Sam was lying, still and silent. Aaron clambered back to his feet and walked towards him. He was sobbing now, his shoulders shaking as he saw the blood staining the snow next to his best friend. His bullet had caught the upper left side of Sam's chest, near his shoulder. It was probably still buried inside him. Sam's eyes were closed, but his chest was rising and falling. He was still alive.

"Sammy?" Aaron dropped next to him. His hands went to Sam's face. "Sam?" he cried. "I'm sorry," he said. "I'm sorry. I'm *so* sorry."

Slowly, Sam's eyes fluttered open. He didn't look over at Aaron, but stared up into the sky. Aaron closed his eyes, forcing out a shaky breath. He needed skin-to-skin contact. That's what he remembered of the transfer – the way a mage could take on the injuries of a human to save their life. Aaron kept his hands on Sam's face and willed the wound he had inflicted on his best friend to transfer to him.

The ache started in the upper left side of his chest. It was a slow burn, as if someone was holding a naked flame to his flesh and gradually pushing it deeper and deeper into him. Sam let out a grunt, which turned into a stifled cry as the bullet pushed out of him. It rolled across Sam's chest and fell into the snow.

Aaron cried out as pain shot across his shoulder and down his left arm, to his very fingertips. He fell back, clutching a hand to his bleeding chest. Sam sat up at once, staring at Aaron with surprise and confusion, the wound on his chest completely healed. But Sam's attention quickly shifted from Aaron back to Kyran. Aaron turned, with jerking, painful movements, to see the Hunters had gathered around Kyran, their guns and weapons aimed at him.

Skyler strode forward, sporting a gash across his forehead, courtesy of Aaron. It was what had knocked him out temporarily.

Aaron tried to get to his feet, but couldn't move, his body held tense and still by agony. He watched as Skyler snatched a gun from Ryan as he passed him and stood before the severely wounded and bleeding Kyran. His fierce eyes were fixed on Kyran, who was glaring back at him with just as much fury. Skyler didn't say anything. He raised the gun and fired a bullet into both of Kyran's knees, then a last one straight in Kyran's chest.

\*\*\*

Aaron couldn't sit still. He paced the length of the room, running his bound hands through his hair. He had two sets of Inhibitor cuffs circling his wrists, to suppress both his Elemental power of Earth and his legacy for Water. As uncomfortable as the thick manacles were around his wrists, it was the heavy, tight pain they induced in his body that was unbearable. Aaron could actually feel the power of his element building inside him, *aching* to get out but unable to. But Aaron only had to endure two. Kyran had three of them, one to block each of his legacics.

Aaron had to force back the onslaught of panic at the thought of his brother. He had no idea where Kyran was, or what was happening to him. They had been separated the moment Skyler shot Kyran, forced the Inhibitors on him and Aaron, and then bundled Kyran in one car and Aaron in another. Aaron didn't even know where he was being driven to, until he was hauled out of the back of the SUV and he recognised the empty streets of Salvador.

Aaron had been forced into a cottage and locked in one of the rooms. If Kyran was in the next room, next cottage, or halfway across Salvador, Aaron had no clue. His state of worry was only worsened when he felt the wound he had transferred from Sam sear in his chest. He had only one bullet wound. Kyran had countless bullets still inside of him. If Aaron was hurting so much with one, not-even-real gunshot wound, then how much pain was Kyran in? Could someone even deal with that kind of agony without losing their mind?

Skyler had brought them to the deserted city, where there was no Scott, no Empaths and no Chris and Kate Adams. Aaron's parents were still in the newly occupied city of Ailsa, oblivious to what was happening to their sons. Even if they found out that both Aaron and Kyran had been arrested, it would take them hours to get to Salvador without the help of portals. What state would Kyran be in by then?

The Blade of Afton was resting in the lake. One of the most powerful weapons of this realm was right here in the city, but Aaron couldn't use it because of the Inhibitors forced around his wrists.

Aaron went to the door and banged on it with both fists. "Hey!" he yelled. "Let me out!"

No one answered him, just like before when Aaron had pounded on the door for endless minutes. But Aaron knew there must be someone outside, guarding him. Skyler wouldn't just leave him locked in a room. He slammed his hands against the door again. "Just tell me where Kyran is," he said. "That's all I want to know."

No answer.

Aaron kicked at the door. Once, twice, three times. He kept kicking and punching, until his knuckles were raw and his feet hurt. "Just tell me where my brother is!" he yelled. "You can't do this!"

"That's where you're wrong."

Aaron stilled, recognising the female voice.

"Skyler can do whatever he likes."

"Bella?" Aaron asked. He pressed his ear to the door. "Bella, please. You have to let me out."

"It's no use," she said. "Even if I open the door, there's nothing you can do for him." A pause, before she said quietly, "Kyran isn't going to make it."

"No," Aaron said quickly, shaking his head as his heart twisted at her words. "Don't say that. Kyran's strong, he'll be fine. He's a mage, he can't be killed by another mage."

"Unless it's by execution," Bella said, and the grief in her voice surprised Aaron. He didn't think any one else cared what happened to Kyran.

"Bella, please," Aaron begged. "Help him. Don't let Skyler kill him, please."

"There's nothing anyone can do," Bella replied. "We didn't want to attack Kyran, but we had to follow orders. Skyler is our leader. Unofficial it may be, but it is what it is." She paused again. "I know Kyran is the Scorcher, everyone knows that now, but we used to be friends. All of us have hunted with him, laughed with him, eaten at the table with him. None of us wants him executed, but Skyler doesn't need our approval."

"Bella," Aaron breathed, his heart racing. "What is Skyler doing to him?" he asked. "Is he planning to execute Kyran?"

There was a stretch of silence before Bella replied, "Yes." Then she took in a heavy sigh. "But that's not the worst of it."

Aaron frowned. What could be worse than death?

That's when he heard it – the faint noise coming from one of the cottages. The sound of Kyran screaming.

\*\*\*

The living room of the cottage had been cleared of all furniture. Even the rugs had been removed, leaving the room bare, except for a metal cage sitting in the middle. Chained inside that cage was Kyran.

Three sets of Inhibitors were locked around his wrists. A short chain was then looped around the three chains of the cuffs and fixed to the top of the cage, forcing Kyran's arms over his head. He was taking short, shallow breaths, recovering from the last assault on his battered and bleeding body. Skyler didn't give him much respite. Slowly, he slid another dagger into Kyran's side, between his ribs. Kyran's groan came from between clenched teeth. Skyler watched him, then twisted the dagger. Kyran's guttural cry rang in the room. Skyler wrenched the dagger back out, leaving Kyran breathless and shaking.

"You know how to make this stop," Skyler said quietly, dropping the bloody dagger to the floor and running his finger over another one in his belt.

Kyran was struggling to breathe, the deep cuts in his sides made each breath feel like he was swallowing fire. He looked at Skyler with bloodshot eyes. Weakly, he shook his head.

"Sky – Skyler," he rasped. "I – I didn't drop – the Gate."

Skyler grabbed his face with both hands. "*Stop* denying it!" he snarled. "Just admit it. Tell me you dropped the Gate." His voice dipped lower. "I want to hear you say it."

Kyran held his eyes. "It – wasn't me," he managed to get out.

Skyler leant in. "It can't have been anyone else," he said. "You're the only mage working for Hadrian. You're the only one who could've let vamages into the city." The anger left his expression, to reveal his pain. "She helped you," he said in a quivering voice. "She healed you after your hunts, Kyran, and you? You're the reason she's *dead*."

Kyran had to fight to get his voice out. "I'm sorry," he wheezed, "about Armana, but – I didn't drop the Gate. It – it wasn't me."

Skyler shoved him back. "Then who was it?" he yelled.

Kyran didn't say anything.

Skyler pulled out a dagger from his belt and stabbed Kyran, in the chest this time. Kyran's cry was lost in his throat.

The door to the room opened and Skyler turned with a snarl, ready to tell whoever had interrupted him to get lost, but stopped short.

Ella stood at the door, staring at him with disbelief. Her eyes moved to Kyran, hanging by his bloody wrists, heaving in shaky breaths before Skyler, whose hands were stained with his blood.

\*\*\*

Ella walked out the front door, with Skyler close behind her. He locked the door and turned to Ella. "How did you find out?" he asked, getting straight to the point.

"We've been friends since we were little, Sky," Ella replied. "So when I woke up after the full moon to find you and half of the Hunters missing, I knew you were up to something." She shook her head. "But I never thought it'd be something like *this*."

The Hunters who had helped Skyler capture Kyran were gathered around the table in the street, but their eyes were on Ella, watching her with Skyler.

Skyler smirked and held out his arms. "Why the judgement?" he asked. "What have I done that's so wrong?"

Ella's mouth dropped open. "You're asking me what you've done *wrong*?" she exclaimed. "Sky, you ordered twenty Hunters to shoot Kyran when he was unarmed, which is as disgusting as it is cowardly. You involved Sam and Rose in the ambush with next to no care if they got hurt or not. You brought Kyran and Aaron here to imprison unlawfully, denied both of them any kind of healing, and I just walked in to find you *torturing* Kyran."

Her stormy grey eyes blazed in anger. "Tell me, which of these things is even remotely right?"

Skyler took a step towards her. "He deserves everything he's getting," he said. "And what does it matter to *you*, what I do to him?"

"It does matter to me, Skyler. It matters very damn much," Ella said. Her hands were curled into tight fists, eyes blazing with fury. "We don't inflict pain on others. We are good. We fight demons, not our own kind." She gestured to the cottage in which Kyran was locked. "You've arrested him. He's unarmed and at your mercy." She stared hard at Skyler. "And you're *hurting* him? You're going against our code as mages."

Skyler scoffed. "The code doesn't apply to him," he said. "He's no better than a filthy demon!"

"No, he's not," Ella said. "That's the point. He's a mage. An Elemental. He's one of *us*."

"No," Skyler vehemently denied. "He's nothing like us! He's fighting for a vamage, he's against the mages. He's our enemy, or have you forgotten that he helped Hadrian *kill* Neriah?"

Ella fell quiet. She stepped towards Skyler. "I'm not denying that he's the enemy," she said. "He's fighting against us in the war, but..." She faltered. "Come on, Sky, this –" she gestured to the door again – "what you're doing, torturing him, it isn't right."

"I don't care," Skyler said.

Ella was taken aback. With a glower, Skyler walked away, heading down the street.

Ella followed after him. "Yes, you do," she called. "You care, I know you do." Skyler kept walking, ignoring her. "You got Kyran. How you did it is another matter, but you've got him under arrest," Ella continued. "But hurting him when he can't fight back is against our morals. We're mages – Elementals. As our leader, you have to set an example."

Skyler stopped and turned around, smirking. "You're right, I am the leader. Which means I make the rules." His smirk slowly fell and a glint of anger lit his eyes. "And I decree that Kyran has to die."

The Hunters at the table shifted, clearly uncomfortable.

"Sky," Ella started, shaking her head.

"At sunset today," Skyler spoke over her, in a voice loud enough for all to hear. "Kyran Aedus will be executed."

From amongst the seated mages at the table, Rose stood up, looking stunned and horrified. "You told me you wanted to arrest him," she said. "You said you could find a way to get to Hadrian if you got Kyran. You didn't say anything about – about killing him."

Skyler smirked. "Did I forget to mention that?" he asked. His expression turned cruel. "Oops."

Rose stared at Skyler with disbelief. "You lied to me," she said.

"I didn't lie," Skyler said. "I chose to only tell you as much as you needed to know."

"You used me," Rose accused.

Skyler walked over to her. "Don't act so innocent, Rose," he said. "You knew what you were doing. *You're* the one who came to *me* the minute you saw Aaron leave the city. We both followed him out and heard their plan to summon the Influence." He smiled. "You didn't have to leave with them, you chose to go – to keep Kyran distracted until I got the rest of the Hunters there. I didn't ask you to do that. Just like I didn't ask you to take all the bullets out of his guns." He grinned and placed a hand on her shoulder. "Nice move, by the way."

Rose pushed his hand away, stepping back, glaring at him. Skyler chuckled. "Face it, Rose. You did what you did because you wanted revenge, and there's nothing wrong with that." His eyes glinted. "He killed your parents after all."

Ella looked at Rose with a frown, and then back at Skyler. "What are you talking about?" she asked.

"I went back to that memory we had extracted from the vamage, Don Kamara," Skyler replied, but his eyes were still on Rose. "Turns out, there was more to that memory than we first thought. I saw that the vamages didn't finish their human victims. Kyran did, with a bullet to their heads."

Rose didn't say anything, but angry tears filled her eyes.

"If you ask Kyran he will probably feed you some crap about putting them out of their misery," Skyler said, "but the fact remains, he was the one who ended your parents' lives." His lips lifted in a cruel smirk. "And to think, their daughter is worried about the execution of their murderer."

Rose dropped her gaze, a breath heaving out of her as she closed her eyes, holding back her pain. Skyler turned to walk away.

"Where are you going?" Ella asked.

"To prepare the bullet," Skyler said.

"You can't do that," Ella said at once. "You know you have to have all the Elementals in agreement of an execution before the bullet is made."

Skyler laughed as he faced her. "All the Elementals?" he asked. "Who are we talking about? There are only five Elementals, excluding Kyran. Two of the Elementals are his blood family, the other one is his adopted father. Which of them will agree to his execution?" He grinned and shook his head, as if Ella was a silly child who had said something ridiculous. "That leaves only me and you as the Elementals not related to Kyran. We are the only ones who can make a decision."

"You're right," Ella said. "And I'm against it."

Skyler's smile fell. "What?" he asked.

"You heard me," Ella replied. "I'm not agreeing to Kyran's execution."

"Kyran is the Scorcher," Skyler said. "It was always planned for the Scorcher to be executed."

"Neriah never wanted Kyran executed," she said. "He forbade it then, and I'm forbidding it now."

"Why?" Skyler demanded.

"Because he doesn't deserve it."

Skyler's eyes widened and mouth opened. "Doesn't deserve it? He deserves worse than death!"

"Why?" Ella asked. "What has he done that sentences him to death?"

"Where should I start?" Skyler spat. "He pretended to be a Hunter to spy on Salvador—"

"During which time he helped in countless demon hunts," Ella interrupted. "And he wasn't spying, he was lying in wait for Neriah."

"Whom he attacked so he could steal the key!" Skyler reminded. "The same day he snapped your neck!"

"He stole the key for the one he thinks of as his father," Ella said. "It's no secret what Neriah did to Hadrian, but locking a mage's power isn't right. Neriah did it because he had no other choice. But you can't fault Kyran for trying to free his father's powers." She straightened up. "And his assault on me didn't kill me. He doesn't deserve death for that."

"He helped Hadrian kill Neriah," Skyler snarled.

"He didn't touch Neriah," Ella shot back. "It was Hadrian who killed him."

"But Kyran made sure no one could go to Neriah's aid."

"That's not a crime punishable by death," Ella said.

"He dropped the Gate!" Skyler shouted, and a ripple of air blasted through the street. Skyler was breathing hard, his hands curled into fists. "He's the reason Salvador was attacked." His eyes gleamed. "He's the reason I lost Armana."

Ella's expression softened. "Sky, you don't have proof that it was him."

"Who else could it be?" Skyler asked.

Ella went quiet, not having an answer. She took a moment and then raised her head to stand tall once again. "You're not killing him," she said. "If you go ahead with the execution, or even so much as *try* to make a bullet with Kyran's name on it, I will gather Scott and all the chiefs of the cities, and demand for you to be banned from becoming the new leader."

Skyler stared at her. "You would do that to me? For him?"

Ella held his eyes. "I would," she said. "But not for Kyran. I'm doing this for *you*," she said. "If you kill Kyran, you'll be killing an Elemental." She stared hard at him. "Just like Hadrian did."

Skyler's rage was felt in the air as it whipped up, sweeping across the street. Skyler was glaring at Ella, but she stood her ground. Without a word, he turned and walked away. The storm died as Skyler strode through the open Gate and out of Salvador.

Ella took in a heavy breath, her eyes lingering on the Gate as it slid shut. Then she looked over at Rose. She took a step towards her but then stopped, as if she changed her mind. She started to walk away, heading to the cottages, but then paused. She turned back and walked up to Rose.

"I don't know what Skyler saw in that memory," she started. "I don't know if Kyran hurt your parents or if he tried to help them, but I do know that he has always protected *you.*"

Rose stood in silence.

"He saved your life," Ella reminded her. "He didn't have to do that transfer when you were attacked by a hell hound, but he did. Any time there's any danger, Kyran has always reached out to protect you, whether by the fire ring he conjured in Balt, or the force of air when we were attacked by Hadrian."

Rose frowned, looking at Ella with confusion.

Ella smiled bitterly. "You didn't even notice that, did you?" she asked. "When Salvador was Q-Zoned and we all ran straight into Hadrian's trap, did you think it was pure luck that nothing hit the car you and Sam were in?" she asked. "The minute the fight broke out, Kyran had a swirl of air circling your SUV. It threw back anything that came near your car."

Rose stared at her in shock, tears falling from her eyes.

"Kyran is my enemy," Ella said, holding a hand to her chest. "I may not want him dead, but I want him held accountable for everything he's done wrong. He deserves to be punished." She held Rose's tearful gaze. "But he didn't deserve your betrayal."

Rose broke at her words, squeezing her eyes shut as tears fell down her cheeks. Ella walked away, leaving Rose crying behind her.

## 25

## INNOCENT

The moment Ella unlocked the front door, Aaron bolted inside the cottage. His hands were still cuffed, but all that concerned him was Kyran. He was losing his mind worrying what state his brother was in. He wasn't even listening to what Ella was saying – what she had been saying ever since she freed him from the cottage he'd been imprisoned in. He had paused briefly when, after unlocking his door, he saw Ella hurry to Bella and hug her, as Bella broke down in sobs. A moment of confusion had swept Aaron up, but he had quickly pushed it aside, focusing on finding his brother first. He could figure out why Bella was so upset later.

Aaron ran into the room Kyran was held in and stopped dead, staring in horror at the sight before him. Kyran was inside a cage, chained and hanging from his wrists. His head was dropped, his front and legs covered in blood. The hilt of a dagger was sticking out of his chest. The smell of blood was so rich it stifled the air.

"Kyran," Aaron breathed, his terror stealing his voice momentarily. "Kyran!"

He ran forward, and tried to wrench the cage door open. Kyran stirred. He lifted his head weakly. His eyes were still closed, his lips dry. "Ace?" he rasped.

"I'll get you out. Just...just hold on," Aaron cried.

He tugged and pulled, but the door remained firmly shut. It was only when Aaron looked away from his brother and down at the door, that he saw that it was locked with a chain and padlock. Ella came to Aaron's side and held on to the chain. It iced over in seconds. Ella gave the chain a hard yank, and it snapped. Aaron pulled the door open and rushed inside.

"Kyran?" Aaron took Kyran's face in his hands. His heart jolted at how warm and clammy Kyran's skin was. Kyran seemed on the verge of consciousness but his eyes wouldn't open. "Kyran," Aaron called, gently shaking him. "Kyran, hey, look at me. Look at me."

Kyran cracked his eyes open.

"You're going to be okay," Aaron said. "I'm not going to let anything happen to you." He looked up at Kyran's chained hands, trying to figure out how to free him. He turned to see Ella was standing at the door. She hadn't come inside the cage. "Ella," Aaron called desperately. "Help me get him down."

Ella stayed where she was.

"Ella, *please*," Aaron begged. "You can't leave him like this. Help me, please."

Ella hesitated and then closed her eyes and forced out a breath as she gave in. She hurried to Kyran's side. She couldn't reach his hands, but she directed her power to ice over the chain holding the Inhibitor cuffs to the top of the cage.

Ella looked at Kyran. "You're going to have to pull," she told him. "As hard as you can."

Kyran didn't look like he had the energy to stand, let alone fight to get free. But he shifted anyway, putting weight on his bleeding, bullet-ridden legs. A hiss of pain escaped him as he tensed his body, and tugged at his arms. Aaron and Ella helped by holding on to his arms and pulling with him. The chain snapped and Kyran almost fell, his legs too wounded to support him. Aaron and Ella guided him to the floor. He rested his torn and bleeding back against the bars of the cage with a groan.

Ella put a hand to Kyran's shoulder, and one around the hilt of the dagger sticking out of his chest. "Just breathe," she instructed.

She pulled the dagger out in one swift move, and Kyran arched in pain, choking out a cry. Ella dropped the dagger but her hand stayed on Kyran's shoulder. Aaron was by Kyran's side, unable to look away from the fresh blood seeping out of the wound the dagger had left.

They had to find a way to stop the bleeding. Aaron couldn't stand seeing his brother hurt and in so much pain. He looked around him, his heart hammering at his insides. But there was nothing that could be useful. The room had been stripped bare.

"Ella," Aaron started desperately, "can't you help him? Do something to stop the bleeding?"

Ella met his eyes angrily. "I'm not an Empath," she bit out. Then almost immediately she looked ashamed. "Mages can heal to a certain degree by themselves," she explained. "But the bullets are still inside him. The bleeding won't stop until the bullets are taken out." She glanced to the bloodied dagger on the floor. "I can take them out, but not without hurting him."

Aaron looked back at his brother. His eyes had slipped shut, his breathing rough and haggard. Aaron's panicked gaze raked over Kyran's body. True to what Ella had said, Kyran was still bleeding from the gunshot wounds, and whatever torture Skyler had put him through.

Aaron shook his head, blinking back the angry tears. "You have to do something. He's bleeding out," he said to Ella.

"He won't die from blood loss," Ella assured. "But he'll become emaciated, weak and unable to move. I can dig the bullets out so he stops bleeding and his wounds can begin to heal. He'll slowly recover with time."

"Aaron," Kyran croaked, making Aaron turn to him.

Kyran's hands were still cuffed with the Inhibitors, the short chain between them not allowing much movement. His arms, like the rest of him, were bloody and wounded, but he slowly lifted them and reached out towards him. Aaron took hold of them with his own bound hands, but Kyran moved past them, his fingers stretched towards Aaron's head. Aaron had no idea what Kyran was doing, until he felt the fingers, caked with dried blood, come to rest at his temple.

With a stomach-lurching jolt, Aaron was pulled into a memory. He found himself standing on a brick road in the middle of the night under a bright moon. Small cottages were lined along both sides of the road. Under a cluster of trees in the middle of the street, stood the Pecosa Aaron now knew to be dead – Grandor, the late Pecosa leader. He was facing Kyran, looking at him with great dislike.

"I have done everything you have demanded from me," he was saying. "I have kept your secret, no matter how many times the Controller has come to me, demanding the Scorcher's identity." He stood tall. "Now it's your turn to keep your word." His eyes glinted with fury. "Release my daughter and my men. Let them come back to me."

"You will get them all back, you have my word," Kyran replied.

Grandor looked at Kyran with narrowed eyes. "How can I trust you?" he asked.

Kyran smirked. "Do you have a choice?"

Grandor didn't speak right away. "We Pecosas are passive by nature," he said quietly. "But even the most gentle of creatures will strike if they and their family are threatened." He held Kyran's eyes. "Remember, Scorcher, you are not the only one who knows how to burn others."

Kyran chuckled. "I'll keep that in mind."

Grandor said no more and walked away. Kyran shook his head with amusement and turned, about to return to the line of cottages when he stilled. His eyes widened. Aaron couldn't understand what it was he was staring at. After a moment or two of following his line of sight, Aaron finally spotted the figure half-hidden in the shadows, dressed in white robes with the hood pulled up, standing at the other side of the street.

Kyran's breathing had picked up, as if seeing the Lurker had spooked him. He took a single step towards him when the Lurker took off, running into the forest behind him.

"Hey! Wait!" Kyran yelled and darted after him. "Wait a minute!"

Aaron ran after them. They entered the forest, with Kyran calling out to the Lurker who refused to give up the chase. Aaron didn't understand what was happening. Why was the Lurker running? Why not just stop and talk to Kyran?

Aaron could see the glimpse of white in the darkness, just ahead of Kyran. The Lurker ran, twisting this way and that, turning in all directions, until Aaron was sure Kyran would lose him. Then Aaron spotted the Lurker come to a stop. In front of him, hovering in the air, was a thin, white line about as long as Aaron's arm, glowing against the darkness. Aaron had never seen anything like it, but somehow he knew instantly what it was: a tear. It was the rip in the barrier that separated the mage realm from the human one. It was where Gates usually stood, to stop the flow of elemental energy seeping out and destroying the human world in the form of natural disasters.

The Lurker turned to see Kyran was catching up. He turned and dived, head first into the tear. The tear opened up like a giant mouth, and swallowed the Lurker whole.

Kyran didn't stop – he followed the Lurker straight through the tear. Aaron took in a breath, but he didn't have to jump into the tear. He was reliving the memory, one that belonged to Kyran, so the moment Kyran passed into the human realm, so did Aaron.

Aaron found himself next to Kyran, standing on a darkened road – a very familiar road. It was only when Aaron looked up and saw the house surrounded in a thick white, pulsing fog, that he realised why. He was facing the back of Sam and Rose's house, on that fateful day he had unknowingly opened the ground to stop the car from running them over, and subsequently alerted the vamages to his presence.

Before Aaron could process the shock of it, Kyran was running, bolting towards the house. Aaron took off after him, on weakened legs. He didn't want to witness Mr and Mrs Mason being killed, but at the same time, he wanted – no, needed – to know what had happened to them.

The windows and doors to the house had been smashed by the vamages, so Kyran didn't have to force his way inside. He ran past the broken kitchen door, Aaron hot at his heels. They ran into the adjoining dining room and came to a standstill, shock and horror rooting both boys to the spot. There, on the floor of the trashed dining room, was Mr Mason. The tall, balding man who always had a kind smile for Aaron was lying dead on the floor of his own home. There was a gash along his neck, where more than one vamage had drunk him dry. His eyes were open, but his chest was still. He was gone.

A scuffling sound had Kyran's attention snapping from the man on the floor to the door at the other end of the room. He ran, wrenching the door open. Aaron found himself in the hallway, where two vamages were huddled on the floor, at the foot of the stairs. It took Aaron a moment to realise what they were doing – and then his stomach turned so violently, it was a miracle he didn't retch.

Lightning fast, Kyran was towering over the vamages. He pulled one vamage up, shoving him aside, before grabbing the second one and throwing him back with so much force the wall dented where the vamage hit it.

The woman they had been feeding on lay in a bloodied mess, her mouth gaping. But she was still alive.

Kyran dropped to his knees next to her. "It's okay," he said, but Aaron could hear the panic in his voice. "You're going to be okay."

Aaron didn't dare come any closer. His chest was aching, seeing the sweet and gentle mum of his best friends lying there, dying, taking her last breaths. She was opening and closing her mouth, trying to speak, but unable to get her voice out. The deep cuts on her neck were leaking blood at an alarming rate. Kyran had taken off his hooded top and was pressing it against the wounds, trying to stop the bleeding. His other hand rested on her cheek and he closed his eyes, concentrating. It hit Aaron, what Kyran was doing, and it left him reeling. Kyran was attempting a transfer – so he could take on the injuries of Mrs Mason in a bid to save her life. But it wasn't working. The transfer would only work if the injuries weren't life-threatening to the mage; Mrs Mason's wounds were too severe.

Nevertheless, Kyran kept trying – squeezing his eyes shut, forcing the transfer to work, but Mrs Mason continued to bleed, her face growing pale.

At last Kyran opened his eyes and heaved out a frustrated breath. "I'm sorry," he said to her. "This should have never happened to you. I'm *so* sorry."

Mrs Mason lifted a hand and Kyran quickly took it, holding on to her.

"My...my...kids," Mrs Mason managed to heave out in a strained voice. "P–Please! S–Save them!" Her eyes moved to the stairs and Kyran looked up to the rooms at the top of the staircase.

Aaron's heart lurched. Mrs Mason didn't know that Sam and Rose had sneaked outside to take him – Aaron – to the Blaze for his birthday. She thought they were still in the house. She was dying, and her last thought was to save her children from the monsters that had attacked them.

Kyran looked back at her, and held her hand tightly. "I won't let anything happen to your children," he said. "I promise, I'll help them. I'll make sure they're safe."

A pained smile came to Mrs Mason's face. She gasped and her body shuddered, before she fell still. Gently Kyran let go of her hand and reached up to close her eyes.

Aaron snapped out of the memory, coming back to the cage, where he was kneeling next to his severely wounded brother. Kyran's hand fell from Aaron's head, just as the tears dropped from Aaron's eyes.

Kyran took in ragged breaths but lifted his pained eyes to look at Aaron.

"I – I don't care what anyone – believes," he said in a scratchy voice, struggling to get the words out. "They can – think what they – they want." He took in a strained breath. "I want *you* to know – the truth. Know that I – I didn't kill them."

"Not even for a second did I believe you had," Aaron said. "I knew you didn't kill Mr and Mrs Mason." His heart skipped a beat. "But I didn't know that you had tried to do a transfer to save Mrs Mason's life."

Kyran closed his eyes. "What good was it?" he asked. "I was – too late."

Ella listened to the brothers in silence, frowning in confusion...wondering what it was Skyler had seen in the memory forced from the vamage, if the truth was what Aaron had just witnessed.

***

Skyler stood at the window, watching the sun getting ready to set. He took in a long breath. "I never thought a day like this would come," he said. "Ella has always had my back, but the time I needed her support the most, she turned on me." He stepped away from the window, turning to look behind him. "But you can understand that. After all, you went through the same thing today with Aaron."

Sam didn't speak. He sat in silence at the foot of his bed, staring at his hands.

"It's a shame," Skyler said. "I remember how loyal Aaron was to you. He would have done anything for you – hell, he even jumped into a collapsing Q-Zone to save you once." Cold blue eyes stared at Sam as he visibly grew upset. "Now that same Aaron shot you to save Kyran."

Sam raised his head, rage in his eyes.

"It's not really Aaron's fault," Skyler said, walking towards Sam. "He's been brainwashed by Kyran, tricked and manipulated into being on his side. Why else would Aaron protect the one who killed the parents of his best friends?"

Sam turned his head away, fighting angry tears, his jaw clenched tight.

"Ella has my hands tied," Skyler said. "Otherwise this would have been Kyran's last sunset," he said, looking out the window. "But maybe there's still a way. I may not be able to execute Kyran, but that doesn't mean he should get to live."

Sam looked at him with confusion. Skyler lowered himself in front of Sam, to look him in the eyes.

"In our realm, the one who has suffered an injustice can take revenge, without any interference from the mages, or even Elementals." He held Sam's stare. "You and Rose are the ones who lost everything because of Kyran," he said. "You are the ones Kyran wronged, so under our laws, you are his judge, his jury–" he pulled out his gun and placed it in Sam's hand – "and his executioner."

# 26

# BLIND VENGEANCE

"What happens now?" Aaron asked, as he walked alongside Ella, heading back to his cottage.

Ella took in a deep breath. "I'm going to keep trying to contact Scott. He only wears his pendant for a short time, to avoid Hadrian spotting him on the Hub, but I'll get hold of him. Once I tell him what Skyler's done, Scott can advise what we should do next." They stopped at the front door of the cottage Aaron was supposed to be in. "For now, just keep your head low and stay inside," she said. "If you behave, I can justify taking those cuffs off."

"Take Kyran's off," Aaron said at once. "He needs them gone more than I do."

The crushing force of the Inhibitors holding back his powers was a deeply uncomfortable sensation. Aaron could only imagine how much worse it was for Kyran to be wearing three of them, and while he was already so badly wounded. Kyran was in so much pain, at least having the cuffs gone would be something.

But Ella shook her head. "His won't be coming off," she said. "Even I know that's a bad idea."

"What can he do in his condition?" Aaron asked, his tone rising with anger.

"Once I get the bullets out, he'll start to heal," Ella explained. "So the cuffs have to stay on if we're holding him as a prisoner. If I take his cuffs off, no one will let me take the bullets out, since that keeps him weakened." She held Aaron's eyes. "You tell me which is worse for him: the cuffs or the bullets?"

Aaron hated himself as he said, "Fine, keep the cuffs on." He held her eyes. "But take those bullets out. He needs to start healing. He's losing too much blood." Aaron couldn't get the horrifying image of his bloodied brother out of his head.

"I'm going right now to the Empath huts to see if they have any numbing salve," Ella said. "It'll help with the extraction of the bullets." She shook her head. "I can't put him through any more torture."

Aaron nodded miserably, his heart breaking at how much pain Kyran had been put through. At least getting the bullets out and giving his wounds a chance to heal would lessen his agony.

"Please keep trying to contact Scott," Aaron said. "The sooner he finds out, the sooner he can get here with my mum and dad." He looked over Ella's shoulder when he spotted several Hunters heading to the cottage that was holding Kyran.

Ella turned too, following Aaron's gaze. They watched in confused silence, as Ryan, Omar and Julian disappeared past the front door. Moments later, they came back out – dragging Kyran with them.

Aaron shot forward at once. "Hey!" he yelled. "What are you doing?"

They had tied Kyran's hands behind his back with the three Inhibitor cuffs. A long chain ran from them to his now shackled feet. It was hardly needed – Kyran could barely stand.

Kyran lifted his head at Aaron's yell, looking to him with bloodshot eyes, but he didn't get a chance to speak to him. Omar and Julian led him away while Ryan stepped forward to catch Aaron, stopping him from following after Kyran.

"Go back inside, Aaron," Ryan said in a voice that betrayed his unease. "You're not going to want to see this."

"Where are you taking him?" Aaron asked, his heart racing. "Kyran!" he yelled, as he saw the Hunters take his brother and disappear down the path that led to the Hub. "Let go of me!" Aaron shouted, struggling in Ryan's hold.

"What's going on?" Ella asked, coming to Aaron's side.

"Skyler's ordered us to bring Kyran to the ring," Ryan replied. He paused, looking deeply rueful. "For his execution."

It was as though the ground had slipped from under Aaron's feet. He gaped at Ryan, his voice lost. He began shaking his head. "No," he choked out. "He – he can't do that."

"I warned him what would happen if he tries an execution," Ella said with fury.

"That's the thing," Ryan said quietly. "He's not the one carrying out the kill."

Ella and Aaron were both confused. That is until they saw Skyler walking down the street, Sam behind him, with a gun in his hand.

Aaron broke out of Ryan's grip and ran towards them. Sam didn't need a personalised bullet to kill Kyran. A normal bullet would kill a mage, as long as it was fired by a non-mage, and it was a killing shot to the head or heart.

"Sam!" Aaron yelled.

Sam stopped in his tracks along with Skyler. A twitch of Skyler's fingers, and a jolt of power struck Aaron in the chest, throwing him to the ground. Aaron rolled onto his front, coughing to catch the breath that was knocked out of him.

The rest of the Hunters were making their way towards the Hub, to watch the execution, but they stopped to look at Aaron. Rose emerged from the Stove, with Mary and Ava. She found a handcuffed Aaron on the ground, gasping for breath. For a single moment, Rose forgot how complicated their friendship had become, and she ran to him. But as she passed Sam, he grabbed her arm, stopping her.

"What's going on?" Rose asked, looking at her brother with confusion. Then she noticed the gun in Sam's hand and her body stiffened. She looked at him with wide eyes. "Sam?"

Sam didn't say anything. His bloodshot eyes were on Aaron, who was picking himself up from the ground.

Ryan caught up with Aaron, just as he stood up. "Come on, Aaron," he said, trying to coerce him back to the cottages, but Aaron refused to move, his eyes fixed on his grim-faced friend.

"What are you *doing*, Sam?" Aaron cried.

"What does it look like?" Skyler said. "He's taking revenge for the murder of his parents."

Rose looked to Sam. "No," she said, horrified. "Sam, you can't–"

"Sam," Ella hurried towards him, passing Ryan and Aaron, and ignoring everyone else. "You don't have to do this," she said to him.

"I don't?" Sam asked with quiet fury. "Would you not avenge your parents' murder, Ella?"

Ella fell quiet.

Sam turned to his sister. "You don't want Kyran to pay for what he did?"

Rose stared back at him. "I do," she said. "But–"

"He shot our parents in cold blood," Sam said. "He deserves the same done to him."

"No, Sam, you've got it all wrong," Aaron started desperately. "Kyran didn't hurt your parents, he tried to save them–"

"Nice try," Skyler said. "But you can't fool him any longer, Adams. Sam knows the truth now."

"What truth?" Aaron spat.

"The truth I found," Skyler replied. His eyes glinted in the setting sun. "I saw Kyran kill their parents. I went back to that memory we extracted from the vamage, and I saw Kyran shoot both the man and woman in the head, killing them after the vamages had attacked them."

Aaron stared at Skyler. "You're lying," he said. "You're lying to them about how their parents died," he said with disgust. "For what? Just so you can find a reason to kill Kyran? Is that how far you've fallen?"

"He's not the one who's fallen," Sam said.

Aaron looked to him. "Sam–"

"Don't," Sam cut him off. "Don't bother. I don't want to hear anything you have to say."

He started walking away, taking Rose with him.

"Sam, wait." Ella came to stand in his way, blocking him.

"You can't stop me," Sam said. "I have a right under your laws to exact revenge."

Ella paused. She gave Skyler a dirty look but quickly turned back to Sam. "I know I can't stop you," she said. "But you're on your way to take a life. There's no coming back from that." She stared hard at him. "Are you sure you want that on your conscience?"

"He's getting justice for his parents' murder," Skyler interrupted. "Why would that weigh down on him?"

Ella glared at Skyler. "You're not thinking straight," she said to him. "Let go of your anger, Sky, and consider what it is you're encouraging Sam to do. Aside from everything else, Kyran holds three legacies. By killing him, you're risking–"

"I'm not risking anything," Skyler said. "When he dies, each of his legacies will find their Elementals. Hadrian will get Fire back, Adams will get Earth, and I'll get what is mine." He smirked. "Justice, in many forms."

Ella looked back to Sam. "Sammy, *please*," she whispered. "Don't do this."

Sam ignored her and walked away, his grip tight on Rose. Skyler gestured to Ryan to take Aaron away.

"Sam?" Aaron yelled, as Ryan began dragging him back to his cottage, to lock him inside until the execution was over.

Aaron fought to get free. His panic and anger was demanding the power of Earth to seep into him, to ready him for a mighty fight, but the cuffs around his wrists kept that power bottled up. He couldn't use his element to stop Skyler and Sam from killing Kyran, even when all the power he needed was right there, waiting for him. It was enough to drive Aaron almost mad with fury.

"Sam! Skyler's lying!" he yelled desperately. "He's *using* you. He wants Kyran dead. You may have the gun but he's the one pulling the trigger!"

Skyler smirked at that, following after Sam and Rose.

"Sam!" Aaron yelled. "Kyran didn't kill your parents. He tried to save them. He tried to do a transfer!"

Rose halted, bringing Sam to a stop too. She turned to look at Aaron, her eyes wide. Even Ryan, stunned by what Aaron had said, ceased his efforts to drag him away.

"He showed me the memory," Aaron said quickly. "I saw it – the attack, what happened." He locked eyes with Rose. "Kyran was telling the truth. He never came with the vamages. He arrived afterwards."

Rose was breathing fast, her stare fixed on Aaron, not daring to look away.

"Don't listen to him," Skyler said in Sam's ear. "He'll say anything to save his brother."

Sam clenched his jaw and tugged at Rose's arm, walking away, following after Skyler as he led the way.

"By the time Kyran got there, it was too late for your dad," Aaron continued. "But he found Mrs Mason; he talked to your mum."

A choked noise of surprise left Rose, as she turned again to look at Aaron.

"He tried to do a transfer!" Aaron yelled so Sam could hear him. "He tried to save her life, but it was too late. She was dying."

"I saw him kill both of them," Skyler said. "He's lying to make you change your mind." He looked to Ryan with blazing eyes and gestured for him to take Aaron away.

Ryan obediently pulled Aaron away.

Aaron fought as hard as he could, as Ryan forced him towards the cottage. "Mrs Mason didn't know that you two were outside!" he continued to shout across to Sam and Rose. "She thought you were upstairs! She asked Kyran to help you, to protect you!"

Rose was hanging on Aaron's every word, her face turned towards him, even while her brother continued to lead her in the opposite direction.

"Kyran kept his promise to a dying woman he didn't even know!" Aaron yelled. "He's always protected you, both of you. You can't kill him, Sam! You hear me? You can't kill him!" He battled against Ryan, as he opened the door to the cottage. "Skyler!" Aaron cried. "If you hurt my brother I'll kill you! I swear, Skyler, I will *kill* you!"

Ryan pushed Aaron into the cottage and closed the door.

Rose came to a stop, forcing Sam to a standstill. "Wait," she breathed. She turned to look at Sam, her eyes searching his for a long moment. "What are we doing?" she asked. "You – you can't do this."

Sam frowned. "Do what?"

"This," Rose said, gesturing to the gun in his hand. "You can't kill him."

Sam's eyes narrowed. "Why not?" he snarled.

"You really want become a murderer?" she asked.

"It's not murder, it's justice," Sam said.

"And what if Aaron's telling the truth?" Rose asked.

Sam's eyes clouded. "You're not falling for that crap, are you?"

"Aaron wouldn't lie," Rose urged, "not about Mum or...or what happened to her."

"You don't know that," Sam said. "If he can shoot me to protect Kyran, he can do anything."

"Face it, Rose," Skyler said, joining the conversation. "You don't know Aaron as well as you thought you did."

Rose turned to Skyler. "I still know him better than I know *you*," she said. "I don't trust you. Maybe you're the one lying about the memory you saw."

Skyler smirked. "Do you really think I would do that?"

"You lied and used me to trap Kyran," she said. "You told me you were only going to get information from him, to get to Hadrian. You didn't say anything about killing him. You tricked me, so yeah, I don't know if I believe you. Ella stopped you from executing Kyran, so you got Sam to agree to it. You're so desperate to kill him, it makes me wonder what else you're willing to say or do."

"I'm not desperate to kill Kyran," Skyler said. "I'm desperate for justice."

"This isn't about serving justice," Rose said. "You hate Kyran. You realised he was unarmed, but you still shot him, ordered the rest of the Hunters to shoot him," Rose said. "You locked him up and then hurt him. How could you *do* that, Skyler?"

Skyler's eyes narrowed and he tilted his head, studying her. "You've got to be kidding me," he said quietly. "You still have feelings for him."

Rose took a moment before shaking her head. "No."

"That's why you're so quick to believe Aaron – because you *want* it to be true," Skyler stated. "You would rather have Kyran as the gallant hero who tried to help your parents than admit the truth: that he's the Scorcher who murdered them." He looked to Sam. "Your sister is so busy listening to her heart she's lost her mind."

"I'm not listening to my heart!" Rose shouted. "If I was, I would *never* have agreed to help you capture him!" She was breathing hard, her eyes brimmed with tears but not a drop fell. "He was unarmed," she said in a broken voice, "because *I* did that to him. He's here, facing death, because of me." She had to fight with all she had not to break down. "And if what Aaron said is true, then I just helped sentence him to death, when he tried to save my dying mother."

"Aaron's lying," Skyler said.

"What if he isn't?" Rose asked. She turned to her brother. "What proof do we have? Skyler's word against Aaron's?" She shook her head. "No, Sam, you're not helping Skyler murder Kyran. I won't let you do it." She reached for his gun. "Give this back–"

Sam gripped her wrist before she could touch the gun. He was staring at her as if he didn't recognise her. "You – you do have feelings for him," he said, with just as much surprise as disgust.

"Sam," Rose started.

"Skyler's right; you're listening to Aaron because you want that to be the truth," Sam said.

"Aaron wouldn't lie to us–" Rose started.

"Aaron *shot* me!" Sam cried. His grip tightened on her wrist as he jostled her. "He put a bullet into me to save Kyran! We don't mean *anything* to him. Aaron will do and say whatever he can to protect his brother."

"Sam," Rose gasped. "You're hurting me."

"You're not standing in my way," Sam said, so lost in his anger, he ignored what his sister had said. "Not you, not Aaron, *no one!*"

"Sam!" Rose cried out as her wrist almost snapped under his grip.

"You can turn your back on your family," Sam spat. "Protect Kyran even though he killed our parents, but I'll never stoop that low!"

Rose swung her free hand and hit Sam, square in the face. Sam shoved Rose back, throwing her to the frozen ground. He moved towards her, but Skyler held out a hand, stopping him. Sam was breathing hard, brown eyes full of unadulterated rage, fixed on his twin sister. She was glaring back at him, just as furious, just as hurt.

Skyler gestured to Ryan, who was standing with Ella, watching them with unhappy eyes. "Take Rose and lock her in one of the cottages too," Skyler instructed. "Until after the execution."

Ryan walked over and helped Rose to her feet.

"Sam," Rose started. "Don't do this."

"Let's go," Skyler said to Sam.

Sam gave Rose a last glower and turned to follow Skyler, disappearing down the path behind the cottages.

"Sam!" Rose yelled. "Don't do this! Please!"

Ryan tried his best to be gentle, as he pulled Rose to the cottages.

"No!" Rose cried. "Sam!" she screamed. "Don't kill him! Sam! No!"

"Shh, Rose." Ryan wrapped an arm around her shoulders and whispered in her ear, trying to calm her. "It'll be over soon. All it'll take is one bullet from Sam, and Kyran will be gone. It'll be instant, painless."

If Ryan thought that was going to comfort Rose, he was very wrong. Rose curled low, as if about to fall to the ground in grief. Then she snapped up, throwing back her head, hitting Ryan in the face. Her elbow struck his midsection, and Ryan fell back with a pained, "Oof!"

Rose started running, screaming after Sam. Ryan was about to chase after her when Ella stopped him.

"Let her go," she said, watching Rose disappear down the path. "She's the only one that has a chance of stopping the execution."

***

Aaron searched the cottage for something, anything he could use to break out. But all he could see was big, bulky furniture pieces, like beds and sofas – nothing he could lift and hurl at the window. So Aaron ran to the bathroom and with bound hands, managed to snap the shower rod off the wall. He brought the metal pole down to the living room and took a full swing at the glass window. It did nothing to it. Not even a scratch. Aaron needed to hit harder.

Aaron pulled back and struck again, and again, and again. His heart was pounding; fear, anger and sheer panic were making his hands shake. Sam might have already reached Kyran by now. He gripped the rod tight and hit the window in a frenzy.

A small crack in the glass made Aaron pause. He stared at it, latching on to the hope it brought. He hit it again and again, mentally calling out to his brother.

*Hold on, Kyran, I'm coming. I won't let anything happen to you. I'm coming.*

\*\*\*

Rose ran as fast as she could, her heart hammering at her insides, her breath coming in great gasps. "Sam!" she screamed. Her feet pounded on the forest ground, through the slush of old snow. She slipped a few times, but refused to stay down. She got back up and raced through the woods.

She couldn't see Skyler or Sam anywhere. They couldn't have reached the ring already, could they? Rose pushed herself to go faster. She sped past the restored workshops and artillery hut. She ran down the hill, slipped and fell, and landed at the bottom in a heap. Her arms and knees were badly scraped and bleeding, but Rose ignored it. She got up and ran forward.

She caught sight of the Hub, the circular building that once housed the table that controlled the hunts of the realm. Outside that building was the ring where the Hunters practised their skills. But today that ring was about to be used as an execution platform.

Rose's heart dropped when she spotted Kyran, bloodied and kneeling inside the ring, his head bowed and his hands behind him. A chain was bolted into the ground and attached to his bound hands and feet, forcing him to stay on his knees.

Rose saw Skyler command the stones to lift and make the arch. Sam stepped inside the ring, the gun clutched tightly in his hand.

Fear stabbed at Rose's insides, making her blood run cold. She bolted forward with a cry. "Sam! No!"

The surrounding Hunters looked over at her. Sam stilled, but he didn't turn around.

Kyran stirred out of his haze of pain at the sound of her voice. He lifted his head, and with bloodshot eyes looked for Rose. He found her moving through the crowd, racing towards them.

"Sam!" Rose screamed. "Don't hurt him!"

She was almost there. She could get to them in time. She would put herself between Kyran and Sam's gun if she had to; she wasn't going to let Kyran die – she couldn't let Sam become a killer.

Kyran was fighting to stay conscious. His breaths were laboured and difficult to pull in. He raised his head to look to Sam, who was standing before him, holding the gun in a white-knuckled grip.

Sam heaved in a steady breath and aimed at Kyran's head.

"No!" Rose screamed. "Sammy, no!"

From the bottom of the path, Aaron came racing out. Ella and Ryan were just behind him. Aaron saw Sam and Kyran inside the ring. His best friend was, once again, holding a gun to his brother's head.

"Sam! No!" he yelled, running towards the ring.

Kyran and Sam could hear the shouts, but neither of them looked away from each other.

Kyran's lips moved. "Sam," he breathed in a pained whisper.

Sam's finger rested on the trigger.

Rose pushed past the Hunters; no one tried to stop her. She was so close, she could see Sam's hand shaking.

"Sam!" she yelled. "NO!"

Sam pulled the trigger, and the shot rang out, bringing Rose to a sudden, heart-wrenching stop.

# 27

## BLEEDING HEARTS

The echo of the gunshot rang in the air. Rose stood transfixed, watching as Kyran slowly turned his head to look at Sam. The barrel of the gun, which had been pointing at Kyran's head a second before, had shifted just as the gun was fired. Kyran had, on instinct, shut his eyes and flinched when the gun went off, turning his face to the side, readying himself for the killing shot. But Sam had diverted his aim at the last possible moment, shooting at the ground instead of Kyran.

Sam was trembling, his eyes were on Kyran, his mouth pressed into a line, but it was no use; the anger, pain, confusion – everything he had been holding back finally came barrelling out and tears fell from his eyes.

Rose darted towards him. Aaron did the same, running past the Hunters. Ella raised a hand to lift the stones so Rose and Aaron could enter the ring. Rose ran under the stone arch and straight to her brother. She clung to him, her arms around his neck, relief drawing tears from her eyes. The gun slipped out of Sam's hand and fell to the ground. Sam wrapped an arm around Rose and sunk to the ground, crying. He hadn't been able to do it. He had pulled the trigger in the heat of anger, when Hunters had ambushed Kyran, but this was different. Having Kyran tied down before him, with all the Hunters standing watching with painful discomfort, and his sister's desperate screams in his ears – Sam couldn't do it. He couldn't kill Kyran. When it came down to it, he couldn't take a life in cold blood, not even for vengeance.

Aaron ran into the ring, passed Sam and Rose, and skidded to his knees in front of Kyran. His hands were tied, so he couldn't even hug Kyran. But he cupped Kyran's face with both hands, as he asked him again and again if he was okay. Kyran didn't answer. He was shaking. Whether it was because of his horrendous injuries, or his near-death encounter, Aaron didn't know.

Skyler stood staring at Sam with great disappointment. His cold blue eyes moved to his Hunters and he gestured to them. They moved into the ring, removed the chain that kept Kyran tethered to the ground, and pulled him to his feet. Aaron went up with Kyran, supporting him so he didn't have to put all his weight onto his wounded legs. Aaron noticed the Hunters were doing the same, only more subtly.

They practically carried Kyran out of the ring. Rose looked up from Sam's arms to find Kyran's eyes were on her. She held his eyes for as long as she could, before Aaron and the Hunters took him to return to his cottage.

Ella came into the ring, and wordlessly coaxed Sam back to his feet. Rose stayed by her brother's side.

Ella reached out to touch Sam's tear-stained cheek. "You did the right thing," she said softly.

Sam looked at her and then dropped his head, closing his eyes. Ella's hand fell from his cheek only to curl around his hand. She led Sam and Rose out of the ring.

"I should have known," Skyler said to Sam. "You don't have what it takes."

"Leave him alone," Ella warned.

But Skyler ignored her, his cruel eyes on Sam. "You had the perfect opportunity to exact revenge," he said. "But you chickened out at the last minute."

"Back off, Skyler!" Ella said.

Sam didn't say anything. He kept his eyes diverted and his head bowed. The Hunters in the area slowly started making their way back. Rose pulled Sam to join them.

"Ignore him," she said to her brother.

"Yeah, just go ahead and ignore me," Skyler seethed. "Ignore everything I did to get that son of a demon here! Ignore how many Hunters it took to arrest him, on the morning after the full moon, when all of us were still recovering from the drain. Ignore the fact that your sister almost got killed by Raoul, in her attempt to trick Kyran – and you just wasted the chance you had to kill him!"

Rose came to an abrupt stop. She turned around to look at Skyler with alarm. "How did you know about Raoul?" she asked.

Skyler didn't speak, but a flicker of unease washed over him.

Rose stared at him, until understanding came to her. "Oh my God," she breathed. "It was you," she said. "*You* dropped the Gate and let the Lycans in. You let them attack us."

The Hunters bristled at the accusation. Ella looked to Skyler, her protest on behalf of her friend almost out of her mouth, but Skyler's response cut her off.

"I had no choice," he said. "Kyran was next to a Blade of Aric, and as long as he stayed there, he would be unable to use his powers," he explained. "I didn't wait for the night to pass. I followed you after you left with Kyran and Adams, and I spotted Lycans roaming the area. I knew that should they attack, Kyran would stay on the other side of the Gate, until he was sure the Lycans were gone." Skyler smirked. "He wouldn't risk your life," he told Rose. "Or his brother's." He straightened up, holding his head high. "So I dropped the Gate, leaving the area open to the Lycans. That way, Kyran was forced to stay put until my Hunters arrived a few hours later."

Rose gaped at him in horror. "How could you do that?" she asked. "You almost got me *killed*."

Skyler's eyes were burning. "Kyran dropped the Gate and I lost the one I loved." He stared hard at Rose. "I figured, worst case scenario, I would only be returning the favour."

Sam went for Skyler with a snarl.

Ella grabbed him, hauling him back. Rose held on to him too, but Sam was fighting to break free, his hands curled into fists, and foul curses dropped from his mouth.

"You risked my sister's life!" he yelled. "You used her – sent her with Kyran, and then endangered her?"

"I took advantage of an opportunity," Skyler said. "I didn't plan for Lycans to show up."

"That makes it better, does it?" Sam spat, fighting Ella and Rose's hold.

"Sam, don't," Ella said. "Go," she urged. "Please, just go."

Rose tugged at a furious Sam. "Come on," she said. "Just leave it, Sam. He's not worth it." She shot a venomous glare at Skyler, who looked unfazed by their anger. Rose managed to take Sam up the path with the help of Zhi-Jiya and Bella, who silently came to Sam's side and held his arms.

Ella looked at Skyler. He didn't quite meet her eye.

"You didn't go back to that vamage's memory did you?" she asked. "You never saw Kyran killing Sam's parents. You made it up so they would help you capture and kill him."

Skyler didn't say anything, but he didn't have to. Ella knew she was right, she could read it in Skyler's expression.

Her mouth formed a line, her grey eyes darkened with anger. She turned and walked away, too disgusted to say another word to him.

One by one, the Hunters left too, looking disappointed in their leader, until Skyler was left standing on his own.

\*\*\*

Rose cautiously opened the door and slipped inside. She came to a sudden halt. She had been preparing herself for the sight of Kyran imprisoned, but it still made her breath choke in her chest. The cage in the middle of the room made her heart jump, and the wounded boy locked inside made it break.

Kyran turned his head to look at her. Rose wanted to move, to run to him, to run back outside, to speak, to apologise, but all she could do was stand there and stare at him.

The coppery scent of blood was thick in the room, the floor of the cage was stained crimson, and Kyran's skin and clothes were covered in it too. Rose took it all in with a bleeding heart, knowing full well she was responsible for Kyran's state.

And yet, at the sight of Rose, Kyran did nothing but smile. His hands were still cuffed, but the Hunters had shown him a small mercy by binding his hands in front of him now. Kyran gripped the bars of the cage and pulled himself to stand up, with great difficulty, gingerly balancing as little weight as he could on his injured legs.

His pained groan was all it took to snap Rose out of her stupor. She hurried forward.

"Don't stand up," she said, coming in front of the cage. "Just – just sit back down."

Kyran leant his head against the bars and closed his eyes, gathering his strength to hold himself up. He looked at Rose and cracked a smile.

"You should always stand when a girl walks into a room," he said in a dry, painful voice. "It's only good manners."

Rose stared at him. Despite her best efforts, her eyes welled up. She shook her head. "Don't do that," she said quietly. "Please, Kyran. Don't make jokes and talk to me as if nothing has happened."

"It's okay," Kyran rasped.

"No, it's not," Rose said. "How can you *say* that? It's not okay, what I – I did to you–"

"You only did what you did because you believed Skyler," Kyran said. "I get it."

Rose fought the stinging in her eyes. "You shouldn't be so understanding," she said. "How can you go through all of this, knowing I got you into this mess, and not hate me for it?"

Kyran looked at her with surprise, his eyes pained and bloodshot. "I could never hate you," he said. "No matter what you do, Rose. You could be the one to pull the trigger and kill me, and even with my dying breath I still wouldn't hate you."

Rose couldn't stop the tears. She squeezed her eyes shut, forcing back a sob. "I'm sorry," she said in a broken voice. "God, Kyran, I'm so, *so* sorry." She wiped at her cheeks. "I know that an apology isn't even close to being enough–"

"It's more than enough," Kyran said. "Rose," he breathed. "I need you to know I didn't hurt your parents–"

"I know," Rose said quickly. "Aaron told me." She stared into Kyran's eyes. "Why didn't you tell me that you had spoken to my mum?" she asked. "And that you tried to do a transfer to save her?"

"You didn't give exactly me a chance."

Rose stilled. He was right. Ever since she found out that Kyran was the Scorcher, she had refused to listen to him. She was so convinced that he would lie to her, she didn't entertain anything he had to say.

"You should have told me to shut up and listen to you," she said.

A weak laugh left Kyran, and it quickly turned into a groan. He pulled in rattling breaths in an effort to dull the pain.

"Next time, I will," he managed weakly.

Rose reached out and held on to the bars, her fingers barely an inch away from his. "Is that why you've been protecting me and Sam?" she asked. "Because you promised it to my mum?"

Kyran looked at her for a long moment. "At first," he whispered. "But very soon it changed to more...selfish reasons." He smiled at her. "I told you once before, I can't stand the thought of anything bad happening to you."

Rose moved closer to the cell. "And Sam?" she asked quietly.

"He's your family," Kyran stated simply. "I couldn't stop what happened to your parents, but I can make sure you don't lose what family you have left."

It took everything Rose had not to break down again. Her fingers touched his. "I never knew Skyler's plan was to try to kill you," she said. "If I'd known this is what he was going to do–" She paused. "I thought he only wanted information from you."

Kyran's expression turned grim. "Not information, he wants a confession," he said. "Problem is, I didn't do it."

"I believe you," she said.

Kyran closed his eyes, leaning his head against the bars. "That's all that matters."

The door to the room behind her swung open, startling Rose. She turned to see Ella hurry inside, with Ryan and Bella behind her. All three had uneasy expressions, their jaws clenched and bodies tensed. Rose opened her mouth to ask what was going on, but then saw the gun clutched in Ella's hand. She looked into Ella's tormented eyes and felt like she couldn't breathe.

"No," Rose whispered, turning to face Ella, her back against the bars – shielding Kyran. "Ella, what are you *doing*?"

"Ending this," Ella hissed and strode towards her. "Get out of the way, Rose."

Rose shook her head and gripped the bars with both hands. She was partly blocking the door to the cage. "Don't do this," she begged. "I thought you didn't want to kill him!"

"Rose, move!" Ella snapped.

"No!" Rose cried. "Ella, please–"

"It's okay, Rose," Kyran spoke from behind her.

"No." Rose shook her head. "I won't let anyone hurt you."

Ella grabbed Rose from the shoulder and pushed her aside, throwing her to the floor. Rose scrambled back up, and in that short time, Ella had broken the chain and lock securing the cage, opened the door and stepped inside.

"NO!" Rose yelled and made to run in after her, but Ryan and Bella blocked her.

"It's okay, Rose," Ryan said, trying to calm her, but Rose was fighting to get past them.

Ella stood before Kyran, breathing hard, her eyes glistening. Kyran had to lean heavily on the bars to stay standing. Ella reached out towards him, and Rose's cry gurgled in her throat. But Ella didn't shoot Kyran. She didn't even aim her gun at him. She undid the three Inhibitors from around Kyran's bleeding wrists, letting the thick manacles fall to the ground with a hard clunk.

Rose fell still, staring in surprise as Ella thrust the gun into one of Kyran's hands. He looked at her with clouded eyes, just as confused as Rose.

"You need to leave," Ella said in a shaking voice. "My bike is outside. Take it and get away from here."

Kyran stood with the gun in one hand, while his other was gripped around the bars of the cage, to keep himself standing. "I don't understand," he said, looking up at Ella.

"Skyler won't stop," Ella said. "He will do whatever it takes to kill you. I can't let him take your life." Her eyes were shadowed. "I won't have an Elemental killing another Elemental. Not again. *Never* again."

Kyran didn't say anything.

"Come on," Ella said, stepping back. "You need to leave – quickly."

Kyran couldn't walk. It was specifically why Skyler had shot him in his knees. The continued blood loss had weakened him so much that he could barely stand without support. Ryan and Bella moved away from Rose and went to Kyran's side to help him out of the cage and across the room. Kyran pulled back before they opened the door.

"Wait," he said. "What about Aaron?"

"He's outside," Ella said. "Waiting for you."

Sure enough, when they opened the front door, they saw Aaron impatiently pacing before Ella's bike. Like Kyran, Aaron's Inhibitors were also gone. When Aaron saw Kyran, he paused, and relief flooded his expression. He darted to Kyran, throwing his arms around his brother, and Kyran returned the embrace just as fiercely.

"We need to move," Bella said, sounding regretful that she was breaking the brothers apart. "Skyler is around here somewhere. We can't have him catch us."

Aaron pulled back, and nodded. "Go," he encouraged.

"What about you?" Kyran asked, holding Aaron by his shoulder, concerned eyes fixed to him.

"Don't worry about me," Aaron said. "Get yourself out of here."

When Kyran didn't move, Ella said, "Aaron will be fine. Scott is on his way here, with Chris and Kate Adams. They'll make sure Skyler doesn't try anything with Aaron."

All of them helped Kyran get onto Ella's bike.

"Driving in the snow isn't going to be easy," Ella said, "but you can't manage a car in your state."

Kyran gave a weak nod of understanding. The bike was kicked into gear by Ella, and she guided Kyran's bloodstained hands onto the handlebars.

Kyran turned his head to find Rose, standing behind the rest. She hesitated for all but a moment, before running to him. She kissed him, her lips on his, full of apology and pain, and the longing she had been battling ever since their first kiss. She pulled back with great reluctance, looking deep into his eyes.

"Go," she whispered, even though her heart was breaking at the thought of him leaving and possibly never coming back.

Kyran didn't look away from her as he pulled the last dregs of stamina from his depleted reserves and prepared to ride. The bike took off. Ella opened the Gate, and the flash lit the city.

At once Skyler came running out of his cottage, his furious eyes on Kyran as he rode towards the Gate. Skyler's hand lifted to send a jolt of power at Kyran, intending to knock him off the bike. But he didn't get the chance. Aaron pushed Skyler back with a ripple, full of fury and anger. It propelled Skyler high into the air before he hit the ground hard. Skyler recovered fast and jumped back to his feet. He pulled out his gun, but before he could fire a shot at Kyran, Ella stepped in front of him, blocking his aim. Skyler paused, his finger on the trigger.

Kyran rode through the Gate and out of Salvador. Aaron choked out a breath of relief. Kyran got away. He could use the portal sitting in the woods and get back home. He would be safe.

Skyler stood where he was with his gun raised, aiming at Ella. Slowly, his arm dropped. He didn't say a word. His eyes were fierce, full of unadulterated anger. Ella stared back at him with clear and unwavering defiance.

Without warning, Skyler struck Ella. Her head whipped to the side by the force of his slap. Aaron and Ryan both darted forward, but Bella grabbed hold of their arms. This was between Skyler and Ella, and Ella Afton could handle her own fights.

Skyler was seething, so angry his hands were shaking. He glared at Ella, who turned her head to look at him with stormy grey eyes.

"Next time, I'll shoot," Skyler warned in a trembling voice.

Ella held his eyes. She reached into her pocket and pulled out her second gun. She held it up for Skyler to see. "Next time, so will I."

\*\*\*

Layla strained to look as far into the distance as she could, but all that met her eyes was the darkness of the night. Her enhanced vision told her not a single entity was out there: no birds in the trees, no wildlife scampering around the woods – no Kyran returning home after more than twenty-four hours away.

A chuckle behind her pulled her attention. She straightened up, rolling her shoulders, but didn't turn around.

"Look at that," Machado's voice purred in her ear. "A golden cat on patrol."

Layla smirked, but kept her eyes fixed ahead. "I'm only out here to enjoy the night," she said. "You're the only dog that guards the front door."

Machado came to stand in front of her. "You don't look like you're enjoying yourself," he said in faked confusion. "You wouldn't be out here waiting for *someone*, would you?" he asked.

Layla ignored him, looking past his shoulder, watching the road that led to Hadrian's manor. Machado grinned widely. "Hadrian warned you not to cross Kyran's path, not after what you did to that Shattered of his."

Layla smiled. "I remember."

"And yet here you are, waiting to get under Kyran's skin the minute he comes home."

Layla turned her head to meet Machado's glittery blue eyes. "You won't understand, Machado," she said. "You have no idea what it feels like to toy with something that is both fierce and dangerous. To prod it, tease it, to know that it's capable of finishing you if you push it too far or get too close." She brushed her long red hair behind her and sauntered close to Machado, looking at him with the lightest of blue eyes. "It's an exhilarating experience. Nothing makes you feel more alive than when you're within an inch of death."

Machado shook his head. "You really are insane," he said with a snigger.

Layla smiled. "Perhaps," she said. "Or maybe I'm just not afraid of death."

Machado lost his smile. He stared at her, and a flicker of something akin to sympathy lit his eyes.

Layla snapped her head to the side, her eyes wide and searching the dark road, her nostrils flared. "You smell that?" she asked, her voice a breathy whisper.

Machado let out an annoyed hiss. "He's up to his usual antics again," he groaned. "I think Kyran may have the same thrill-seeking problem as you, only he likes messing with vamages."

Layla didn't seem to hear him. Her vampire senses were on full alert. Her searching gaze found the single beam of the headlight in the distance, coming towards them. Layla watched it, growing restless. Her breath caught.

"He's bleeding," she said, stunned, as if the very idea was somehow ludicrous.

"Nothing new," Machado said, sounding bored. "He's made a habit of it, just to torment us."

Layla watched as the headlight grew bigger. The purr of the bike reached their ears, and both Layla and Machado picked up instantly that it wasn't Kyran's bike, Lexi. But the slightly slumped figure on the bike was definitely Kyran; the scent of his blood confirmed that.

Layla took a step forward, her eyes narrowed and fixed on the dark outline driving the bike. The figure swayed, the bike trembled, and then the rider fell off.

"Kyran!" Layla cried and darted forward.

Her vampire speed had her at Kyran's side before the bike clattered to the ground, its wheels still spinning.

Kyran had landed on his front. He was breathing hard, fighting to take in air. There was blood *everywhere*. It was seeping out to pool under him. The sheer amount of injuries on him had Layla's heart racing with fear, and a thirst she couldn't even think of quenching.

She turned to see Machado had followed her, and was staring at Kyran with shock. This wasn't Kyran trying to annoy the vamages by coming home bleeding. He was seriously hurt this time.

"Get Hadrian," Layla said with urgency. "Go!"

Machado took off at once. Layla turned back to Kyran, but didn't know what to do. Her hand hovered over his bleeding, torn back, but she didn't touch him. She knew Kyran didn't like her touching him.

"Kyran," she called. She leant over him, trying to catch a glimpse of his face, to see if he was even conscious.

The pounding footsteps made Layla look up to see Hadrian running towards them, Machado at his heels.

Hadrian saw her crouched over Kyran and small sparks flew in the air. "Get away from him!" he snarled.

Layla scampered back, and Hadrian fell to his knees at Kyran's side. He turned Kyran over, gathering his son's injured body into his arms. Kyran's eyes were closed.

"Kyran," Hadrian breathed, horrified at the state of his son. His vamage senses had picked out every bleeding wound on Kyran's body, and it left Hadrian alarmed, and dangerously furious. The very air began to smell like smoke.

Kyran's eyes opened to no more than thin slits. He was barely conscious, but he managed a dry, throaty rasp. "Father?"

"I'm here," Hadrian said. "I'm here, Kyran. You're home. I've got you, son. I've got you."

Kyran's eyes slipped shut and his head lolled back.

Hadrian hugged Kyran, cradling him to his chest. His eyes were a liquid gold as his anger spiralled out, making lightning storm across the dark sky. Some of the bolts fell to the ground, sizzling the air, leaving the ground scorched. Machado and Layla would have run to safety if they weren't rooted to the spot by sheer fear.

Hadrian didn't know who was responsible for Kyran's injuries, but he promised himself the *entire realm* would pay.

No one got away with hurting Hadrian's son.

No one.

# 28

# PAYBACK

The door opened and Scott poked his head inside the busy room. "We have another group on the way," he said. "They should arrive in the next hour."

Aaron held in his groan. Another influx of injured mages coming to the City of Ailsa for refuge. They still hadn't finished healing and settling the last crowd, and here was Scott informing them of more.

"Scott, wait," Ella called, as Scott pulled back to leave. She gestured for Ava to come forward. "Here, hold this." She guided Ava to hold the cloth to the bleeding shoulder of the mage seated before her. "Apply a little more pressure," she said. "That's it. Just stay here; I need a quick word with Scott."

Ava nodded, and Ella got up and hurried to Scott, stepping outside with him.

Aaron looked back to his own charge: a small seven year old with a broken arm and first-degree burns. A huge gash in his leg had been bleeding, but Aaron had taken care of that, tying a belt above the wound to slow the blood loss. He had a cloth held to the cut, but that was more to hide the sight of it, so the little boy didn't start crying again.

"You doing okay?" Aaron asked. The boy sniffed, but didn't speak. Aaron looked to the Empaths at the other side of the room, attending to the other victims, healing one after the other. He turned back to the boy and smiled. "It's almost your turn," he said. "You're a champ; you can manage a few more minutes, yeah?"

The boy didn't say anything, but nodded his head as he clutched his broken arm to his chest, dried tear tracks on his face.

Aaron looked to the Empaths again. He knew there was nothing that could be done. The Empaths were working as fast as they could, making their way through the long line of injured mages, attending to the critical and small children first, but there were just so many of them.

Hunters and other mages were crammed inside the cottage, helping the wounded and keeping them as comfortable as possible until an Empath became available to heal them. Mages with minor injuries were in the rooms upstairs, resting and healing on their own.

Aaron lifted the cloth to check the boy's leg, and was relieved to see it had stopped bleeding. "Not long now," he said to him, spotting Amber finish healing a young girl and move onto the last victim in the line. He stood up to see if any of the other Empaths were done, and could help the little boy next. "You'll be healed in no time," he said distractedly. "Just a few more min—"

"What's a Scorcher?" the boy asked in a small voice.

Aaron turned to him. The fear in the child's wide eyes was heartbreaking. "Why?" Aaron asked, managing to keep his voice steady despite how fast his heart was racing.

"That's what it said," the boy said in a haunted voice. "In the sky, before...before the fire started."

Aaron didn't need any further explanation.

It had been two weeks since Kyran escaped Salvador and returned to Hadrian, and the very next morning the massacres had started. City after city was Q-Zoned. Sometimes it was three, four cities in the one day. And every time, when the terrified residents opened the Gates to escape their Q-Zoned city, they found vamages waiting on the Gateway. Some cities were burnt to the ground, their residents – including the blind Empaths and young children – killed before the forty minutes it took for the Q-Zone to collapse. Others were killed by vamages.

And in each and every city that was attacked, moments before the white walls of the Q-Zone appeared, flames burst into the sky spelling the same message: *Touch the Scorcher and you will burn.*

How Aaron managed it, he didn't know, but he smiled at the boy and shook his head. "You don't have to worry about that. You're safe now."

That, of course, was a lie. Nowhere was safe as long as Hadrian had the Hub. He could Q-Zone the City of Ailsa, if he found out that was where they were all hiding.

Aaron turned to see Amber step back and wipe a hand over her sweaty brow. She was clearly exhausted, having spent hours and hours over the last two weeks healing victims of Hadrian's brutality. But she still turned to face the room with blind eyes and called for the next patient. Aaron lifted the young boy and carried him to the bed, propping him onto it as gently as he could. Leaving him in Amber's care, Aaron walked to the door, needing a moment to himself.

He stepped outside, and caught Ella and Scott arguing.

"What do you want me to do?" Scott was asking, his brow furrowed and eyes dark with annoyance. "Turn my back on them? Tell them to go and find a place on their own?"

"No, of course not–" Ella started.

"Then what, Ella? What do you want from me?" Scott asked. "They're wounded and traumatised after losing their families and their homes. I can't just dump them in some abandoned city with no Empaths and no food – they'll die. I have to bring them here."

"Scott, we're running out of resources," Ella said. "Everyone has given their cottages and their beds to the wounded, but even that's not enough now. I had to put blankets on the hard floor last night for the injured to sleep on. Mary is struggling to feed everyone on her own as every Hunter and mage here is helping the Empaths tend to the wounded." She held Scott's troubled eyes. "Salvador was a sanctuary that Neriah built. No matter how many came asking for refuge, we gave it without question, and we handled it. I'm an Afton too – I will never turn my back on those who need help." She shook her head. "But we're drowning, Scott. We need help to handle this many survivors."

"I'm doing all I can," Scott said. "I've called in as many Empaths as I could from other cities. I've moved the healed and healthy mages out to the City of Nigh. It's not a small city, but it's been abandoned for almost four decades. Hadrian will never think to attack it. I don't know what else to do to ease the congestion. I know there are too many of us here, but it's out of my control."

Aaron could hear the pain in that last statement; for the realm's Controller to admit things were out of his control.

"We just have to ride this out," Scott said. "Hadrian is acting out of anger–"

"Because of what Skyler did to Kyran," Ella finished for him. "I know, Scott, I know." She fell quiet for a moment. "It's Skyler's fault," she said. "The realm is burning because of Skyler's stupidity."

"Skyler crossed a line," Scott said. "He should *never* have hurt Kyran like he did. But Hadrian's using it as an excuse to destroy this realm, and the human one. His vamages force mages to drop their Gates at the time of the attacks, so every city of ours they destroy, the human realm pays the price too." He shook his head, blue eyes dark with pain. "Hadrian is killing both realms, just like he always threatened he would, once he got his powers back. If Skyler hadn't attacked Kyran, Hadrian would have found another reason to do this same thing."

Ella went quiet. After a moment or two she asked, "Have you heard from him?"

Scott shook his head. "No. He's refusing to speak to me, or anyone, actually."

Ella didn't say anything but jerked her head in an awkward nod and took a step back. "I'll start what preparations I can for the newcomers," she said, and hurried back to the cottage they were using as the Empath huts. She passed by Aaron without looking at him, her head bowed to hide from him, but it was in vain. Aaron felt her tears as they leaked out of her eyes.

***

It was chaos: children screaming, stalls broken, clothes and toys trampled under the feet of the panicked mages trying to run, to escape. Kyran's ears were ringing, a noise was slowly deafening him. His chest felt tight, too tight; he couldn't breathe. There was a moment of dizzying confusion before Kyran realised the noise was a scream – *his* scream. He couldn't breathe because he was screaming, and he was screaming because Raoul had his claws in him. He looked down, his stomach turning when he found Raoul's claws had disappeared into his flesh, embedded deep inside his waist. His jeans and shoes were drenched with blood, trickles of it dripping and pooling on the road below his dangling feet. Startled, Kyran looked up, straight into the terrified blue eyes of his mother.

"BEN!" Her cry shattered whatever numbing daze he had been in and the pain slammed into him like a speeding train.

Red-hot agony spread throughout his body. Waves of excruciating pain ripped through him. Kyran could hear Raoul growling in his ear, the single most terrifying sound he had ever heard. His arms were trapped in his mum's hands. She was pulling him one way, Raoul was dragging him in the other, and Kyran knew he was going to be torn in half.

Then his mum let go and he slipped through her fingers. Raoul threw him to his dogs. Teeth. Horrible, unforgivingly sharp teeth bit into his flesh, tearing chunks out of him. Kyran wanted to scream, but instead he was choking on warm blood that gurgled up into his throat.

Kyran snapped awake, breathing hard. His darkened bedroom came into focus and Kyran realised he was at home in the mansion, not in Marwa being attacked by Raoul and his Lycans. He could feel his heart beating short and fast, thudding against his rib cage. He focused on breathing – pulling in long, deep inhalations and pushing them back out, calming himself down. His body ached, sharp stabbing pains in his sides, stomach and arms made Kyran groan. They were only phantom pains, brought on by his nightmares, by him reliving the trauma he had suffered.

Shaking, Kyran wiped at his face, feeling the moisture against his fingers. He hadn't dreamt about the Lycan attack in years, but now he had seen, and felt, the assault for the fourth time this week. Kyran knew the reason why his nightmares were back. He had met Raoul again, faced him for the first time since he was four years old. It was bound to remind him of the horror he had lived through.

For a little while after awakening from the nightmare, Kyran could feel each and every bite, rip and scratch that he had endured that day fourteen years ago. It died down quickly, but it was enough to leave Kyran rattled and at the edge of maddening fury. If Aaron and Rose hadn't been there – if Kyran hadn't been more focused on keeping them safe – he would have taken his revenge on Raoul then and there.

Kyran tried to go back to sleep, but couldn't. He lay in his bed, staring at the ceiling. He had spent the day training, putting his recently healed body through its paces, building his strength back to what it used to be before Skyler's ambush. He was forcing himself through a tough regime, so he should be exhausted and easily able to fall back asleep. But it wasn't happening. It wasn't just because of the nightmares. He was worked up, and he had no idea why. Kyran closed his eyes and breathed out a sigh. That wasn't completely true. He knew why. It had been two weeks since he saw or spoke to his brother. He had become so used to having Aaron around when they'd been researching the legacies together that being away from him for so long now felt odd.

Kyran eventually gave up on sleep and got up. Wincing at the dying phantom pains in his body, he pulled on a top over his pyjama bottoms, and walked out of his room, heading to the kitchen. He would eat something and go train, put his insomnia to good use.

Making his way through the dark and silent manor, Kyran entertained the idea of sneaking out to meet Aaron instead. He could probably make it there and back before dawn. All he needed was five minutes to check Aaron was okay, that Skyler hadn't tried anything after he had escaped on Ella's bike. But then he remembered his father's fury when he was digging bullet after never-ending bullet out of his body, and he squashed the thought of going to Aaron. If Hadrian found out he had gone anywhere near the mages again, he would stay true to his promise and barricade Kyran inside the manor. Kyran shuddered at the thought. He would lose his mind if he was forced to stay inside, with Layla and the vamages working his last nerve. Seeing Aaron was going to have to wait.

Kyran walked into the kitchen and waved a hand, lighting the lamps. When the flickering glow filled the room, Kyran saw the figure sitting at the table, and it startled him so much he came to a sudden stop.

"Father," Kyran breathed in recognition. Then he frowned. "Why are you sitting in the dark?"

A tired-looking Hadrian only smiled, a steaming mug before him on the table, as well as a covered plate. "I couldn't sleep," he said. "So I thought I would come downstairs and start on breakfast."

Kyran frowned. "Since when did you start cooking again?" he asked. "What happened to your staff?"

"They're still here," Hadrian said. "But I felt like making breakfast, the way I used to when you were younger."

Kyran smiled and walked over to him, distractedly rubbing a hand across his side, soothing the twinge of pain still lingering from his nightmare. He sat down at the table. "Why would you do that? I seem to remember you saying that was the worst time of your life."

Hadrian chuckled. "It was," he answered. "Cooking wasn't a skill I possessed before I met you."

Kyran ducked his head. "I know," he said. He gave Hadrian a cheeky smirk. "I remember those half-cooked meals."

"Cut me some slack, Kyran," Hadrian said, leaning back in his chair. "When you came to me I was living alone. I didn't have a vamage staff to help me then. I was barely looking after myself. I wasn't in a position to look after a kid. But there you were, and I had to do the best I could."

Kyran nodded, sombre at the reminder of how he came to be with Hadrian. He gave Hadrian a tight smile. "You did good."

"No, I didn't." At Kyran's frown, Hadrian shook his head. "I'm not foolish enough to think you don't remember how hard it was at the beginning; how evident it was that I didn't want you staying with me."

Kyran did remember. He remembered with the utmost clarity, overhearing Hadrian's heated conversations many a times.

*I can't do this! You have to take him.*

*I can't, Hadrian, you know that.*

*You're the one who brought him to me, you can take him away.*

*Hadrian, you know it's not safe.*

*He's working my last nerve!*

*He's a kid. Can you blame him after what he's lived through?*

*I'm not cut out for this. He's better off staying with you.*

*He's the safest with you. It's just for a little while. Chris will come for him. We both know he will.*

Kyran pulled himself out of those memories. The same conversation had happened more times than Kyran cared to admit. He noted the way Hadrian was staring at him, waiting for him to speak. Kyran shrugged as nonchalantly as he could. "It's understandable," he mumbled. "I wasn't your responsibility."

"That shouldn't have mattered." Hadrian said. "It's no excuse, but I was in a bad place. I was alone, the only one of my kind. And my former friends – people I thought of as my family – were trying to kill me." He smirked, but his eyes showed his pain. "I was so wrapped up in my own misery I didn't give you much thought. I just wanted Chris to come and take you away, so I could get on with my life." He looked up at Kyran. "I didn't see it until later but before you, I wasn't living, not really – I was only surviving." His face darkened. "Neriah took away my ability to be a mage, so I lived like a demon, drinking blood to sustain myself. I was...paralysed in a sense. I couldn't feel anything; didn't care to feel anything." He looked at Kyran and the corners of his mouth turned upwards into a small smile. "That is, until you came into my life and forced me to feel again, to live again."

Kyran tilted his head as his eyes narrowed at Hadrian. "What's with all the sentiment all of a sudden?" he asked. "What's got into you?"

"It's not what's got into me, Kyran," Hadrian said. "It's what you had in you when you came home." His eyes were burning, but not with anger this time, but pain. "All those bullets, those cuts that could only have come from a blade." Kyran shifted uncomfortably, avoiding his father's intense eyes. "You were in such a bad state, I had to call the Empaths in my zones to come to your aid, something I never thought I would have to do." Hadrian paused. "The hours you spent unconscious, I sat by your side and thought about the last fourteen years – the way you came to be in my care, how reluctant both of us were to become each other's family, and how incapable I am now of living without you." A rare flash of vulnerability lit Hadrian's eyes. "If something happened to you, if I lost you–"

"Mages can't kill me," Kyran reminded. "I was never in any fatal danger." His father didn't need to know about the bullets Skyler had prepared with his name on them, or how close Sam came to executing him.

Hadrian was watching him closely. "I know about the Shattered ones with the Hunters when you were ambushed."

Kyran's face dropped. "How did–?"

"It's not important," Hadrian said. "You can keep what happened from me, but I know you didn't simply *run* into Hunters. They were lying in wait for you. They attacked you." Again he paused, and the gold glints in his eyes shone brightly. "You are the holder of three legacies. There must be a reason you couldn't fight back, and there are only so many explanations that make sense." He shook his head when Kyran opened his mouth to speak. "I don't want to know what happened. It doesn't matter now. But there were Shattered ones there, who could have attacked you, could have *killed* you." His eyes were staring so deep into Kyran's it was as if he were probing his mind, to see that exact moment when Sam almost shot him in the head. Kyran dropped his gaze.

"The fact that you could have been killed in that ambush, that I came close to losing my son–" Hadrian forced in a breath, closing his eyes – "I don't know how to deal with that," he confessed. "And I'm afraid my anger might end up burning this realm to the ground."

Kyran snapped his head up, a jolt of panic running through him. "You said you wouldn't do anything," he said quickly.

Hadrian held his eyes. "I did," he said. "But rage doesn't remember promises."

"Father," Kyran started, shifting in his seat, sitting taller. "What happened is between me and the Hunters. It's *my* fight; *I* will handle it. You don't need to get involved. I want your word that you won't do anything to the Hunters or any of the mages in Neriah's zones."

Hadrian lowered his eyes so he didn't have to look at Kyran as he lied to him. "You have my word," he said quietly, and raised the mug to his lips.

Kyran let out a breath of relief, visibly relaxing.

"You need to remember one thing, Kyran," Hadrian started, putting down his drink. "I never have, and never will, tolerate anyone or anything hurting you. I've worked hard, spent years training you, making damn sure that you can take on any foe and walk away without a scratch." His eyes glinted gold. "So when you come home, wounded beyond description, and refuse to tell me how you got into that state—"

"Father," Kyran cut across him. "I told you it's my problem. I'll deal with it. You don't have to worry." He smiled with reassurance. "It won't happen again."

"Good," Hadrian said. "Because you may have come in to my life uninvited, but I don't know how to live without you now."

Kyran smiled. "I'm not going anywhere, Father. You can stop worrying."

"Never," Hadrian replied. "With a son like you, there'll always be some reason to worry."

"What's that supposed to mean?" Kyran asked with a short laugh.

Hadrian took a moment to look at Kyran. "I've waited for a week, Kyran," he said with a sigh. "When were you planning on telling me?"

Kyran looked lost. "About what?" he asked.

"About the nightmares."

Kyran tensed, the smile slipping off his face. He looked surprised.

"You think I can't tell when you've had a nightmare?" Hadrian asked. "I've brought you up, Kyran. There's very little you can hide from me. You might have forgotten, but I'm the one who stayed in your room all those nights you were too afraid to sleep, in case you relived the attack in your dreams. I'm the one who guided you through the phantom pains, taught you how to deal with them, how to get rid of them." His gaze dropped to Kyran's side, where he knew the most pain usually originated, before looking back at Kyran. "Why didn't you tell me the nightmares were back?"

Kyran took a moment to answer. "I can deal with them now," he said. He attempted a smile. "I'm all grown up, Father. I don't need you to chase away my demons. I can face them on my own."

"You'll never be on your own, not while I'm around," Hadrian said. He leant forward and Kyran could read the worry clear in his eyes. "Why are the nightmares back?"

Kyran paused. He had to be careful with what he said. Hadrian didn't know about him taking Aaron to the Blade of Adams in an attempt to meet the Influence. He had to keep it that way. "I saw him," he admitted. "Raoul. I met him."

Hadrian looked surprised. He sat back in his chair, staring at Kyran. "When?"

"Shortly before I ran into the Hunters," Kyran said. "I guess that's why the dreams are back."

Hadrian wasn't satisfied with that brief answer, Kyran could see it in his expression, in the tight line of his jaw. But he didn't push for more. Instead he asked with a quiet fury, "Did Raoul attack you?"

"No," Kyran replied. "It was a very brief encounter, but I think it was enough to jog the memory." He shifted in his seat, under his father's intense stare. "It's fine, though. The nightmares will die down eventually." He smiled at Hadrian. "It's nothing I can't handle."

Hadrian didn't look at all pleased. "Kyran—" he started, with a shake of his head.

"We have bigger things to worry about," Kyran interrupted.

Hadrian clicked his mouth shut, studying his son silently. Then he nodded and sat back, letting the topic go, for now. "You're right," he said. "And that's why I'm sending you on an assignment in the morning."

Kyran was surprised. "I thought you wanted me to stay in and *rest*." Kyran emphasised the word with great distaste.

Hadrian chuckled. "I can see how much *resting* you're doing, out on your training grounds. If you've got so much energy, you may as well run an errand for me."

Kyran nodded his head. "As you wish, Father."

"But first —" Hadrian reached over and lifted the napkin covering the plate on the table— "have some breakfast."

Kyran let out a laugh at the misshapen potato lumps lying on the plate. "Alphabet bites," he said fondly.

"Just like the ones you insisted you wanted when you were five," Hadrian said with a smile. "I couldn't make them then...and I can't make them now."

Kyran lifted a strange R-shaped one, that could very easily have been a B or maybe it was a P. He bit into it. "At least they're cooked this time," he said, smirking.

"Experience teaches us all," Hadrian mused, lifting his mug in a mock toast before draining it in one go.

\*\*\*

"There's another group on the way," Scott told the crowd as it gathered before the Gate guarding the City of Ailsa. "Their city was attacked just after dawn this morning," Scott continued. "A large number of them managed to get out in time, and get past the vamages. That's the good news. The bad news is most of them are injured. We need to get them to the Empaths as soon as possible."

Standing in the midst of mages and Hunters, Aaron listened to Scott's instructions. He noted how tired Scott looked, his pinched face seemed even paler in the early morning light. As Aaron gazed through the gathered crowd, he saw that everyone seemed just as weary as their Controller. They had been dealing with the aftermath of Hadrian's relentless attacks for too long. Taking care of those who came to Ailsa, hours after losing family and friends, in physical and emotional pain, was soul shattering. The harsh cruelty of war was wearing everyone down; taking the light from their eyes and the smiles from their lips.

Aaron's gaze rested on his parents. They looked just as worn down as the others. But there was another reason for the lines on their brows. They had rushed to Salvador with Scott at the news that Kyran had been captured and was badly injured at Skyler's hands, but they never got to see their son. They arrived an hour after Kyran had escaped. Since that day, neither Chris or Kate had slept properly. Aaron could hear them, night after night, pacing the length of their room, talking to one another, fretting and worrying about Kyran.

Kate met Aaron's stare with tired blue eyes and forced a half-hearted smile. Aaron gave her just as empty a smile and looked away. He spotted Rose at the other side of the street. Aaron took another look around, but couldn't find Sam anywhere. Aaron hadn't spoken to Sam ever since Kyran was almost executed by him a fortnight before. Rose had revealed to Aaron what lies Skyler had told them, how he convinced them that Kyran had murdered their parents, just to get them to turn against him. Aaron understood that Sam and Rose were tricked into taking part in Kyran's arrest, but that didn't mean he could forget what Sam had almost done. The memory of seeing the gun in Sam's hand, the barrel aimed at his defenceless brother, it was something Aaron could never forget, and never forgive Sam for either.

"They're here," Scott said, holding on to his pendant.

He slipped the chain over his head and pocketed it, having to limit the time he spent wearing it in order to keep hidden from Hadrian. Scott waved a hand and the Gate slid open. Aaron moved with the crowd to wait at the open Gate.

Aaron's stomach turned when he saw the all too familiar sight of wounded, bleeding, traumatised mages making their way down the Gateway of Ailsa. Their pain-filled moans and cries pierced through Aaron. He moved closer to the Gate. Some of the Hunters, including Ella, stepped past the threshold of the Gate, to help the mages that were struggling to walk. They guided them into the city, supporting them to the Empath cottages. Some were injured so badly, they were levitated in the air.

Aaron caught sight of one of the mages, right at the back of the line, who was limping rather badly. A ragged and singed scarf covered his head, his hands and clothes covered in soot, he weakly made his way forward. The man stumbled and fell, hitting the ground hard. Aaron hurried past the mages entering the city and ran down the Gateway.

He reached him and bent down to put a hand to the man's shaking shoulder. "Are you okay?" he asked.

He mentally kicked himself. Every time he had to help someone, he asked this same stupid question. Of course they weren't okay. But it was force of habit; an instinctual question that came to his lips when seeing someone in distress.

But the man under the scarf chuckled. "I will be," he said.

He raised his head and Aaron met the glittery blue eyes of the vamage, Machado. Aaron's body seized. Panic and disbelief fell over him. He pulled back, but Machado swung a hand at him, knocking the hilt of his gun into Aaron's head, and propelling him into darkness.

*\*\**

Aaron awoke with a throbbing pain in his head. He moaned and reached up to touch the sore, bruised spot on his forehead. He blinked in surprise and confusion at finding himself in a lavishly furnished room, seated in a comfortable armchair next to a fireplace, which had flames heartily dancing in them, washing the room with warmth. Aaron still got goosebumps, though, as he spotted a large painting of Kyran and Hadrian hanging over the fireplace.

"Good afternoon," a voice greeted him, startling Aaron.

He turned and his heart almost leapt into his mouth.

Hadrian was sitting in the chair next to him, calmly watching him, with a twisted smile. "I'm so glad you're finally awake."

# 29

## DEALINGS WITH THE DEVIL

Hadrian sat relaxed in his chair, one leg crossed over the other, the fingers of one hand at his temple. Sharp hazel eyes took careful note of Aaron, who in comparison was tensed in his seat, staring back at him in shock and surprise.

"Can I get you anything?" Hadrian asked. "Something to drink, perhaps?"

Aaron swallowed hard, fighting back his panic. He kept his eyes on Hadrian, even though his senses picked up the presence of other vamages dotted in the corners of the room, half hidden in the shadows.

Aaron gathered all the bravado he possessed and injected it into his voice, to keep it steady as he asked, "Where am I?"

Hadrian's hand lifted and gestured to the room. "My home, of course," he said. "Where did you expect to wake up? In a dank, miserable dungeon?" His eyes darkened with amusement. "That was my first choice, by the way." He reached over to the side table to pour a dark red liquid from a bottle into a glass. "But I couldn't do that, not to you." He brought the glass to his lips but his eyes stayed on Aaron. "My boy wouldn't have liked that." He took a sip.

Aaron resisted the urge to shudder. He looked around the room, so he wouldn't have to watch Hadrian casually drinking blood as if it were any other beverage. There was a door at each wall of the room. Which was the way out? Even if he figured that out, did he stand a chance of reaching it? He was unarmed, surrounded by vamages, with their leader seated in the chair next to his.

Aaron steeled himself and met Hadrian's eyes. "You brought me here so you can kill me and take the legacy," he said. "So what are you waiting for?"

A slow smile spread over Hadrian's face. He chuckled. "You're more like Chris than I thought," he said. "He has a penchant for stupid questions too."

Aaron felt a jolt of anger make it through the pit of fear inside him.

"Maybe I haven't brought you here to kill you," Hadrian said, putting down his glass. "Maybe, you're here as retribution." The gold specks in his eyes started to lighten. "Hunters took my son and hurt him. Why shouldn't I do the same to you?"

Aaron had heard the phrase *sick with fear*, but this was the first time he actually understood it. He had to fight to keep his breakfast down. His body was quivering with nerves, but Aaron would be damned if he showed it. He sat as rigid as he could, eyes fixed on Hadrian.

"I didn't hurt Kyran," he said, not in a bid to escape Hadrian's wrath, but to make that point known: he could never harm his brother.

"You may not have been the one to physically assault him, but you're the reason he was ambushed," Hadrian replied. "Kyran can keep his secrets, but I know he was attacked when he took you to the Blade of Adams. I also know that he contacted the Influence, and if I were to guess, I would say it was to find a way to get the legacy out of you without it killing you."

Aaron didn't say anything, neither to confirm nor deny Hadrian's words. Rose may have taken the bullets out of Kyran's guns, but if Kyran hadn't been next to the Blade of Adams, he would have been able to fight the Hunters using his powers. He had three legacies after all. It was because of Aaron that Kyran went to the Blade of Adams, and was left defenceless when the Hunters attacked. Hadrian was right; it *was* Aaron's fault.

Hadrian shifted in his seat, both feet on the ground now as he leant towards Aaron. "I know you weren't born in this realm," he started, "so you didn't grow up hearing stories about the cruel vamage that was once an Elemental. You know nothing about this war, what instigated it, and what it will take to end it." His eyes were slowly changing from hazel to amber. "But I want you to know that this war is not my doing. I never intended to make this realm burn, never meant to make it *bleed*. It was Neriah who started this, and I had thought it would end with him, but he passed that death sentence onto you." His gaze felt heavy on Aaron, as if it were a physical thing weighing down on him. "Even if I tried, I wouldn't be able to make you understand how *badly* I need that last legacy residing inside you."

The flames in the fireplace crackled loudly beside Aaron.

"I have spent the last sixteen years exiled from those I thought of as my family because of these legacies," Hadrian continued. "I have given up *everything* in the quest to have the power of all four elements. The only thing standing in my way is you."

Aaron had to force himself to stay sitting. Every fibre of his being was screaming at him to get up and run. To use the power of Earth, to fashion a weapon, to do *something* before Hadrian came in for the kill. But Aaron couldn't move, couldn't even look away from the powerful vamage seated next to him. Fear had him rooted to the spot.

"But it's here, this exact point, that presents a conundrum," Hadrian said quietly. "You have the legacy I want, the last piece I need to conquer this realm. But by killing you, I inevitably hurt the one who matters most to me."

Aaron watched as Hadrian sat back in his seat. His eyes were on Aaron, his gaze piercing through him. Aaron didn't need anyone to say it; he could see how much Hadrian *hated* him. His hand lifted and Aaron tensed, ready to throw himself out of the way of the fire Hadrian was about to direct at him. But Hadrian didn't point at him. He aimed at the door to his right and it swung open.

"Go," he said.

Aaron looked to the door, then back at Hadrian in stunned disbelief.

"Leave," Hadrian said. "I'm giving you the chance to get up and walk away from here, unharmed. I won't come for you, and neither will any of my vamages."

Aaron didn't move. "You're letting me go?" he asked, his heart hammering at his insides.

"I'm letting you *live*, but on a set of conditions," Hadrian said. "You will leave this realm for good. You will go back to the human world you grew up in. You've lived there all your life, you can spend the rest of it there too. Take your parents and leave, and never come back here." His eyes glinted a perfect gold. "And *never* meet Kyran again."

Aaron stilled as understanding filtered through the shock.

"You will disappear from Kyran's life," Hadrian continued. "You will leave today, without contacting him, without explaining anything to him. You won't answer if he calls to you. You will ignore him, and by doing so, you will get to live out the rest of your days in peace. Once you die a natural death, your legacy will move to an Afton, and I can take the legacy from there." He lifted his glass and looked away from Aaron. "Go now," he instructed. "Leave."

Aaron didn't move. He stared at Hadrian. The fear that he had been fighting evaporated in an instant.

"My invitation won't last forever," Hadrian said, filling his glass again. "Once that door closes, so does your opportunity to live."

Aaron stayed where he was. In a quivering voice, Aaron spoke, his voice barely above a whisper. "You were a mage once. An Elemental, and you changed to a vamage, just so you could take the legacies and become the only leader of the realm." He stared at Hadrian. "And now, after fighting a war for sixteen years, when you have just one more legacy to steal, you're giving it up?"

Hadrian turned his head to meet Aaron's stare, his eyes blazing, but he smirked and said, "I told you my reasons."

"No." Aaron shook his head, his voice louder, stronger. "No, I don't think you did. You're not letting me go because you don't want to hurt Kyran," he said. "If that was the case, you would never have instructed him to kill me. You want me gone because you're scared if I stay, Kyran will choose me and not you."

The flames in the fireplace shot up and crackled with force at Hadrian's anger, but Aaron ignored it.

"If you kill me for the legacy, you'll lose Kyran," he continued. "If you don't kill me, you'll never get all four legacies and rule the realm. You can't control the realm with only three legacies at your command, but you still want me gone from this realm. Why?" He held Hadrian's golden eyes. "Because of Kyran. Because he's more important to you than the legacies you've been fighting so long for."

The vamages in the room were growing restless as the flames in the fireplace licked the top of the hearth, about to spill out into the room. Aaron didn't care. He was too far gone to stop now.

"You're so terrified that Kyran is going to leave you, that he's going to come back to his *real* family, that you're trying to bribe me into leaving," he said, his voice picking up in volume. "You know that as long as I'm here, Kyran will have a connection to his true family, and you don't want that. That's why you're giving me a way out. You want me gone from his life, because you know when it comes down to it, Kyran will always choose me. Because no matter how strong the sense of loyalty is, blood will *always* be thicker."

The glass in Hadrian's hand cracked under his grip. The only sound to follow the sharp tinkle was the crackling of the flames and Aaron's quick breaths. Anger had replaced his fright, and Aaron was raging; furious that Hadrian was trying to distance Kyran from him.

Hadrian put the broken glass down on the side table and leant towards Aaron. "Out of that whole speech, can you pick out the *one* word you probably shouldn't have said in front of me?"

Aaron smirked back. "I'm not afraid of you," he said, and he meant it. "Go ahead, kill me, drink my blood. You can do what you like, but I'm not leaving this realm. I won't abandon my brother. So if you want to kill me, go ahead," he challenged. "I'll die knowing you've lost Kyran forever."

Hadrian didn't say anything. For a moment he didn't move, just stared at Aaron with nothing but absolute fury. Then his gaze darted behind Aaron, to the vamages in the corner, and he nodded at them. Aaron was grabbed by both arms and hauled out of the chair almost instantly. They held him in place as Hadrian stood up.

"I was planning on killing you as swiftly and as painlessly as possible, should you not take up my offer," he said, walking towards him. He waved a hand and the door he had opened shut with a bang. "But after what you just said, it's only right that you suffer." He stopped before Aaron. "But I want you to understand one thing." He lowered himself to look Aaron in the eye. "No one will take Kyran from me," he said. "Not your parents, and most definitely not *you*." His eyes blazed. "Kyran will be upset at your demise, and I wanted to save him from that pain, but with time he will get over it. He won't leave me. He needs me, just as much as I need him."

"He may think of you as his father," Aaron said. "But I'm his brother. He will never forgive you if you kill me."

Hadrian chuckled as he stood tall. He gently patted Aaron's cheek. "Foolish boy," he said. "Kyran will never come to know who killed you. He will believe whatever story I offer to him. He will also believe that after you died, the legacy went back to Ella Afton." He gave Aaron a smug smile. "And after I kill her, Kyran will believe I have the last legacy. He will never know I got it from you."

Aaron stared at him, too disgusted to find his voice and talk back. Hadrian turned to his vamages. "Do what you like with him," he said. "Just make sure not a drop of his blood spills." He looked back at Aaron. "That honour will be mine."

***

For the third time in the last ten minutes, Kyran came to a stop, feeling the all too familiar ache deep in his core. He took a moment to steady himself, holding a hand against a tree for support and closed his eyes. He understood the strange sensation inside him, this heavy feeling in his bones; his brother was calling out to him.

"Is there a problem, Scorcher?" a vamage asked him.

Kyran straightened up. He turned and gave the four vamages accompanying him an annoyed look. "I don't know why Father insisted that you lot come with me," he grouched. "I can do this on my own."

"We're not exactly pleased with this arrangement either," one of the vamages replied tersely.

"Guess that makes it a little more bearable then," Kyran said.

He pushed himself to keep walking, until they came out of the forest and onto a stretch of empty land. The recent rainstorm had left large puddles in the uneven ground, which

Kyran and the vamages trod through as they made their way forward.

Kyran felt another desperate call of Aaron's and he closed his eyes, wincing. *Damn it, Ace,* he thought to himself. *Not now. I can't come just yet.* His father had sent him on an assignment with four vamages by his side. He couldn't leave and go see Aaron. His brother was just going to have to wait.

It was as Kyran climbed to the top of the hill, that he saw him – the figure in a hooded white robe, on the other side of the mountain. Kyran came to a halt, his eyes fixed on the Lurker. It was the same Lurker he had been seeing all over the realm. Kyran didn't know how it was possible that he knew it was the same person, but somehow he did.

"What's wrong now, Scorcher?" a vamage asked, sounding tired as well as annoyed.

Kyran looked to them. They were staring at him with impatience, eyes narrowed and mouths set in grim lines. The Lurker was clearly visible on the cliff behind Kyran. Were they really this blind? Couldn't they see a Lurker had spotted them?

"Look over there," Kyran prompted, tilting his head to the other side of the cliff. "What do you see?"

The vamages glanced behind Kyran and then met his eyes with a bored expression.

"I don't know," one said. "Grass?"

"It's the way we came," another said. "We got to the other side of the mountain. Good for us," he mocked.

Kyran turned around to see the Lurker was gone.

"We still have a long way to go," another vamage was saying, but Kyran was barely listening. His gaze searched the hillside, squinting in the sun to find the white-robed man. "We need to keep moving if we're going to reach the camp," the vamage finished.

Kyran found the Lurker, further down the mountainside, standing next to the mouth of the woods Kyran had just walked out of. The Lurker lifted an arm and pointed at something. Kyran followed the direction to see he was gesturing to the portal Kyran and the vamages had used to arrive here.

Kyran frowned. What was going on? Why was the Lurker gesturing to the portal? Was he asking what the portal was doing there? Or was he pointing it out to Kyran? Trying to suggest he should use it and go back?

Aaron's call tugged at Kyran's heart, and Kyran forced in a deep breath. He shook his head, to clear it. When he looked up, the Lurker was gone.

"You know what," Kyran started, facing the vamages. "I don't think I'm up to this."

The vamages looked confused. "What do you mean?" one asked.

"I'm going home," Kyran said. If he left now, he could quickly go and see Aaron before returning to the manor. "The assignment isn't urgent. It can wait a few days." He took a step to go back but found to his shocked surprise, all four vamages blocking his way.

"Hadrian said he wanted this assignment completed today," one vamage said.

"And I'm saying it can wait," Kyran said.

"But it's a simple task," he replied. "All we have to do is get to the Pecosa camp and deliver Hadrian's letter to the chief."

"Then you do it," Kyran said, taking the letter out of his pocket and throwing it to the ground. "I'm going home."

The vamages blocked him again.

"You're coming with us," one vamage said.

Kyran frowned. "Since when do *you* tell *me* what to do?"

"You have to go to the camp," another vamage replied. "That's Hadrian's orders."

"And my orders are to *back off*," Kyran warned.

Two of the vamages had their hands on their belt, ready to draw their weapons. Kyran looked at them with sharp green eyes. "Have you lost your mind?" he asked. "You're going to try to attack me?"

"We don't want to," one said, his voice a little shaky, "but we've been instructed to take you to the camp, by any means necessary."

Kyran's eyes widened with surprise. "Really?" he asked. "By who?" His gaze flitted from one vamage to the next. "Machado put you up to this?"

The vamages didn't reply.

"You must have done something exceptionally stupid to annoy Machado so much that he's trying to get you killed at my hands," Kyran said. "Lucky for you, I don't want Machado to get what he wants. Get out of my way."

Kyran moved forward and all four vamages pulled out their guns, aiming at Kyran.

"Sorry, Scorcher," one said, "but you're coming with us. We can't let you go back yet."

Kyran stilled. He turned to look at the vamage. "What did you just say?" he asked.

"I meant, you have to complete the assignment first," the vamage said, trying to cover his mistake.

But it was too late. Kyran glanced at the other three vamages to see their agitation and sheer nervousness at their fellow vamage's slip up. Aaron's call pulled at Kyran's core, and a sudden suspicion grew in Kyran's mind. Why did the vamages not want him going back home? At the same time when Aaron's calls were growing in desperation? What if...?

Kyran stumbled back a step. No, it couldn't be. His father would never do that. He couldn't. But Kyran couldn't push away the doubt clouding his senses. Every fibre of his being was screaming at him to go and find his brother. Kyran's eyes darkened. He strode forward. The vamages took aim, but Kyran's jolt of air pushed them aside, throwing them to the ground before even one of them could fire their weapon. A swift kick to one's head and a punch to another had two knocked out. The other two vamages got to their feet, but seconds later Kyran let their unconscious forms hit the ground. Kyran took off, bolting for the portal that would take him back home.

***

Aaron threw himself to the ground to avoid the fireball one vamage sent at him, and rolled out of the way of another. The vamages crowded around him laughed, amused by his attempts to escape their attacks. They cheered whenever a fireball caught Aaron, or a jolt knocked him to the ground. But Aaron got up every time, refusing to take their abuse lying down.

Aaron's hands were bound by two Inhibitor cuffs, so he couldn't retaliate. His only defence was to try to avoid getting hit. The vamages took it in turns to throw jolts of power at him. They weren't allowed to kill him or make him bleed, but that didn't mean they couldn't break his bones.

Two jolts of air caught Aaron, slamming him to the ground with brutal force. A shock of pain ran down Aaron's back, making him cry out. He didn't get the chance to recover, as another jolt crashed into his side, snapping one of his ribs. Aaron curled to the side, gritting his teeth. He heaved himself onto his hands and knees, but couldn't climb back onto his feet.

Two pairs of hands grabbed him by the arms and Aaron was hauled up. His bruised and battered body protested violently, but there was nothing Aaron could do to stop them. A vamage sauntered up to Aaron with a gleeful smile on his face. He took a fistful of Aaron's hair and pulled, forcing his head back so he could look into Aaron's eyes.

"You had enough, boy?" he asked. "Or are you willing to play a little longer?"

Aaron spat at him, catching him right in the eye. The vamage viciously backhanded Aaron before grabbing him by his hair again, wrenching his head back so far, Aaron thought he was going to snap it clean off.

"You're lucky we don't have permission to kill you," the vamage snarled in Aaron's face. "Or I would have made you pay for that."

Aaron's mouth was filling with blood – he could taste it. He gave the vamage a bloodied grin, before spitting at him again.

The vamage struck him in the stomach and Aaron doubled over, unable to breathe. He gasped and coughed, wheezing to suck in air. The vamage cleaned Aaron's blood off his face, before grabbing him with both hands. He threw Aaron to the ground and kicked him as the surrounding vamages cheered the ruthless attack on.

The vamage finally pulled back, breathing hard. Aaron lowered his bound hands from trying to protect his head, but made no attempt to get up. His body felt like it was on fire. Every breath was a struggle and he couldn't move without causing himself pain. Still, he turned his head, his gaze flitting past the vamages to rest at the door at the very end of the chamber.

The vamage followed his gaze and chuckled. "Who are you looking for?" he asked, a glint of deep amusement in his cruel eyes. He knelt down beside him. "You really think your brother is going to come for you?" he asked. "He's not here," he told Aaron with great pleasure. "The Scorcher has been sent from the manor, and everyone knows to keep him away until your last breath. By the time he gets back, there will be no trace of you left." He smiled at Aaron, showing his fangs. "He's not coming to save you. No one is."

Aaron closed his eyes, and deep in his mind, he called for Kyran one last time.

The doors Aaron had been watching flew off their hinges and slammed into the adjacent wall. Kyran stopped at the threshold. His darkened eyes scanned the chamber until they found Aaron, lying limp on the ground in the midst of vamages.

Kyran's gaze shifted to the vamages, all of who stilled, their eyes growing wide at the sight of the Scorcher. The four lines across the back of Kyran's right hand began to glow, as did the circle on his chest. Then, like a hurricane, Kyran descended upon the vamages.

# 30

## COMPLICATED RELATIONSHIPS

There was no need for Hadrian to walk into the chamber. The doorless entry showed him the bodies of his vamages – scattered across the vast hall, lifeless and still. Kyran had drained the life out of them, taken Aaron Adams and left the manor. A small number of vamages that had been torturing Aaron managed to run before Kyran got to them, but most of them didn't make it.

The sound of doors slamming reached Hadrian. He straightened up and turned around, just in time to see Kyran appear at the end of the corridor. He looked livid: his eyes were dark slits of poison green, his jaw was clenched, and his hands curled into balls.

"What did you think you were doing?" Kyran snarled as he walked up to him.

Hadrian tilted his head to gesture to the chamber behind him. "I could ask you the same."

Kyran was breathing hard, rage emanating from him in thick waves as he came to stand before his father. "You tried to have Aaron killed!"

"And you went ahead and killed many of my men," Hadrian said.

"I would have killed *all* of them," Kyran spat. "If my priority hadn't been to get Aaron out, I would have made sure not even *one* of your vamages survived."

"They were only following orders." Hadrian didn't try to cover it up. He couldn't fool Kyran now, not when Kyran had caught Aaron with the vamages – he had to admit he attempted to kill the last legacy holder.

"You played me," Kyran said, sounding just as hurt as he was angry. "You sent me on a useless mission so I wouldn't be here when your vamages attacked Aaron. You told your men to keep me away, so I couldn't help him." He glared at Hadrian with venomous eyes. "You went behind my back."

"Don't act like this is a surprise, Kyran," Hadrian said. "I gave you a month, at your behest, to try to *save* him." He said the word with disdain. "Yesterday was the thirtieth day of that agreement. I told you I wanted the boy on the thirty-first day. You didn't act on that instruction, so I did it for you."

Kyran's eyes darkened a shade further. His balled hands were shaking with the effort it took to hold back his rage. "That legacy will be yours," he said, his voice low and guttural. "But you will never try anything like this again," he warned. "If your vamages so much as cross Aaron's *shadow*, I will bleed them out – the whole lot of them."

Hadrian stepped forward, his face inches from Kyran's, the gold specks in his eyes glowing with anger. "And what about me?" he asked. "What if *I* go for him? What will you do then?"

Kyran held his eyes. "Understand one thing, Father," he said quietly. "I will break the hand that reaches for my brother's throat, no matter whose it is."

Hadrian stilled, his expression full of shock. He stared at Kyran with stunned disbelief. He hadn't expected that – not from the obedient son who always put his father's needs before all else.

With a glower, Kyran turned and walked away, leaving Hadrian on his own.

\*\*\*

It didn't take long for Aaron to be healed. Amber took all of ten minutes to fix his broken bones and heal the bruises littered all over his body. His parents stayed with him during the treatment, refusing to leave his side. They had been in the street, arguing with Scott, when Aaron had gingerly made his way into the city. Kyran had to hold back on the Gateway, but Aaron knew he wouldn't leave until Aaron was inside the city. Aaron had caught a glimpse of Kyran watching him just as the Gate was sliding shut, moments before he was engulfed in a hug by his mum and dad.

"You need to rest; you're very tired," Amber said, still holding Aaron's hand, her unseeing eyes staring past Aaron's ear.

"It's been an eventful day," Aaron said.

"Don't make jokes, Aaron," Kate said.

"Who's joking?" Aaron asked.

Amber let go of his hand and sat back in her chair. "A few hours of sleep is all you need to get better."

Aaron nodded, then mentally kicked himself. The blind Empath couldn't see him. "Okay, thanks, Amber."

He got off the bed, shrugging away his parents' helping hands. "I'm fine," he insisted. "I'm not made of glass."

They walked out of the Empath's cottage, heading to the line of cottages.

"Can we talk now?" Chris asked.

"I already told you everything," Aaron said. "I don't want to keep going over it."

"You didn't tell me what it was that son of a demon said to you." Chris said. There was such rage in his voice it unnerved Aaron.

Aaron had run through his ordeal as briefly as he could. He didn't have it in him to go through it word for word. He didn't explain to his parents exactly how he was rescued. He just said Kyran arrived and saved him from the vamages. He didn't tell them how Kyran bled out the vamages. They didn't know about their son's special power, and Aaron didn't want to be the one to tell them.

Aaron suppressed a shudder as the memory of Kyran killing the vamages resurfaced in his mind. It was a terrifying sight, seeing the light glow from his chest and hand, those black lines spreading up Kyran's hand and arm, the vamages falling to the ground, dead from Kyran's touch. It was something Aaron would never forget, and as thankful as he was that Kyran saved his life, he would rather pretend it had never happened.

"Aaron?" Chris called, bringing Aaron out of his thoughts. "Tell me, what did Hadrian say to you?"

"I already told you," Aaron mumbled. "He wanted me – us – gone so he got to be Kyran's only family."

A pink flush of anger was spreading up Chris's neck and face. He didn't say anything more, which Aaron was thankful for. Aaron didn't want to keep everything Hadrian had said to him a secret necessarily, but he didn't want to get into it right now. All he wanted at this moment was to fall into his bed and sleep.

"Is there a bed available?" he asked his mum, remembering the injured mages that were recuperating in the city.

"Yes," Kate replied. "Scott's started the evacuation, moving mages out of the city in groups."

Aaron looked around at her with surprise. Then it made sense to him. Machado had come to the Gateway of Ailsa and taken Aaron. That meant Hadrian and his vamages knew about the city being habited by mages. It was no longer a hiding place, so they all had to move, again, to stay off Hadrian's radar.

"When are we leaving?" Aaron asked, with a heavy heart. They hadn't even finished setting the city up, and now were moving in case Hadrian tried to kill them with a Q-Zone.

"In a few hours," Chris answered. "You rest. We'll wake you when it's time to go."

Aaron didn't say anything. There was no way he would be able to sleep, knowing they were moving to another city so soon. Is this what life was going to be like for them? Moving from city to city, never having a home, never being able to settle down because they had to stay one step ahead of Hadrian?

"Aaron!"

Aaron turned at the call. He found Rose running towards him. She threw her arms around him, hugging him tight. "Thank God!" she breathed. "Ella told me you were back." She pulled away to look at him with frightened eyes. "What happened? Are you okay? Where did that vamage take you? What did–"

"Slow down, Rose," Aaron said with a tired smile. "I'm fine. I'll tell you all about it later." His gaze went behind her to Sam, as he stood awkwardly in the middle of the street, staring at him.

Sam didn't speak, but his expression alone told of his relief at the sight of Aaron. He didn't come any closer though. He just stood there, his shoulders tensed and eyes so heavy with regret, they couldn't hold Aaron's gaze.

Rose looked between the two friends. "Sam was really worried about you," she said. "He was arguing with Scott, saying we needed to go out and look for you. Your dad and Sam were about to go out on their own–"

"Yeah, that's great," Aaron said, interrupting her. He looked away from Sam. "I'm very tired, Rose. I'll see you in a bit, yeah?" He turned and walked away, leaving behind a dejected Rose, and a heartbroken Sam.

\*\*\*

Aaron was on top of the mountain. Sitting in front of him was a young Kyran, with his arms draped around his knees, and his eyes fixed to the tear in the distance. The wind blowing gently across Aaron's face was warm, even with the sun beginning to dip out of view. Aaron took a few steps closer to his brother's younger self. He lowered himself onto the rocky ground, sitting next to the memory of Kyran. If Aaron had to guess, he'd say Kyran looked around eight years old. His eyes were an impossible shade of blue and green, his features resembled less of Ben now and more of Alex. He was sitting in silence, just watching the tear, his gaze heavy and full of pain.

Footsteps approached them from behind. Aaron didn't need, nor did he want, to look around and see who it was. He knew it could only be Hadrian. Kyran didn't have anyone else in his life at this point.

Sure enough, Hadrian came to sit down on Kyran's other side. A great surge of hatred rose in Aaron at the sight of the vamage, the one who had tried to make him disappear from Kyran's life. Hadrian didn't speak for long minutes, and Kyran didn't even act like he had noticed his arrival. He stayed as he was, with his chin resting on his knees, eyes staring dead ahead.

Eventually, Hadrian took in a breath. "We need to go," he said quietly. "It's almost sunset. You know what kinds of beasts come out when it's dark."

Kyran didn't answer him, and he didn't move either.

Hadrian looked into the far distance, his eyes on the tear that had all of Kyran's attention. Moments stretched into silent minutes, but no one got up to go. Then, in a quiet, broken voice, Kyran spoke.

"They're not coming back, are they?"

Hadrian turned to look at Kyran, first in surprise and then in stunned stupor. Aaron saw the emotion that flickered on Hadrian's face. He looked, only for a single moment, just as heartbroken as Kyran. It threw Aaron. He had never spared any thought on what Hadrian had felt about Kyran's abandonment. He had just assumed Hadrian wouldn't have cared if Chris and Kate had left Kyran behind and didn't come back for him. But it seemed Hadrian did. He cared and, right now, it showed in every inch of his being.

Hadrian was struggling to answer Kyran. Aaron could see the dilemma in the vamage. Should he lie to the child? Or should he give an honest answer and break the eight years old's heart? Hadrian looked to the skies and closed his eyes.

"Yes," he said softly. "They're coming, Ben. They are coming." He looked over at the young boy next to him. "Chris is going to come back for you, I know he is. Your dad is just – he's trying to work things out. They're in a new world, it's probably difficult to set things up, and that's why he's not come for you yet."

Kyran turned then to look at Hadrian. "You're lying," he said in a rough, tearful voice. "I can tell. You're lying to me." He glanced to the tear and shook his head a fraction. "They're not coming. They're never going to come back for me." He went quiet for a moment. "He's right, I'm on my own. I'm...I'm an orphan." The word struck Aaron like a knife in his chest. "He told me I'm an orphan because I don't have any family," Kyran said, "He's right. I'm alone. I am an orphan."

Hadrian's hand closed on Kyran's arm, not tight enough to startle him, but firm enough for Kyran to focus on him. "Listen to me," he growled, and Aaron was stunned to hear the anger laced in Hadrian's voice. "Machado doesn't know what he's talking about," he said. "You're *not* an orphan, and you're not alone. How can you be alone when you have me?"

Kyran stared at him. Hadrian's expression softened.

"Ben, I know what it's like to be alone," he started. "I've been left on my own for a long time now, but *you* are not alone. You will *never* be alone. I will always be here, and I'll always look after you." Hadrian glanced at the tear and sucked in a deep breath. "I know your mum and dad. I know them very well, and I can promise you, Ben, they would never leave you behind."

Kyran tried to hold back, but his pain came out as a choked, strangled sob. He dipped his head, hiding behind his knees, curling tight into himself.

"I know you're tired of waiting for them to come back. And that's okay, Ben. It's okay to be tired," Hadrian said. He ran a hand over Kyran's head, ruffling his hair gently. "You are not an orphan, Ben. Don't ever let yourself believe that. You have a family. You have a mum and a dad, and – and me."

Kyran raised his head, his dark lashes soaked with tears.

"You took my legacies." Hadrian smiled. "And a little bit of my core. That makes us family now. In a way, that makes you my...my son." He breathed the word out, like it was something precious, something that took all of Hadrian's heart to say out loud. "I know, like you've told me a thousand times now, that I'm not your dad," Hadrian said. "And that's fine. I can look after you even if I'm not your dad."

Kyran didn't speak, but continued to stare at him, tears rolling down his cheeks.

"I'll come up here with you, every day, and together we'll wait for your mum and dad to come back for you," Hadrian said.

"And if they don't?" Kyran asked, his voice cracking with fear.

Hadrian held his eyes. "You'll always have me."

Kyran's sob broke through his resolve and he moved towards Hadrian, hugging him. Hadrian closed an arm around Kyran, and with his other hand, he caressed the top of Kyran's head.

"It's okay," he said, his voice low and soothing. "It's okay, I've got you, Ben. I've got you. You're going to be okay, I've got you."

Even as the dream slipped away and Aaron woke up, Hadrian's voice continued to echo in his head for several moments. He couldn't stop thinking about it. The vamage he hated was the one who'd comforted his brother when he had no one else. What was Aaron supposed to feel for him now?

There was no way Aaron could go back to sleep. He looked out the window to see the sky grey and overcast, sprinkling nothing more than a drizzle. It was just after sunrise. With a sigh, Aaron got up, careful not to disturb Sam and Rose as they slept on the ground next to him. Aaron's packed bag sat against the wall. Aaron hadn't bothered to unpack it. It had only been a few days since they moved from Ailsa to the City of Yara, but Aaron didn't know how long they were going to spend there. If Hadrian found out their location, they would have to leave again. Was there any point in unpacking?

Aaron got up. Maybe a walk outside in the light rain would do him some good.

It was as he passed his mum and dad's room that he noted the lamp hanging from the ceiling was lit. The door was open, so Aaron walked over, pausing at the doorway. His mum was sitting on the floor, leaning against the wall, her legs crossed, and a small box was lying open next to her. His dad wasn't in the room. Aaron could hear him downstairs.

Aaron glanced at the box next to his mum, holding back his grimace. He recognised it. It was where his mum kept Kyran's – Ben's – cloak, the one he'd worn when he was attacked by Lycans. It was from that cloak that Aaron had witnessed the memory of the brutal attack that had convinced his mum and dad their son had died. That same cloak was in his mum's hands right now, as she sat staring at it, unaware that Aaron was standing in her doorway.

"Mum?" Aaron called.

She looked up at him with wet eyes. "Aaron," she said with surprise. "You're up early." She quickly folded the cloak, putting it back in the box and closing the lid. She stood up, wiping at her face. "Are you hungry? I can make us an early breakfast."

Aaron spotted the half unpacked bags next to where she had been sitting. She had obviously taken the box out to put away but was finding it difficult.

"Why do you still keep that thing?" Aaron asked."You know Kyran's alive now. Why torture yourself with the memory on that cloak?"

Kate didn't speak right away. She turned to look at the box, sitting innocently on the floor. "I've not kept his cloak because it holds the memory of Ben being attacked," she explained. "I don't need a physical reminder for that. I can just close my eyes and relive that nightmare." She looked at Aaron with bright blue eyes. "I kept it because it was the only thing I had of his when we left this realm. It's all I could hold on to when he was snatched out of my arms. I couldn't bring myself to let go of it. It's all I had of him." Her eyes brimmed. "It's still all I have of him."

"Mum," Aaron whispered, moving close to hug her. "It's not always going to be like this," he comforted. "It'll get better, very soon, you'll see." He pulled back to look at Kate. "Kyran can't stay mad at you forever," he said. "He'll give in, I know he will. He can say what he likes, but he does care about you. He saved you and Dad when he didn't have to." He walked over and picked up the box. "This is not all you have of him," he said. "I won't let that be true. Kyran will come home. Our family *will* be together again. I promise."

***

The weather was changing. As the end of August approached, the cold, wet days became warmer and drier. The sun was out longer, meaning Aaron had to wait hours before sneaking out at night to meet Kyran on the Gateway.

As Aaron walked to the end of Yara's Gateway – a stretch of uneven path, just as broken and ragged as the city it led to, he found Kyran waiting for him, his arms crossed at his chest, leaning against Lexi.

"Hey," Aaron greeted.

Kyran nodded in response. "You took your time." It wasn't a complaint, just a comment.

"It took ages for the rest to call it a night," Aaron explained.

"Everyone asleep?" Kyran asked.

"I think so," Aaron said. "I don't exactly check before sneaking out–" Kyran shifted a little, breaking his gaze, and that's when it hit Aaron what Kyran was *really* asking. He shook his head with amusement. "Why don't you just ask me outright?" he chuckled. Kyran didn't say anything, but Aaron answered him anyway. "Rose was asleep," he informed. "Otherwise she would have followed us out by now."

Kyran smiled at that, and ducked his head.

"Is that why you're here? Waiting an hour on the Gateway to see if Rose is still awake?" Aaron teased.

Kyran didn't say anything right away. He straightened up before looking at Aaron with serious green eyes. "I think I might have found another way," he said.

Aaron's mirth left him. His body tensed in apprehension. "What is it?"

"At this point, nothing more than a theory," Kyran said. He uncurled his arms and reached into his pocket to pull out several leafs of paper, full of his handwriting. "I found a study completed by a group of scholars," Kyran started. "They argued that should two legacy-holding Elementals marry, the cores of their offspring would be designed to take either one legacy, or the other. They didn't know that a core can carry more than one." He paused briefly, before pushing on. "They presented a theory that if one of the Elemental offspring were to get a legacy from their parent that wasn't quite suited to them, there stood a danger of the legacy disconnecting from the core."

Aaron frowned. "Is that even possible?"

"It makes sense," Kyran said. "Legacies move from one generation to the next, but each legacy is associated to one Elemental family. You're an Adams. Your core calls to the element of Earth. So if you were to carry a legacy, it would be the legacy for Earth. That's what your core expects; it's what it's designed to connect to."

Aaron nodded to show he understood.

"But the legacy you got was for Water. It's connected to your core, but it doesn't quite fit," Kyran said. "The legacy is lodged into your core, but it's the wrong one – think of it as a round object wedged into a square opening. Exert enough force, and the legacy should free itself."

"And how do I do that?" Aaron asked.

"That's the bit I'm working on," Kyran said. "In theory, you can force the legacy out by pushing your power for the element of Water beyond its limit. How exactly that's achieved, I'm not too sure."

"That's what you're researching now?" Aaron asked.

"Pretty much."

Aaron felt a surge of guilt well up in him. "I want to help you," he started, but Kyran was already shaking his head.

"You can't."

"But–"

"No, Ace," Kyran cut him off. "I can't risk it. You're safer here. If I take you with me..." He trailed off.

"Hadrian might find out and try to kill me again," Aaron finished for him. He saw the look of anger and hurt flash on his big brother's face. He hesitated for a moment before asking in a quiet voice, "Have you spoken to him yet?"

Kyran shook his head.

Aaron couldn't help it. Ever since witnessing that Inheritance moment between Hadrian and an eight-year-old Kyran, Aaron couldn't help but feel some empathy towards the most hated vamage of their realm. Hadrian might be a monster, but he was also the one who'd looked after his brother.

"Maybe you should," Aaron said. "Speak to him, I mean."

"Why?" Kyran asked, raising his eyes to glare at Aaron. "So he can lie to me again?"

"Kyran," Aaron placated.

Kyran moved, stepping away from Aaron and his bike, running a hand through his dark locks.

"I asked him – specifically *requested* him – not to attack the realm," Kyran said. "And he gave me his word that he wouldn't, but he went behind my back and attacked them anyway. And he did it in *my* name. That's what makes this a hundred times worse. So many innocent mages killed and made homeless because he thought he was avenging me."

"And yet, you still want the last legacy for him so he can rule this realm," Aaron said.

Kyran snapped around to look at him with angry eyes. "The only thing I'm focusing on right now, is getting that death sentence off your head," he said. "Once the legacy is out of you and back to Ella, I can focus on what to do next."

"What does that mean?" Aaron asked.

"It means I'm going to have a heart-to-heart with my father," Kyran glowered.

Aaron had been the one to tell Kyran about the havoc Hadrian had unleashed on the realm. He'd told Kyran about the cities being Q-Zoned, how survivors dragged themselves and their injured children for days to seek help; all because Hadrian wanted to punish the realm for what Skyler and his Hunters did to Kyran.

Aaron had told Kyran everything the night he rescued him from Hadrian's attack. That was almost two weeks ago now. And since then, Kyran hadn't spoken one word to his so-called father. Apparently, he was waiting until Aaron was legacy-free before confronting Hadrian.

Clearing his throat, Aaron looked to the ground. "Mum and Dad are really worried about you," he said.

Kyran looked taken aback by the abrupt change in topic.

"They've been upset ever since Skyler's attack," Aaron continued. "They're desperate to see you, to make sure you're okay."

Kyran squared his shoulders and then shook his head. "That's not a good idea."

"Kyran, please," Aaron begged. "Let me tell them you're here. All they need is one minute—"

"No," Kyran cut him off. "I don't want to see them."

"But they want to see you," Aaron said. "Ever since they rushed to Salvador with Scott to help you, they've been on edge. All they talk about is you, finding you, meeting you, talking to you. They don't sleep, they don't even eat much, they're so desperate to see you."

Kyran met Aaron's eyes with blazing eyes. "I was desperate to see them too," he said. "I learnt to get over it; they will too."

\*\*\*

The days were getting longer, and much warmer now that September had arrived. It worked in the mages' favour: they needed as many daylight hours as possible to fix up the ruined city they had taken refuge in. It was by far the worst of the cities Aaron had yet seen.

When they first arrived in the City of Yara, they walked onto nothing more than charred, barren land. There was no orchard, no Stove, no table in the middle of the street, and only broken, damaged cottages. Everything had been demolished in whatever attack had killed the city decades before.

But no one had said a word about it. They all walked in, dumped their meagre belongings in one corner of the street and quietly, without protest, started working. They built everything from scratch. Aaron helped his dad and Drake revive the ground, breathing life into it. Ella, Kate and the rest of the Hunters – and Sam – set about repairing the houses. Michael constructed a fire pit, so Mary and her helpers could cook food. Rose helped Mary arrange simple meals, as they didn't have any livestock, and had to rely on the fruit and vegetables harvested from the new orchard.

A week later, the city was looking better. The cottages were mostly restored, the orchard was blossoming, and Mary was getting inventive with her meals – but it still wasn't home. Aaron missed Salvador fiercely, which was strange considering that ten months before he hadn't even known it existed. Now, it was the only place he considered home.

The mages had done an incredible job rebuilding the cottages, but when it came to furnishing them, they were lost. There were no beds, no sofas, no tables they could line up in the street. The mages made small platforms out of wood as bed frames, and used hay to cushion them instead of mattresses. That made sleep a little more comfortable than the rough, bare floor.

For Aaron, though, it made no difference. He couldn't sleep on the floor or the makeshift bed. He was too keyed up to be able to rest. It had been a week since he had seen or spoken to his brother, when he'd told him about the theory of forcing the legacy out of him by exerting his power. Aaron told himself

Kyran was probably making arrangements to test this theory. He would come when he was ready. He would come to see him. He had to.

"Aaron?"

Aaron looked up to meet his dad's eyes.

"Yeah?"

Chris gestured to the ground. "I think you're done."

Aaron looked down, past his outstretched hands, to see the fully grown ears of corn. He quickly pulled his hands back. "Yeah – uh – sorry," he said.

Chris knelt down, a dagger in his hand. "What were you thinking about?" he asked, cutting the corn loose and throwing it into the wide basket by his side. "You looked a little lost there."

Aaron opened his mouth, about to tell his dad about Kyran's visit, when a flash lit the city. Chris and Aaron turned to see the Gate slide open. Neither of them were prepared to see who had rode inside.

# 31

## CATCHING SHADOWS

Everyone was out on the street, working on either building furniture for the cottages or bringing baskets of fruit and vegetables from the orchard to the fire pit. They all stopped to stare in surprise as their supposed leader, Skyler Avira, rode into the city, weeks after storming out on them and leaving them on their own to deal with Hadrian's wrath in retaliation for *his* actions against Kyran.

Skyler slowed to a stop, but didn't get off his bike. He scanned the street, searching through the mages until he found the one he was looking for. Ella was crouched before a half-built bed, her eyes on Skyler, looking like she was battling the desire to throw the hammer in her hand at him or go running to hug him.

Aaron didn't have that dilemma. He knew exactly what he wanted to do. Aaron was ready to go for Skyler with nothing more than his fists, but Chris stopped him by holding onto his arm. Aaron looked to his dad, whose green eyes had darkened and jaw clenched as he stared at Skyler. Aaron knew his dad was beyond furious with Skyler for what he had done to Kyran, but he was holding back, waiting to see why Skyler had returned.

Skyler stayed on his bike, his blue eyes glued to Ella's. His smirk was missing, his shoulders dropped, as he looked to his childhood best friend with eyes full of remorse. Behind him, two trucks arrived, loaded to the top with beds, sofas and chairs.

No one moved. They watched in silence as the trucks pulled up on either side of Skyler. The Hunters looked to Ella, waiting for her instructions. Skyler may have been the eldest Elemental and the one who would be the new leader of the realm, but Ella was the one the Hunters followed. Not just because she was Neriah's niece – the only descendant of their last leader – but because she was fair and level-headed. She hadn't lied to them, used them, or forced them to attack a fellow mage – another *Elemental* – to satisfy the need for vengeance as Skyler had with Kyran.

Ella slowly stood up, the hammer still in her hand. Skyler pulled himself off the bike and stood, staring back at Ella.

Scott broke the tension. He was the only one to welcome Skyler to Yara, albeit not as warmly as he perhaps would have once done. It was on Scott's instructions that the mages moved to the trucks to unload them with the essentials Skyler had brought. It was a peace offering, and everyone knew it, but no one commented on it.

Ella dropped the hammer and turned around, heading to her cottage.

"Ella, wait," Skyler called. In a few long strides, Skyler was standing behind her. "Ella," Skyler held her arm, to turn her around to face him.

Ella whirled around of her own accord and pulled her arm out of his grasp before shoving him hard in the chest. "Don't touch me," she snarled.

The mages stopped unpacking the trucks, watching Ella and Skyler instead.

"Ella, please," Skyler started quietly.

"Why are you here?" Ella asked venomously. "We don't need you. We're doing fine on our own."

"I'm sorry," Skyler said. "I shouldn't have walked out on you, on all of you."

Ella scoffed at him. "There's a hell of a lot that you *shouldn't* have done, Skyler."

Skyler's expression clouded with guilt. "I was angry," he said. "I said things I didn't mean."

"I'm not talking about what you said to me." Ella shook her head. "It's what you almost did to Kyran, what you almost made Sam do to him."

Skyler's expression hardened.

"You lied about Kyran killing Sam's parents, just so you could convince Sam to execute Kyran. You told the Hunters the same thing, so they would attack Kyran at your command." She glared at him with glistening eyes. "You ambushed Kyran, tried to kill him, tried to manipulate Sam into killing him. You dropped a *Gate* to let Lycans in and attack Rose. And all for what?" she asked. "Answer me!" She shoved him again, this time with so much force Skyler stumbled back a step. "How could you stoop so low?" she asked. "Is this what Armana would've wanted?"

"I don't know," Skyler said, and there was fury underlining his words. "Armana's dead, and it's all because of Kyran."

"You don't *know* that!" Ella exclaimed. "You don't have any proof. And without proof, you can't execute someone."

Skyler looked away from her, dropping his gaze to the ground. "I'm sorry," he said.

"I'm not the one you should be apologising to." She looked to Aaron and his dad, standing at a little distance, watching them.

Skyler followed her gaze. Without another word, he turned and walked towards Chris and Aaron.

Aaron freed himself from his dad's grip and stepped forward, the ground shuddering with his anger.

"Aaron," Chris called from behind him. "Don't."

Aaron forced himself to stay, to obey his dad, but his furious gaze didn't move from Skyler, who was ignoring the trembling ground under his feet. He walked straight up to Aaron.

"Adams," he started, looking at Aaron and ignoring Chris. "I'm sorry that I tried to have Kyran executed," he said. The blue of his eyes turned cold. "I should have just killed him myself."

Aaron lunged forward with his teeth gritted and his fists tight. But Chris was suddenly by his side, a grip on his arm. Chris pulled Aaron behind him and stepped in front, facing Skyler.

For a moment, neither of them spoke. Skyler smirked with his usual disdain for Chris Adams.

"You know, ever since I met you, Skyler, I've felt nothing but sorry for you," Chris started in a quiet voice. "Not because you lost your parents, or because you had to watch them die, or because you were forced to grow up without your family. I felt sorry for you because you never got a chance to know your father."

The smirk fell from Skyler's face, and he looked genuinely shocked that Chris was bringing his dad into this.

"You never got to see how just and fair Joseph was," Chris continued. "You can never know his kindness, or his compassion for protecting others."

"Don't talk about my father," Skyler warned, and a gust of wind accompanied his threat.

"He was my best friend," Chris continued regardless, "and my Elemental brother. He was a good person and he didn't deserve to die like he did."

"I'm warning you, Adams!" Skyler snarled, and the wind picked up with gusto, swirling into a vortex.

"I remember how excited he was at your birth," Chris said.

The whirlwind died. Skyler was staring at Chris with unblinking eyes.

"He couldn't get over the fact that he had a son," Chris said. "Joseph was very proud of you." Chris held Skyler's eyes. "Would he be proud if he saw you now?" he asked.

Skyler didn't speak. He just stared at Chris.

"Despite what you think, you are just a kid," Chris said. "A kid who happens to be the son of my best friend. Believe me, Skyler, that is the only reason you're still left standing after what you tried to do to my son." He took a step closer. "Joseph's memory won't protect you forever," he warned. "Try anything like that again, and I will be the one who kills you."

For once, Skyler didn't have a snarky response. He just stood and stared at Chris, who turned and walked away, taking Aaron with him.

*** 

Tension was in the air. Everyone was talking about Skyler's return, and what Christopher Adams had said to him. As the city unpacked the trucks Skyler had brought, Scott called for an Elemental meeting, taking Skyler, Ella and Chris into a room, to try to settle their dispute in private.

"Why aren't you in there with them?" Zhi-Jiya asked Aaron, jutting her chin towards the cottage that Scott had chosen. "You're an Elemental too, shouldn't you be a part of the meeting?" she asked as she lined up the chairs to the table that now sat in the middle of the street.

"My dad asked me to sit this one out," Aaron replied, doing the same as her on the other side of the table.

"Why?" Zhi-Jiya asked.

"'Cause if I go anywhere near Skyler right now, I won't be able to stop myself from tearing him apart," Aaron answered.

Zhi-Jiya gave a brief nod. She hesitated for a moment, giving Aaron a glance before clearing her throat. "I heard Ryan saying that Scott and Ella are calling the chiefs of the realm. There are talks of Skyler possibly losing his chance to become the next leader."

Aaron paused, the chair in his hand forgotten. "Really?" he asked.

"It's what I heard." Zhi-Jiya shrugged. "Aside from trying to unlawfully execute Kyran, Skyler did other things that can get him in a lot of trouble."

"Like?" Aaron pressed.

"Like dropping the Gate," Zhi-Jiya said. "He was the one who let the Lycans into the area that holds the Blade of Adams. Dropping Gates is a punishable crime in our realm."

Aaron could feel the tension build between his shoulders. "So what, now Skyler's going to be the one facing execution?" he asked. "Not that he doesn't deserve it," he bit out, "but this has to stop. I thought mages weren't keen on killing other mages?"

"We're not," Zhi-Jiya said. "And no, Skyler's not going to be executed, but he might lose his leadership. No one has faith in him any more. How can he lead us if he's so readily able to lie and manipulate us?"

Aaron didn't speak right away. He let out a deep sigh. "So then, that means Ella would be the next leader?"

Zhi-Jiya nodded. "If that's what the Elemental council and the rest of the chiefs decide," she said. "Technically, it's supposed to be the next eldest who takes over, which actually is..." She trailed off, giving Aaron an awkward look.

"Kyran," Aaron said in realisation.

Zhi-Jiya nodded. "Seeing as we're fighting for Kyran's side *not* to take over and rule the realm, it would have to be Ella."

Inexplicably, Aaron felt himself smile. Then he was chuckling, shaking his head. He raised his face to the skies and closed his eyes, hands on his waist. He let out a sigh. "It can never be simple, can it?"

Zhi-Jiya gave him a lop-sided smile. Her expression changed as she spotted something behind Aaron. "Talking about things that are complicated." She nodded for Aaron to look behind him.

Aaron turned and stilled.

Sam stood awkwardly, a chair in his hand, having brought it from the pile next to the unloaded truck.

"Sort things out," Aaron heard Zhi-Jiya say to him. "It's painful to see you both like this." She walked away, leaving Aaron and Sam standing, looking at each other.

Sam shuffled forward, lifting the chair. "Thought I'd help," he said quietly.

Aaron nodded. Without saying a word, he turned and walked away, leaving Sam to finish on his own.

"Aaron, wait," Sam called after him. He left the chair in the middle of the street and hurried over to him. He stood in front of Aaron, blocking his way. "Please," he started. "I can't do this any more. I can't." He looked close to tears. "I need you to talk to me."

Aaron looked at him. "What do you want me to say?" he asked.

"Come on, Aaron," Sam pleaded. "You know that I'm sorry."

Aaron nodded. "Yeah, I know you are," he said. "And I'm sorry too. But that doesn't change what happened." He held Sam's guilt-ridden eyes. "You almost killed my brother."

"Because I thought he had killed my parents," Sam explained. "Skyler played me and I fell for it. It was stupid, I know. I should never have believed him." He looked at Aaron desperately. "But he told me he had seen it, that he watched that vamage's memory and I – I don't know – he was so convincing–" He closed his eyes and shook his head. "I know that I messed up, and I'm sorry."

"It doesn't matter," Aaron said. "You can be as sorry as you like, but that doesn't change the fact that you would have shot Kyran in the head if I hadn't stopped you."

Sam's expression hardened. "Yeah," he said. "You stopped me by shooting me. You put a bullet in me, Aaron, but I've forgiven you for that."

A humourless laugh left Aaron. "Mighty big of you, Sam," he said. "But I was never going to leave a bullet in you. I planned to do that transfer and heal you, before I even pulled the trigger. I never wanted to hurt you, but you were ready to hurt me by killing my brother." He started walking away.

"Why are you being like this?" Sam called after him. "I said, I'm sorry!"

"It doesn't matter," Aaron snapped, turning around to face him. "Saying sorry doesn't change anything."

"So what, you're going to be mad at me forever?" Sam asked. "I told you I was tricked by Skyler. I would never have attacked Kyran otherwise, you know that."

"I thought I did," Aaron said. He paused, struggling to keep himself together. "I thought I knew you, what you were capable of. Guess I was wrong."

Sam's anger left him, evaporating in the air. He hurried forward. "Aaron, please," he begged. "You can't hold this against me, I was played."

"I know you were," Aaron said. "And because of that, I can forgive you. I can work past it." Aaron paused, his green eyes glistening. "But what I can't deal with is that you didn't believe me. You took Skyler's word over mine. You didn't even want to hear what I had to say, Sam. You were so sure I was lying." He held Sam's eyes. "You were my *best* friend. I've known you all my life, and you thought I would *lie* to you; that I would side with Kyran if he had killed your parents?"

Sam couldn't hold his gaze. He looked away, ashamed.

"You didn't come to me after Skyler filled your head with lies, because you didn't *trust* me," Aaron continued, his pain shaking his words. "How can we be friends if you don't trust me? What did I do that made you lose faith in me, Sam?"

"Aaron," Sam's voice cracked, as he raised his head to look at him with tear-filled eyes. "I'm – I'm sorry."

Aaron gathered himself and nodded. "I'm sorry too," he said. "I'm sorry it had to end like this."

Sam didn't say anything, but watched as Aaron walked away, leaving him standing alone and heartbroken.

*\*\*\**

The tavern wasn't as busy as it had been weeks earlier, when the weather was cold, wet and miserable. With the sun out, most mages preferred to be outdoors, soaking in the sunshine. Kyran was sitting at the bar on his own, the drink before him forgotten. He let out a frustrated sigh and dropped his head, rubbing at the nape of his neck. It had been over a week since he'd met Aaron and told him about his 'forcing out the legacy' theory, but he hadn't come any closer to figuring it out. On top of that, he still wasn't speaking to his father. He didn't want to. He was afraid he would lose the fragile hold on his temper if he exchanged words with him. Kyran was already beyond furious with him for attacking Aaron, but after learning about the Q-Zone attacks in the realm, Kyran's anger had peaked to new heights.

In an attempt to avoid his father, Kyran had been spending a lot of time out of the manor. He wanted to meet Aaron, but he was afraid his father's vamages might follow him and find

Aaron again. He had decided to only go to Aaron once he found a conclusive way of forcing the legacy out of him.

Kyran felt lost. He hated what his father had done to the mages, what he allowed his vamages to do to Aaron, but he still felt hopelessly bound to him. He couldn't walk away from his father, he wouldn't abandon him, he would *never* do that. But how could he trust his father again? He had lied to his face about not attacking the realm. And he had gone after Aaron behind Kyran's back. Kyran brushed his fingers across his forehead, soothing a headache. Chris and Kate Adams were forever lost to Kyran, but he would never let Aaron go. He would always protect his brother, even from his father.

"You want something else?" the bartender asked, pointing to Kyran's barely touched glass.

Kyran shook his head.

The woman lifted the glass and took it away. She put an iron mug in front of him with a frothy top. "Here," she said. "This will give you a bit of a kick."

Kyran gave her a half-hearted smile and lifted the silver mug. It was so shiny, Kyran could see his reflection in it. He caught the flicker of movement in it – someone dressed in white moved behind him. Kyran whipped around, sharp green eyes scanning the pub. The few mages there were all sitting at their tables, enjoying their drinks while they chatted with one another. And none of them was dressed like a Lurker.

Kyran turned in his seat completely, looking from one corner of the tavern to the next. He was sure he'd seen a Lurker pass by him. How that was possible, in his father's zone, he didn't know, but it was what he'd seen.

His searching gaze spotted the Lurker walk past the window, outside the tavern. Kyran shot out of his seat to run after him. He came out of the pub but lost sight of the Lurker in the crowd of mages bustling along. Kyran headed down the street, looking for the white-robed Lurker. He caught a glimpse of him, on the other side of the road, just turning the corner. Kyran pushed past the mages, going after him. He'd had enough of these hide and seek games. He was going to get this Lurker today, once and for all.

Kyran saw the Lurker head into the small orchard at the very end of the road. Kyran ran in after him. Again, it was as if the Lurker had disappeared. Kyran searched the trees, struggling to see past the thick branches, hanging low with fruit ready for picking. He was tensed, his heart pounding, as he hunted for the Lurker. Finally, he spotted the white-robed Lurker standing before a glowing portal.

Kyran took a step towards him and the Lurker turned, as if taken by surprise. His face was hidden by the low hood, only his bottom lip and chin were visible, but Kyran knew the Lurker's eyes were on him.

Kyran held up both hands. "I'm not armed," he started, inching closer. "I just want to talk."

The Lurker turned and dived headfirst into the portal.

Kyran cursed and ran in after him. He came out at the other side on rocky ground, high on a hilltop. Kyran frowned, looking around at the strange, yet somehow familiar, surroundings. He knew this place. Kyran momentarily forgot about the Lurker he was chasing, and took a few steps to the edge of the hill, to look at the street below. It was lined with fancy houses behind well-kept front lawns. A long, rich mahogany table sat in the middle of the street.

It was as if the air had vanished, leaving Kyran unable to breathe. He knew where he was now. He could never forget this place. The portal had somehow brought him to the City of Marwa – the home Kyran left when he gave up waiting for his parents' return, ten years before. He hadn't come back since.

Kyran heard the sound of feet scraping against rock and he forced himself to look away from the house – the home he grew up in – to see the Lurker running full speed to the other side of the hill.

Kyran had had enough. He pulled out his gun and chased after him.

"Hey!" he yelled. "Stop!"

The Lurker kept running, his long white robe flapping behind him as he sped forward.

Kyran had shortened the distance between them, but if he didn't get to the Lurker soon, he would lose him again, as they approached the steep decline that led to the street below.

Kyran skidded to a halt and raised his gun. "Stop, or I'll shoot!"

The Lurker came to a sudden stop.

Breathing hard, Kyran took a few steps forward, keeping his gun aimed.

"Turn around," Kyran said. "Hands where I can see them."

The Lurker raised his hands and turned around. His face was still hidden.

Kyran gripped his gun tighter. "Lower your hood," he instructed.

Slowly, the Lurker's hands moved to the hood, and he gently pushed it back, letting it fall.

Kyran's breath caught in his chest. His eyes widened as his arm fell to his side, the gun in his hand forgotten.

It couldn't be.

The Lurker standing before him was his uncle, Alex Adams.

# 32

# LEX

The gun slipped from Kyran's slack grip and fell to the ground with a thud. He barely noticed. His attention was on Alex. Kyran didn't understand; he had felt his uncle die. He had awoken after the Lycan attack with a deep sense of loss, that he knew – even at the innocent age of four – was because his uncle 'Lex' was gone forever. So how could Alex be standing before him now? It wasn't possible when Kyran had felt – could still feel – the hole in his soul that Alex left behind.

It was when Kyran's shock dulled that he realised Alex looked *exactly* like he had the last time Kyran had seen him. From his youthful appearance of a twenty-two year old to the Lurker robe he had worn to match Kyran's Halloween costume that fateful day – *fourteen* years ago.

It hit Kyran like a tidal wave. He understood what it was he was seeing. It wasn't Alex – it was his echo; an imprint of him left in this world. But even as Kyran came to that conclusion, the rational part of his mind rejected it. Echoes retraced the steps they took when they were living; they didn't follow others around. They didn't take part in chases. They didn't pretend to be Lurkers and guide you to places you needed to be. Echoes weren't supposed to even be *visible* for more than a fleeting glimpse. And they certainly didn't stand there and stare at you with pained eyes and a bittersweet smile.

Alex started walking towards Kyran.

Echoes didn't do that either.

Kyran was completely lost. It couldn't be his uncle because he was dead, but it wasn't his simple echo either. So who – what – was this then?

Alex came to stand before him, an identical copy of Kyran in every physical sense. Kyran couldn't speak. He stared at the face he saw every day in the mirror. Alex didn't say anything, but for a moment just held Kyran's eyes. Then his hand shot out and he grabbed Kyran's hand.

Kyran was thrown into a whirlwind of spinning images. He couldn't make anything out at first – just a blur of colours as Alex dragged him into his memories. Then everything slowed down, and Kyran found himself inside the Adams manor – the home he'd lived in for the first four years of his life.

The front door was open, Alex was standing at the threshold dressed as a Lurker, grinning as he held up a miniature matching Lurker cloak. Kate was at the door, a hand on her pregnant belly, as she laughed with her head thrown back. The sound of it travelled through Kyran, making his heart ache. He loved her laugh. It's what he remembered most about her, and one of the things he missed so fiercely of her.

The door to the living room opened and Chris appeared. Clinging to his arm, bouncing up and down with excitement, was the four-year-old child Kyran once was. It was such a strange sight, seeing himself like that. Kyran actually remembered this – this *very* moment – early in the morning of his fourth birthday, hours before he lost his family.

Chris stopped at the sight of Alex at the door. His eyes widened with surprise, and a look of disbelief crossed his features as he gave Alex a head-to-toe look. Alex smiled, and again Kyran's heart twisted with grief. He had forgotten how full of life his uncle's smile used to be.

Alex gestured to his Lurker robes and looked to his brother with raised eyebrows. "Too soon?" he asked.

Kate laughed again and Chris shook his head. "Very funny, Alex," he admonished. "You crushed my dreams by not becoming a Lurker. The least you could do is not tease me about it."

Alex grinned and tilted his head, a gesture that simply said, *Sorry, can't help it.*

Kyran saw his younger self let out a squeal of "Lex!" and run to the door, jumping into Alex's arms.

"Got one for you too," Alex said as he balanced his nephew on his hip with one hand, and draped the Lurker cloak around the small shoulders with his other.

The memory changed, and Kyran found himself outside, in the midst of bustling mages enjoying the Halloween fair. There were stalls everywhere, displaying everything from clothes, to toys, to tasty sweet treats. Alex was at a stall, looking at a long chain with a gold pendant, which Kyran knew must be for Alaina.

Kyran searched the street, finding himself with his parents a little way ahead, going to the toys stall. His already racing heart sped up. He knew what was coming. He remembered it only too well – lived this moment again and again in his nightmares. With a thudding heart, Kyran searched the distance and saw the Gate fall. Lycans were bounding across the street, coming straight for the unsuspecting mages. Chaos fell upon them when the Lycans charged at the mages with bared teeth and claws.

Alex was one of the first few Hunters, as well as Chris, to snap into action and start fighting the Lycans. He grabbed a sword from a nearby weapons stall and leapt into battle, swinging the blade with great precision, wounding several Lycans. But there were too many Lycans, and not enough mages. It was a fight they could never have won.

Kyran didn't want to see it happen – he had lived through it, he couldn't do it again. But there was no way for him to leave the memory, and so he had no choice but to stand there with gritted teeth and curled fists, as the memory replayed how he was snatched from his mother's arms. Kyran watched with darkened eyes, as Raoul dug his claws into his small body, making him bleed. His own screams were ringing in his head and Kyran felt the phantom pains start again, spreading through him, marking each and every spot on his body where Lycans had once sunk their claws and teeth.

Forcing himself to stay upright, Kyran watched as Raoul tried to drag him away from Kate, who wasn't letting go of him. Raoul kicked her, right in her pregnant stomach, and Kyran's indignant cry echoed in the air. He didn't remember that happening to her. In his memory, and in every one of his recurring nightmares, he only saw Raoul pull him out of his mother's arms. He had been so lost in his own pain and panic, the attack on his mother never registered. But now he had seen it, and it made his insides twist with rage. He saw his mum hit the ground, one hand on her abused stomach, the other clutched around the Lurker robe that was all that was left in her hand as she tried to hold on to him.

"Kate!" Chris cried.

Kyran turned to see Chris and Alex fighting the Lycans, trying to get to Kate. But Alex's attention quickly went from his fallen sister-in-law to his four-year-old nephew, who was thrown to the Lycans to devour. Kyran read his brutal attack in Alex's horrified eyes and the growing panic in his expression.

"NO!" Alex was crying out. "NO! NO! BEN!"

Not too far away, Chris was yelling the same thing as he slashed at the Lycans. Kyran could see the anguish, the torment on his dad as he tried with every last fibre of his being to get past the Lycans and to his son. But there were too many of them, blocking his way.

Kyran turned back to where the attack was taking place to see his bloodied body being tossed from one Lycan to another as they bit into his stomach and arms, shaking him like a rag doll. Kyran remembered, with agonising clarity, the slice of those fangs as they had chewed through his flesh and snapped his bones. He could remember the taste of his own blood, gagging him, choking through his screams.

This was as far as the memory went for Kyran, since his four year old self had lost consciousness at this point, unable to take any more of the pain. Even his nightmares ended here.

But this was Alex's memory.

The Lycans continued playing their sick game of catch with Ben's limp body, taking him further up the steep hill, and disappearing from sight when they reached the top. Alex and Chris were fighting to get past the Lycans and run after them. They swung their swords and sent jolts of power at the demons. The ground was shaking under their command, but no matter how many Lycans they fought, they couldn't follow after Ben. His other uncle, Michael – Kyran noticed – had reached his sister, and was protecting her from the surrounding Lycans.

Something happened then, because his parents and both uncles stilled at the same time, their backs arched and faces frozen in complete and utter terror. Then Kate screamed – a blood-curdling cry that made Kyran's stomach twist. Chris stumbled back a step, before a furious, agonised cry left him too. The earth shook violently from his pain, and then tore open. Alex turned to look at the hill, where the Lycans had taken Ben; his eyes darkened and his jaw clenched. Michael looked like all his strength had left him at once, and he fell to his knees.

Kyran had no idea what had happened, why all four of them had reacted like this. He looked from one to the next, seeing nothing but anguish on them. Then Alex let out a rage-filled yell and charged forward, swinging his sword with all his might. He cleared a path and darted up the hill, taking out whatever Lycan crossed his path. Chris was trying to follow behind him but it was as if every Lycan was targeting him. They swarmed around him, making it impossible for him to move forward.

Kyran's surroundings changed when Alex got close to the top of the hill, shifting with his memory. Kyran made his way to where Alex was crouched with tear-filled, bloodshot eyes fixed to the top of the hill, his sword clutched close to his chest, preparing to attack however many Lycans were at the top. Alex moved and raised his head, only just enough to have a peek. Kyran saw what Alex witnessed, and it was as if the air had vanished, stealing Kyran's breath.

At the top of the hill, sitting before his crumpled, bleeding four-year-old body, was Hadrian.

Kyran gaped at him, while his heart and mind told him over and over again that this wasn't possible. Hadrian hadn't been in Marwa when it was attacked. He was home, hiding from the mages – hiding from Neriah. But his eyes were showing him a different story. Hadrian was sitting calmly next to Ben's unconscious, unmoving body. The Lycans had evidently just dumped his small, wounded self to the ground without a care. Kyran could see he was lying on his side, one of his arms extended outwards, his leg bent – clearly broken. Blood was steadily staining the rocky ground under him.

Hadrian was holding a hand over Ben's head, and for a fleeting moment, Kyran believed Hadrian was trying to heal him – attempting a transfer to save his life. But for a transfer, there needed to be skin-to-skin contact, and Hadrian's hand was hovering above him, not touching him.

A tall, white-haired man came to stand beside Hadrian, and Kyran felt like the earth had moved from under his feet. He stumbled back a step, staring in disbelief.

"Is it not done yet?" Raoul asked Hadrian with impatience.

"It would have been, if you hadn't injured him so badly," Hadrian said, a bite to his tone. "I had to waste time healing him, before I could detach the link."

Raoul didn't look like he cared. He paced, his eyes fixed on Hadrian. A number of Lycans, still in their beast form, lurked at the edges of the hill, obviously standing guard. A few Lycans tottered up the hill, dragging dead mages with them. They threw the bodies close to where Hadrian was sitting. Even in his shocked state, Kyran noticed the body of another little boy, similar in age to his four-year-old self.

Raoul looked over the edge of the hill at the street below, where his Lycans were still killing mages. He smirked. "It sounded like it was done," he said nonchalantly. "If those screams were anything to go by."

"It's almost complete," Hadrian said. "The bond he shares with his family is broken." He smiled as if deeply satisfied. "His family thinks he's dead. Everyone in the world who shares his bloodline just felt him die." He cast a quick look at the mangled corpse of the other little boy beside him. "When they find that body, they'll have no problem believing it's their son."

The words hit Kyran like punches, leaving him winded, in pain, and unable to breathe. They had been telling the truth; his mum and dad weren't lying. They had felt him die because Hadrian had fooled them into thinking that. Hadrian had been the one to sever the bond between him and his family. His parents, his uncles – they'd all felt him die. Hadrian had even prepared another body to trick his family into believing was his.

"Now, I just have to make sure his side of the bond remains," Hadrian said.

"Why?" Raoul asked.

Hadrian kept his hand where it was but turned to look at Raoul. "It's the most important part of this whole process," he said. "He has to *feel* his family, know that the bond is still there, and believe that his parents can feel it like he can, otherwise my plan will never work." He looked down at the wounded child lying before him. "If I don't break his heart, I will never own it."

Kyran stared at the scene with dumbfounded disbelief. This couldn't be real. It couldn't be. Hadrian would never do this, not to him. He wasn't this cruel.

"What did you have to give to the Influence to learn this trick?" Raoul asked with a grin.

Hadrian pulled his hand back and stood up. He turned to face Raoul. "That is none of your business," he said.

Raoul chuckled. "Tell me, was the Influence the one to tell you about his special powers?" he asked, nodding to the small boy lying at their feet.

"No," Hadrian said. "He's born with the mark. I knew what it meant the very first time I saw it on his chest, even if no one else did. They all thought it was nothing more than a birthmark, and I was happy to let them believe that."

"So you could use the boy for yourself?" Raoul asked. "I have to say, Hadrian, I like you a lot better as a – what did you say you were now? A *vamage*?" He grinned. "You're a lot more fun than when you were a mage."

Hadrian didn't say anything.

Raoul stepped forward, holding Hadrian's gaze. "The thing is, I know what that dark circle on his chest means too," he said. "I know this boy will grow up with the power to drain life out of others. The moon will not affect him, which is why he's immune to our venom." He looked at Hadrian without a hint of amusement. "I'll keep my end of the deal, if you remember to keep yours."

Hadrian smirked at him. "What's the matter, Raoul? You don't trust me? I got you inside Marwa, didn't I?"

"And I got you the boy in return," Raoul said, "Just as you asked. So when the time comes, I want you to do what I have asked."

"I will," Hadrian said.

"Good." Raoul smiled. "Now, before I go, how about a taste?" He moved towards the bloodied body of Ben.

Alex leapt up from his hiding spot and charged at Raoul with a cry, his sword drawn. Kyran was numb, watching his uncle race forward to protect him. He had grown up believing that no one had tried to save him, that his parents had got scared and left him to die, that his uncle Alex died fighting Lycans. He never knew that Alex had been fighting for *him*, in a bid to save him from Raoul.

Raoul ducked to avoid the swing of the blade, and Hadrian was quick to move out of the way too. The Lycans that had been on all fours, circling Hadrian and Raoul, bounded forward with their teeth bared and claws out. Alex fought all of them, keeping them not only back but away from the spot where a little Ben lay, bleeding out. Alex killed three Lycans, slicing their heads clean off.

Raoul transformed into his wolf form, his cold cobalt eyes fixed on Alex. But he didn't come for him. He howled and his Lycans pulled back. They formed a tight group, but didn't charge at Alex. They backed away, their sharp eyes on him.

Alex was breathing hard, the sword held fast in his hand. His gaze was on the Lycans, watching them in case they came forward to attack, as he reached for his wounded nephew on the ground.

"Ben–" he called.

Alex arched all of a sudden. The sword he had been fighting with fell from his hand. Alex's cry choked in his throat, his green eyes widened with surprise first, then clouded with agony. Protruding from the middle of his chest was the tip of a sword.

The sword pulled out and Alex fell to the ground with a groan. Kyran's breath left him completely when he saw who it was who had stabbed Alex in the back. Hadrian stood holding the bloodied sword, his cold, cruel eyes fixed on Alex, who was trying to get back up but couldn't. Alex was trembling on the ground, not far from where Ben lay, blood pooling under him and spreading quickly across the ground.

Alex raised his head to see his little nephew. Raoul and his Lycans were closing in on them again, now that Alex couldn't fight them. Slowly, and in great pain, Alex inched forward, dragging himself closer. He reached out to hold Ben's hand, his fingers closing over the back of Ben's right hand, his thumb under it. "Ben," he gasped.

When Hadrian's shadow fell on Alex, he turned his head with difficulty, his breath ragged and uneven. When his eyes met Hadrian's, Alex's whole body seized in shock. He looked at Hadrian with disbelief.

"H-Hadrian?"

"Sorry, Alex," Hadrian said, and Kyran could hear the genuine regret in his tone. "I never meant for you to be a part of this." He gripped his sword with both hands and raised it high.

"H-Hadrian," Alex breathed. "N-No!"

Hadrian plunged the sword into Alex, through his back and into his heart. Alex's last breath rushed out of him, and as it did, a light glowed under his fingers and four silvery lines formed across Ben's hand, directly under Alex's fingers.

Kyran came out of the memory just as suddenly as he had gone into it. He blinked the tears out of his eyes and stared at Alex, who was still standing before him, holding his hand, the placement of his fingers matching the lines on the back of Kyran's hand.

The four silvery marks Kyran had grown up hating, thinking they were scars left by the Lycans, had actually come from his uncle Alex. They weren't scars at all; they were imprints, left on him when his uncle died but refused to let go of him.

Kyran realised the spot he was standing in right now, the place Alex's echo had brought him, was where Alex had died, fourteen years ago. This was the same hill, where Hadrian had taken Alex's life, where he had used the knowledge he got from the Influence to break Kyran's bond with his parents.

Tears rolled out of Kyran's eyes, as he looked to his uncle's echo. He tried, but his voice wouldn't come out. With difficulty, Kyran managed to utter a single word.

"Lex."

Alex smiled, and his hand lifted from Kyran's hand to cup his face. His mouth opened, and a whisper of, "*Ben*," rang in the air, just as he faded before Kyran's eyes.

# 33

## CONFESSIONS

Hadrian was not accustomed to visitors, and certainly not uninvited ones. So when his doors opened and the swarm of men marched into his chamber, Hadrian was surprised to say the least. He stepped away from his desk and moved towards them.

He raised a hand. "That's close enough, Raoul."

The leader of the Lycans came to a stop, his men stationed behind him. Hadrian gestured to the vamages that came running in after them, weapons in hand.

"There's no need," he said, coming to stand before Raoul. "You can go. This will be a short visit."

His vamages obeyed, and left Raoul and his Lycans with Hadrian.

Hadrian stood tall, matching Raoul's height. "I hope you have a good reason to come barging in here," he said.

Raoul was livid, his brown eyes sparkled red with fury. "We had an agreement, Hadrian," he said.

"We still do," Hadrian replied.

Raoul let out a snort, that sounded more like a growl. "It's already been breached. That *boy* has been killing my men! Every full moon, I've been losing my numbers, but I didn't know it was him until recently."

"Kyran likes to hunt," Hadrian said nonchalantly. "It's nothing unusual. Most mages are natural-born Hunters, and Lycans are their most popular prey. Kyran isn't the first mage to hunt Lycans, so why would that bring you to my door?"

"Because he doesn't hunt them, he *drains* them," Raoul spat furiously.

Hadrian fell quiet, his surprise evident in his expression.

"My men can fight back if he hunts them like mages usually do," Raoul said. "But there's no defence against his draining powers." He pointed a finger at Hadrian. "You told me that *boy*—"

"Kyran," Hadrian said, his voice cooling considerably. "His name is, Kyran. Refer to him as such."

"Fine. You told me *Kyran*—" Raoul grit out— "would never use his powers on my men. That was part of our agreement. I would get you the child, and you would give us immunity from his draining powers when he got older." He looked away from Hadrian, shaking his head. "I *knew* I shouldn't have listened to you. I should have killed that *brat* instead of handing him over to you."

"If you had killed him, you wouldn't have survived until now," Hadrian said.

Raoul stilled, looking at him with fury.

Hadrian took a step forward. "Don't forget you are where you are today because of *me*," he said with quiet anger. "I'm the one who gave you free reign over ten zones. You can walk into any zone you like because *I* open portals for you. My vamages don't attack your *dogs* because I've instructed them not to, otherwise your kind would have been long extinct." He smirked as Raoul's face darkened with anger. "I gave you everything you have today, and I did it only because you helped me get Kyran. If you had killed him, you would still be scampering from one zone to the next, looking for a big enough hole to hide in."

Raoul snarled, and his men shifted behind him, ready to transform in a heartbeat and attack the leader of the vamages. But Raoul didn't do anything. He just stood there, panting with rage, eyes fixed on Hadrian, who smiled back at him.

"Bark all you want," Hadrian said. "You know what will happen if you try to bite."

Raoul pulled back, but he looked no less angry. "Warn him to stay away from my men," he growled.

"Keep your men away from my son, and you'll have no problems," Hadrian replied.

"Your *son*?" Raoul asked, hissing the word as if it belonged to a language he didn't understand. "Aren't you taking this pretence a little too far?" he asked. He stared at Hadrian, his anger fast turning to surprise. "Unless...you don't really think of him as your own, do you?"

"What concern is it of yours?" Hadrian asked.

Raoul gaped at him with his mouth open. "Have you lost your mind?" he exclaimed. "You actually think he's your son?" He shook his head so vehemently his silvery white-hair bounced along his back. "Snap out of it, Hadrian! How are you going to kill him if you think of him as your own?"

"Who says I'm going to kill him?" Hadrian asked.

Raoul was dumbstruck. His eyes gleamed red and his jaw clenched. He took a step towards Hadrian. "You can't change your plan midway," he warned. "You told me the boy had to be nineteen before you could kill him; that if he died before his core matured, his power to drain life would go to another, along with his legacy. I thought you were only biding your time, so that his power to bleed out life died with him." He stared at Hadrian with wide eyes. "He has to die, Hadrian. You and I both can't afford for him to come into his full powers."

"No, *you* can't," Hadrian corrected. "I don't have a problem with it any more. I'm his father now. He defends me against all others. If anything, I'm looking forward to him getting his full powers."

Raoul's expression tightened with fury as he looked into Hadrian's smirking face. "You played me," he said. "You used me to get the boy. You were never going to kill him." He shook his head. "You son of a—"

"Calm down, Raoul," Hadrian cut him off. "I didn't trick you. Truth is, I had every intention of killing him, especially when he took my legacies from me. I wanted them back, but I had to wait until he came of age." He paused as a small smile came to him. "But he was still Benjamin then. After he became Kyran, things…changed."

Raoul narrowed his eyes at him. "How?" he barked.

"He became an Aedus," Hadrian replied. "Kyran Aedus — my heir, my son." He held up a hand, when Raoul opened his mouth to argue. "Kyran does what I say." He pushed away the small voice in his head that said, *unless it has anything to do with Aaron Adams.* He shifted uncomfortably before standing tall to meet Raoul's eyes. "I will tell him to stop killing Lycans. You won't lose any more of your men at Kyran's hands."

"That's not enough," Raoul said. "His ability to drain—"

"Will not affect you or your kind," Hadrian interrupted. "Kyran will not use it against Lycans again. You have nothing to worry about."

"Yes, I do," Raoul said. "We are creatures of the dark. We get our power from the moon, a force even the mages fall weak against — all except *him.*" He shook his head slowly. "He's too dangerous to be allowed to live. The only reason I haven't killed him yet is because I don't want his power to drain life going to another. I will wait until his core matures. But if you won't destroy him, then I will." He smirked. "He may be immune to our venom, but that doesn't mean I can't rip his heart out."

The air filled with the smell of smoke. The Lycans became restless, their eyes on Hadrian, who was looking at Raoul with golden eyes. "Touch him, and I'll make sure it's the last thing you do," Hadrian warned.

Raoul grinned, and stepped back. "Fourteen years of a secret truce between the Lycans and vamages," he said, walking back to his crowd of men. "It was never going to last." His expression turned cold, the smile dropping from his lips. "Do what you can to save him, Hadrian," he said. "But the day he comes of age, I'll be holding his beating heart in my hand."

Hadrian's fury came as a huge wave of fire, roaring at Raoul, engulfing the room with smoke and flames. When it cleared, several Lycans were dead on the ground, but Raoul wasn't one of them. Hadrian's eyes moved to the door, through which Raoul and the rest of his Lycans had escaped.

***

The sun was about to set and Kyran still hadn't come home. Hadrian was fretting, pacing the length of his room. His eyes kept drawing to his arched, floor-to-ceiling windows, desperate to see his son arrive, riding on his motorbike. But there was no sign of Kyran. Hadrian muttered curses under his breath. He was on edge, had been ever since Raoul left. Hadrian felt the grip he had on his temper slipping at the mere memory of what Raoul had said. He promised to himself that he was going to find Raoul and do to him exactly what he'd threatened to do to Kyran. He wasn't going to let Raoul get away with threatening *his* son.

Something moved outside his window. Hadrian came to a stop, and his vamage vision scanned the vast landscape stretched before him. He couldn't see anyone. For a moment, nothing happened. Then the willow tree just outside the window swayed violently. Hadrian didn't get a chance to move out of the way. The window smashed, glass raining down on Hadrian, as a thick branch of the tree forced its way inside and wrapped itself around Hadrian's waist, and yanked him out of the room.

Before Hadrian could make sense of what was happening, the branch pulled back and flung him across the garden. Hadrian hit the ground hard, rolling to a stop. Before he could take in a breath, vines were growing out of the earth and slithering towards him. They twisted around his arms and legs like rope and pulled him up and backwards, until he slammed into a tree and was held there. Hadrian conjured his own element, and the vines began to weaken as flames licked across them.

Branches from the trees on either side of Hadrian began to grow, stretching out like long arms. They twisted around and shot forward, piercing through Hadrian's flesh, burying deep into his chest and stomach, effectively impaling him to the tree. Hadrian grunted, his breath lost as pain clouded his senses. He could free himself, he just had to ignite the wood embedded in his body, and the coils of vine holding his arms and legs in place.

But before he could push the pain away and clear his mind to focus on freeing himself, he heard footsteps approaching. He looked up, and a great surge of relief flooded him.

"Kyran!" he called, as he saw his son walking towards him. "There's someone here!" he warned. It had to be a mage with the element of Earth who had attacked him like this. No, not just a mage, it could only be an Elemental who had the power to manipulate their element with this much force. "Chris," he breathed in realisation. "Kyran, Christopher Adams is here!" he said.

Kyran didn't react in any way. He continued walking, at a rather slow pace.

"Kyran," he called. "Hurry up and free me." He couldn't believe he had to actually say the words. What was wrong with Kyran? Was he this angry at him over Aaron Adams that he was purposefully dragging his feet when Hadrian needed his help?

At his call, Kyran raised a hand. The vines tightened around Hadrian's arms and legs, and the branches embedded in his torso pushed in a little deeper. The pain came afterwards. It was the sense of disbelief and shock that crushed Hadrian first, choking a cry of surprise from him. He stared at Kyran with wide eyes.

"Kyran?" he breathed.

Kyran came to stand in front of him, and it was then that Hadrian noticed his green eyes were so dark they looked almost black. Kyran was breathing hard, his chest heaving as he glared at Hadrian.

"Why?" Kyran asked, and the question hit Hadrian like a tsunami.

He knew, without Kyran saying anything else – Hadrian knew *exactly* what Kyran was asking. He could practically read it in his darkened eyes. His fury, his behaviour, his attack on him – it had to mean only one thing: Kyran had found out the truth about the Lycan attack that separated him from the Adams. Nothing else would make Kyran lash out at him like this.

Hadrian's carefully crafted world, one he took fourteen long years to build, came crashing down at Kyran's one word.

"Kyran," Hadrian started, trying to move towards him, momentarily forgetting he was pinned against the tree. Pain held him still, unable to do anything but stare at Kyran.

"Why did you do it, Hadrian?" Kyran asked.

Hadrian was surprised how much that hurt – more than the pieces of wood forced into his flesh, more than the humiliation of being tied down, more than anything he had felt before. Hearing Kyran address him by his name and not as 'father' was more painful than Hadrian ever thought possible.

Kyran, it seemed, was oblivious to Hadrian's agony. He leant in. "Tell me," he said quietly. "Offer me an explanation. I want to hear you try to justify what you did."

Hadrian didn't say anything. He could see, with the dwindling light in the sky, how little green was left in Kyran's eyes. They were dark with fury, with unadulterated rage, with unimaginable pain.

"Tell me why?" Kyran asked. "Why did you do this to me? What could I have done to you, for you to take me away from my family, to *break* their bond with me?" His jaw clenched. "You watched me call out to them, day after day, knowing all along they couldn't hear me. You let me suffer for *years,* encouraged me to keep waiting, just so I would grow to hate my parents for not coming back, all for what?" he spat. "So you could break my heart, only then to own it?"

Hadrian felt his blood run cold at the exact words he had spoken on top of that hill all those years ago.

"I know what you did," Kyran confirmed. "I know you broke the bond, but kept my side of it alive, just so you could turn me against my family and into your obedient servant."

"No," Hadrian fought back, pushing himself to speak past his horrified daze. "Not a servant, you were my son."

Kyran smirked, but even this was full of anger and pain. "Son?" he asked. "I'm nothing more than a weapon to you. You took me because of this!" He tugged the neckline of his top down to reveal the dark circle on his chest. "You told me my power to drain life came from the Lycans, but it's got nothing to do with them. I was born with his power." He lifted his hand, showing Hadrian the four silvery lines across it. "This didn't come from Raoul." He paused, and Hadrian saw tears in his dark, dark green eyes. "It's from Alex. The mark he left on me when he tried to save me, even while you were *killing* him."

Hadrian's panic was making sparks flicker in the air. How could Kyran know all of this? Who told him? Who could have exposed all of Hadrian's secrets?

"You killed Alex," Kyran seethed. "You severed my bond with my family. You took me away and turned me against my own blood. Just so you could use me because I have a power no one else has?"

Hadrian didn't need to answer. He could see that Kyran already knew he was right. He had worked it out.

"I was desperate, Kyran," Hadrian said. "My powers were locked. I needed someone like you by my side. I was the only one who knew what that birthmark meant, and I wanted to take advantage of that." He shifted, his instinct told him to hold on to Kyran, to make sure he didn't walk away before he got a chance to say what he needed. The vines held fast, pinning his hands to the tree, and his chest throbbed in agony with the smallest of movement. "I admit, at the start, I wanted you for your powers," Hadrian said, speaking past his agony, both physical and emotional. "But that was before I understood what it was like to have you in my life." He held Kyran's eyes. "I arranged the attack on Marwa, on the place that was my *home*, because I needed you."

"Not me," Kyran corrected. "Only my power." He shook his head with disgust. "You should have just killed me and took the damned powers for yourself! That would have been more merciful than what you put me through!"

Hadrian didn't speak, tried really hard to keep his guilt out of his expression, but Kyran saw it anyway. He stilled, and his eyes widened. All those months of researching legacies and how they interacted with the core had given Kyran an acute understanding of them. Hadrian could practically hear Kyran's heart break.

"That's what you were planning," Kyran said in realisation, his voice barely above a whisper. "You're just waiting for me to come of age. You didn't want to risk taking my core before it matured, in case the power to drain life didn't come with it."

"Kyran–" Hadrian started.

"You were going to kill me," Kyran stated. "Another two months, and I would have been dead."

"That was my plan *years* ago," Hadrian said. "But after living with you, I changed my mind."

"Yeah?" Kyran growled with so much fury it rattled the ground. Hadrian felt the vibrations in each and every wound. "Is this the part you tell me you started caring for me? That your pretence changed to reality?" He moved forward and snarled, "Save it. I don't want any more of your lies."

"It's not a lie," Hadrian said. "I planned to take you away from Chris and Kate, and make you believe they abandoned you. I wanted you as my ultimate weapon, and yes, once you came of age I had every intention of taking your life *and* power with it." He stared at Kyran, holding his furious, heartbroken gaze. "But I never planned for you to take my legacies," he admitted. "When you drained them from me, you took a piece of my core with them. It's inside you, Kyran. My core is connected to yours, making you as much my heir as you are Chris's. You're a part of my bloodline, a part of *me*." He stared at Kyran with desperation. "And every time you called me father, you made a little more room for yourself in my heart until you had taken over it completely. Before I knew it, you had become my son in every sense of the word." He shook his head, as much as his condition allowed it. "I brought you up, thinking of you as my own. I could never hurt you, Kyran. You *are* my son."

"I was," Kyran said, "up until a few hours ago. Now, I'm your worst nightmare." A bitter smirk twisted his lips. "You're going to wish you had killed me when you killed Alex."

Hadrian stared into Kyran's eyes, searching for even a *sliver* of green. There was none.

Kyran's hand rested on the tree, next to Hadrian's head and he leant in. "You used me to take over this realm," he said quietly. "I took zone after zone in your name, building your empire. It's what you crave the most, isn't it? To rule this realm. To have complete control of it." He looked deep into Hadrian's eyes. "That's what I'm going to take from you," he said. "Do what you can to save your kingdom, Hadrian, before I burn it to the ground."

He pulled back and turned around, walking away.

"Kyran?" Hadrian called after him. "Kyran? Kyran!" he yelled. "No – wait!" He was struggling against his restraints, so focused on Kyran he didn't realise how badly he was tearing at his flesh. The pain didn't register, not when his mind was reeling from the fact that his son was leaving him.

"Kyran!" he shouted. "No – don't go! Kyran, wait!" He came to his senses and called to his element. Fire flared across the vines and up the branches, weakening them. Hadrian fought against them, freeing himself at last. He scrambled forward, with sticks of wood still embedded in his chest and stomach. Hadrian barely noticed. "Kyran!" he cried, stumbling forward to run after him.

But Kyran was gone. All Hadrian could hear was the fading sound of his bike as it sped far away. Kyran had left Hadrian standing alone, with the burning tree behind him.

# 34

## ALLEGIANCES

Although Skyler was in the city, he wasn't seen much. Whether he was sulking in his cottage all day or going over battle strategies with Scott, Aaron didn't know. He didn't care either way. As long as he didn't cross his path, Aaron was content to obey his parents' request and 'ignore' Skyler's existence.

"Hey, Aaron."

Aaron turned to see Ella walking towards him. The warmer weather had prompted her to start wearing her cropped tops again. Her lily flowers tattoo was clearly visible, going up her side and across her stomach. Now that Aaron knew Ella's mother was named Lily he understood her tattoo design, and it made his heart ache for her.

"Hey," he replied.

Ella stopped beside him, smiling at the tree Aaron was standing under.

"You almost done?" she asked.

Aaron looked up at the shiny red apples, hanging from the branches. "Almost," he replied. He held his hand to the trunk of the tree, and fed it his power, so the apples could grow to maturity.

"Rose said Mary wants to try baking apple pies in the pit," he said in explanation.

Ella smiled and shook her head. "Got to hand it to Mother Mary," she said. "Give her a hole in the ground and a naked flame, and she'll pull pies out of it."

Aaron chuckled. He picked the apples from the branches and loaded the basket at the foot of the tree.

"You know where Drake is?" Aaron asked. "He's been missing all morning."

"I think Scott may have sent him to help other refugees in hiding," Ella said. "I heard something about poor food growth in a few of the abandoned cities." She gave Aaron a rather uncomfortable look before dropping her gaze to the ground. "There's something I need to talk to you about," she started, but then hesitated, as if she couldn't find the words or the courage to go on.

Aaron paused. "What is it?" he asked.

Ella gathered herself and met his eyes. "Skyler's birthday is at the end of the month," she said. "Because he's coming of age, there's supposed to be a ceremony of sorts. And since he's the new leader–"

"He might be your leader," Aaron interrupted, "but he's not mine." He yanked the next apple off, rattling the branch.

Ella put a hand on the tree, leaning in to speak to Aaron. "I know you were hoping for Skyler to be banned from becoming the leader, but Scott and the rest of the chiefs decided–"

"That the homicidal maniac would make a great leader, yeah, I get it," Aaron said. He tore another apple off the branch.

Ella stared at him. "I know you're upset–"

"I'm way past upset," Aaron said. He looked at Ella with blazing eyes. "He tried to have Kyran *executed*. My brother almost died because of him."

"I know," Ella started. "What he did was wrong–"

"It's not just wrong, it's unforgivable," Aaron said. "He blatantly lied to my friends, and the Hunters, to turn them against Kyran. He tried to shoot Kyran with a personalised bullet *twice*, and after taking Kyran down in an unfair fight, Skyler *tortured* him."

"I know—"

"If you know, then why are you here?" Aaron asked. "Why are you trying to justify what he did?"

"God, Aaron, will you just let me talk?" Ella said, annoyed.

Aaron crossed his arms across his chest. "Go ahead," he said. "Talk."

Ella took in a breath. "I know Skyler messed up," she started. "What he did to Kyran was...It was unspeakable. Mages can't kill other mages, and Skyler used that to hurt Kyran, to inflict pain on him." She paused. "But Skyler wasn't in his right mind. That's why he was excused by Scott and the rest of the realm's chiefs. Ever since Skyler lost Armana, he's been...not quite Skyler. I know him, Aaron. I've been with Skyler all my life. We grew up together. No one knows him better than I do, and I'm telling you Skyler could *never* do what he did to Kyran if he wasn't hurting over the loss of Armana."

"So that's it?" Aaron asked with a shrug. "That's your excuse? He was missing Armana, so he tried to kill Kyran?"

"He blames Kyran for the attack on Salvador," Ella started.

"Kyran had *nothing* to do with it," Aaron snarled.

"I believe you," Ella said. "I know Kyran would never jeopardise you, or Rose, in a vamage attack. He came to warn Rose, to tell her to take you and Sam, and leave Salvador." She held Aaron's eyes. "To me, that says there's no way he would have allowed vamages anywhere near Salvador when he knew you and Rose were still there."

Aaron's anger dulled at her words.

She stepped towards him and put her hand on Aaron's crossed arms. "I know that you will never forget what Skyler did to Kyran, and I'm not asking for you to either," she said. "But we need to stand united. We have to have solidarity." Her eyes clouded with pain. "We're already fighting one war with an Elemental; we can't have another."

Aaron dropped his arms, but only so Ella's hand would fall. "I didn't start this fight," he said. "Skyler did."

"But if you attend his ceremony you'll be ending it," Ella said.

"Why should I end it?" Aaron asked. "You can tell yourself whatever you want, Ella, but I *know* what Skyler's like. He's always been cruel and vindictive. He stuck knives into Layla when she was tied down–"

"Layla's a *vampire*," Ella exclaimed. "And Skyler only did that to keep her from fighting back."

"What good did that do?" Aaron asked. "She still got away, and she killed two Hunters for good measure."

"Aaron," Ella breathed, visibly reaching the end of her patience. "Please, don't compare how we treat demons to how we treat each other."

"I'm not," Aaron said. "I know the difference. Skyler's the one who doesn't."

Ella fell quiet. She couldn't fight that truth. Skyler had treated Kyran worse than any demon they had hunted.

"Just think about it," she said quietly. "That's all I'm asking."

"I don't need to think about it," Aaron replied. "The answer's no." He began walking away.

"Aaron, please," Ella called after him.

"What's with you?" Aaron asked, coming to a stop and turning to face her. "Why are you fighting so hard for this?"

Ella held his angry stare. "Everyone attends the coming-of-age ceremony of an Elemental," she replied. "All mages, the Controller, the rest of the Elementals, absolutely everyone. And with Skyler, it's also his inauguration to becoming the new leader of the realm. It's tradition for the other Elementals to be there, by the leader's side, paying him their allegiance. Without you and your parents, I'd be the only Elemental there."

"You shouldn't be there either," Aaron said. "He lashed out at you for helping Kyran escape, or have you forgotten about that?" His eyes narrowed. "What is it, Ella? He comes in here with a few beds and chairs, and you're ready to bury the hatchet?"

"No," Ella said with a furrowed brow. "That's got nothing to do with it."

"Then why are you suddenly on his side again?"

"I'm not on *his* side. There should be no sides!" Ella exclaimed. "We are all supposed to be together, fighting against demon-kind. That's it. That's all it's meant to be. No sub-divisions with some mages backing one Elemental, while the rest go with another."

Aaron smirked, the lines disappearing from his brow. "So that's what's happening," he said. "The Hunters don't want to follow Skyler. He's alienated all of them by lying to them about Kyran. That's why you want me to publicly appear at his inauguration, so it seems like everything is forgiven and forgotten, so they can do the same?"

"You're going too deep into this," Ella said. "I just want everyone to be together. True power lies in unity, that's what Aric taught us."

"No amount of power can make me stand with Skyler," Aaron said. "And my allegiance will always be to my family, to my *brother.*"

Aaron tore his furious gaze away from Ella and started walking. Ella followed after him.

"Aaron—"

Aaron spun around. "I said, NO!" he snapped, and the ground between them split with a loud *crack*.

Ella stared at him, stunned. The gap was only an inch wide, barely two metres long, but it was there all the same, separating Aaron from Ella.

Everyone who was working outside ran up to them.

"What's going on?" Mary asked in alarm. Her hands were covered in soot from working with the fire pit, her cheek and forehead streaked with it too. "You both are fighting?" she asked Aaron and Ella in disbelief.

"Looks like Aaron's winning," Ryan teased with a playful smirk, looking to the crack in the ground.

"Aaron," Rose came to his side, looking alarmed. "What are you doing?"

Aaron was breathing hard, but the anger that had bubbled up in him was fast evaporating, leaving him feeling regretful. The look of hurt on Ella's face made shame well up in him.

"Ella," he started. "I'm sorry—"

Three loud bangs in quick succession drowned out Aaron's apology.

Everyone turned to look at the Gate, where the sound had come from, wearing expressions of surprise and dread in equal measure. The Gate remained firmly shut, but the echo of the hits against it hung in the air.

"Was that...a knock?" Rose asked.

"No one ever knocks," Ella said in a breathless whisper, taking out her gun from its holster.

In a matter of seconds, the Hunters were armed with guns and blades. Chris, Kate and Michael appeared in the street, as did Scott and Skyler, guns clutched in hands and eyes on the

Gate. Skyler was the first to approach the Gate, followed closely by the Hunters, including Ella and Aaron.

On a silent count of three, Scott opened the Gate and the Hunters took aim, ready to take out whatever force was outside the city, trying to get in.

But there was no one there. Skyler lowered his gun, as did the Hunters, staring in shock at what lay beyond the Gate. Scott pushed his way to the front, gaping in disbelief. Aaron saw for himself what had taken everyone's breath away, and he too, found himself rooted to the spot in sheer surprise.

"It can't be," Scott whispered, as he stepped out and touched the gleaming round table – the Hub that had been taken from them so many months ago.

***

Hadrian could barely move. He sat at the steps leading to his balcony with his head bowed. Guilt surged in him like fire, igniting a pain he couldn't anchor in any way. He was left reeling. He buried his face in his hands, trying with all his might to calm down. He had messed up – *really* messed up. Kyran was gone, and Hadrian didn't know how to recover from that.

A knock sounded on his door, but Hadrian ignored it. He didn't have the presence of mind to deal with anyone right now. The door creaked open, and to his utter bewilderment Hadrian saw Kyran walk in. Hadrian stared at him, at the ten-year-old boy standing awkwardly at the threshold of the room. He looked a lot calmer, but there was still some hesitation in his expression. Hadrian didn't move, didn't utter a sound, but Kyran still walked inside and shut the door behind him. The sound of the door thudding closed snapped Hadrian out of his shocked daze.

"You came back?" Hadrian asked, his voice barely above a whisper.

Kyran frowned. "You thought I wouldn't?" he asked.

Hadrian's heart flipped in his chest. "I was sure you had...had left for good. The way you ran–"

Kyran looked away. "You took me by surprise, that's all," he said. "I didn't expect you to attack that Abarimon demon like – like...that."

Hadrian was up and moving towards him. "Kyran," he started, his mouth awfully dry. "I'm sorry. I know I scared you. The Abarimon came for you and I – I panicked. If I had control of my powers, I would have killed that demon before his shadow even crossed yours, but the only weapon I have now is my vampire abilities." He paused, shuddering at the memory of how Kyran had looked at him, the fear in his eyes as he saw the blood of the Abarimon staining Hadrian's lips. He forced himself not to think about it. "I should have told you who I am – what I am – but...I wasn't sure how you would take it," he confessed.

Kyran reared his head up, green eyes with just a hint of their previous blue, pinned Hadrian to the spot. "You thought I would hold it against you?"

"Why not?" Hadrian asked, and his voice finally cracked. "Everyone else did."

Kyran went very quiet. He shifted his weight from one foot to the other. "This is why Neriah locked your powers, isn't it?" he asked.

Hadrian's hands curled into fists. He had to swallow hard before a strained, "Yes," made it out.

Kyran nodded, as if finally understanding the full story. He glanced up at Hadrian. "I always knew there was something different about you," he said.

Hadrian stepped closer. "I know this isn't something that can be easily accepted," he said. "Now that you know that I'm...That I have this...this dark side, does it change things for you? Does it make you want to leave?" His throat closed up at the very thought, but he stood rigidly, watching the young boy, waiting for an answer.

Kyran looked down at his hands, at the four silvery lines across the back of his right hand. "Everybody has a dark side," he said quietly. He raised his eyes to meet Hadrian's with a tight smile. "So you're half vampire." He shrugged. "So what? The other half is still a mage, right? That counts for something."

Hadrian almost sagged in relief. "I was so sure..." He shook his head, displacing his fear of being rejected by the boy he now thought of as his own. "I didn't mean to keep it a secret," he said. "I just – I was scared that if you found out I was a vamage, you'd leave me."

"I'm not going anywhere," Kyran promised. "Whatever you are – part vampire, part mage – you're still my father." He held Hadrian's eyes. "I'd never leave you."

Hadrian let out the breath he hadn't been aware of holding. He should have known Kyran wasn't like the rest of the mages. He should have trusted Kyran enough to know he would accept Hadrian in all his darkness. He wouldn't do to him what Neriah had; he would never turn on him. Kyran would always be by his side. He would never run from him. He would never leave him...

"Sir? Sir?" Machado's voice drifted to him, piercing through the memory Hadrian had been replaying in his mind over and over again.

"Did you hear what I said?" Machado asked.

Hadrian gave him a slow nod. "Yes, Machado. I heard you." He had to gather his strength to repeat what had been reported to him. "Kyran–" He had to force himself to speak past the bubble of hurt, pain and anger that swelled at the back of his throat – "attacked five of our men, killing them before taking the Hub."

Machado nodded. "What are your orders?" he asked.

Hadrian didn't speak right away.

"Sir?"

With a sigh, Hadrian looked at him. "The same as before: gather your men and track him," he said. "Capture Kyran, and bring him back to me."

Machado's brow furrowed. "Sir, you know that's impossible."

"Nothing is impossible," Hadrian returned.

"Sir, you know what the Scorcher is capable of. Without using force, we can't–"

"I will not give the order you're after, Machado," Hadrian told him with quiet venom. "Bring me my son back *alive*."

Machado nodded. "Yes, sir. But you know as well as I do how difficult it will be to fight the Scorcher when he can bleed us out, but we're not allowed to harm him."

Hadrian's jaw clenched, and sparks sizzled in the air. "Do what you have to," he said, forcing the words out, "but stay within a limit. I want Kyran back in one piece, do you understand?"

Machado dipped his head. "Yes, sir."

He walked out of the room, passing Layla at the door. She watched him go, before turning to look at Hadrian with a smirk. "You do know what's going to happen?"

Hadrian held up a hand. "Not now, Layla," he warned.

Layla leant against the door with her arms crossed at her chest, mischievous eyes fixed on Hadrian, greedily drinking in his anguish.

"You're going to get all your vamages killed," she said. "You know as well as I do that they can't capture Kyran. And even if they do, you know that you won't get Kyran back. Your men can force him here, but he'll never *come back* to you." Her eyes gleamed with delight. "You've lost your son for good."

Hadrian didn't speak. He dropped his head. "I know," he admitted in a whisper.

"And yet, you're still protecting him?" Layla asked. "You don't want him hurt." She looked at Hadrian for a long moment. "Guess I was wrong about you," she said quietly. "You do know what love is. You love him."

Hadrian closed his eyes.

"He's declared war on you," Layla said. "He left you, and he took the Hub from you. He will kill your men every chance he gets, and still you want him back alive."

"I do," Hadrian said in a quiet voice. "I want him back. I need him returned to me alive." He turned his head to look at Layla with golden eyes. "But it's not for the reasons you believe," he said. His heart twisted in his chest. "He has my legacies," he said. "And to get them back, I need him alive." He met Layla's slowly widening eyes. "Because I have to be the one who kills him."

# 35

# TURNING TIDES

Aaron couldn't help but grin as the Gate slid open, and the sight he had sorely missed, greeted him like an old and dear friend. Salvador was lying in wait for its residents. The mages walked in with big smiles, carrying their belongings. They were back home at last.

The moment Aaron stepped past the Gate, his eyes went to the lake in the distance. He could make out the whirlpool from where he stood – the Blade of Afton was happily resting in its element.

"Easy! Take your time. Don't drop it!" Scott fretted, guiding the mages levitating the Hub into Salvador.

"Yeah, okay," Alan puffed, along with the six others who were carrying the table. "We've brought it all the way from the City of Yara without incident, but we're going to damage it at the last stretch."

Scott frowned at him. "Do I look like I can take a joke right now?" he asked.

"When can he ever take a joke?" Zhi-Jiya murmured to the surrounding Hunters.

Aaron dumped his bags in the street and followed after the table as it was levitated down the path, heading for its resting place. Aaron wasn't in the least bit surprised when the others did the same. Everyone wanted to witness the moment their Hub returned to where it belonged – sitting in the middle of the round chamber, in all its glory. Even Sam and Rose joined them. They all followed Scott and the floating table, down the path, past the workshops and carefully down the hill, to get to the circular glass building that had been named after the Hub.

Scott had nearly two heart attacks along the way, and another one as the table was manoeuvred up the steps and into the corridor.

"Do you have to hit *every single* corner?" he asked Alan, exasperated.

"It's a round table going down a narrow corridor," Alan protested. "There's going to be a few bumps."

"There'll be more than a few bumps on your head, if you don't stop knocking my Hub into the walls!" Scott warned.

"Put the table down," Skyler called from amidst the crowd.

Everyone fell silent as Skyler made his way past the mages. Alan and the others didn't say anything but lowered the table to stand in the middle of the corridor and stepped away. Skyler raised a hand and the table glided up into the air. Effortlessly, he guided the table down the corridor – without it touching the walls or knocking into anything – and to the chamber. No one spoke a word, but followed behind him in silence. Skyler gently lowered the table to stand exactly where it used to. It locked into position with a satisfying click.

Skyler stepped back, raising his head to look at the others.

Scott stepped forward and patted him on the shoulder. "Thank you," he said to Skyler. He turned his eyes to the gleaming table and grinned. "We have our Hub once again," he said to the mages filling the chamber. "Now we don't have to hide from Hadrian, going from one abandoned city to the next. We don't have to run. We can fight back." Scott walked over to stand before the table. His hand rested on the edge, and the Hub glowed brightly under his touch. "It's not just the Hub that was returned to us," Scott said, "but our fighting chance against Hadrian, and for that, each and every one of us should be grateful."

Scott didn't say it, and neither did anyone else. There was no need for it really, for everyone knew there was only one person who could have returned the Hub to them.

*Kyran.*

It was Kyran who had come, left the Hub at their doorstep and disappeared before the Gate opened. With the Hub back in their possession, Hadrian was no longer able to trap and kill mages with Q-Zones. Mages that had been hiding in ghost cities could finally go home. Survivors of Hadrian's attacks could be settled in new cities. The mages owed this victory to Kyran, but some of the mages didn't quite know how to deal with that. Mages like Skyler. He had barely spoken a word since they found the Hub. Neither did he look in Aaron's direction, as if afraid to meet his eyes.

Scott instructed everyone to go and rest after a long trip back home.

It was as Aaron, his parents and Rose turned to open the door to their cottage, that they realised Sam was heading to another one.

"Samuel?" Kate called. "Where are you going?"

Sam stopped to look at her. "Ella said there's an empty cottage I can take." He glanced once in Aaron's direction, but didn't look directly at him. "I figured it would be better if I stayed there."

Kate looked over at Aaron, wanting him to respond.

Aaron was looking at Sam, but he didn't say anything. He didn't call to him, didn't tell him it was fine and that he wanted him to stay with him. Ever since coming to this realm, Sam and Aaron had always stayed under the same roof...up until Sam tried to kill his brother.

"You're welcome to stay with us, Samuel," Kate said, when there was no response from her son.

Sam was watching Aaron, waiting for him to speak.

"Samuel," Chris called, his tone strict. "You're staying with us. Come inside."

Sam hoisted his backpack higher on his shoulder and shook his head. "No, Mr Adams, I'm not."

He looked over to his sister, who was standing next to Aaron. He didn't ask her to come with him, but Rose gave Aaron's hand a tight squeeze, and walked over to join her brother. The twins headed to the cottage at the very end of the street.

Aaron turned and walked into his own cottage without looking back at them.

*** 

Two weeks passed, and everyone fell into their usual routine at Salvador. Mary worked at the Stove with her helpers, happily preparing meals. Chris, Aaron and the orchard workers made sure the ground and trees were thriving with life, giving fresh and delicious produce. Empaths were back at their huts, recuperating after their hectic workload of healing the injured survivors of Hadrian's terror.

The Hunters spent their time with Scott and Skyler, planning out strategies. Now that Hadrian didn't have the Hub, he wasn't actively fighting, so it was a good time to plan their move.

Aaron didn't attend those meetings. He helped his dad run the orchard instead, as Drake was yet to return to Salvador, still helping other cities improve their food growth. Aaron was glad for the extra workload; it was a good way to keep a worried mind occupied. He had spent the last two weeks trying to contact Kyran. He wanted to thank him for returning the Hub to them, and talk to him, make sure he was okay. He just wanted to see his brother. But no matter how many times Aaron called, Kyran never answered.

It was bothering Aaron; Kyran *always* answered his calls, no matter where he was or what he was doing. So why was he ignoring Aaron's call now?

"Hey, Aaron."

Aaron came out of his thoughts at Ella's voice. He turned to see her walking towards him. He gave her a nod. "Hey."

"You not done yet?" she asked, eyeing the full basket at Aaron's feet.

Aaron wiped an arm over his sweaty forehead. "Almost," he said, and pulled the last of the oranges off the branch, casually tossing it into the basket.

"How are you?" Ella asked.

Aaron narrowed his eyes. "Why are you asking?"

"Just making conversation," Ella replied with a shrug.

"Are you?" Aaron asked.

Ella looked at him with a frown, before she gave up on her act. "Okay, fine. I'm trying to gage how annoyed you are to see if I can talk to you again about coming to Skyler's inauguration next week."

"Still angry," Aaron said. He picked up the basket and started to walk away. "So don't bother."

"Aaron, please," Ella said, walking alongside him. "If you come, so will your mum and dad."

"None of us are coming to Skyler's inauguration," Aaron told her.

"Aaron—"

"Drop it, Ella."

A burst of light distracted them both. They looked up to see Aric's mark form in the sky. It was the distress signal sent from Scott. Aaron flung the basket of oranges aside as he sprinted up the street behind Ella. Several Hunters joined them, as they all raced to the Hub.

The chamber was full by the time Aaron and Ella arrived. Aaron spotted his mum, dad and uncle Mike in the midst of Hunters and mages.

"Scott!" Ella called, hurrying her way through the crowd. "What happened? What's wrong?"

Scott was leaning over the table, his head bowed. He straightened up and pulled back. "Take a look," he said.

Ella leant in to survey the table, as did practically everyone else in the room. Aaron didn't understand what it was he was supposed to be looking for. All he could see were lines and zone numbers. He looked up to see everyone around him seemed just as lost as he felt. That was a first. Usually Aaron was the only clueless one.

Scott waved a hand over the table and the image changed, going from the intricately lined map of the realm to the simpler map with a red $H$ or blue $N$ on the black lined zones, to show who owned which zone.

A gasp of surprise echoed around the room. The Hunters stared at the map with wide eyes. Aaron was deeply confused. The last time he had seen this map, there had been seven zones marked as Neriah's safe zones – ones that had a Gate to protect the human realm from the elemental energy the mages released when they used their powers. Hadrian had the other nineteen zones. Since the war started, Aaron had prepared himself to see a lot more red zones on the map. But what he saw, in fact, were still seven blue zones marked with $N$ for Neriah, but only thirteen zones with a red $H$ for Hadrian. Six zones were now marked with a white symbol – a circle with an inverted V in the middle, three wavy lines behind it, and a spiral between the legs of the V – Aric's mark.

"I don't understand," Zhi-Jiya started. "What is this?"

"I didn't understand it either," Scott said. He paused for a moment, before looking down at the table. "Since we got the Hub back, I've been noticing some growing anomalies on the map – changes happening in Hadrian's zones. These–" Scott touched the zones with Aric's symbol– "are zones that belonged to Hadrian. Why they now have Aric's mark instead of Hadrian's initial, I don't know. I sent a team of Lurkers to scope what was happening in three of these six zones. Ten minutes ago they informed me that these zones are now Gated."

"We've seen that before," Ryan said. "There was a Gate in Hadrian's zone when we went with Neriah to get the Hub back."

"Yes, but that Gate never showed up on the map," Scott said. He pointed to a white marked zone, right next to a blue N zone. "This is where Neriah died," he said. He met Ella's eyes. "You all saw the Gate that was there."

Ella nodded to confirm.

"There had been a Gate there all along, but it never revealed itself on the Hub. It was always marked as one of Hadrian's red zones – ungated and unsafe." His gaze darted to Aaron. "Kyran put that Gate up, but he hid it, so we'd never know it was there. But now, it's showing up on the Hub as a white zone.

Aaron felt his skin prickle with something akin to dread. He looked to his parents to see they were looking just as unnerved.

"Why it's changed, I don't know," Scott continued. "But the Lurkers have scanned the zones and reported that there are no vamages there. These six zones have been taken from Hadrian, cleared of demons and then Gated." He looked to Skyler, standing next to him. "Someone is doing our job for us."

Aaron's heart skipped a beat.

"This one, Zone P." Scott pointed at another white marked zone. "This one never had a Gate. I know that because it's one of the hotspots for causing disasters in the human realm. But now, it's been Gated." He looked to the Hunters. "These zones are being taken from Hadrian but not claimed. Instead, they're being freed, given back to the realm. The Gates that have been put up are surging with immense power."

Murmurs started from the gathered mages, exclaiming their surprise and confusion.

"But wait," Ella said, "if we're not the ones doing this, then who is?"

Scott took in a breath. "I have a strong suspicion." He held on to the Hub. "Gates can only be set up by a mage," he said. "And there's only one mage who isn't working for us. One mage who knows how to access Hadrian's zones. He's the only one powerful enough to put up these kinds of Gates."

A moment's silence rang in the room before Skyler's drawl broke it. "You've got to be kidding me." Skyler glared at Scott. "Kyran didn't do this."

"Then who did?" Scott asked.

"I don't know, but I know it's not the *Scorcher*," Skyler seethed.

"Stop calling him that ridiculous name," Chris said.

"Oh, I'm sorry, would you rather I call that murdering son of a demon, *Ben*?" Skyler asked.

"Skyler, that's enough," Ella intervened before things got heated between Skyler and the Adams again.

"Oh, come on, Ella, listen to this. It's insane!" Skyler said. "Kyran is the one who took these zones from Neriah to give to Hadrian. Why would he take them back to give to the realm?"

"The same reason he returned the Hub to us," Scott said. He paused for a moment to look through the crowd. "I think Kyran has turned against Hadrian."

His words sent Aaron spinning in a vortex of unimaginable relief. He wanted – more than anything – for his brother to leave Hadrian and return to his family. But Aaron had seen how devoted Kyran was to Hadrian, how fondly he spoke of his adoptive father. What could have happened to make Kyran rebel against Hadrian like this? It had to be something big to make Kyran walk away, make him lash out, and have him ready and willing to turn against the one he called *father* for most of his life. As much as Aaron wanted Kyran away from Hadrian, he didn't like the idea that Kyran had been hurt by the one he cared so deeply for.

"We have to make contact with Kyran," Scott was saying to his Hunters. "If Kyran has changed loyalties, we need to get to him before Hadrian does."

Aaron's heart dropped like a stone. Of course Hadrian wasn't going to let Kyran walk away. He would rather kill Kyran than let him go, especially if Kyran was going around taking Hadrian's zones from him.

Scott was laying out strategies but Aaron tuned him out. He ignored everything and everyone around him and concentrated on calling out to his brother. He kept at it throughout the rest of the day. That night, he went out onto the Gateway and waited at their usual spot.

Kyran never came.

\*\*\*

Hadrian stood at the high-arched windows, staring out at the night. His mind was struggling to process the latest incident. No matter how many times he repeated it, it still didn't make sense to him. Kyran was taking zones from him. His Kyran. The son who had worked day and night to build Hadrian's empire was the very same boy who was now destroying it. Even though it was what Kyran had threatened to do to him, Hadrian hadn't really believed it, not until now, when he had lost six of his zones.

"Sir?" Machado's voice drifted to him, as if from far away, even though he was only standing a mere few steps behind him. "What are your orders?"

Hadrian turned around to look at the vamage, but he didn't speak.

"We have to do *something*," Machado said. "He's actively attacking us. Kyran has bled out *every* vamage in six of our zones. He's put up Gates so we can't get in. We need to find a way to stop him."

"Yes," Hadrian said quietly. "Kyran has to stop." He looked at Machado. "Use all our numbers; he can't fight all of you."

"We need to find him first," Machado said. "Over the last fortnight, we've exhausted our contacts trying to locate his whereabouts. No one knows where he is, or when he's going to attack next, or which zone he's going to target. How can we capture him?"

"If you can't get to him, make him come to you," Hadrian said, walking past Machado, heading to the side table next to the fireplace so he could pour himself a much-needed drink.

"And how do you propose we do that?" Machado asked.

Hadrian fell quiet for a moment. "The thing you have to know about Kyran, is that he's fiercely protective of those he cares about," he said quietly. His gaze flickered to the portrait of him and Kyran hanging above the fireplace. He looked away abruptly, and snatched up the bottle to pour the drink into his glass. "Target those who mean something to him and Kyran will come running."

"You mean the Adams?" Machado asked. "But we can't get to them either; they're too well protected. They're in Salvador and we can't get past their Gate, not now—"

"Then smoke them out," Hadrian said. "Once you have the Adams, you will have Kyran."

"But how can we lure the Adams out of Salvador?" Machado asked. "They don't have any family left to target."

"Yes, they do," Hadrian said. He turned to Machado, the gold sparks in his eyes were like flickering flames. "Family doesn't always mean blood."

Machado looked confused, then the lines on his brow disappeared. He nodded at Hadrian. "Understood, sir." He swept out of the room.

Hadrian looked to the portrait again, his gaze lingering on Kyran's face. Watching him, he downed his drink in one go.

# 36

## HOLDING ON

Aaron hurried to the Empath huts. It was dead of the night, everyone was sleeping in their cottages, including the Empaths. Casting a quick look around, Aaron opened the front door and snuck inside.

He headed straight to the room that once belonged to Armana and closed the door behind him. He scanned the darkened room until he found the cabinets against the far wall. A whole array of small, thin glass vials, filled with coloured liquids were neatly arranged inside. Aaron wondered how the Empaths, without the ability to see, could differentiate between the vials. It was only when he looked closely that he saw the small etchings on the glass. Each vial was marked with a series of dots – Braille, Aaron realised.

Aaron spotted the vial he was after instantly. It was the only one with a clear liquid, while the rest were blues and reds. Aaron carefully lifted the vial, staring at it with a pounding heart. He had never done this without the help of an Empath, and he had no idea of the dangers involved, but Aaron didn't care. He had to do this, and he had to do it alone. He didn't want Amber or any of the other Empaths reporting to Skyler that Aaron had gone to speak with Naina. Skyler was a lot of things, but stupid wasn't one of them. He would know Aaron's trip to another plane of existence was to do with locating Kyran. Aaron was certain even Scott would push Aaron to find out what information Naina had about Kyran's whereabouts, since he was desperate to have Kyran on their side, fighting against Hadrian. But until Aaron had spoken to his brother, he didn't want anyone knowing where he was.

Another week had passed with Aaron calling out to Kyran every day and every night, but Kyran still hadn't answered. That wasn't like him. Kyran didn't ignore Aaron, not for this long. That had to mean Kyran was in some sort of trouble, and with Hadrian's vamages after him, that was a very real possibility.

His parents, both of them, along with Michael were out every day searching for Kyran, trying to find him before Hadrian did. Scott had dispatched teams of Lurkers and Hunters to track Kyran down, but so far none of them had found him.

Aaron couldn't just sit about and wait. Not when he knew that Hadrian was looking for Kyran too. What if he had already got to him?

Aaron shook himself out of that terrifying thought. He could feel his bond with Kyran. His brother was alive. But where he was, what condition he was in, that Aaron could only find out with the help of Naina.

Aaron took the vial and hurried back to his cottage. He was alone at home, his parents and uncle were out looking for Kyran. No one would be there to interfere. Taking a deep breath, Aaron sat on his bed. He stared at the vial, hoping he didn't get lost and could find Naina without the help of an Empath. He uncorked the vial and brought it to his lips. He squeezed his eyes shut and tipped the glass bottle back, swallowing the liquid quickly. Lowering himself down, Aaron kept his eyes closed and his mind focused on only one thing: meeting Naina.

\*\*\*

A cool breeze brushed along Aaron's cheek, and he could feel the warmth of the sun on his skin. He opened his eyes to find himself no longer in his room but on a hilltop. He was standing on rocky ground, looking out over a city. The wind ruffled his hair as he squinted in the bright sunlight, looking at the houses lined along the street below. He frowned. The street looked exactly like–

"Hello, Aaron."

He turned to see Naina walking over to him. There was a little grey in her blond hair, a few lines around her bright blue eyes and her mouth. She wore a long dress with a shawl draped around her shoulders. She walked up to Aaron, smiling as though he were a dear friend she hadn't seen in a long, long time.

"I've been waiting for you to come and see me," she said.

"It's only been a few months since I last met you," Aaron replied.

She had been young then, in her early twenties. But Aaron knew she had aged not because time moved differently on this plane of existence, but because Naina grew older every time Aaron came seeking answers from her. He felt bad, but he had to come. Kyran wasn't responding to his calls, and he had no idea how to reach him. Naina was his only hope of finding Kyran.

Naina smiled at him, before laughing softly, reminding Aaron of wind chimes. "It's okay, Aaron, don't feel guilty about it," she said. "This is inevitable. Every time you come to me, I grow older."

Aaron frowned. "You can read minds too?"

"I don't need to read your mind, Aaron. You wear your guilt freely for everyone to see," Naina said. "It's one of the many remarkable things about you."

Aaron refrained from snorting. "Yeah, okay," he said. "Looking guilty is a real feat."

"It is," Naina said. "Others hide their guilt; they go to great lengths to justify their wrongs, and in doing so they taint their souls. You, on the other hand, show your guilt. You feel remorse, even when it's not your doing. That is what keeps you pure."

"I don't know about that," Aaron muttered. "But I do feel bad about coming to you, and ageing you in the process," he admitted.

Naina smiled. "Keep in mind, though," she said, "age may only be a number, but it's not infinite. You have one, perhaps two, visits left."

"What do you mean?" Aaron asked. "Are – are you saying if I keep visiting you, you'll grow old and…die?"

Naina smiled. "It's the way it has to be."

Aaron shook his head, horrified. "That's not fair."

"I never said it was," Naina replied.

"Naina," Aaron started, "I can't be responsible for *killing* you."

"You won't be," Naina assured. "I will grow old and be gone from your life. But I will not die. That concept doesn't exist for me. When another being asks for my help, I will meet them as I did you – as that young, *annoying* child." She laughed. "But I will be gone from your life, and no longer able to meet you. I will be dead for *you*." Her eyes softened. "And that, Aaron, is the true tragedy of death. It's not the one who is gone from this world, but the ones they leave behind, alive but in mourning, that deserve sympathy."

Aaron understood what she meant. The ones who died, they were gone. Pain was only felt by the ones left living.

"I promise, Naina, I won't come to you again," Aaron said. "This will be my last visit. But I need your help. Kyran–"

"Isn't answering your calls," Naina finished for him with a small nod. "And you're worried he might be in trouble."

"You showed me the memories of Kyran's childhood and that time he came to rescue Layla," he said. "You always seem to know what's happening." He held her eyes. "You know Kyran has turned against Hadrian."

It wasn't a question, but Naina nodded anyway. "I do."

"Do you know where Kyran is?" Aaron asked.

She didn't reply, but her eyes lowered. Aaron felt his heart lurch. "Please, Naina," Aaron said. "I need to know he's okay."

Naina's expression filled with sadness. "He's not okay," she said. "He's not hurt physically, but he's suffering. He's surrounded by nothing but pain, and it's swallowing him whole."

Aaron felt his blood run cold with fear. "Where is he?" he asked. "How can I find him?"

But Naina shook her head. "You're asking the wrong questions," she said. "You can only help your brother once you learn the reason behind his pain."

Aaron watched as her eyes welled with tears. She looked over at the rocky ground to her right. Aaron followed her gaze, and his stomach turned.

There was a puddle of blood on the ground, stretched wide and long. Crimson drops were streaked around it. There was *so* much blood. Someone had died here, that much was brutally apparent.

"Before you can make sense of the present, you must understand the past," Naina whispered.

Aaron staggered a step towards the blood. "What happened here?" he asked.

"You already know," Naina replied. "You've figured it out."

Aaron felt like he couldn't breathe. He looked back at Naina, past her to the street below. "We're – we're in Marwa," he said.

He had recognised the street. He even picked out his house. He turned back to the blood. He remembered the Lycan attack he had watched from the memory held on Ben's cloak. He could still hear his dad's broken voice narrating what had happened.

*I don't know how, but he managed to get ahead of me. He raced after the Lycans, blinded by rage.*

"Uncle Alex," Aaron breathed. "This – this is where he died."

Naina came to stand by his side. She put a hand on his shoulder.

"Brace yourself."

That was all the warning Aaron got before the empty ground before him changed. The blood was still there, but this time there was a dark-haired man lying face down in it.

Aaron almost leapt back in shock.

"No!" he cried. "Naina, please! I don't want to watch this!"

Naina wasn't next to him any more, but her voice echoed in his ear. "You must. You have to see what happened. It's the only way."

Aaron's breaths were becoming laboured as he took in the horrific scene. His uncle Alex was dying, right before his eyes. The uncle who looked so much like Kyran, it was as if Aaron was watching Kyran die.

"Naina, *please*, stop this!" Aaron cried, clenching his eyes shut. "I can't – I can't see him die!"

"You have to," Naina said. "Kyran saw this. You must too."

Aaron opened his eyes, forcing himself to look. Blood was pooling under Alex as he struggled to move, to inch forward. He reached out with a shaky hand, trying to get to the small, unconscious boy before him. Aaron's knees almost buckled under him. He had been so focused on Alex, he hadn't noticed his brother. There were other bodies there too, strewn across the ground. Other men, women – Aaron even spotted another little boy, dressed similarly to Ben, lying not too far from Alex.

Aaron's focus was on his brother. Ben's eyes were closed, his chest rising and falling, but his body was covered in horrendous bites, making him bleed profusely. Chunks of his flesh had been ripped out. Aaron heard a growl behind him and turned to see the Lycans, led by Raoul – easily distinguishable as the only red-furred beast – approaching Alex and Ben.

Alex managed to drag his wounded self closer to Ben. His fingers locked onto the back of Ben's hand.

"Ben," he called out in a hoarse whisper.

Someone came to stand before Alex, a bloodstained sword in hand. Aaron raised his eyes to see who it was, and the sight almost knocked him to the ground. Hadrian was staring at Alex, a mix of regret and anger on his face.

"H-Hadrian?" Alex called, in shocked, pained disbelief.

"Sorry, Alex," Hadrian said. "I never meant for you to be a part of this." He raised his sword.

"NO!" Aaron yelled.

"H-Hadrian–" Alex breathed. "N-No!"

The sword went through Alex's back, but Aaron felt as though it were him who had been stabbed in the heart. His body trembled in shocked horror as he watched Alex take his last breath. Everything went dark. Aaron didn't move. His body wasn't in his control any more. He could do nothing but stand transfixed. The darkness lifted, and Aaron's breath, once again, left him in a surprised gasp.

Alex was no longer on the ground. He was sitting with the four-year-old Ben gathered in his lap, hugging him close. They were still on the hilltop, but it looked like no one else was there. No Hadrian, no growling Lycans, no bodies of fallen mages, just Alex and Ben, both wounded and bleeding.

Alex, Aaron noted, was still holding on to Ben's hand.

"Lex," Ben whispered, his voice ragged with pain.

"It's okay," Alex whispered back. His gaze darted from edge to edge of the hilltop, looking, searching, but there was no one else there.

"Lex," Ben moaned. "It hurts."

"You'll be okay," Alex said, cradling him, holding him tight. "I've got you. I won't let anything happen to you."

"Lex, I'm scared." Ben started to cry. "I wanna go home."

"It's okay," Alex said softly, rocking him in his arms. "I'm here." Aaron could see the tears in Alex's eyes. "I'll get you home. I promise, Ben. I'll get you home."

"Lex," Ben's voice lifted with panic. "Lex, Lex!" He was arching in Alex's arms, writhing in pain. "Lex! Don't let go! Don't let go, Lex!"

"I won't," Alex said, tears falling from his eyes as he closed them tight. "I won't let go of you."

"Lex!" Ben was screaming. "I'm scared, Lex. Don't leave me!"

"I won't," Alex said, as the little boy in his arms started to fade, his body slowly becoming transparent. "I won't leave you."

"LEX!" Ben's cry lingered in the air as he disappeared. Alex faded with him. Everything went black once again.

This time when the darkness lifted, Aaron saw Alex's body lying in the pool of his blood again, his hand still closed around Ben's tiny hand. A light glowed under his fingers, moments before Hadrian walked over and picked Ben up. Alex's lifeless hand fell from Ben's, but the imprint of his fingers remained on Ben's skin as four silvery lines. Hadrian carried Ben away, leaving the Lycans to close in on Alex's body.

The image thankfully faded there, before Aaron had to endure the sight of Lycans attacking Alex's dead body. Aaron was left staring at nothing. The pool of blood was gone, leaving the ground empty and innocent-looking, as if such atrocities had never occurred upon them.

Naina was once again by Aaron's side. Her hand lifted from his shoulder and Aaron felt like someone had sapped all his strength out of him. He almost fell to the ground, his legs shaking under him. He bent low, his hands on his knees to keep himself steady, and took in several deep, shuddering breaths. He was shaking, his stomach curling. Hadrian had killed Alex. It hadn't been the Lycans, like everyone believed. It had been Hadrian.

Naina's soft hands helped Aaron to straighten up. It was only when Aaron turned to look at her that he realised his vision was blurred by tears. Naina cupped a hand to Aaron's cheek.

"I'm sorry," she said. "But you had to see it to understand what it is your brother carries with him, what those marks really mean."

Aaron's already broken heart twinged with pain. "They're not scars," he said, his voice cracking with grief.

"They are scars," Naina corrected, "but not from the Lycans, as Kyran believed. They are imprints, left on him when his uncle's soul departed from his body, but refused to move on. Alex couldn't leave Ben in the clutches of Hadrian and the Lycans. He couldn't ignore Ben's pleas for him to stay with him, so Alex held on to Ben, never letting go, even in death."

Aaron stared at her. "Uncle Alex stayed with Kyran?" he asked in disbelief.

Naina smiled, but it was one full of sadness. "Why else do you think Kyran resembles him?"

Aaron was rendered mute.

"Alex's presence lingers in Kyran," Naina explained. "The marks he left on Kyran's hand weren't the only ones. His imprint is on Kyran's very *soul*. Over the years it manifested, so as Kyran grew up, more and more of Alex became apparent in him. Alex is the shadow that stays with Kyran, who helps Kyran fight against Hadrian's complete control. Without Alex, Kyran would have been lost to Hadrian's thrall."

Aaron remembered what the Pecosa Rukhsana had told him.

*There's a darkness in him. It's a part of him, a shadow he cannot escape. Its influence weighs down on him.*

That's what Rukhsana had sensed in Kyran's aura. The darkness wasn't anything sinister. It was simply Alex's imprint.

"When Alex died, his soul – spirit, energy, whatever you want to call it – his very *essence* clung to Kyran's, unwilling to leave him," Naina said. "By choosing to stay with him, Alex bound himself to Kyran. That's why he can interact with Kyran like no other echo can." She paused, and a tear slid down her cheek. "That's why, even when Alex is there, no one other than Kyran can see his echo."

Aaron's thoughts raced to Alaina, the woman who had spent her life waiting for a glimpse of Alex again.

"There has to be a way," Aaron said. "A way for others to see uncle Alex's echo."

"There isn't," Naina said. "Not until Alex's purpose is fulfilled. Only then can he move on from Kyran, and only then will those who loved him finally be able to catch a glimpse of him."

"What's his purpose?" Aaron asked. He would do anything, *anything*, to give his uncle's soul his freedom, to end Alaina's wait, to complete the story of the Waiting Bloom.

"His purpose is the same as yours," Naina said to Aaron. "To save Kyran from Hadrian and reunite him with his family." She held Aaron's eyes. "The last thought to cross Alex's mind, just before life rushed out of him, was to save Ben and get him home. That's his purpose. To get Ben back home."

Aaron couldn't find it in himself to speak.

"As Alex's soul left his body, he met Ben's, just for a brief moment. That's what you saw. Alex sacrificed not only his life, but his peace in death for Kyran. He's been with Kyran for the last fourteen years, but he can't speak to him. He can only reveal himself to Kyran in locations his echo can walk – cities he once lived and breathed in. That's why Kyran only spotted him after he joined the mages under the pretence of being a Hunter. Every time Kyran went on a hunt and entered a city Alex had once hunted in, he saw Alex's echo; he just didn't understand what he was seeing." Naina looked to Aaron with glistening eyes. "Alex has been guiding Kyran, keeping him from slipping into the darkness Hadrian encouraged. But now that Kyran has learnt of Hadrian's deceit, even Alex can't hold him back."

Aaron's heart skipped several beats. "What do you mean?"

The sky above them turned grey, as clouds moved to block the sun. Naina hurried a step closer.

"We don't have much time left." She held on to Aaron's arm with a firm grip. "You have to stop him."

"Who, Hadrian?" Aaron asked.

"Kyran," Naina said. "You have to stop Kyran."

"Stop him from what?" Aaron asked.

A fork of lightning hit the sky.

"The ability Kyran possesses to drain life is not something he got from the Lycans," Naina said. "It's a power he was born with. The mark on his chest is proof of that. It's an immense power that comes from Aric himself."

"What?" Aaron asked. "Wait – you're saying Aric had the same ability?"

"He did," Naina said. "He could drain the life of a demon with a touch. Kyran isn't the first mage to inherit that ability from his forefather. There have been others in the past. But Kyran will be the first to destroy himself if he doesn't stop using this power."

Aaron's stomach clenched with fear. "What do you mean?" he asked.

Thunder boomed in the sky and the ground began to tremble under them. Naina tightened her grip on Aaron's arm as a fierce storm started from nowhere. Aaron's hair and clothes ruffled in the strong wind.

"The power to drain life was only ever meant to be used against demons," Naina said, raising her voice to be heard over the howl of the wind. "Aric used to bleed out demons, taking their life and gaining victory, but Kyran is using that same power on vamages. When he drains the life of a vamage, he is not only taking the life of a part-demon, but also of a part-*mage*." She shook her head. "This power to drain life was *never* meant to be used on another mage. Mages aren't supposed to kill one another."

The ground under Aaron cracked. The wind pushed Aaron back, threatening to topple him off the hilltop. Aaron felt the pull just at his navel. He was about to be wrenched off this plane of existence and slammed back into his own. Naina held him by both arms, saving him from being dragged away.

"Stop him, Aaron," she said desperately. "By draining the lives of part-mages, he's tainting his soul. If Kyran continues to bleed out vamages, he'll lose the purity that makes him a mage and—"

Her terrified eyes were the last thing Aaron saw before he was finally yanked away from her. He shot up in bed, breathing hard, and Naina's last words echoed in his head. "*– and he'll turn into the worst kind of demon your realm has ever seen.*"

## 37

# THE BURNING BLOOM

Aaron waited at the door, nervously pacing before it. He couldn't stop trembling. His heart was still racing, his palms clammy. The last words Naina had said repeated on a loop inside his head. He had to find Kyran. He had to stop him from massacring vamages before it destroyed him. How many had Kyran killed so far? Was the damage already done? Aaron recalled Scott reporting that the newly gated areas were suspiciously vamage-free. Had Kyran killed every last vamage in those zones? Or had some escaped back to Hadrian? Aaron found himself praying the latter was the case. Then he still had a chance of saving Kyran, of *keeping* him Kyran, and not losing him to darkness.

The street was slowly filling with mages getting ready for the day, and preparing breakfast. A few of them gave Aaron strange looks as he paced outside his front door, but Aaron was too keyed up to care. A flash of light lit the street, and Aaron stopped mid-step. His eyes narrowed at the Gate as it slid open to reveal the very people he was fervently waiting for. His mum, dad and uncle's tired, dejected faces were visible even from a distance. They had returned from another failed search for Kyran. Aaron took off at once, running towards them.

Chris looked up as Aaron came nearer. He shook his head at Aaron, thinking he was coming to ask if they had found any trace of his brother.

"Chris!"

Before Aaron could get out a word, Scott's shout had all of them turning to see him hurrying towards them. He looked worried – which was mostly how Scott looked these days, but there was a particular urgency in his movement, as if he couldn't get to Chris quick enough.

"Scott?" Chris frowned. "What is it? What's wrong?"

Scott was talking before he even reached them. "I just got a call from my Lurkers. The Gate at Zone J has fallen. The Lurkers have spotted a number of vamages in the vicinity, but they're not spreading out to take the zone. All of them are heading in the one direction." He met Chris's eyes with dread. "They're heading for J-26."

Aaron felt a stirring in the pit of his stomach. That zone sounded familiar, but he couldn't figure out why, until he saw his dad pale to the hue of a ghost. Behind him, Kate and Michael looked equally horrified.

Chris staggered back a step, and shook his head. "No," he breathed, his eyes wide and full of fear. "Please, God, no."

*** 

Her garden was thriving with life. Flowers were in full bloom, filling the air with their sweet scent. The mix of vibrant colours brought a smile to Alaina's face as she guided her power to sprinkle the flowers with water. It had taken her years to learn how to control it and not drown the poor flowers in too much of her element. She remembered how Alex used to laugh every time he had to revive her dead garden. She smiled at the memory, her heart aching to hear his laughter again, even if only for a moment.

It came over her all of a sudden: the feeling of his presence – enveloping her whole being, like a warm blanket on a cold winter's night. Alaina lowered her hands, her heart somersaulting in her chest. Her eyes fluttered closed as she relished the moment, the one she had been waiting for *so* long. A smile tugged at her lips.

"I knew it," she breathed. "I knew you would come."

She turned around, opening her eyes slowly to brace herself but her heart skipped a beat anyway when she found him standing before her. Alex looked just like he had the last time she had seen him – from the small, sweet smile on his face, right down to the white Lurker robe he had worn to match Ben's Halloween outfit, and of course to annoy his brother, Chris.

"I knew you would find your way home," Alaina said.

Alex stepped forward, his soft green eyes on her. "I was never lost."

His voice soothed Alaina. It felt like an aching, burning wound had finally been healed. It took a moment before what he said made sense to her. She frowned slightly. "What?"

Slowly, Alex walked over to her. "This isn't the first time, Alaina," he said. "I always come home to you. Every time you close your eyes, I'm here. You just don't remember it once you wake up."

Alaina jerked back a step. She looked around her. The sweet smell of her garden, the warm air on her face, the distant whoosh of waves crashing, Alex finally finding his way to her – all of this...was it real? Or was it just something her desperate mind had made up? Her breathing quickened. "This – this is just a dream?" she asked.

Alex looked like he would give anything to tell her no, but instead he nodded. Alaina felt like she couldn't breathe. Her vision started to blur, but she blinked the tears out of her eyes so she wouldn't lose sight of Alex.

"No," she urged. "It can't be a dream."

"It is," Alex told her sadly, coming to stand before her. "It's the only way I can meet you. It's how we've been meeting for a long time. But the minute you wake up, you forget." His eyes glistened as he stared at her. "You wait for my echo every day; blame me for not coming back to you, question my love for you, not knowing that I'm here – you just can't see me until your eyes are closed."

Alaina stared at him in disbelief. "Why?" she asked, her voice cracking. "Why can we only meet when I'm asleep? Why can't I see your echo when I'm awake?"

Alex's expression clouded with pain. "I've told you why," he said. "Countless times."

Alaina shook her head. "Tell me again."

"Alaina–"

"Tell me," Alaina demanded. "Why can't I see your echo? Why can't I feel your presence?" A tear slipped down her cheek. "Why do I have to dream you to meet you?"

"I'm not a figment of your imagination," Alex explained. "I'm here, Alaina. I'm really here. It's not in your head. I'm really here with you."

Alaina reached out, her hand trembling, terrified that he would disappear if she touched him; that she would wake up and lose him all over again. Her hand rested on his chest – firm, solid: real. A moment later, his hand was covering hers. Alaina moved into his arms, hugging him tightly, breathing in his scent, letting herself finally believe he was really here. A sob broke past her resolve as she was held by him again, nestled in his warm embrace after fourteen long years. Even if what he was saying was true, to her this felt like their first embrace in over a decade.

"Alex," she wept. "Don't – don't leave. Please, stay with me."

Alex tightened his hold on her. Alaina was sure that if he were to loosen his arms, she would fall to pieces.

"I don't know how to live without you," she told him brokenly.

"Yes, you do," Alex said. "You do, Alaina. You know what you have to do." He paused for a moment. "You have to let me go."

"No." Alaina locked her arms around him. "I can't do that. I can't. Don't ask that of me."

She felt him pulling back so he could face her. He cupped her face in his hands. "Alaina." His voice was soft and gentle but it only made Alaina cry harder. "Listen to me," he pleaded. "You don't remember these dreams once you wake up. Everything we talk about, all I've told you, explained to you, nothing seems to stay with you the moment your eyes open. But you have to focus on what I'm about to say, okay? Please, Alaina, remember what I'm about to tell you. You *have* to remember this time – please."

Alaina took in long breaths to stem her tears, and nodded.

Alex looked her dead in the eyes, his expression growing to one of sheer desperation as he whispered, "Run."

Alaina frowned, blinking at him with confusion.

Alex nodded at her. "Run, Alaina. Run!"

Alaina snapped awake, the book in her lap fell to the floor with a thud. Her heart was racing, tears drying on her face. She sat up in the chair she had fallen asleep in, and stared around the living room. Everything was still and quiet. Alaina took in a deep breath. Why was she feeling so panicked? Had she had a nightmare? She must have been asleep, dreaming, but for the life of her she couldn't remember about what. Whatever it was that left her feeling shaken right down to her core had slipped away from her the moment her eyes opened.

Taking a deep breath to calm her erratically beating heart, she wiped at her face, erasing the tear tracks. Sniffing, she bent down to pick up the book she had been reading before falling asleep. Her fingers barely touched the book before a tremendous blast of fire shook her house. Her front door was smashed, reduced to nothing more than splintered wood. Had Alaina not been leaning down, she would have been hit by the rubble flying across the room.

Instinct made Alaina duck to the floor, covering her head with her arms. She looked up to see several men – vamages, she realised a heartbeat later – striding into her home. Fear and confusion froze her. What was happening? Why was she being attacked? Her city was as small as it was unremarkable. Why would it be targeted? Why would *she* be targeted?

Alaina got to her feet, her hands held out before her. "I'm not armed," she said.

"We know," a vamage with glittery blue eyes replied with a grin.

Alaina didn't stand a chance. The vamages attacked as one, their jolts pushed her bodily into the air. She smacked into the far wall and fell to the floor. Her head spun, her cry lost as all the air was knocked out of her. Groaning, Alaina raised her head, trying to stop the room from spinning before her eyes. She caught the glow of something red and orange, hurtling away from the vamages and striking her walls in all directions.

The room exploded. Her walls went from soft cream to black in the blink of an eye. Alaina's breath choked in her throat. Her horrified gaze went straight to the wall above her mantel, where flames were hungrily devouring the pictures she had lovingly displayed – the memories she had of Alex.

"No," she croaked, her shock momentarily stealing her voice. "No, NO!"

She was up and running, her element spilling out around her, battling the fire with earnest. If she hadn't been one mage against twenty vamages, she might have had a chance of putting out the fire.

Alaina tried. She wasn't a fighter but she tried to defend herself against the vamages. Her wave of water, while not as big and not even a fraction as powerful as Neriah's or Aaron's, rushed forward, trying to knock back the vamages and salvage some of her burning photos. The vamages put a swift end to it. Her panic and growing desperation to save Alex's pictures made it almost too easy for the vamages to overpower her and pin her to the ground, laughing as she struggled under their hands.

"No!" she cried, straining against them as they held her arms behind her back. Her head lifted, and with bloodshot eyes, she saw flames turn each and every picture she had to charcoal. "Please!" she cried. "Please, stop, please! It's all I have of him. Please, it's all I have!"

The vamages paid her desperate pleas no heed, laughing while they kept her trapped in place so she could helplessly watch the images of Alex being swallowed up in flames. Alaina's whole house was ablaze. Every room, every corner; everything she owned was burning, turning to ash.

Machado gave the order and the vamages holding Alaina pulled her to her feet and began dragging her out of the house. The acrid stench of the fire made her cough and splutter as she dragged more smoke than air into her lungs. Her already tear-filled eyes stung with the smoke, but Alaina fought to stay.

"No!" she screamed as the vamages pulled her towards the door.

She couldn't leave. She couldn't let the house she had lived in – the house that held so many memories of not only Alex but also of her family – burn to the ground. She had to stay. She had to save her home.

She fought with all the strength she possessed, kicking and scratching at the vamages, but it made no difference. They dragged her out of the house and across the porch before throwing her viciously to the ground. The rough edge of the last step leading to her porch caught Alaina, cutting along her temple. She tried to sit up, holding a hand to her bleeding forehead, but a kick to her back had her falling face forward again.

She was grabbed by her hair and yanked up to her feet. She found herself looking into Machado's cruel eyes.

"Why are you doing this?" she cried. "What do you want?"

Machado only tightened his grip and pulled her closer, grinning at her. "Nothing personal, Alaina," he said, revelling in her look of surprise that he knew her name. "This isn't about you."

Machado began walking, dragging Alaina by her hair. She fought him every step, striking him in the chest and neck with curled fists, but Machado only laughed in return. Without warning, he pushed her to the ground. Panting, Alaina looked up to see her house, engulfed in flames behind the vamages. Her angry eyes settled on Machado, who raised his hands to aim at her. The vamages behind him did the same.

"You made the wrong people your family," Machado said. "The Adams are the ones to blame for this. They must know by now that this zone's Gate has fallen. You're going to suffer until they come to your rescue." He smiled to reveal his fangs. "Once they arrive, you can die."

Alaina wanted to move, to get up, to run, to use her element to block the attack that was about to come her way, but she couldn't. Her head felt fuzzy, warm blood trickling down the side of her face from the cut on her temple. Fear had her weighed down, unable to get up.

Time seemed to slow for Alaina. She saw the flicker of the fireballs forming in the vamages' hands. Sparks flew in the air before a stream of fire came at her as all twenty vamages attacked her as one. Alaina was transfixed in terror; she couldn't even look away as the rush of fire came at her. She felt its searing heat even at a distance.

But it never reached her.

Someone came to stand before her, blocking the attack before a single fireball could hit her. Alaina stared in surprise as a boy stood with his back to her, hands raised, his wall of fire swallowing each and every one of the fireballs that had been thrown at her. Holding the fiery shield in place, he turned his head, just enough to glance at her, and Alaina felt the ground slip from under her.

Vivid green eyes met hers. His face was one she could never forget – had not forgotten, even in fourteen long years. He was the spitting image of Alex, down to every last feature. The same face, the same hair, but somehow he also wasn't Alex. Alaina knew, even in that first nanosecond their eyes met, she knew he wasn't her Alex. The eyes gave him away. Her Alex had had soft, kind, green eyes that lit up every time he smiled. But these green eyes staring back at her were fierce, full of rage, full of a darkness Alex had never known. Alaina's heart broke when realisation flitted through her shock.

"Ben," she breathed.

Kyran tore his gaze away from her, unable to hold the weight of her tear-filled eyes any longer. He turned his attention to the vamages that had stilled at the sight of him. The last of the fireballs disappeared and Kyran lowered his hands, ending the shield. His poison-green eyes swept through the crowd of vamages, pausing briefly on Machado. Hadrian's right-hand vamage looked thrown. They were expecting Chris and Kate Adams to show up, not Kyran.

The burning house was the last thing Kyran noticed. He raised a hand, and the vamages flinched, visibly terrified. Kyran clenched his hand into a fist and the flames destroying Alaina's house died, killed in an instant.

Kyran turned back to the vamages. His eyes darkened and the mark on his chest began to glow, as did the four lines at the back of his hand. With a growl, Kyran went for them, just as Machado gave the signal for his men to surround the Scorcher.

\*\*\*

Aaron ran out of the portal at his dad's heels. His mum arrived a second after him, with his uncle Mike right behind with a team of Hunters, including Skyler and Ella. The first thing Aaron registered was the smoke. The street was full of it, but Aaron could still make out Alaina's house in the distance, charred black with thick dark clouds twisting up from it into the sky. Everyone took off towards it at once, weapons in hand.

Aaron felt as though his heart was sitting in his mouth. He was utterly petrified at the thought of vamages hurting Alaina. He could see they had torched her house. Was she still inside? What if they had already killed her? Aaron forced himself not to think like that. He couldn't afford to think like that.

As they ran on, they heard yells and grunts, and what was unmistakably the thump of bodies hitting the ground, coming from somewhere beyond the house. They couldn't see anyone though; the smoke from the fire was obscuring their sight.

Skyler was already working on clearing the air, forcing the dark clouds to dissipate as they ran forward.

The smoke thinned, and the first thing Aaron spotted, with immense relief, was his aunt Alaina, sitting on the path that led up to her house. She was wounded, one side of her face stained red with blood. But she was sitting up, so that had to mean she wasn't too badly injured. She wasn't moving, though; she was just sitting there, staring at something in front of her. Chris reached her first, kneeling down beside her. Aaron came to her other side.

"Alaina? Alaina, are you okay?" Chris asked, his voice shaking as badly as his hands as he touched her shoulder.

Alaina didn't give any response. Aaron turned his head to follow her gaze.

What he saw would never leave him.

Kyran was there, surrounded by vamages. He was fighting them. The beam of light shining from his chest, glowing through his clothes, was as bright as a full moon in a starless sky. Aaron's breath choked in his chest. Kyran had no weapons; his hands were all he needed. The four lines at the back of his right hand were gleaming white as Kyran grabbed vamage after vamage, bleeding the life out of them in mere seconds, each lifeless body dropping to the ground.

It took a moment for Aaron to understand what was actually happening. The vamages had all thrown their weapons to the ground. They were no longer fighting Kyran; they were trying to escape, but Kyran had them trapped by fire, and a current of air that pulled them back to him, no matter how far away they got.

"What?" Ella's gasp brought Aaron out of his horrified daze. He looked up to see her standing behind Alaina, staring at Kyran with horror. "What…what is that? What is he doing to them?"

She wasn't the only one to be brought to a sudden stop. Everyone had stilled at the sight of Kyran bleeding out the vamages. It was clear from their shocked and terrified reaction that they had never seen anyone using the kind of power Kyran possessed.

Aaron's gaze darted to his parents, ignoring the others. He couldn't care less what the Hunters thought of Kyran, but he didn't want his parents and uncle to get freaked out.

Too late.

His heart sunk to the soles of his feet when he saw the fearful looks on their faces. They were staring at Kyran as if they couldn't believe their eyes. Aaron couldn't really blame them. It was a sight beyond any horror. The way the vamages arched with pain – their backs curved, mouths open in silent screams – as Kyran's hand glowed on their chests, dark lines travelling under their skin, racing to Kyran's fingers, across his hand and up his arm to the light in his chest – it was a sight that chilled Aaron's blood.

Aaron wanted to explain, to assure to his parents that this wasn't a sinister power Kyran had – that it was something Aric had wielded; a power that came from the first mage himself. But Aaron didn't have the clarity of mind to do any explaining right now. Naina's warning was ringing in his head...

*If Kyran continues to bleed out vamages, he'll lose the purity that makes him a mage and he'll turn into the worst kind of demon your realm has ever seen.*

Aaron was up and running full pelt towards Kyran.

"Aaron!" Several cries erupted after him, including his mum and dad's. "No!"

Aaron ignored them, racing as fast as he could. He brought forward the element of Water to extinguish the flames that circled the vamages.

"KYRAN!" he yelled. "STOP!"

Kyran either didn't hear him or completely ignored him. Aaron had to step over dead vamages to reach his brother's side. Two successive ripples shoved back the vamages nearest to Kyran. Aaron reached Kyran and grabbed him by the top of his collar and arm, pulling him around to face him.

Aaron's heart almost stopped. Kyran's eyes were no longer green. They were black – a complete, bottomless black. Thin black lines that looked like blood vessels were visible from his hands, all the way up both his arms, disappearing under the sleeves of his top. Bleeding out so many vamages, taking the life of part-mages, had already taken a toll on Kyran. He looked less human, and more like a demon.

"Kyran," Aaron choked. "You have to stop. You can't kill them. They're part-mage—"

Kyran yanked his arm out of Aaron's hold.

"Kyran–" The rest of Aaron's words never made it out as Kyran's jolt of air threw him across the street.

Aaron fell with a hard thump. His mum and dad were instantly by his side, helping him back up. They had run after him, leaving the rest of the shell-shocked Hunters huddled around Alaina.

"What's happening?" his mum demanded, looking at Kyran and the terrified vamages. "How is he killing them?" she asked.

"He's not just killing them," Aaron panted. "He's killing himself in the process."

Aaron hadn't had the chance to tell his parents about Naina's warning. They were too distracted coming to Alaina's rescue. His parents didn't understand what was happening, or that Kyran was destroying himself.

His dad gave a desperate look in Kyran's direction. "How do we stop him?" he asked Aaron.

Aaron shook his head. "I...I don't know."

"Simple." Skyler's voice sounded from behind them. Aaron and his parents turned to see him staring at Kyran with cold eyes. "We take him out." He looked to the Hunters, his gaze stopping on Ella. "Still think I was wrong to try to kill him?" he asked. "I told you he wasn't a mage. He's worse than a demon!"

Ella had no reply. Her clouded grey eyes moved to stare back at Kyran.

A group of vamages tried to attack Kyran together, but he threw them off, his jolt of air sending them spinning upwards before hitting the ground, winded and in pain. Aaron recognised one of them; it was the glittery-blue-eyed vamage, Machado.

Kyran drained one vamage, then another, and then another. He looked crazed, lost in his rage, killing without reserve, without thought. Aaron was running again, his blood turning cold with fear. He had to find a way to stop him. He had to stop Kyran before it was too late.

Machado was on his feet now, and tried to swing a sword at Kyran. His strike was dodged and the sword knocked out of his hand. A jolt of air pinned Machado against the scorched wall of Alaina's porch, holding him in place as Kyran reached for Machado's throat to bleed him out.

Aaron stepped in the way, putting himself between Kyran and Machado. Kyran halted. His hand was a hair's breadth away from Aaron's chest. Kyran was panting, his black-as-night eyes fixed on Aaron. Kyran pulled himself back, tilting away from Aaron. His hand dropped to his side, the light in it fading, as well as from his chest. The black lines that had spread like a vine up Kyran's arms disappeared. His eyes finally went from black to their usual green.

Aaron watched him carefully, seeing comprehension dawn slowly on him. He stepped forward. "Kyran?"

Kyran didn't speak, but it was as if a haze was being lifted from before his eyes, as if he had finally come to his senses. It took Aaron putting himself in Kyran's way for him to snap out of his murderous rage. Now Kyran's expression was one of painful awareness as he looked at Aaron.

Aaron reached out for him, but Kyran backed away, moving out of his reach. "Kyran," Aaron called again.

Kyran looked around him, his gaze darting through the assembled group of Hunters, Alaina, and Michael, until they rested on Chris and Kate Adams. Kyran froze. For a moment that seemed to last forever, Kyran did nothing but stare at his parents. His eyes glistened a true green. Chris and Kate took a step in his direction, and Kyran immediately stumbled back a step. He shook his head. Kate and Chris came to an immediate halt.

A click, then a bang, and just like that, a bullet came speeding at Kyran. It sliced the skin of his shoulder, just nicking him. It was enough to snap him back to the present. All eyes turned to Skyler as he aimed another shot at Kyran.

"Sky, no!" Ella cried.

But before Skyler could fire his gun again, Kyran's furious jolt caught him, throwing him back with tremendous power. He hit a tree and fell to the ground. Clearly dazed, Skyler picked himself up but still raised his gun, blindly aiming for Kyran.

But Kyran had already took off.

"Kyran!" Aaron bolted after him.

The remaining handful of vamages – including Machado – scampered off, running in the opposite direction, using the distraction to get away from the Scorcher and the Hunters.

Kyran raced to the portal he had used to arrive, Aaron hot at his heels. The ground was shaking – Chris using his powers to fight Skyler no doubt – but Aaron didn't stop to look back. He kept running, chasing after Kyran, refusing to let his brother go after weeks of searching for him.

Kyran jumped into the portal, touching the top of the ring as he did so, igniting the portal to close behind him. Aaron didn't stop. He raced forward and threw himself into the ring of fire, passing through it mere seconds before the portal disintegrated into nothing.

## 38

# NEVER LETTING GO

Aaron stumbled into a deserted street, the crumbling buildings and debris around him suggesting it was another abandoned city. He didn't have the time to take in more as his attention snapped to Kyran the moment the portal shut behind him with a bang.

Kyran turned to him with a snarl, a hand pressed to his wounded shoulder. "What do you think you're doing?" he growled. "Why did you follow me?"

"To make sure you're okay," Aaron said, panting a little to catch his breath.

Kyran pulled his bloodied hand from his shoulder and waved it in the air. A portal opened up behind Aaron. "Go," Kyran commanded. "Get out of here."

"No," Aaron replied. "I'm not leaving you."

Kyran strode towards him, the action full of threat. "*Get out,*" he hissed the words.

Aaron shook his head. "No."

Kyran shoved Aaron, hard enough to make him stagger backwards. "Go!" he yelled.

Aaron stood his ground. "I told you, I'm not leaving you."

Standing so close to him, Aaron could see how dark Kyran's eyes had turned. They were also red-rimmed and bloodshot. His face seemed paler. He looked ill. It took a moment for Aaron to realise he probably was, at least partially as a result of not answering Aaron's calls for *weeks*.

"I don't want you here," Kyran spat. "Leave me alone." He pushed Aaron towards the portal again. "Go!"

Aaron almost toppled backwards into the glowing Aric's mark. He straightened back up, gaining his footing. "Not a chance, Kyran. I'm not going anywhere."

Kyran grabbed him by his collars, shaking him. "Don't you understand?" he bellowed. "You have to go! You have to stay away from me." Sparks were spitting around him, crackling in the air. "He's looking for me. If he finds you with me, he'll kill you, like he killed Alex." His breath caught in his chest and, for a heartbeat, Kyran's whole body sagged under the crushing weight of guilt. "He killed him, because of me. It's my fault...it's all my fault." His grip tightened and he pulled Aaron closer, growing fierce once again. "Leave, and don't ever come back. Don't call to me, don't look for me." His eyes were a dark green, full of pain and regret. "Go back to Salvador and stay out of the way. I'm taking Hadrian's zones, and I won't stop until he's left with *nothing!*"

"What about me?" Aaron asked. "What will I be left with if your revenge costs you your life?"

Kyran's grip slackened, but his eyes didn't lose their darkness.

"There's only one way this can end," Kyran said, his voice quieter now. "And you're going to have to make your peace with it."

"Make peace with the fact that you're going to get yourself killed?" Aaron asked incredulously. He shook his head. "No. I don't accept that. I don't. You don't have to do it this way. You don't have to fight Hadrian on your own. All of us – all of the mages – want Hadrian defeated. You can help–"

Kyran let go of him, moving back, running his hands through his hair. "You don't get it."

"I do," Aaron said.

"No, you don't!" Kyran yelled. "You have no idea why I have to do this on my own. You don't understand."

"Then explain it to me," Aaron said.

But Kyran only shook his head. "You won't understand," he repeated in a broken voice. "You don't know what he did."

Aaron's chest seized with pain. "Actually, I do," he said quietly. "I saw it, Kyran – what Hadrian did." He met Kyran's eyes. "It wasn't Lycans that killed uncle Alex. It was Hadrian."

Kyran's eyes were still dark, but they glistened with pain so raw it stole Aaron's breath. "That's not all he did," Kyran said. "Hadrian's the reason Marwa was attacked that day. He teamed up with Raoul. He let the Lycans destroy the city. Everyone that died that day, it was all because of Hadrian. It was him, from the very start. He planned it all." He paused for a moment. "He broke the bond, Ace," he said, heaving the words out. "He made them think I was dead. He tricked them – tricked Mum and Dad, just to make me hate them – to make me believe they had abandoned me." Kyran's head bowed, and Aaron could see how badly this revelation had broken his strong and fearless brother. It made Aaron's heart bleed. "They never heard me," he said. "All that time I was calling out to them, four years of me begging them to come back for me, hating them for ignoring me, but they never heard any of it. They never heard me." He closed his eyes. "They'll never hear me," he said in a hollowed voice. "Hadrian broke their bond with me. That can never be undone. My parents will *never* be able to feel my presence, feel their bond with me again. I don't *exist* to them."

"You know that's not true," Aaron said at once. "They know you exist, Kyran. They know and they love you. They're fighting to get you back and they won't stop until they do. They will never give up on you, and neither will I."

But Kyran was shaking his head. "Our bond connects us to one another. It's what makes us whole. What makes us a family. Hadrian's ripped me away from my family, and no matter what

I do, what anyone does, that can never be fixed. The bond is broken." Kyran was distraught, his hands curled tight, his eyes bloodshot and brimming with tears. "I'm not a part of my family any more."

"No, that's not true," Aaron said. "Hadrian may have broken the bond so Mum and Dad can't feel you…" He held Kyran's glistening gaze. "…but he messed up. I hadn't been born then, so whatever he did, it didn't affect me. Our bond still exists, Kyran, and it's strong. Mum and Dad are connected to you through me. We *are* a family, and nothing can ever change that."

Kyran closed his eyes and a few drops spilt down his cheeks. He shook his head. "What he's taken from me, I can never get back," he said quietly. "Hadrian made me hate my own parents, made me resent them for something they didn't even do." The guilt in his eyes turned to rage. "I'm not going to let him get away with it. I'm going to take everything away from him: his zones, his power, his vamages. I'm going to kill *every last one* of his men until he has no one left!"

Aaron's stomach swooped with fear. "You can't do that," he said. "They're part-mage, Kyran. Taking their life means you're corrupting yours. If you keep on draining them, bleeding them out, you'll end up becoming a demon too."

"I don't care," Kyran said.

Aaron stilled, staring at him in shock. "But I do," he said. "I care, Kyran. I won't let you destroy yourself."

"I grew up believing I was part-demon," Kyran said. He glanced to his hand – at the four lines across the back of it. "So what if it actually comes true? It'll be worth it, taking Hadrian's army down with me."

"You can't let your revenge change who you are," Aaron said.

Kyran quietened for a moment. Then in a tortured voice, he said, "I don't know who I am any more."

Aaron held on to his arm. "You're my brother," he said. "And I'm not losing you – not to demons, not to Hadrian, not even to your own powers."

"Why not?" Kyran asked. "I'm a weapon. I have the power to drain life. It makes sense to use it. And if I take out all of his vamages, it makes the war easier for your side to win."

"Kyran," Aaron choked. "What good is winning the war if I lose you?"

Kyran fell silent, not having a response.

"You have to stop," Aaron said, swallowing his fear. "You'll destroy yourself if you kill any more vamages."

"I know," Kyran said. "I can feel it, deep in my core; every time I bleed out a vamage, it kills a little more of me." He locked fierce eyes with Aaron. "But it's a price I'm willing to pay. I'm dead by the end of this war anyway, either at the hands of Hadrian, or Skyler and his Hunters, so why not take Hadrian's numbers with me?"

Aaron grabbed Kyran by his collars. "You're *not* going to die," he said, shaking him. "You hear me? I won't let anyone hurt you, not Hadrian and definitely not Skyler. And if taking out Hadrian means I have to lose you to darkness, then I won't let you fight Hadrian either."

Kyran looked at him with surprise.

"Hadrian is my enemy," Aaron said. "He ripped my family apart – made my parents grieve the son who never died, took you away from us, and brutally murdered my uncle. Hadrian's the reason I didn't grow up in this realm, didn't grow up with my brother. Trust me when I say I'll do anything – anything – to defeat him. But the one thing I won't do is risk *you*." He stared at Kyran. "I'm not going to watch you turn into a demon, Kyran. Losing you is not an option. I'd rather lose the war."

Kyran didn't say anything, but he stared at Aaron with genuine surprise. It was clear he didn't expect that from Aaron: didn't expect someone to fight so hard to save him.

Aaron gathered himself, letting go of Kyran and standing back. "Tell me you won't drain another vamage," he said. "Swear it on my life."

"Ace–" Kyran breathed in protest.

"Do it, Kyran," Aaron said. "Swear on my life, that no matter what happens, you will not bleed out another vamage ever again."

"I have to make Hadrian pay," Kyran said.

"And we will," Aaron said. "But not at the expense of your soul."

Kyran looked at him for a long moment before finally giving in. He nodded.

"Say it," Aaron demanded.

"I swear," Kyran said.

"The full thing," Aaron pressed.

"I swear on your life, Ace, I won't bleed out any more vamages," Kyran promised.

Aaron felt like he could finally breathe again. It was as if an invisible weight had been lifted from his chest. He nodded, and then smiled. "Good." His hands moved to hold Kyran's arm. "Now come on, we're going home."

Kyran didn't look at him, but slowly shook his head. "I don't have one."

Aaron's smile slipped. "Why are you saying that?" he asked. "Of course you do. Your home is where your family is, where we are."

"And where is that?" Kyran asked, meeting his eyes. "In Salvador? Marwa? Cities that are controlled by mages – by the soon-to-be new leader, Skyler Avira?" He looked at his shoulder, where Skyler's bullet had grazed it, splitting a line across his skin. He turned to look at Aaron again. "You know I can't. If I walk into one of their cities, I won't leave it again." He stepped back, out of Aaron's reach. "And I have too much to do – too many zones to take from Hadrian. I won't bleed out his men, but I'm still going to destroy his kingdom."

"Skyler can go to hell!" Aaron spat. "He can't stop you from coming home."

"Yeah, he can," Kyran said. "I gave up my home, Ace. I gave it all up when I chose to stay with Hadrian, chose to call him my father." A flash of pain crossed his features before Kyran fought it down. "Too much has happened. I can't expect Skyler, or any of the mages, to look past my crimes."

"What crimes?" Aaron asked furiously. "You've not done anything wrong."

"I have," Kyran confessed. "I have, Ace, I've done plenty." He paused, before heaving out a breath. "I'm the reason Hadrian has his powers again. I let him take control of the zones, carry out attacks on cities. I was so focused on protecting Hadrian that I let him kill Neriah." His eyes were full of remorse, full of self-loathing. "I'm the reason this realm is falling apart. I have to be the one to fix it."

"But you don't have to do it alone," Aaron said. "If you come to Salvador and tell Scott, tell Ella and the rest of the Hunters that you want to help them – that you want Hadrian defeated – they'll forgive you for all you've done in the past. Even Skyler won't be able to do anything to you, not without the support of the rest of the mages. He got away with it once, but it won't happen again." He stepped closer. "*Please*, Kyran, come back with me," he begged. "Scott knows you've turned against Hadrian. He knows you're taking Hadrian's zones and putting up Gates. He's been trying to find you, to ask for your help in defeating Hadrian. He knows they can destroy Hadrian with your help."

"That's the problem," Kyran said. "I want to take Hadrian's zones. They want to take his life."

Aaron stilled, staring at Kyran, unable to keep the shock out of his expression.

"I know he deserves it," Kyran started, "for everything he's done. I want Hadrian to pay, I want him to lose this war, lose control of this realm. I want him to suffer." He paused, and a breath choked in his chest. "I loved him, Ace," he said. "He was my father, my best friend, the one person I thought I could always depend on." His eyes clenched shut. "But it was nothing more than a lie – an act he put on, biding his time until he got what he really wanted." He looked down at his hand, at the four lines across it. His hand curled. "I hate him," he whispered, but Aaron heard him, felt his pain ache in his own chest. "I hate him. I should want him dead, but...I don't. I should hate him more than I ever loved him, but...but I don't. I'm taking his zones, the one thing he cares about – the only damn thing he cares about – and giving them back to the realm. I'm out to destroy his rule, his chance of being the sole leader of this realm. I'm his enemy now, but if he's captured tomorrow, I'm scared I'll go running to save him." He held Aaron's gaze with tortured eyes. "I don't know why. I don't understand it. It's as if the need to protect him is a part of me, and as much as I want to, I can't get rid of it. I can't help Scott, or the Hunters, because I'll never let anything happen to Hadrian." He shook his head, running a hand down his face. "It's stupid, I know. It's dumb and it makes no sense–"

"No, I get it," Aaron said quietly. "I get it." A small, sad smile crossed his face as he nodded at Kyran. "I've felt something similar."

Kyran didn't say anything.

"I get what you're saying," Aaron said. "I understand why you don't want to come home—"

"It's not a matter of what I want," Kyran cut him off. "I want nothing more than to be able to come home, to see Mum and Dad again, to tell them face-to-face how sorry I am," Kyran paused. "But I can't."

"You have to," Aaron stressed. "You have to find a way, Kyran. You don't know how important it is for you to come home."

Kyran's brow furrowed.

Aaron steeled himself, taking in a deep breath. "Uncle Alex," he forced the words out, "died saving you. After Hadrian killed him, his...his soul, it didn't move on." He saw the first flickers of panic pass over Kyran. Aaron held on to his arm to keep him grounded. "He stayed with you. That's why you...you look...like him." Aaron had to push himself to keep going. "That's why no one has seen Uncle Alex's echo – because he's bound to you. You're the only one who can see him. Uncle Alex can't move on, not until the purpose of his staying with you is fulfilled." He held Kyran's eyes. "And his purpose is to get you back home, back to Mum and Dad."

Kyran stared at him with wide, unblinking eyes. "How do you know this?" he asked.

"Naina showed me," Aaron said.

"Wait. Naina?" Kyran frowned. "You've met her?" he asked with disbelief.

Aaron nodded. "She showed me the attack, and how Uncle Alex was murdered by Hadrian. She told me Alex never moved on, that he stayed with you, to try to get you away from Hadrian and back home."

Kyran was silent for a moment, his brow creased, green eyes narrowed as he tried to work it out.

"Why?" he asked at last, and his voice cracked with anger. "Why would he do that? Why would he forsake his peace, his afterlife, just to stay with me?"

Aaron held his eyes. "Because he wanted to. Because you asked him to."

Kyran stilled. He started shaking his head, denying it.

"I saw it, Kyran," Aaron said. "Naina showed me." Aaron forced himself to go on. He had to tell him, however painful it was. His brother had a right to know. "It was just after Uncle Alex died, or maybe it was as he was dying – I don't know, but...but I saw him with you. He was holding you, comforting you. Naina said it was your souls meeting." Aaron shook his head, biting back the tears that were resurfacing at the memory. "You were so scared. You were confused, and in pain, and terrified of being left alone. You were begging Uncle Alex to stay with you, to not let you go." Alex's gaze dropped to Kyran's hand – to the four silver lines across the back of it. "So he didn't."

Kyran stared at him. Shock, disbelief, pain – all of them flashed across his features. He shook his head weakly; his lips parted but no sound came from them. His hand came up and he gripped onto Aaron's arms, steadying himself. He looked ready to collapse, visibly reeling from Aaron's words. He lost the battle and sunk to the ground, his head in his hands. Aaron knelt by his side.

"Kyran," Aaron called softly. "Kyran, come on." His voice shook. "Don't, please."

An angry Kyran, Aaron could handle, even a violent Kyran, but a *broken* Kyran – Aaron couldn't begin to deal with.

"Kyran," Aaron called, his voice cracking with his own grief. He put a hand on Kyran's uninjured shoulder, shaking him gently. "You can't fall apart, okay?" he said. "Please," he whispered. "Don't fall apart."

Kyran dropped his hands, tilting his face up towards the sky, his lashes wet with tears. "I'm sorry," he heaved out, and Aaron knew he wasn't talking to him. "I'm so sorry. It's all my fault. It's all my fault."

Aaron couldn't stop himself. He pulled Kyran into a hug, holding him tight in his arms. "It's not your fault," Aaron told him. "It's not your fault, Kyran. Uncle Alex chose to stay with you. He wanted to save you, to get you back home to Mum and Dad, and that's what we're going to do." He pulled back to look at Kyran, but didn't let go of him.

But Kyran was shaking his head. "I'm the reason he died," he said in a hoarse voice. "Not only did he give his life for me, he gave up his afterlife too. And I've spent my life believing no one cared enough to help me, that my family didn't try hard enough to save me." He closed his eyes, reaching up to cradle his head.

Aaron tightened his grip on Kyran. "Hadrian tricked you," he said. "He manipulated you into thinking like that. It's not your fault."

Kyran didn't look like he agreed. "That's why I can see him," he croaked, seemingly talking to himself. "That's why his echo is different, why he can follow me, why he can lead me to places." He was looking at his hand, tracing the four lines across it.

Aaron looked at it, at the mark Alex had left. "That's how you came to help Aunt Alaina," he said in realisation. "Uncle Alex led you to her, didn't he?"

Kyran closed his eyes, reaching up to wipe at them. "I've never seen him so...so frantic before," he said. "He kept flickering in and out of sight. I opened a portal and he led me through it to arrive in Halia, to see Machado hurting her." His hand curled into a fist and his head dropped.

"Kyran," Aaron said, pulling him a little to get his attention. "We can make this work, okay? Uncle Alex wanted you to get away from Hadrian. You've done that. All that's left is for you to return home. We can do that too. In two days' time, it's Skyler's inauguration. Every mage in the realm is going to be attending the ceremony, everyone except our family. I can make an excuse; say I don't want to be there while the ceremony is taking place. I'll get Scott to open a portal to Marwa. I'll take Mum and Dad, and come home. You can meet us there. The whole of Marwa will be empty, so no one will know. Maybe you coming home, to Marwa, to our actual house will be enough for Uncle Alex and he'll be able to move on."

Kyran didn't say anything for a long moment. He tilted his head, looking at Aaron. "Skyler's inauguration?" he asked.

"Yeah, it's his birthday. At his coming of age ceremony he's going to be declared the new leader," Aaron supplied. "Ella said everyone will be attending, that it's a big deal of sorts. She's been trying to convince me to go too, but I told Ella straight up I'm not going to his ceremony."

"No," Kyran said. "No, don't do that," he said slowly. He paused before nodding to himself. "You should go to the ceremony."

Aaron looked at him as if he had grown two heads. "Are you insane? You think I'd go to his celebration after everything he's done to you?"

"Don't think about that," Kyran said.

"How can I not?" Aaron asked. He gestured to Kyran's wounded shoulder. "You're still bleeding from his last assault." His eyes hardened. "Skyler's not my leader, so why should I go to his inauguration? I'd much rather spend that time in Marwa, with my parents and my brother, trying to bring peace to my uncle."

"Inauguration ceremonies are always held in Marwa," Kyran supplied, somewhat distractedly. "It's the city of the Elementals. That's where new leaders are appointed."

Aaron couldn't hide his disappointment. "Okay, so then...then we'll hold back in Salvador. You come once everyone leaves for Marwa. It should still work; you're still coming back to your family, even if it's not your actual home. Uncle Alex—"

"Home was only ever Marwa, Ace," Kyran cut him off. He was talking to Aaron, but his eyes were far away, working something out. "Go to the ceremony."

Aaron's eyes narrowed. He had spent enough time around his brother to know when he was putting together a plan. "What are you thinking, Kyran?" he asked.

Kyran straightened up, wiping his sleeve across his eyes. "Get yourself to the inauguration," he said. "Make sure Mum and Dad are with you too."

"There's no way in hell any of us are going to that lunatic's ceremony," Aaron returned.

"Please, Ace," Kyran said, looking to Aaron. "Do it for me. Go to Marwa and attend the ceremony." Something akin to hope glinted in his pained eyes. "We can use this opportunity to right a number of wrongs, Ace, and give everyone what they rightfully deserve."

# 39

## THE INAUGURATION

It was the last day of September, and the day that Skyler finally came of age. Residents of Salvador had piled into Marwa in the early hours of the day. Ella and Scott had instructed mages to prepare the city days before, so when Aaron walked into the City of the Elementals with his parents by his side, he saw the whole of Marwa was dressed for the occasion. There were silver and white lanterns floating in the air, adorned with the spiral symbol for the element of Air. Huge banners with Skyler's name on them hung in the air, and the table was set for a mighty feast. A raised platform in the town square made a stage for Skyler to be hailed as the new leader of the mages.

During the course of the morning, mages from all over the realm came to the city, dressed in their best outfits. Long, flowing dresses mingled with high collared suits, in bright, vibrant colours. Lurkers arrived in hooded robes, wearing a silver sash across their torsos. Everyone looked like they had made the best effort to look smart for the occasion.

Aaron, in his jeans and T-shirt, stood against the wall of one of the many ornate buildings in Marwa. He may be attending the inauguration ceremony at his brother's behest, but he would be damned if he didn't show his distaste for it. Skyler hadn't taken the stage yet. His iconic white Elemental coat, with the silver studded spiral on the back, was waiting for him; floating in the air above the raised platform. Aaron tried not to look daggers at it.

He glanced around the bustling street, to the mages huddled around the extra long table, or standing in groups, chatting happily, drinks in hand. It did indeed seem as if the whole realm was there, crammed into one city, to watch their new leader take the pedestal. Even Sam and Rose had come, since Scott point blank refused to leave them on their own in Salvador. But they didn't want to be a part of Skyler's celebrations, and so were keeping their distance.

Aaron didn't get to see much of his friends lately. Rose took every opportunity to speak to Aaron, but Sam hadn't tried talking to him after their last conversation. He had been keeping his distance, staying in a separate cottage with Rose, and working in the orchard whenever Aaron wasn't there. Aaron wished he could say it didn't bother him, but it did. He missed Sam something fierce, but he couldn't bring himself to forgive him for what he'd done.

Aaron watched as more mages entered the city, joining the party. The gathering was spread across the street, all the way up to where the houses were. It was only thanks to his family bond that Aaron could find his family among such numbers. His parents and uncle Mike were seated midway down the table.

Aaron wanted to tell them. He *really* wanted to tell them about Alex: the truth about how he had died. He knew his dad felt guilty; felt that there had been something lacking in his training that resulted in his brother's death. Aaron wanted to ease that guilt. He wanted to assure his dad that there was nothing wrong with what he had taught his brother – that Alex had been a more than competent fighter, and that his death was because Hadrian attacked him. But try as he might, Aaron couldn't bring himself to do it.

It had been mentioned to him more than once that Alex and Hadrian had been close; that Hadrian had looked out for the youngest Elemental. Finding out that Hadrian had killed Alex was going to hurt Chris, and Aaron couldn't do that to his dad. He was already so stressed out, Aaron didn't want to add to his mental trauma. His parents were struggling to deal with the fact that their eldest son had left Hadrian but couldn't return to them because of the complications with the mages. Aaron had told them that much – how Kyran wanted to come home but couldn't because of his affiliation with Hadrian. He told them that Kyran now knew that he hadn't been abandoned by them, that it was Hadrian that had severed their bond. It had been a tough enough conversation on its own, and Aaron just didn't have it in him to tell them everything; especially that it was Hadrian who had killed Alex.

Aaron saw his dad lean in towards Alaina, seated next to him. He asked her something and she gave a small nod in return. Aaron found he couldn't tear his eyes away from her. Alaina seemed as forlorn as two days before, when Aaron had returned to Salvador after meeting Kyran and found her in the cottage with his parents. Alaina had lost her home and all her earthly possessions, so Chris and Kate had brought her to Salvador to stay with them.

Aaron would never forget how she had looked at him the moment he had walked into the cottage. She wanted to speak with him, Aaron could tell that much from the way she had risen from her chair at the sight of him, but she couldn't get a word out. Even while his parents were crowded around him, asking frantically about Kyran – where he was, how Aaron got back to Salvador, if Kyran was as badly injured by Skyler's attack as they feared – all Aaron could focus on was Alaina. Eventually he had walked over to her, and without saying a word, he wrapped his arms around her. He held her as she cried, not just because of all she had lost that night at the hands of vamages, but because of what seeing Kyran for the first time had done to her. She had been shaken to her very core. Alaina had sobbed in his arms, her words unintelligible, except for one she had kept repeating – *Ben*.

Aaron could still feel the tears that had fallen on his neck, like a phantom pain, aching in his very being. Aaron owed her a painful conversation. He had to tell her the reason why she hadn't seen Alex's echo. He was planning on telling her, but not just yet. She was too fragile at the moment, utterly emotionally exhausted. He wanted her to recover a little before telling her.

"There you are."

Aaron found Ella next to him, looking very unlike her usual self – in a pale blue gown that swept to the ground, and her long dark hair gathered up into a bun. "I've been looking all over for you," she said.

Aaron pushed his hands deeper into his pockets and stayed as he was, leaning against the wall. "Why?"

"It's almost time for the ceremony," Ella said. "Come onto the stage with me."

Aaron gave her a withering look. "Don't push it, Ella," he said. "I'm here. Let's just leave it at that."

Ella smiled and moved closer, putting a hand on his shoulder. "I'm so proud of you, Aaron," she said. "You chose to be the bigger man by coming today. You even got your parents to come, which I never thought would be possible after...after what happened between Chris and Skyler."

Aaron looked away, shifting his weight as his feet shuffled under him. That had not been easy. When Aaron had returned to Salvador, it was to find that Scott had sent Skyler away from the city, so that Chris and Kate could calm down. It was probably the best thing to do, as Chris was fuming over Skyler shooting Kyran – again. Convincing them to come to Skyler's inauguration wasn't something Aaron ever thought he'd do, but he'd argued and cajoled to the best of his ability – and solely for Kyran.

"This is good," Ella was saying. "It'll smooth things out between Skyler and the Adams."

Aaron turned his head to look at her with sharp green eyes. "You do realise 'the Adams' includes Kyran too, yeah?" he asked, his voice uncharacteristically harsh.

Ella faltered, her smile slipping. "Aaron," she started, "you can't blame Skyler for attacking him. You saw what he was doing to those vamages–"

"He was protecting Alaina," Aaron said, feeling his face heat up with anger. "She's a part of our family, Ella, and those vamages were attacking her. Kyran was only defending her."

"That wasn't defence, that was an annihilation," Ella said. "What he was doing, draining the life out of the vamages–" She shook her head – "that's not how mages fight. We fight with honour."

Aaron scoffed. "Seems like you don't know mage history as well as you think you do, Ella."

Ella frowned. "What's that supposed to mean?"

Aaron straightened up. "It means that the power Kyran was using to kill those vamages is something that came from mages – from Aric himself, actually."

Ella had never looked so offended. "How can you say that?" she asked with narrowed eyes. "Aric would never–"

"Yes, he would, and he did," Aaron said. "If you don't believe me, dig a little deeper into the great Aric's history. You might be surprised by what you find."

Aaron walked away, leaving Ella to stare after him. He got maybe four, five steps away before he felt guilty. He was in a rotten mood, but that didn't mean he could take it out on Ella. It was clear from the mages' reaction to Kyran bleeding out the vamages that they weren't aware mages could possess such a power. Even his parents didn't know anything about it until Aaron explained it to them. Aaron knew the truth because Naina had told him, but not all mages had the privilege of meeting a higher being that lived on another plane of existence, let alone conversing with her.

He was about to go back and apologise to Ella when he heard Scott's voice carry through the air.

"If I could have everyone's attention, please."

Aaron turned to see Scott on stage, wearing the brightest smile Aaron had seen on him since...since before Kyran was revealed as the Scorcher. Next to him stood Skyler.

"I would like to invite all the Elementals to please join me, so we can start the ceremony," Scott said, manipulating the air so his voice would carry to all corners of the street.

Aaron really didn't want to go up there. He had dragged himself to Marwa, but couldn't make himself take the last few steps to the stage. He looked at his dad, who was still seated at the table, looking as reluctant as Aaron felt.

A warm hand slipped into his, and Aaron turned to find Ella beside him. She smiled at him, seemingly not holding his harsh words against him. She gently tugged at him and Aaron went with her, not seeing the sense in fighting her on this. They climbed the platform and faced the packed street. Aaron didn't look in Skyler's direction. Aaron's gaze settled on his dad instead, still seated at the table. He didn't look happy.

A united front – those were the words Aaron had used to convince his parents to come. They had to show solidarity. It was a borrowed argument from Ella, but it worked in the end, and his parents, along with Alaina and Michael, had joined Aaron in Marwa.

Chris held Aaron's eyes for a full thirty seconds before giving in. He came to stand stiffly next to Aaron, not looking in Skyler's direction either.

"Thank you," Ella whispered to him, to which Chris only nodded curtly.

Scott was giving a speech – something about the numerous responsibilities of a leader, the qualities they all knew Skyler possessed, and the expectations the realm had of him at such a crucial point in their history. Aaron was tuning it all out. He stood with his hands tucked behind his back, clenched into fists, and his head bowed so he wouldn't have to look at the assembled crowd before him, or at Skyler's arrogant face as he revelled in his moment of glory.

Aaron's skin prickled with goosebumps all of a sudden. His hands felt clammy, his stomach swooped – as if he had missed a step going downstairs – and his heart skipped a beat. Aaron snapped his head up, green eyes scanning the tightly packed crowd before him. Aaron understood the sensation passing over him. He knew the signs pretty well by now. Kyran was here, and he was calling out to him.

Green eyes met green, and Aaron had to fight to remain still and silent, so as not to raise suspicion. There, in the midst of the crowd of mages, stood his brother. Kyran was wearing a Lurker's robe, the hood pulled up just enough to partly shadow his face. But Aaron knew it was him; his core was telling him it was his brother. The hood shifted, just for a brief moment, and Aaron saw Kyran smile at him. His head tilted in the direction of the houses lined along one end of the street. Aaron understood. He gave the tiniest, most discreet of nods, and then dropped his gaze to the ground again.

His heart was going a mile a minute. Kyran was *here*. He hadn't told Aaron he was going to come here. Wasn't this too risky? What if someone spotted him – a Hunter, one of the cities' chiefs, Scott, *Skyler*?

Aaron looked over to see Scott had presented the Elemental coat to Skyler, slipping it on him, earning a deafening cheer and applause from the rest of the mages. Skyler stood with his head held tall, his chest puffed out. His eyes were the lightest blue Aaron had ever seen them.

Skyler met Aaron's gaze and the smirk he gave him was enough to make Aaron's blood boil. Aaron looked away, counting the seconds in his head. The ceremony came to an end with the Hunters firing their guns in the sky, and Skyler demonstrating his full powers by creating powerful whirlwinds at a twitch of his finger, which caught the bullets and had them spinning around inside them. Mages were cheering, laughing and clapping with joy. Scott hugged Skyler, the first to congratulate him.

As Ella walked over to embrace Skyler, Aaron took his dad's arm and hurried him off the stage.

"Aaron, what are you–?" Chris started, sounding annoyed at being dragged around.

"Just come with me, please," Aaron said.

He pushed his way past the cheering crowd, heading to the table for his mum. The crowd of mages had started to break apart now that the main ceremony was over. Most of them were heading towards the stage to offer their good wishes to the new leader. Some were making their way to the houses to bring out the food for the feast. It made manoeuvring through the crowd all that more difficult.

Aaron couldn't see Kyran, but he knew the longer he was out here with the rest of the mages, the greater the risk of discovery. He had to hurry. He found his mum leaving the table, following Mary towards one of the houses.

"Mum!" he yelled. "Mum, wait!"

There was no way she would hear him, not with the Hunters still firing their guns in celebration and the commotion of the crowd around them. Aaron's panic had him use his bond to call out to her, like he did with Kyran all the time. Sure enough, Kate came to a stop. She turned, her blue eyes scanning the crowd, until she found him. She looked at Aaron with a worried frown. Her head lifted once, asking him without words what was wrong.

Aaron pushed his way towards her, Chris trailing after him.

"What's the matter?" Kate asked the moment Aaron reached her.

"Where's Uncle Mike and Aunt Alaina?" Aaron asked instead of answering her.

"Mary asked them to help set out the food," Kate said. "Why?"

Aaron slipped his hand into hers. "You have to come with me," he said.

"Where?" she asked.

"Just come. Hurry."

Kate had but a moment to share a confused and somewhat concerned look with Chris before Aaron was pulling her down the street. They merged with the crowd that was now bearing platters of food Mary and her helpers had spent all morning cooking.

Aaron darted to the only house in the city that hadn't been used to prepare the feast, seeing as the Adams were clearly unhappy to attend the ceremony, and so wouldn't be keen on helping cook food for Skyler's celebration.

"Aaron, what are you doing?" Kate asked. "Why are you bringing us home?"

Aaron didn't say anything. He opened the front door and ushered both his parents inside, before closing the door with a firm thud.

"Aaron," his mum started. "What are you–?"

Her words died in her throat when she noticed the Lurker in her hallway. Chris stilled next to Aaron, who stood mutely by his parents' side, not having it in him to speak a word of explanation.

Kyran pushed the hood down as he turned to face his parents and brother. Chris and Kate froze. There was complete silence. No one spoke. Both Chris and Kate were staring at Kyran with disbelief, before a slow realisation came to them: this wasn't a hallucination. Their estranged son was really there, standing in their very home, looking at them with tense trepidation.

Kyran's gaze went from one to the other, looking between his parents, as if debating who to approach first. Guilt sat heavily in his eyes, so much so that he eventually dropped his gaze to the floor.

Kate took a step towards him, then another, and another, her breathing picking up the closer she got. She stopped in front of him, her eyes fixed on him, her lips trembling. She extended her hand slowly, hesitant at first, almost as if she were afraid he would disappear if she touched him. Very lightly, her hand came to rest on his chest. She let out a choked breath that sounded more like a sob. She looked into his face as he raised his head, his vivid green eyes glistening. Her hand moved from his chest to cup his face.

"Ben," she breathed. "You're...you're really here," she said. "You're here."

Kyran reached up and held on to the hand resting against his cheek. "Mum," he whispered.

That one word of his broke her. Her head dipped and sobs racked her frame. The next moment Kyran had her in his arms, hugging her. Kate held her son tightly in her embrace. He had been four years old the last time she'd had the chance to hold him. Fourteen years had passed and not a day had gone by when her arms hadn't ached to be around her little boy.

"I'm sorry." Kyran's breath brushed past her ear and Kate sobbed harder. She shook her head.

"*I'm* sorry, Ben," she said. "I'm *so* sorry."

Aaron wasn't fighting to hold back his tears. There was no point; he wouldn't win that battle. He looked to his dad, who was still standing beside him, his eyes on his wife and son. Kyran raised his head, meeting his dad's eyes.

Aaron could see how much Kyran didn't want to, but he pulled himself back from Kate, unfurling his arms from around her. His eyes were glistening with tears that somehow hadn't fallen yet. He stepped towards Chris.

That's all it took – Chris shot forward, reaching Kyran in a few strides. Both father and son opened their arms for each other, hugging with a desperate yearning. The tears in Kyran's eyes finally fell as he held on to his dad. Chris had a hand at the back of Kyran's head, cradling him as he whispered his relieved thanks over and over again.

Kyran squeezed his eyes shut, gripping at his dad with both hands. "I'm sorry," he choked out. "I should have believed you. I should have listened–"

"No, no, Ben, no. Don't apologise," Chris said. He pulled back so he could look Kyran in the eyes, but his hands were still on Kyran's arms, unwilling to let him go. "You're here now, that's all that matters." His expression grew concerned almost at once. "You took a great risk coming here today, with the inauguration."

"The best way to hide is in a crowd," Kyran said. A small, bittersweet smile came to Kyran, even while his eyes gleamed with fresh tears. "Besides, I told you, I'm not afraid to take risks." He glanced to Aaron. "Especially when it comes to my family."

"No more risks," Chris said. "You don't have to take any more, ever again." He looked to Kate. "I'm going to go find Scott, say we're not feeling up to the celebration. The ceremony is over anyway. We'll take the portal back to Salvador." His eyes settled on Kyran again. "We can talk and figure out a plan."

Kyran didn't say anything but nodded.

A knock at the door made Aaron jump. A moment of panic swept through the room, before everyone snapped into action.

Chris pushed Kyran down the hall. "Hide in one of the rooms," he instructed.

Kate wiped at her face, drying her tears, as she hurried to the front door.

Aaron joined his brother, and both boys ducked into the kitchen. They waited behind the door, listening to the front door open.

"I've been looking all over for you." Ella's voice drifted into the house. A pause before she asked, "Is...everything okay?"

"Yes." It was their mum who replied. "We just needed a little break from all the commotion. What can we do for you, Ella?"

"The food is about to be served..."

Kyran pulled Aaron away from eavesdropping. He beckoned for him to follow and headed to the back door. Aaron frowned, but went after him. Kyran pulled his hood back up and slipped outside. Aaron walked out after him.

"What are you doing?" he asked, walking shoulder to shoulder with him. "Where are you going?"

"I couldn't stay," Kyran replied.

"Because of Ella?" Aaron asked.

"No," Kyran said. He pulled his hood further down, but the mages were still queuing up to congratulate Skyler, or settling at the table – no one was looking their way. "I didn't come here to stay."

Aaron's heart dipped. "Then why did you come?"

Kyran turned his head, looking at Aaron with a grim expression. "To see them."

*One last time*, went unsaid but not unheard.

Aaron came to a stop, forcing Kyran to do the same. "I'm not going to let you walk away and disappear again," he said. "You can't do that to Mum and Dad; you can't show yourself for thirty seconds and then leave before they even have a chance to talk to you. That's not fair."

"I know," Kyran said. He looked back to their house with remorse. "I know it's not fair, but it's how it has to be."

"Why?" Aaron asked. "Why can't you let them handle things now? They'll figure out a way, I know they will. They'll speak to Scott and Ella; they'll explain that things are different now. They'll make the others accept you–"

"Aaron, look around you," Kyran said. "Where are we right now? What just happened *minutes* ago?" His eyes were fierce, full of anger and pain. "Skyler Avira is the new leader of the realm. There is nothing Scott, or Ella, or even the rest of the mages can do if Skyler doesn't want to do it. You know as well as I do how desperate Skyler is to put a personalised bullet in me. I'd rather not give him that chance."

"Skyler may be the leader, but he can't make a decision the rest of the Elementals are against," Aaron said, repeating what Scott had told him.

Kyran scoffed. "Don't be so sure, Ace," he said, and his eyes glinted. "Skyler is an Avira. He's going to follow in his family's footsteps."

Aaron frowned. "I'm not sure what that means."

Kyran looked away. "It doesn't matter."

"Kyran?" Aaron stepped closer but Kyran cut him off.

"We don't have a lot of time," he said. "Mum and Dad are probably already out here looking for me." He closed his eyes, forcing out a breath. "I don't have it in me to keep walking away from them." He scanned the street, before looking back at Aaron. "Now listen closely, and do *exactly* as I say," he instructed. "If we pull this off, we'll be able to right at least one wrong today."

# 40

## MUTE-ELLES

Kyran pulled his hood lower as he made his way through the crowd of mages, heading to the other side of Marwa. Aaron had left to do his part, and as long as he completed it without attracting too much attention, everything would fall into place.

Rose caught his eye rather suddenly. She was standing on her own, under a cluster of trees at the far end of the street, making it painfully obvious she wasn't willing to be a part of Skyler's celebrations. Kyran came to a standstill. His green eyes drank her in, taking note of every little detail: the sunshine kissing her hair, the downward corners of her mouth as she surveyed the packed street with narrowed eyes, her arms crossed at her chest. She looked very unimpressed, and it drew a smile from Kyran – something he hadn't done in weeks.

Kyran knew he should walk away; he didn't have much time, and he couldn't risk anyone spotting him, but Kyran just couldn't do it. No matter how hard he tried, his gaze wouldn't shift from her. Kyran started towards Rose, his steps full of haste, but then came to a halt. What would he say to her? As much as Kyran wanted to meet her, talk to her, *kiss* her, he knew it would only end in heartbreak. He couldn't be with her, not when his death was certain now – at the hands of Skyler or Hadrian. What right did he have to invade Rose's life when his days were so shortly numbered?

Sam appeared from behind the trees, coming to stand next to his sister, holding out two apples from the armful he'd collected. Kyran watched as the twins kept their distance from the rejoicing mages, choosing to eat the fruit of Marwa and not the feast prepared to honour Skyler. A laugh choked at the back of Kyran's throat. Rose sure knew how to hold a grudge.

The rational side of Kyran's mind urged him to leave. Aaron was probably on his way to their meeting spot. He had to go too, otherwise his plan would fail. Kyran afforded himself one last look, his eyes glinting as he committed Rose to his memory, before he forced himself to step back. It was better this way. Kyran couldn't give her what she deserved, couldn't give her the *simple romance* she had once said she wanted, but he could walk away from her, so she could have that uncomplicated love with another.

Kyran was fighting with himself not to turn back. He had to focus. He was almost out of time. He had to get across the city before Aaron. He had to be there waiting before Aaron arrived. A glimmer of white grabbed his attention. Kyran looked over to see Alex walk past the crowd – pass right through them. Kyran's heart clenched. So his brief visit home hadn't done enough for Alex. He was still bound to Kyran.

Kyran had figured as much. Alex wanted Kyran to truly come home – to be safe again, to live with his family. But that was impossible for Kyran now. He couldn't be safe with the mages, and he couldn't be with his family without dragging them into his mess.

Alex was looking at him, glancing in his direction as he headed down the packed street. Kyran didn't stop, but his steps slowed as he watched, following the echo with his eyes, wondering what it was his uncle Lex wanted to show him. Alex walked until he crossed paths with Christopher and Kate Adams, then faded from sight, leaving Kyran to stare at his parents. It was clear they were searching for him in the crowd. Others would think they were looking for Aaron, to tell him to sit at the table to eat, or join the mages that had flocked to the magnificent waterfall of Marwa with their filled plates, to enjoy the sight as they tucked into their feast.

Kyran lowered his head as their frantic gaze passed over him. They hadn't spotted him. Kyran's heart lurched once again at the reminder of their broken bond. If Hadrian hadn't severed their connection, his parents would have found him in a heartbeat. But here they were, moving through the crowd with him, so close that Kyran could reach out and touch them, and they didn't know. They were looking for him with such desperation, but they couldn't feel him. They would *never* feel his presence again, even if he was right before their eyes.

The pain only strengthened Kyran's resolve. He wasn't going to let Hadrian get away with what he had done to him, to his family. Kyran hurried away, leaving his parents searching for him.

*\*\**

Aaron made his way down the street, past the crowds of mages drinking in Skyler's honour. He found who he was looking for after searching for almost twenty minutes. Scott was at the other end of the table, talking with Mary, a drink in his hand and a smile on his face. Aaron hurried over to him.

"Scott, I need to talk to you," he called.

"About what?" Scott asked pleasantly, turning to him.

"Can we go somewhere private?" Aaron asked. "Please?"

Scott grew concerned almost at once. "What's this about?" he asked, putting down his drink.

Aaron didn't answer right away. "I'll explain everything, just...just please come with me."

He led Scott away from the table and around the back of the platform where Skyler was still meeting mages, shaking their hands and laughing with them.

"Is something wrong?" Scott asked. "You're scaring me, Aaron."

Aaron was scaring himself. "I'll tell you once we're alone," he replied, and kept walking.

Aaron led Scott around the back of the houses and up the hill that led to the acres of land used as Marwa's orchard. Aaron didn't stop until he led Scott to a secluded spot, just behind the impressive grapevine. He turned to face Scott, who looked more than a little worried.

"What's going on?" Scott asked. "Is everything okay?"

"Scott," Aaron started, his mouth dry with nerves. "I'm...I'm so sorry."

Scott was too busy looking at Aaron with concerned eyes to realise someone was behind him, until he felt the sharp tip of a dagger rest at the small of his back.

"Not a sound, Scott," Kyran's voice urged in his ear. "Just stay calm and quiet, and this'll go a lot smoother."

Scott's blue eyes darted to Aaron, full of shock at his betrayal. "Aaron?"

Aaron's shame made him wish the ground would open up and just swallow him whole. And since he was an Earth Elemental, that wasn't exactly out of the realm of possibility.

He hurried towards Scott with his hands up in a placating manner. "It's not what you think," he said. "We just want to talk."

"At knife-point?" Scott scoffed. "I can only imagine what the topic of discussion will be."

"Trust me," Kyran said. "You're not going to like it."

With a hand on Scott's shoulder and the dagger still resting at his back, Kyran steered Scott forward. Aaron followed behind him. They made their way through the orchard, until Scott saw the small portal ahead, sitting ready and open for them.

"Where are you taking me?" Scott asked, and Aaron hated how anxious Scott sounded.

"Home," Kyran said. "Stay close, Ace," he called behind him, just as he stepped into the portal.

Aaron hurried in after him, and found himself in the forest outside the Gateway to Salvador.

No one spoke as Kyran led Scott through the Gate – opened by Aaron – and down the streets of Salvador, until they reached the glass building. Kyran hurried Scott inside, only coming to a stop when they were in front of the gleaming white table that was the Hub.

Kyran finally let go of Scott and stepped away. He took off the Lurker robe he had been wearing, throwing it aside, so he was left in his dark shirt and jeans. He pocketed the dagger and pulled out a slip of paper. He dropped it onto the table.

Scott looked at it with dread. "What is that?" he asked stiffly.

"Co-ordinates," Kyran replied. "To where I need to go."

Scott reached over and picked up the folded piece of paper. He opened it and read the numbers. His brow furrowed before his eyes widened. He snapped his head up to look at Kyran. "No," he breathed. "This is – this place doesn't exist, not any more."

"I assure you, it does," Kyran replied. "I've been there before but only once. So I need *your* help to open a portal there."

Scott's jaw tightened. "You don't seem to have any problems opening portals on your own," he said.

"I can open portals, but only in places where they have been opened and closed countless times." Kyran nodded at the paper in Scott's hands. "This isn't a very popular location – which is why you're going to help me create a portal using the Hub."

Scott was staring at Kyran with lines on his brow. "You know the name that was given to this place, don't you?"

"*Mute-elles*," Kyran replied. "Mouth of hell."

Aaron's already nervous stomach jolted in horror.

"Yes, the mouth of hell." Scott nodded. "The very spot demons supposedly first entered this realm. It was rumoured to have been destroyed by Aric himself, but if it's really still standing, why would you want to go there?"

"Because that's where Aaron needs to go," Kyran said, glancing to his brother. "So he can force the legacy out of himself, and back to Ella."

Scott stilled. His eyes narrowed. "Is that what this is all about?" he asked, looking from Kyran to Aaron in surprise. "You're trying to give Ella back her legacy?"

Kyran smirked. "I'm sure you had it all figured out in your head – a nice, selfish reason for the Scorcher to go to the mouth of hell. Sorry to disappoint you."

"Kyran." Scott shook his head. "I'm sorry. I knew you had left Hadrian's ranks, but I didn't know you were trying to help Aaron and Ella." He stepped around the table, to walk over to him, but came to an abrupt stop when Kyran aimed a gun at him.

"Back to the table, Scott," Kyran instructed.

Scott held up a hand. "You don't have to do it this way, Kyran," he said. "We're on the same side now. I want to help Aaron and Ella too. I want Ella to regain her birthright."

"Then make the portal," Kyran said.

Scott looked terribly conflicted. He looked at the Hub and then back at Kyran. "I can't let you and Aaron go there by yourselves. It's far too dangerous."

"I can take care of myself and my brother," Kyran assured.

"Let me call the other Hunters," Scott said. "Once I explain everything to them, they'll be happy to have you back again–"

Kyran chuckled. "I'm sure they will," he mocked. "Might just welcome me with a firing squad, like last time."

"Kyran," Scott said. "I'm not going to let anyone hurt you."

Kyran's smirk was still in place, but his eyes were gleaming. "There's not much left to hurt, Scott." He motioned to the table. "Create the portal."

Scott stood where he was with clenched fists. "I'm the Controller," he said. "I took an oath not to willingly endanger mages." He shook his head. "I can't send you to the mouth of hell on your own, with no back up–"

Kyran cocked his gun. "You don't have a choice."

Scott looked at the pistol in Kyran's hand. "Go ahead," he said. "We're both mages. Your bullets may hurt me, but they won't kill me."

Kyran faltered, before lowering his gun. "You're right," he said. "I can't kill you with this." He shifted the gun to his other hand, before lifting his right hand up, just as the four lines started to glow bright. "But I can with this."

Aaron's breath choked in his chest. He gaped in surprised horror as Scott froze on the spot, staring at Kyran's hand with wide eyes.

"Kyran–" Scott started.

"Don't think I won't do it, Scott," Kyran said. "I'm desperate enough to kill you. There's *nothing* I'm not willing to do to get that legacy out of my brother."

Scott swallowed heavily. "If you kill me, who will open your portal?" he challenged.

"I'll figure out another way to get to Mute-elles," Kyran said.

Scott didn't move.

Kyran stepped towards him, his hand glowing bright, the circle at his chest shining through his dark shirt. "Don't make me do this," he said, a note of pleading in his voice. "Create the portal, please."

"Scott," Aaron called to him, his voice shaking. "Please, just do it."

Scott didn't say anything, but he moved to the table, making both Kyran and Aaron breathe out a sigh of relief. Scott looked at the paper Kyran had given him and correlated the co-ordinates to the map on his table. He worked in silence, with Aaron and Kyran waiting, watching him.

The light dimmed in Kyran's hand and chest. After a moment or two, Scott's fingers worked their magic and a portal burst open in the middle of the room. Kyran almost smiled at the sight of it. He turned back to Scott.

"Thank you," he said.

"I'm asking you again: *please* don't go. It's not safe," Scott said.

Kyran walked over to Scott, standing before him. "Don't worry, Scott," he said. "By the time you wake up, Aaron will be back here, hopefully minus one legacy."

Scott frowned. "Wake up?"

Kyran swung the gun in his hand, whipping it across Scott's head. Scott went down instantly.

"Scott!" Aaron cried, running to him, but the Controller was out cold, the attack catching him by surprise. He turned to his brother. "What the hell, Kyran?" he snapped.

"Come on," Kyran gestured, pocketing the gun. "We have to go."

"I'm not leaving him like this," Aaron said.

"Don't worry," Kyran said. "Neither am I." He pulled a set of familiar-looking manacles out of his back pocket and moved towards Scott's prone body.

\*\*\*

Kyran and Aaron walked out of the portal onto dry, cracked land. The air was hot and stifling, and stank of brimstone. Acres of desolate land stretched before them, with dark mountains in the distance.

Kyran shut the portal behind him. "Come on," he said. "It's best not to linger here."

Aaron walked alongside him, his mind still racing over Kyran's behaviour with Scott. "I can't believe you attacked Scott like that," he said.

"What were you expecting me to do?" Kyran asked. "If I didn't knock him unconscious he'd have a team following us here by now."

"I know," Aaron muttered, hating how easy it was for him to accept and justify their reasoning. "You could have been gentle about it, though."

Kyran looked at him. "That *was* gentle," he said.

Aaron grumbled low in his throat. "And what was with threatening to *kill* him?" he asked, glaring at Kyran.

Kyran shrugged. "I was never going to do it," he said. "I just wanted him to think I would, so he would make the portal."

A part of Aaron already knew Kyran could never bleed out someone in cold blood. He had taken life before, yes, but it was never in such a calculated and ruthless manner. And it was demons Kyran hunted and drained, never mages – at least he didn't think so. Vamages were technically part-mage, but they were also dangerous part-demons, so did that count? Aaron rubbed at his head. Pain was blooming just behind his eyes, and if he kept thinking about Kyran killing different beings of the realm, he would have a full-blown headache.

He glanced around his surroundings.

"So, what exactly am I here to do?" he asked, partly to distract himself, and partly because he really wanted to know.

"It's simple enough in principle," Kyran said. He stopped and pointed to a mountain in the far distance. "You have to turn what lies in that into water."

Aaron turned his head to look at him. "You're having me on," he said. "You want me to go inside a *volcano*, and turn lava into water?"

"I know it's difficult–"

"No, no, it's not difficult," Aaron mocked, batting a hand at him. "All you're asking for me to do is change the properties of a substance to the complete opposite of what it is – have you lost your mind?" he snapped. "How do you expect me to change lava into water, Kyran? It's impossible."

"That's the whole idea," Kyran said. "Since the legacy you hold isn't a right fit for your core, the hope is that if you push it to its absolute limit, you might be able to dislodge it out of your core," he explained. "The legacy has nowhere to go but to Ella, since she's the last Afton."

"That actually makes sense," Aaron admitted. He took in a breath. "Okay, but how do I do it? I mean, I know how to command water but this is lava. It's a completely different thing."

"Wait until you're standing before it," Kyran said. "You'll know what to do. Your instincts have never failed you yet."

"Yeah, *yet*," Aaron muttered. He felt his heart thud with uncertainty. He had no idea how he was supposed to try and manipulate lava to try and turn it into water. Even if he figured that part out, would he be able to get his power to breaking point? Would trying to do the impossible really force the legacy out of him and send it to Ella? He glanced to his brother. If Kyran thought it would, then it must. He had to trust his brother, which was the easiest part of this whole ordeal. "Let's get to it, then," Aaron said. "Somehow, I don't think I'm going to figure it out on the first try."

"We've not got a lot of time, Ace," Kyran said. "At any minute, someone might notice Scott's not in Marwa, and come to Salvador looking for him. If they find him, they'll find out about us coming here. Scott can open another portal to send Hunters after us." He rubbed at his forehead, sighing. "I'm hoping everyone is busy getting drunk and having too much fun to notice their Controller is missing," he said. "But if anyone does go to Salvador looking for Scott, they'll find him chained to the railings in the Hub."

Aaron groaned, shaking his head. "We're so going to hell for that one."

"We're already at its doorstep," Kyran mused.

Aaron couldn't help but shudder. "Is this really the mouth to hell?" he asked. "I mean, actually, literally, hell?"

Kyran kept walking. "Hell is everywhere, Ace," he said quietly. "It's not a place; not like a city in a zone. Hell exists all around us." His eyes darkened. "What felt like your home for years can turn out to have been hell all along – and you just didn't see it." He dipped his head, visibly gathering himself. He nodded at the far distance. "It's a well-believed myth that the mouth of hell opened here and that's how demons came to be in this realm. They lived here for hundreds of years, fighting the barrier that separates the realms. Once they tore their way into the human realm and started killing innocents, mages came into existence."

Aaron scanned the darkened grounds. "I can see why," he said. "The whole place gives off a creepy, end-of-the-world kind of vibe." He looked at Kyran. "You said you've been here once before. Why would you come here?"

Kyran's expression tightened. "It's where the Blade of Aedus was kept, before I claimed it."

Aaron didn't say anything.

Kyran came to a sudden stop. His eyes narrowed. He spun around and threw out his hands. It wasn't a moment too soon. The wall of fire he had conjured shielded him and Aaron from the onslaught of sudden jolts of power – everything from fireballs to daggers of ice.

A sea of dark-clothed figures was spilling out from a glowing portal in the distance behind them.

Vamages.

Vamages were here and they were coming right at them.

# 41

## THE LAST LEGACY

The vamages were racing towards Kyran and Aaron, throwing jolt after jolt of power at them. Kyran's fiery wall blocked the attack, but it was clear it wouldn't last. Kyran's strong arms were trembling with the effort to keep the wall up.

Aaron's power gathered like a storm and rushed out as a tremendous wave of water, gushing across the dry, chapped ground. The wave knocked the vamages down, swirling around them. Kyran lowered his hands, dropping the shield.

The portal was still spewing out dark figures. There must have been almost a hundred vamages already, and more were coming. Hadrian had sent his full force after Kyran.

"How did they know we were going to be here?" Aaron asked, holding his hands out, putting more force into his wave, knocking as many vamages as he could to the ground.

Kyran didn't offer an answer. Instead, he clenched his hands into balls, and a mighty tornado came alive. It tore across the ground, spinning into a vortex, swallowing vamages in its path. But more vamages continued pouring out of the portal, armed with weapons as well as their powers.

Jolts of power rained down on Kyran and Aaron – countless fireballs, shards of ice, as well as invisible blows of air aimed to knock them to the ground. Kyran's shield came back up, but the accumulated power of the attack almost threw Kyran off his feet. He skidded back, barely managing to stay upright. His hands shook as he struggled to hold up the shield; the flames flickered to the point of almost extinguishing.

Aaron sent another blast of water, aiming to knock out the vamages targeting Kyran. The vamages fought back, not staying down for long.

"What's the plan?" Aaron asked.

Kyran turned his head to meet Aaron's eyes. "We're not leaving until we get that legacy out," he said. "If we leave now, we'll never be able to come back here. Hadrian will have this place surrounded. Once you get rid of the legacy, Hadrian will have no more reason to hunt you." His hands curled into fists. "You ready, Ace?"

Aaron nodded. "Ready."

Kyran dropped the shield and threw his fists into the ground, as did Aaron. The ground shook and cracked, surging with the power of the two Earth Elementals. It was as if a mighty earthquake had hit them. The vibrations spread out every which way, throwing vamages clean off their feet. Large chasms formed, forcing vamages to back off – for the time being.

"Run!" Kyran cried and both brothers took off with a burst of speed.

Dodging the jolts being thrown at them, Kyran and Aaron ran towards the dark mountains. The vamages couldn't get past the gaps in the ground, so took to the skies instead. A cloud of white fog flew over the chasms and chased after Kyran and Aaron, closing the distance at a frightening pace. Kyran turned and aimed at it. Forks of lightning fell from the sky and hit the cloud, stopping it in its place.

The vamages didn't give up.

They raced after the brothers on foot, throwing everything from jolts of power to bullets and blades at them. A jolt of air hit Kyran like a punch, right between his shoulder blades, throwing him to the ground headfirst.

"Kyran!" Aaron rushed to his brother's side.

Kyran picked himself up, looking a little dazed. The jagged, rocky ground had made a cut across Kyran's temple. A line of blood ran down his face. Aaron looked horrified.

"You okay?"

"I'm fine," Kyran said, sounding winded. "Come on, keep going."

Aaron turned around instead and built an enormous wave to tower high above him. Using all the force he could muster from his fast depleting reserves, Aaron turned the wave solid for a moment, before thin, spear-like icicles formed – thousands of them. Aaron saw the realisation dawn on the vamages as they came to a screeching halt. But it was too late to avoid it. Aaron gave the silent command, crushing his hands into fists and the spears shot forward.

Aaron didn't see how many were attacked. Kyran had pulled him into a run and they hurried away, leaving the vamages screaming behind them.

***

They reached the line of mountains, but Kyran kept going, racing forward.

"Where are you going?" Aaron panted. "We're here."

"No, we need a particular one," Kyran said.

"What do you mean?" Aaron asked.

Kyran didn't stop to explain. He kept running until he spotted the mouth of a cave, at the base of one dark, almost black, rocky mountain.

"This is it," he said with relief. "This is the one."

"How can you be sure?" Aaron asked.

"It's the one I found the Blade of Aedus inside," Kyran replied. "It's the fiercest volcano of them all. This is the one we need to make this work. Come on."

As they sped along the cavern trail, they heard scraping sounds against the rough ground; vamages were not far behind. Aaron's spear-spitting wave hadn't managed to keep them back for long. The brothers picked up their pace.

The cave was dark, too dark. Aaron could barely see his own hands in front of him, never mind Kyran. He had to rely on his hearing to keep up with his brother. The heat in the cave was unbearable. It made even breathing difficult. His lungs were aching for air – for fresh, breathable air – but Aaron didn't let that slow him down. He kept running, blindly following Kyran, turning corners this way and that.

His muscles were screaming in protest, begging for him to slow down, to stop, to catch his breath. But Aaron knew the vamages had probably already reached the cave, having followed the scent of Kyran's blood from his head injury. There was no time to take breaks.

Aaron heard Kyran's footsteps slow down. He looked up, blinking the sweat out of his eyes. He saw a faint glow of red ahead of him. Kyran was running again, and Aaron quickly raced after him. They were heading for the red mark, watching it get bigger and brighter as they approached it, and Aaron realised it was an opening to the centre of the volcano.

Kyran led Aaron through it, and both boys came to a gasping stop. Aaron could barely stay standing. He doubled over, his sweaty hands on his trembling knees, trying to keep himself steady and not fall to the ground in exhaustion. He took in deep breaths, tasting the ash in the air. Panting, he looked up to take in his surroundings – but he already knew what he would see. He had witnessed this moment, several times, in his dreams months before – even before he knew the truth about who he was. The sea of lava before him churned sluggishly; a deep red and orange magma. There was no way to get across it and reach the other side. It filled the entire cavity of the volcano.

"This is it," Kyran said.

Aaron turned to meet his brother's eyes. The cut on his forehead was still bleeding, the trickle reaching down to his jaw. Kyran motioned to the fiery sea before them, panting to catch his breath.

"Do it," he said.

Aaron looked to the molten lava before him. What was he supposed to do? How did he even begin trying to change this into water? He had thought he would have time to work it out, but with the vamages close behind them, Aaron had mere minutes – if even that – to figure this out. He wracked his mind, but couldn't come up with a way to challenge the lava and push the legacy beyond its capability.

"I…I can't," he said, in horrid realisation.

"Come on," Kyran said, looking behind him for the vamages that were no doubt searching the caves for them. "You have to hurry."

Aaron was panicking. This was lava, not the element of Water. How was he supposed to control it?

"I don't know *how*!" Aaron cried.

"Aaron." Kyran stepped closer, staring at him with vivid green eyes. "Focus. You can do this. I know you can."

Aaron waited for his instinct to kick in, to do the impossible, like he had when Raoul was attacking the Pecosas and he had conjured a tower of water without being fully aware of it. But this time, nothing was happening. Aaron shook his head, then dropped it in exhausted defeat.

"I can't."

"Aaron?" Kyran reached out to hold on to his arm. "Aaron? Aaron, look at me."

Aaron raised his head to meet his brother's eyes.

"The whole point of this is that it's impossible. I don't want you to change the lava into water, I just want you to *try*," Kyran said. "Focus, and demand your will. Call to the element of Water and *make* it obey you. Push with everything you have, and the legacy will be forced out of you."

Aaron let out a slow breath, fighting to calm himself down, and turned to look at the lava. He held out both of his hands, casting all his doubts aside, repeating Kyran's words to himself and focused, closing his eyes.

He reached out with his mind. He allowed the heat radiating from the molten lava to sear his skin, forcing beads of sweat from his very pores. The thick stench of sulphur filled his nose. He could see the rich red and orange colours of the magma from behind closed eyelids. Aaron breathed out, and raised both hands.

The sound of vamages searching the caverns was getting louder. They would find them any minute now. Aaron felt Kyran shift from beside him, hurrying towards the opening. A moment later a rush of heat came from behind him, as Kyran barricaded the entrance with flames. Aaron could hear them roaring, but he forced all of his attention on the task before him.

He pushed his power out, tentatively first, then gradually building force behind it. It latched onto the lava. Aaron could feel his core working, chugging inside of him as he willed the magma to change form. His stomach quivered, the muscles in his body tensed. A fine sheen of perspiration that had nothing to do with the stifling heat covered him from heat to foot. Aaron's limbs jerked as the legacy inside him twisted in protest to what Aaron was demanding from it. Aaron locked his knees to remain upright. He pushed harder, panting as his breathing raced and his heart hammered against his ribs. He gathered every last ounce of power he possessed and lashed out, trying to surpass his capabilities, so the legacy would break free and leave him and go to Ella – to its rightful owner.

He was doing it, he could sense it. The legacy was working furiously, twisting and turning, thrashing inside him. It couldn't possibly keep this up. It was going to break. It was going to leave him and go to Ella. Then he felt the dip in the temperature. The magma in the cave was somehow cooling.

Aaron opened his eyes in time to catch the breathtaking moment when the sea of red, fiery lava transformed into a pool of calm blue water. The air chilled instantly. Aaron blinked at the sight in disbelief, staring at the water as it lapped gently at the charred and burnt edges of the ground.

He had done it.

But he wasn't supposed to do it.

He wasn't supposed to succeed in changing lava into water. The legacy was meant to be forced out of him. Maybe it had? Maybe the transformation of lava to water had broken the legacy free.

Aaron didn't feel any different. Shouldn't he be able to tell if the legacy had left him? He had felt unimaginable pain when the legacy had come to him. Shouldn't he feel maybe even a fraction of that pain when the legacy left him? Breathing hard, Aaron stared at the water, and tentatively, held out a trembling hand. The water lifted at once, coming up to almost touch his palm, before falling again. Aaron's heart dropped like a stone.

Turning, he saw Kyran at the opening, holding his fiery block in place, stopping the vamages from coming in. But Kyran's eyes were on him, darkening as all the hope left them.

It hadn't worked.

Aaron had turned lava into water, but either that wasn't enough to force the legacy out of him, or it had been a theory that was never going to work in the first place.

The vamages outside the entrance were putting up one hell of a fight with Kyran's flames, trying to extinguish them and get inside. Kyran pushed more of his power into the fire, strengthening them.

"We're going to have to find another way out," Kyran said, and even his voice sounded crushed. "There's too many of them for us to fight." He nodded at the water. "Jump in."

Aaron faltered. "What if it's still actually lava?" he asked. "I've never transformed anything before. What if it only looks like water, but it's actually still fire?"

Kyran was struggling to hold his block in place. "Guess there's only one way to find out." He tilted his head towards the water and then to the opening he was currently blocking.

Aaron nodded and held out his hands, ready.

Kyran dropped his hands, extinguishing the flames, just as Aaron directed the water pooled inside the volcano to lift up and rush across, hitting the vamages that were trying to get in. They were hit full blast, and fell backwards, but their lack of agonised screaming told them Aaron had done a thorough job. It was water.

Kyran turned, grabbed Aaron and dived into the pool. They stayed under the surface, hiding from the vamages that rushed inside, having recovered from Aaron's strike. They were eventually going to come into the water. Aaron knew it. There was nothing else in the cave. The element of Water guided Aaron to a tunnel to one side of the underwater pool. He and Kyran swam through it, resurfacing in another chamber inside the volcano. Kyran and Aaron quickly pulled themselves out of the water and ran, using their element of Earth to find another way out.

They eventually found one, and came out onto rocky foothills at the base of the mountain. They had come out at the other side. They breathed in the open air, shielding their eyes from the daylight. The area was clear; no vamages in sight. Both boys took a minute to catch their breaths. They were still damp from the water, their clothes sticking to them, but neither seemed to care. Their failed attempt to get rid of the legacy was weighing heavily on their minds, not allowing room for anything else.

"It was worth a try," Aaron said quietly.

Kyran didn't speak. He leant against the rough wall of the mountain and closed his eyes. Giving himself a shake, he looked over at Aaron. "Come on, we have to get out of here."

They had taken no more than a few steps when a white, pulsing fog surrounded them. Countless vamages walked out of the cloud, guns and blades in hand. Kyran and Aaron were trapped. Kyran pulled Aaron behind him. The lines on the back of Kyran's hand started to glow, but Aaron grabbed his wrist.

"Don't," he said at once. "You swore, Kyran."

If Kyran drained even a small fraction of the vamages present here, he could lose his purity and be left with nothing but darkness. Aaron would rather face death than lose his brother.

The light faded from Kyran's hand, but the ferocity in his eyes did not. His gaze was flitting through the crowd, watching the vamages, daring them to step forward and try to attack them. No one did.

Another cloud of fog hit the middle of the circle the vamages had created, directly before Kyran and Aaron. Out from it stepped Hadrian. Aaron felt Kyran stiffen. There was absolute silence. No one dared move or make even the smallest of sounds, as Hadrian and Kyran stood across from one another. Hadrian's hazel eyes were on Kyran, and Kyran alone.

There was a shift in Kyran that Aaron noticed. He was no less tense, but the brazen urge to fight was gone from his stance the moment Hadrian's eyes met his. Aaron knew Kyran could fight anyone else who crossed his path, be it demon or mage, but not Hadrian. Kyran wouldn't raise his hand, or call forth the elements, to fight the person he had called father for so many years.

Hadrian was staring at Kyran, his expression guarded, but his eyes spoke volumes of pain and disappointment. "I knew you would come here," he said.

Kyran bristled at the sound of his voice.

Hadrian glanced once at Aaron, his gold-flecked eyes turning cold, before looking back to Kyran. "It was never going to work. You can't force legacies out." His gaze softened. "Your fight is over," he said. "Don't make this harder than it has to be. Step out of the way."

Kyran didn't move.

"It's a lost battle, Kyran," Hadrian said. "You can't save him now. I'm giving you a chance to turn away, to not witness his death as I take the last legacy from him." His eyes gleamed gold. "*Move* out of the way."

Kyran shook his head. "You're going to have to kill me first."

Hadrian's expression grew fierce. "It'll be your turn soon enough," he said. "But not just yet. You have a little more time." His eyes blazed. "Move, Kyran. Or I'll change my mind and *make* you watch as I kill him."

Aaron's stomach twisted into knots. He was half willing to push Kyran out of the way and face Hadrian with his head held high. If only he could work his mind past the crippling fear.

"You know you can't win this," Hadrian said. "There's nothing more you can do," he told Kyran. "It's over."

Kyran stilled. His shoulders relaxed and he raised his head. "No," he said quietly to Hadrian. "There's one last thing."

He turned and slammed his hand against Aaron's chest, just as the four lines at the back of his hand lit up. Aaron's body seized with pain of the likes he had never experienced before. His insides were being scraped out; something was hollowing him with the sharpest blade in existence. Aaron's vision turned white. He was blind. He couldn't see. He couldn't *breathe*. Then his entire centre of gravity shifted and Aaron found himself on the ground, his arms and legs twitching as the excruciating agony slowly dulled. His vision returned, first cloudy and blurred, then clearing.

He was flat out on his back, and still surrounded by vamages. He was shaking, trembling as aftershocks raced through him. Aaron's chest felt like it was on fire. Tilting his head was all he could manage. That's when his eyes found Kyran, on the ground before him, and Aaron forgot all about his pain.

Kyran was dying.

Aaron could see it – he could *feel* it. Kyran's body was convulsing so hard it was lifting off the ground. Trails of blood were seeping out of his nose and ears. His screams weren't getting out; he didn't have the breath for them. He was writhing on the ground, the rough, jagged rocks cutting into him, but it didn't look like Kyran was even aware of it. He was distracted by worse pain.

Aaron knew why. Even in his half-lucid, pain-wracked state, Aaron knew Kyran had done a half-bleed – taking the legacy out of him but not his life. The result was that both of them were on the brink of death.

Using the last drop of his strength, Aaron rolled over onto his stomach and inched forward, reaching out to hold on to Kyran's hand.

"K-Kyran," he stammered. "It's – it's okay," he whispered. "I'm here. I'm right here. I'm n-not going to – to leave you."

Aaron didn't know if Kyran could even hear him, but he wanted to say it, to tell his brother that they were in this together. He wouldn't leave him, even if he left this world.

"I'm not going to leave you," Aaron repeated, even as Hadrian's vamages grabbed him with unkind hands. "Kyran," Aaron choked out, as he was wrenched away, his hand slipping out of Kyran's.

Aaron was thrown at Hadrian's feet. Wearily, Aaron lifted his head to look at the vamage. The anger on Hadrian would have been terrifying if Aaron wasn't already dying. One of the vamages handed Hadrian a sword, and he took it, his golden eyes on Aaron. He raised the sword high, holding it with both hands.

Kyran's voice, thick with pain, came from behind Aaron. "Kill him, you kill...both of us!"

Hadrian paused. His glistening eyes went to Kyran, filled with fury. In his haze, Aaron recalled Kyran telling him a half-bleed joined the two life forces, if only for a short period. If one died, so would the other.

Hadrian threw the sword aside and stepped away, leaving Aaron where he was. Aaron could do nothing but watch as Hadrian walked over to where Kyran was. His vamages reached down and grabbed Kyran up.

Aaron wanted to yell, to scream, to make any possible sound as Hadrian's vamages dragged Kyran away, but he couldn't. Just to keep breathing was turning into a losing battle.

Aaron's vision was darkening around the edges. He was drifting away, but he stubbornly fought it, keeping his eyes open to focus on Kyran as his brother was hauled towards the glowing portal Hadrian had opened. He watched until Kyran disappeared into the bright Aric's mark, along with Hadrian and his vamages. The portal vanished.

Aaron was left on his own, dying in the place dubbed the mouth of hell. Only Scott knew he was there, but how long would it take for someone to find Scott, and free him so he could send Hunters here?

But even if Aaron was saved, what about Kyran? His brother was gone, taken by Hadrian. Aaron knew Kyran would be killed for the four legacies he now held. Aaron had lost him. Hadrian had won. The feeling of utter hopelessness spread through Aaron. He stopped fighting. His eyes slid shut and finally, Aaron succumbed to the darkness that was eagerly waiting to swallow him up.

Look out for Book Four, *Scattered To The Wind*, in the Power of Four series by SF Mazhar.

Printed in Poland
by Amazon Fulfillment
Poland Sp. z o.o., Wrocław